THRONE *of the* HEAVENS

Books by Connilyn Cossette

OUT FROM EGYPT

Counted with the Stars
Shadow of the Storm
Wings of the Wind

CITIES OF REFUGE

A Light on the Hill
Shelter of the Most High
Until the Mountains Fall
Like Flames in the Night

THE COVENANT HOUSE

To Dwell among Cedars
Between the Wild Branches

THE KING'S MEN

Voice of the Ancient
Shield of the Mighty
Splendor of the Land
Throne of the Heavens

THE KING'S MEN

4

THRONE *of the* HEAVENS

CONNILYN COSSETTE

BETHANY HOUSE
a division of Baker Publishing Group
Minneapolis, Minnesota

Published by Bethany House Publishers
Minneapolis, Minnesota
BethanyHouse.com

Bethany House Publishers is a division of
Baker Publishing Group, Grand Rapids, Michigan

Printed in the United States of America

Library of Congress Cataloging-in-Publication Data
Names: Cossette, Connilyn author
Title: Throne of the heavens / Connilyn Cossette.
Description: Minneapolis, Minnesota : Bethany House Publishers, a division of Baker Publishing Group, 2026. | Series: The king's men ; 4
Identifiers: LCCN 2026022673 | ISBN 9780764238949 paperback | ISBN 9781493454150 ebook
Subjects: LCGFT: Christian fiction | Novels
Classification: LCC PS3603.O8655 T47 2026
LC record available at https://lccn.loc.gov/2026022673

Cover design by Jennifer Parker

Author is represented by the Steve Laube Agency.

Baker Publishing Group publications use paper produced from sustainable forestry practices and postconsumer waste whenever possible.

26 27 28 29 30 31 32 7 6 5 4 3 2 1

For Chad, my first and forever hero.

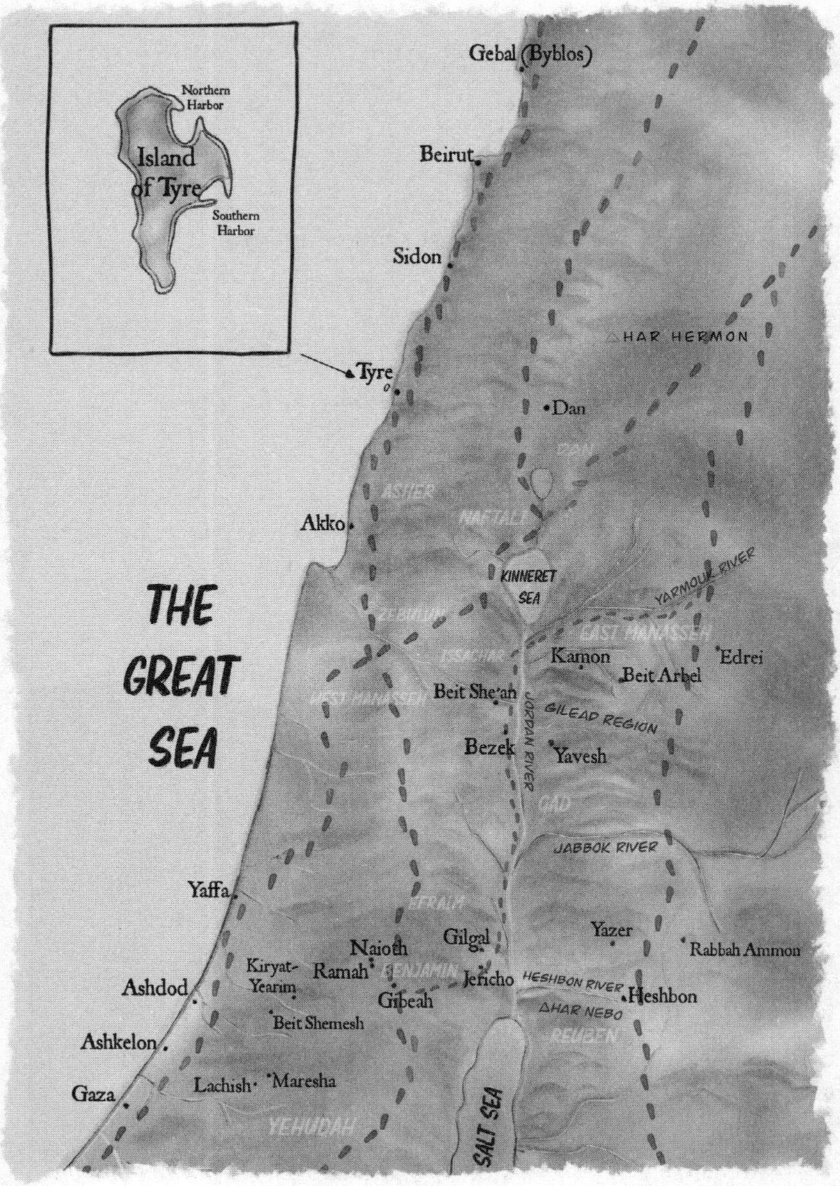

Northern Harbor
Island of Tyre
Southern Harbor
Gebal (Byblos)
Beirut
Sidon
HAR HERMON
Tyre
Dan
DAN
ASHER
NAFTALI
Akko
KINNERET SEA
YARMOUK RIVER
THE GREAT SEA
ZEBULUN
EAST MANASSEH
ISSACHAR
Kamon
Edrei
Beit Arbel
WEST MANASSEH
Beit She'an
JORDAN RIVER
GILEAD REGION
Bezek
Yavesh
GAD
JABBOK RIVER
Yaffa
EFRAIM
Yazer
Gilgal
Naioth
Rabbah Ammon
Kiryat-Yearim
Ramah
BENJAMIN
Jericho
HESHBON RIVER
Heshbon
Ashdod
Gibeah
HAR NEBO
Beit Shemesh
REUBEN
Ashkelon
Lachish
Maresha
Gaza
YEHUDAH
SALT SEA

Then Samuel went to Ramah, and Saul went up to his house in Gibeah of Saul. And Samuel did not see Saul again until the day of his death, but Samuel grieved over Saul. And the LORD regretted that he had made Saul king over Israel.

1 Samuel 15:34–35 ESV

A psalm of Ronen ben Avidan

The anointed one shall abide by the counsel of the
Most High,
The voice of the Ancient One to light his every step.

A shield to both the humble and the valiant,
His mighty fortress offers refuge to all who call on the
Name.

From ashes and dust shall his glory arise,
a diadem of splendor to grace the head of the lowly.

His scepter lifted high shines justice across the Land,
Heavenly righteousness, like a river of gladness, flows
from his throne.

Selah.

1

Mattaniel

Sardinian Sea
1032 B.C.

I was going to die, and I did not even know my own name.

A towering wave crashed over the port side of the ship, sweeping me from my feet. I went down hard, mouth full of brine. I clung to the rigging line with raw palms as two terrified crewmen washed overboard not five paces from me, their pitiful screams overpowered by the roar of the storm as the sea consumed them.

The ship suddenly tilted starboard, the water rushing the other direction. Flung sideways, I scrabbled for a foothold on the slippery boards, knuckles white as I tightened my grip, but the angry sea shifted again and I hit the cabin wall with a thud. Pain spiked through my head, my eyes going bleary and my ears ringing. But the sound of Adin's hoarse voice screaming my name broke through the haze.

Blinking the burn from my eyes, I peered into the dim. A flash of lightning illuminated his form huddled on the deck, clinging to the leg of a rowing bench. There was nothing I could do for my young friend. Even if I let go, I'd never reach him before the ship tilted into the next enormous wave.

"Hang on!" My throat burned as I shouted. "Don't move!"

There was no choice but to hold on with all our might until this violent storm blew itself out. It was not the first one this ship had weathered during the last year we'd been at sea and wouldn't be the last. It was, however, the first I wasn't sure we'd survive.

A horrific crack split through the howling winds, and the ship shuddered.

"Watch out! It's coming down!" someone bellowed.

I tightened my grip on the rigging but twisted to see the center mast, made from a sky-scraping Tyrian cedar, shattering in half with a spray of splinters. It careened sideways between Adin and me, its wind-shredded sail billowing as the top half tipped over the side of the ship into the black water.

With a jolt the ship righted itself, and frantically I tried to catch sight of my friend through the driving rain, but the place where he'd been clinging to the bench was empty.

Thunder rumbled as my insides went icy. *No!*

"Throw it all over! Everything!" My master's desperate command somehow cut through the wind.

We'd spent months trading goods along the frigid northern coasts and were heading back to Tyre with a load far more dear than when we'd departed. Raphad would never willingly throw cargo overboard unless it was the only way to keep us from going down with it.

So, with my chest hollow from the loss of my only friend, I peeled my shredded palms from the rigging and ran to help what was left of the crew throw everything into the sea. Jugs of ale, crates of tin ingots, bags of precious salt, baskets of exotic textiles, jars of resin and costly perfume, and anything else not secured to the deck were greedily devoured by ravenous black waves.

But before I could catch my breath, the ship plowed headlong into another vicious swell. Pleas to various gods went up from the sailors as the vessel pitched upward, and I skidded across the deck toward the railing. A blinding flash of lightning splintered the sky, outlining the horse-head prow at the front of the ship in sharp detail.

Gasping, I reached for something to stop myself, but the world tipped sideways and then everything was black and cold, swirling around me. I kicked and flailed against the pull of the furious sea, unsure which way was up. My lungs ached, my head spinning as I fought for one more breath—a battle I was quickly losing.

"Stop struggling so hard" came a voice from somewhere deep inside. *"Relax your body."* The image of a boy with bright green eyes rose up in my addled head. He leaned close with an encouraging smile. *"Let the water carry you."*

Although uncertain whether it was a long-ago memory or simply a product of my broken mind, I obeyed the vision and ceased fighting the whirling sea, willing my body to go limp even as my lungs screamed for air.

When my head broke the surface a few moments later, I dragged in a painful breath while I treaded water, blinking salt water from my bleary eyes. Something floated by and I grabbed for it on instinct. A wooden crate, empty of whatever costly item it once held. Holding on with every bit of strength I had left, I searched the blackness for the ship. But all I could see was scattered detritus on the surface of the rolling waves. The vessel must have been swallowed by the sea while I was underwater.

Satisfied with its victory over us, the storm sped into the distance as I clung to the flimsy crate in the middle of the Great Sea. Nothing but water and sky all around and the terrifying deep below.

Perhaps it would have been better if the Sidonian traders had left me to die in the wilderness where they'd found me ten years ago, with no memory of who I was or where I'd come from. It was my fault Adin had come aboard Raphad's ship in the first place. I'd been desperate for a friend after so many years of loneliness and encouraged his thirst for adventure and freedom. And now he was dead because of me.

"What was the point of keeping me alive at all?" I croaked out to Yahweh. "Why let me be rescued then, only to sink to the bottom of the sea as a nameless slave with no past?"

No answer came as I bobbed up and down while the sky brightened with the encroaching dawn to reveal no sign of other survivors among what remained of the wreckage. I grabbed for a stray oar, glad for something else to hold on to, when a voice floated across the water.

I blinked as I searched the graveyard of debris around me, wondering if I was hearing things in my desperation for rescue. But then it came again, a little louder.

"Mattaniel!"

Relief crashed over me. I recognized that hoarse voice. Heart pounding, I whirled around to find Adin floating a short distance away, holding on to a crate like my own.

"Are you hurt?" I called out through the burn of emotion in my throat.

He gave me a feeble smile. "Bruised but otherwise fine."

I kicked my feet, angling toward him as I clung to the crate with one hand and the oar with the other. Once I was within reach, I stretched out the oar so he could grab hold. With his light brown hair plastered to his face and his blue eyes wide with shock, he looked far younger than his twenty years. "What do we do?"

I had no answer. What remained of the storm clouds were breaking apart to reveal patches of gray on the horizon, but only water stretched around us in every direction. I'd not seen land since we'd passed through the straits at the mouth of the Great Sea and we'd been days from the next port.

"What's that?" He gestured to something dark on the surface about twenty paces away. My heart stuttered as I imagined some hungry sea creature stalking us, but it was only the figurehead from the prow of Raphad's ship.

The imposing head of a warhorse had been a masterpiece of woodworking. Mouth gaping to reveal bared teeth, eyes inlaid with onyx, and decorated with vivid shades of red, blue, and purple, the exquisite carving had been the hallmark of Raphad's prized ship. Now it may be our only salvation.

After kicking our weary legs toward the cedar prow, I held it still as Adin pulled himself atop it, then I handed him the oar so I could do the same, hoping I did not dump both of us back into the water. But although it bobbed and trembled until we adjusted our balance, it held both our weight.

"Are we the only ones alive?" Adin's expression was grim as his eyes traveled over the lonely sea.

I nodded my head wordlessly. The silence around us spoke for itself. I'd been traveling with Raphad and his crew for years and knew every one of his men by name. Some had been kind to me, some had not, but none deserved to die in such a horrible way.

"Look . . ." Adin pointed in the direction of the rising sun. "Do you see that?"

I narrowed my eyes against the glare, heart squeezing. *Land.*

A small island jutted out of the sea to the east. Far enough away that it would take effort to get there but close enough to offer the first shred of hope that we might actually survive.

"Should we try to row there?" asked Adin.

"It'll be difficult enough to keep this thing from tipping over. We'll just have to pray the tides guide us there." At least the wind was at our backs. I let the long oar drag behind us in the water, a makeshift rudder. But if a crosswise current caught us, we'd be at its mercy.

"Forgive me, Adin," I said after a long stretch of fraught silence.

He peered over his shoulder. "For what?"

"I should not have talked you into coming on this voyage."

He huffed. "There was nothing you could have said to deter me once I latched on to the idea. It was my chance to start a new life and I took it."

"A lot of good it did you," I murmured, my eyes tracking over the endless blue toward the west.

"I have no regrets. If I'd remained in Israel, I'd have been under my father's thumb for the rest of my miserable life. If I die now, at least I'll die a free man."

I had no true memory of what it was like to be a free man. From the moment I'd awakened in the bed of a wagon, bloodied and confused, I'd been a slave.

The Sidonian traders had heard my cry while passing by on the road and ran off the pack of hyenas encircling me. They'd said I'd probably fallen from the ridge above and struck my head on a rock. Why I'd been up there, in the middle of the wilderness, was one of many questions that filled my head on sleepless nights. I remembered nothing, aside from disjointed and blurry visions of people and places I could not name.

Something appeared on the choppy surface a short distance from us. My bleary eyes, burning from the salt water, narrowed as I peered across the water at what looked to be a ring of inflated bladders dipping and swaying in rhythm with the waves. And within that circle was the head and shoulders of a man.

I caught my breath, pointing at the still form. "Adin. Look! Someone's out there."

His gaze tracked back and forth between the person and the island. "Whoever it is isn't moving. He's probably dead, and we might be swept farther out to sea if we try to get to him."

"We can't just leave him." I carefully pulled the oar across my lap, gently stroking with its tip to steer us northward, hoping the current would be in our favor. Yet when I realized that the man floating on the ring was none other than Raphad, my master, I went still, considering what it meant for me if he still lived. But almost immediately, a wave of guilt slammed into me. I could not leave him to die.

Unconscious, Raphad was bleeding from the head, but when I shook him by the shoulder, he moaned, eyelids fluttering for just a moment before he went still again.

"There's no way we can pull him onto this prow, Mattaniel."

Adin wasn't as tall as I was, but we were both fairly lean.

Raphad, however, was as stout and round as the jugs of strong ale he preferred.

"We'll just have to pull him along and hope his floats will keep him aloft." And that no predator from below would see his limp body as a meal. Pushing away that horrific thought, I set my eyes on the island ahead. The rocky outcropping appeared mostly barren, more like a giant boulder jutting from the sea than any sort of inhabitable land, and the closer we came, the more my worries grew. The waves pushing us toward the shore crashed hard against a rocky reef, spraying white foam into the air. I pressed the oar deep into the water, trying to aim for a less dangerous landing spot, but the waves were too strong. We would be dashed to pieces before we even reached land.

"Get off the prow! Swim!" I shouted.

During his brief time as an aide in the Israelite army, Adin had learned the lesson of unquestioned obedience well. He tipped into the sea without a word. I dropped the oar and followed him into the water, grateful that whoever that green-eyed boy in my liquid memories had been, he'd taught me to swim.

Grabbing hold of either side of Raphad's bladder floats, Adin and I kicked hard against the insistent press of the sea until we were clear of the worst of the devilish reefs. Then, with limbs numb from cold and exhaustion, we let the tides carry us the rest of the way.

By the time the azure sea spit us onto a narrow white-sand beach, there was nothing left in us to even drag our bodies, along with Raphad's, more than a few paces onto dry land. We dropped to the ground on either side of my insensible master, staring up at the canopy of brilliant blue, then let sleep wash over us.

When I awoke, Adin was gone. Panic welled as I weakly pushed to standing, noting Raphad was still unconscious a couple of paces away. Hand blocking the blazing sun overhead, I surveyed the beach where we'd landed. My friend's footprints tracked along the water's edge and then disappeared around the rocks.

Raphad mumbled something, his eyes peeling open to stare up at the bright sky above us.

I knelt beside him in the sand. "It's all right, master. We've made it to land. You are safe."

It felt like an obvious lie, since without food or water none of us would last long. A deep cut slashed down the middle of Raphad's face, from his hairline to his jaw. He needed a healer, soon.

"Matta . . . niel?" he croaked, turning his battered face toward me.

"Yes, my lord. Adin and I found you floating after the ship went down. We made it to an island."

Raphad's reddened eyes wheeled about for a moment and then to my astonishment, he began to cry. "I'm not dead?"

"No. We survived. Well, at least the three of us did."

"Thank you," he wheezed, tears mixing with blood to cascade down his craggy face. "Thank you for saving me."

"Think nothing of it—"

"No," he interrupted, eyes going wide. "You didn't have to. You could have left me."

I considered the moment I'd recognized him floating out there on the sea. It shamed me to admit, even silently, that my first thought had been if Raphad was dead I would no longer be a slave.

I shook my head, not meeting his eyes. "I would never have done so."

And it was true. No matter that I'd hesitated, I'd known deep in my bones that had I willingly left him to perish, I'd have been shackled to guilt for the rest of my life.

Before Raphad could respond, Adin called to me. Hip-deep in the water, he was pushing one of the huge jugs once stowed in the belly of Raphad's ship toward the beach. I ran down to the shoreline as he rolled the large vessel onto the sand.

"It's still sealed," he said. "I think it might be wine."

It was astonishing the jug had not sunk to the bottom of the sea with the rest of the wreckage. It must not have been filled completely, containing enough air to keep it afloat. What likely was meant to cheat my master of his full purchase was now a blessing from the heavens.

Together we rolled the vessel to where Raphad still lay flat on his back, gaping at the sky. Then, using a sharp rock, Adin broke the thick beeswax seal and tipped the contents into his hand. Deep red wine from one of the first cities we'd ported on the western coast of Galicia filled his palm.

We drank our fill, bringing handfuls of wine to Raphad's mouth, until dazed by strong drink under the harsh sun, one by one we passed into blessed oblivion.

Words in a language I'd never heard before looped strangely through my dream as I ran through a densely wooded forest, following three boys with wooden swords in hand. Then something nudged me hard in the side as more unintelligible words encircled me. My eyes fluttered open, and I blinked against the sunlight. Shadows moved over me, then changed to unfamiliar faces as my hazy vision cleared.

A group of strangers hovered over us, talking in a language I could not understand. My pulse pounded as I took in the bronze-tipped spears pointed at my chest. Four more well-armed men had encircled Adin, who'd awakened to the same horror.

"What do we do?" he whispered as one of the men bent to examine Raphad, his well-weathered skin wrinkling as he poked a long finger into my master's chest. Raphad moaned but did not wake.

"Show them we are unarmed," I said. "Lift your palms. Slowly."

We both raised our empty hands. The strangers chattered to one another, and my curious ears strained to catch a pattern within the lilting syllables, but it was like no other language I'd ever heard, undulating like the waves that had carried us here.

Two men reached for my wrists and pulled me to my feet while others did the same for Adin, both of us covered in sand and reddened from the sun. The rest of my skin itched, tight from the dried salt water, and my tongue was like wool.

One of the men gestured toward the sea, moving his arm in a simulation of the waves.

"Yes," I said in the language of my master. "We came on a ship, from Tyre." I moved my hand in the same manner and swirled it to emulate the storm. Then, cupping my palms like the hull of a boat, I plunged them downward.

The strangers launched into a conversation I desperately wished I could understand. They were dressed simply, either sporting rough-spun tunics or standing bare-chested with thin woolen kilts. Most wore long braids in their hair and beards, some laced with tiny shells or stone beads. Their skin, although darkened from the sun, was a shade or two paler than Adin's, and three of them had hair the color of sun-ripened wheat.

Two of the men, one older and one nearer my own age, seemed to be arguing over our fate. The younger one snapped out what sounded like a command and gestured down the beach to where a few more men stood in the surf securing two longboats, their curious gazes on us. Every one of these strangers was tall, lean, and well-muscled, not to mention armed with a variety of deadly weapons. Adin and I were no match for any one of them, especially in our weakened state.

Four of the men surrounded Raphad, each taking one of his limbs, and hoisted my portly master into the air with shocking ease. Then, with him strung between them like fresh game, they headed for the boats, the eldest of the group in the lead, looking annoyed.

The younger man, who seemed to have championed the decision not to kill us, said something to me in his language and waved toward the boats. With a quick glance between us, Adin and I wordlessly agreed that these rough and dangerous men were our only hope of survival.

By the time we reached the boats, the others had settled Raphad atop a pile of sodden nets stinking of seaweed. Adin and I climbed in to sit on either side of him, careful not to step on the many silver fish strewn about the wide hull. Our rescue had obviously interrupted a return trip with an impressive catch of tuna. After a flurry of discussion in their fascinating language, some of which seemed to be an argument over who would ride in which boat, the youngest ones pushed the vessels out into the waves, then slithered up into the boats with amazing dexterity.

Someone handed me a waterskin and I nearly wept as the first drop touched my parched tongue. I gulped the tepid liquid, then handed Adin the skin. Another man offered us each a thick filet of dried fish and a golden apple, which we devoured as our rescuers dipped their long oars into the water. Someone else began a rhythmic chant that quickly transformed into a boisterous song in cadence with their powerful strokes.

Raphad stirred at the noise, gasping as he took in the strange sights around him. I placed my hand on his shoulder. "It's all right, master. We have been rescued by local fishermen."

"We're saved?" Raphad's voice warbled.

I had no real answer. They could be taking us back to their village to sacrifice us to their gods for all we knew.

"They've given us food and water. Why don't you take a drink?"

Adin held the skin to Raphad's lips as I propped my master up enough to take a mouthful. He coughed, choking at the rush of water until his face went deep red, so I propped him onto his side to let him catch his breath.

"I owe you my life," he said between coughs.

"You don't owe me anything," I said. "I only wish I could have done something to save the rest of the crew." *If only they would not have laughed at my warnings.*

He cleared his throat, shaking his head. "No. I owe you, Mattaniel. You have been the best of slaves these past few years. Far more valuable to me than any other."

This I knew. Raphad bragged to everyone he could about my ability to speak a number of languages and learn new ones with little effort. He treated me well, far better than the vast majority of other slaves I'd come into contact with during my time in bondage. I'd become more of a personal scribe and translator than anything. But I was still a slave. Still owned by Raphad.

"And to thank you for saving me, when we get back to Tyre—if we find a way—I will set you free."

My pulse raced, thumping in my temples as I stared at him in astonishment. "You . . . you will?"

He let out a rusty chuckle and another cough. "I guess, even if I don't make it, you'll no longer be a slave."

My jaw gaped. I'd been enslaved for ten long years. I had no idea what I would even do if I had the choice to go my own way. I did not know where I came from or where I belonged.

I looked up to find Adin grinning at me. At least I would have a friend to help me in the search.

In the distance, land came into view, a wide expanse of green sprawling to the north and south. Atop one of the hills, a stone tower rose to seemingly impossible heights, a column of smoke drifting upward from its tip. As we came closer, the water turned from deep blue to a vivid turquoise so clear I could see the coral reefs below.

Villagers gathered on the white beach, waving to the fishermen and calling out excitedly, some of the children already splashing into the surf to meet the boats. Whether these people would welcome or enslave all of us was yet to be seen, but at least for the moment, we were alive. And if by some miracle we found our way back to Tyre, I would finally be free. Perhaps Yahweh had heard the desperate call of this nameless slave after all.

2

Elissa

City of Tyre
1029 B.C.
Three Years Later

"Do not dishonor the king by letting the hem of your skirt drag over the threshold, Elissa."

I winced as Magin's admonishment echoed through the empty room but lifted my fringed hem higher as I stepped into the cedar-paneled Grand Hall. Head held high and features schooled into pleasant apathy, I passed the pool in the center of the room, which glittered under the soaring skylight overhead. With measured steps, I approached the empty throne and the three eunuchs scrutinizing every move of my kid-leather slippers from the dais. Once I stood before them, they surveyed me head to foot with varying expressions: Magin, with his usual sour frown; Shamzur, with polite disinterest; and Abenasser, with a vaguely apologetic look on his round face.

Frustration buzzed in my chest. I'd followed every instruction. My bearing was straight, my grooming impeccable. I'd even worn the gaudy gown Shamzur had selected without complaint. But there was little pleasing the head of the palace eunuchs.

Abenasser lifted a well-sculpted brow, his dark eyes dipping to the floor meaningfully. Realizing my mistake, I sank to a deep bow, chin tucked, and recited the fawning greeting I would offer my father, the king of Tyre, tomorrow night before a room full of dignitaries and sycophants. Then, mustering every drop of grace the eunuchs had drilled into my head since I was a child, I set my forehead to the cool tile and held myself prostrate.

I dared not even peek up at Seriyah, my older half-sister, who had glided into the room ahead of me like one of the exotic black swans in the palace gardens. With hair the color of midnight and eyes of sun-drenched ebony, she was the embodiment of her mother's royal Egyptian heritage and destined to sit on a throne herself one day soon. An honor I did not begrudge her.

"That will do," Magin barked, then called for the next sister in line to enter. I arranged a pleasant expression on my face as I rose and went to stand among the unlit lampstands and empty vases on the opposite side of the dais from Seriyah, as was befitting a daughter of a once-favored concubine.

Thalassa entered the throne room next. Another princess, this one belonging to my father's second wife and granddaughter of the king of Chalcis to the north. Thalassa knew her place, never failing to hold herself apart from those of us not born of pure royal blood. Although she was my half-sister, she and her mother rarely associated with us, so I barely knew her. Once she stood next to Seriyah in their elevated position to the right of the dais, Melita entered the room, eyes lowered.

Melita was a concubine's daughter as well, a few months younger than me and my favorite among all my sisters—though I'd never admit such a thing to the rest. However, given the tight set of her shoulders and the strain on her face, she was not at all ready for the eunuchs' scrutiny.

Halfway up the aisle, Melita tripped on the fringe on her skirt. My stomach lurched as she wobbled dangerously toward the edge of the pool, but she caught herself before she pitched into the water and finished her slow march up to the dais without further calamity. With tears in her big, brown eyes, she bent low to offer the customary salutations and grandiose exaltations of our father's greatness but stumbled over the flowery words before losing her place in the recitation entirely. My instincts screamed that I should run to shield her from Magin's undisguised disdain. But it would only make things worse, so I held myself in check.

"You should have had this memorized weeks ago," the head eunuch snapped.

Melita dipped her wobbling chin. "I have tried, I promise. The words refuse to stay in my head."

"So you will shame your father?"

"Of course not . . ." she began, blinking furiously against more tears.

His piercing gaze dropped to her bare toes. "And where are your slippers?"

She shrank at the harsh demand, voice small. "They keep sliding off my feet."

Magin huffed an aggrieved sigh, turning to Shamzur, whose duty it was to tend our wardrobe.

The eunuch gave a tight-lipped nod. "I'll take care of it."

Looking down his long nose, Magin snapped his fingers to regain Melita's attention. "Don't stoop."

She flinched but obeyed, stretching her long, graceful neck and straightening her shoulders. With shining golden hair and an enviably statuesque form inherited from her Hittite mother, she was a striking woman. Yet her timidity made her a frequent target of Magin's disapproval.

I willed her to look at me once she finally took her place at my side, but her eyes remained on the floor, pale cheeks pink as a sunrise. I desperately wished I could slip my fingers into hers but refused to draw any further attention her way. Three more of the king's daughters entered the room—Nikka, Zorina, and Ramina—all performing well enough to avoid harsh criticism.

However, unlike the rest of us, none of them were old enough yet to be married off to further our father's political machinations. There was still plenty of time for the eunuchs to mold them into dutiful treaty brides.

"The Feast of Awakening is *tomorrow* night, ladies," said Magin, once the younger girls were in place. "You will present yourselves as soon as the men return from the sacrifice."

I'd always loved the fire ritual that launched the Days of Awakening, when an effigy of Melqart was immolated in the city square to symbolize the end of the stormy season. But only men were allowed in the temple on the third day, when they celebrated the resurrection of the deity and secured his blessing over the seafaring months with secretive rituals.

"And remember . . ." Magin's gaze raked over all the girls before lingering on Melita and me. "You are daughters of the king of Tyre. A direct reflection of His Majesty. Do *not* dishonor your father or your people by taking that responsibility lightly."

We'd heard this all many times before. Each of us had been tutored by the eunuchs since childhood for the express purpose of securing advantageous marriages. We'd learned to speak, dance, dress, and entertain with graceful poise solely to glorify our father's throne. Highborn or not, we all knew our duty from our earliest years.

Once finished with his rant, Magin stepped off the dais and led Shamzur and Abenasser out of the room. Although all three eunuchs had oddly soft features, smooth faces, and voices pitched like those of women, each held a coveted position and were entrusted with the king's women and children, a rare honor. They were highly educated, deadly with weapons, and trained to spot a threat from a hundred paces away. Such sharp-eyed vigilance, along with the fringed black robes that flapped in their wake like feathers, meant they were called the Crows by most everyone in the palace, and had been since long before my birth.

The moment they were gone, an army of servants streamed in to prepare the hall for tomorrow night's feast. Overnight, the room would transform into a paradise of food, flowers, and glittering entertainment. Abibaal never did anything by half-measures.

Melita turned, dropping her forehead to my shoulder with a groan. "I'm going to make a fool of myself."

I patted her cheek. "You will not. I'll help you."

"As will I." Seriyah approached with the same elegance she'd employed to float into the room. She was perfect in face, form, and manner. If only I could summon a hairsbreadth of hatred for her. But alas, she was as kind as she was lovely and had never treated Melita and me as anything less than full-blooded sisters. In fact, it wasn't until I was eight years old that I'd even realized some strict lines between us were absolutely not to be crossed. A concubine's daughter was not on the same footing as the offspring of a queen, no matter how much I adored my older sister.

"I plan to tell my mother how terrible Magin was today, Meli," Seriyah said, a rare edge of frustration in her voice. "It was uncalled for."

"There's no need." Melita sighed. "He's right. No matter what I do, I either trip over my skirts, my slippers, or my words."

"It would only make it worse, Seri," I said. "You know how he can be."

It was not only Thalassa who held herself in high regard in this household. One would think Magin himself was of royal blood the way he stared down his nose at us.

She glared at the doorway. "He deserves censure after humiliating her."

"You know as well as I that your mother will not agree." The queen was not likely to see Magin's admonishments as anything but helpful critique. It was his duty to teach us, after all, to help us become the accommodating brides we were destined to be. And for as condescending as he was, none of the Crows dared lay a hand on any of us.

"But don't worry," I said, sliding my arm around Melita's waist to pull her close. "Seri and I will spend every hour between now and then helping you practice."

Melita's chin wobbled as she leaned into me. "Thank you, Lissi."

"You know we'd do anything for you, sister," said Seriyah, grasping Melita's other hand and squeezing it tight.

My throat burned. I loathed the idea of Seriyah being sent away from us, but Abibaal had already negotiated a lucrative trade agreement with the king of Gebal. And our older sister was the beautiful seal on that covenant. Her marriage to the prince was set to be announced tomorrow night at the feast, so I had only a few months to prepare to let her go. Thank the gods the man pursuing my own hand was a local merchant whose extensive holdings were just across the water on the mainland of Tyre. I'd only be a short ferry ride away.

"Pardon the interruption."

I turned to find my mother's maid, Danice, approaching us. She bowed low. "Apologies, my lady, but your mother is asking for you."

Gut clenching at the strain in her voice, I dropped my arm from Melita's waist. "What's wrong?"

Danice peered up at me, her dark eyes brimming with all-too-familiar concern. "She needs you . . . *right away*."

Needing no further explanation and knowing my sisters would understand, I ran.

I'd lost my slippers somewhere along the way but did not care when my mother's cries could be heard across the courtyard. Ignoring the icy cold of the limestone and the stares of a few concubines and their children, I ran past their game of Serpents and Stones, my only thought to reach her. Danice would not have left her alone unless things were very bad.

I flew through the door into the dim chamber. Curled in a ball in the center of the large bed, where she'd been for the past few days, my mother's body shook, face hidden in the tangle of her hair as she sobbed. Tipping my head back to beg the gods for calm, I willed my breaths to slow before speaking. It would do no good for her to sense my panic.

"*Ama*, it's me. I'm here."

As if she'd not heard me, she continued wailing.

"Everything will be all right," I crooned, crawling onto the bed to lie close beside her. "I'm here with you now."

Her body jerked when I slipped my arm around her, and she dragged in a shuddering breath, peering at me through a mess of auburn locks, her pale skin streaked with tears and the remains of kohl. My heart pinched as I slicked hair away from her face. No matter how many times I'd seen her in this state, it never failed to hurt.

"Elissa?" she croaked, her wet lashes fluttering. "You're here?"

I forced my mouth into the semblance of a smile. "Danice said you needed me."

Her breath hitched, another painful sob racking her body. I pulled her closer, murmuring quiet assurances as she pressed her face into my shoulder and soaked my expensive gown with tears while I stroked her back. I winced at the ripple of her bony spine under my hand. I knew Danice did her best to make my mother eat, but she was far too frail after so many days in this bed. During times like this, I worried she might simply waste away and disappear.

Sometimes I wondered if she *meant* to disappear.

After a while, her sobs eased. And although her body still twitched whenever she took a labored breath, she went quiet, and the tense set of her shoulders softened. I thought perhaps she'd drifted into sleep when she blinked up at me with hazy eyes, frowning.

"Your gown, I've ruined it." She frowned at the yellow fabric, now spotted with black tears.

"That's all right. It makes me look like a boiled citron anyhow." I tried to smile. "Shamzur made me wear it."

Her breath hitched, her eyes going wide. "Oh no, I took you away from something."

I shook my head. "We were done anyhow."

A leftover tear dripped onto her sodden pillow. "I'm sorry, I should not have—"

"I'd much rather be with you." I curved my palm over her cheek, swiping at one dark streak with my thumb. "You know what a wretch Magin can be during event preparations. I cannot wait for it to be over."

Her chin wobbled. "The Feast of Awakening is tomorrow?"

I nodded, wishing I had a different answer. No matter how many years had passed, this season was always a difficult one for her.

"I can't . . ." Her blue-green eyes filled with tears again, her voice small. "He won't make me go, will he?"

I stroked her hair. "Of course not."

Regardless of the king's demand that his entire household make an appearance tomorrow night, my father knew better than to insist she take part. He'd learned that lesson years ago when she'd had to be carried out by the eunuchs after collapsing in a hall full of exalted guests. And now that I was old enough to represent her during official events, he never asked for her presence at all. It was almost as if he'd forgotten she even existed, let alone had once been his favorite concubine.

Her watery gaze lifted to the altar at the end of her bed and she gasped. "The flame! It's gone!"

Danice darted into the room as if she'd been listening at the doorway, her black curls slipping free of her ever-present blue headscarf. Snatching the oil lamp from the table beside the bed, she revived the blackened wick in the tall one set directly between the golden form of Astarte and a silver statue of Eshmun on the altar.

"Apologies, mistress," Danice murmured, her expression pained as she dropped her chin. "It must have gone out while I fetched your daughter."

My mother did not answer, the flickering light reflecting in her glassy stare as her mouth moved in what I knew to be silent prayer to the gods.

"Don't leave me," she whispered after a long while, still staring at the flame.

My throat ached as I held her frail body close, wishing I could bring myself to pray too. "Never, Ama. I promise."

3

Mattaniel

Enclosed by towering limestone walls, the city of Tyre crowned the island in splendor, the white-clad palace shimmering like a diamond at its crest. Deep purple and scarlet banners dripped from multileveled rooftops and from every tower atop the ramparts, flapping lazily in the sea breeze as if beckoning us forward.

At my side, Adin stared with open-mouthed wonder as we trailed Raphad up the bustling main thoroughfare, both of us hefting heavy-laden leather packs. The royal fortress had always been impressive but was even more spectacular now. The port, too, had been expanded, with enormous sea breaks to protect the northern harbor from the frequent storms that battered this coast.

Abibaal had obviously grown in both power and influence over these past four years. Not a surprise—the king of Tyre was famous for his ambition to build what had been a moderately profitable seaport at his crowning into the most affluent kingdom in the region. It seemed he was well on his way to accomplishing that goal.

Although his rich green robes were fit for an audience with the king, Raphad's pallor was sallow after the short trip from the mainland, highlighting the pale scar across his face. My master's brush with drowning had stolen his former love of the sea. It had taken a fair bit of convincing for Raphad to even board the Cypriot ship that unexpectedly landed on the shores of Shardana three months ago, and even then he'd spent the majority of the journey back to Tyre belowdecks with the cargo. He'd practically kissed the shore when we made land a few days ago. If Abibaal had not sent him a personal invitation to the Feast of Awakening today, I doubted he would have set foot on the ferry at all. But there was no ignoring an edict from the king of Tyre.

If it were possible, the inside of the palace was even more of a marvel than its exterior. As Abibaal's servants ushered us into the Grand Hall, Adin and I gawked at the massive cedar beams soaring overhead. Every wall was paneled in the same rich material. The enveloping smell of the wood stirred some deep-seated memory: cloud-scraping trees towering above me, leaves crunching beneath my feet, the hint of smoke lingering in the air.

"Can you believe we are here, among royalty?" Adin's voice melted away the inexplicable nostalgia for a place I did not remember.

I raised a brow. "You've been living among royalty for the past three years, my friend."

Adin scoffed as his gaze tracked over the purple curtains fluttering at the windows. "Not like this."

A smile quirked my lips. "Uvaldo would be quite offended to hear you insult his kingliness."

In truth, the leader of the Shardan would expire from envy if he were here now. His dream of being on the same footing as the other powerful kings around the Great Sea was something of an obsession. Which was why, before bargaining our return passage with the Cypriots, he'd made Raphad vow to wield his influence with the king of Tyre and negotiate trade between the two kingdoms. Perhaps tonight my master would have a chance to fulfill that promise.

We passed two intimidating guards standing at attention in the portico, dressed in well-polished bronze armor and with neatly trimmed facial hair. Adin rubbed at his clean-shaven chin. "I miss my beard."

All men on Shardana wore long braids and unkempt beards. We'd not thought much of it until Raphad's wife, Portea, nearly fainted at the sight of the three of us at her door, looking like savages come to ravish her. We'd far more resembled the rough-edged pirates we'd been living with for three years than the well-manicured people of this cultured city.

"We would not have been allowed to accompany Raphad looking like wild men."

"Still . . ." Adin frowned. "I haven't been without hair on my face since I was twelve."

I slicked my palm over my own clean-shaven jaw and the divot in my chin that had been hidden for so long I'd nearly forgotten it was there. I, too, felt naked without my beard and my shoulder-length locks, which the women of the island regularly braided and oiled while filling my ears with village gossip. They'd always made much of the streak of silver above my right brow, calling it the kiss of the gods, so while I'd submitted to having my hair cut nearly to my scalp this morning in preparation for today, I'd kept that singular silver braid as a reminder of my time on Shardana.

"We can let it grow after today. No one will care."

His deep blue eyes locked on me. "You really are coming with me, then?"

I'd been weighing his plan to return to Israelite territory for weeks now. Adin had decided to join the army of Israel, the very thing he'd eschewed before he fled Gaza, on account of his brute of a father. But regardless of the skills I'd learned from the Shardan, I had little interest in war. I was far more suited for halls of learning than battlefields. Raphad had offered to keep me on as a paid scribe once the manumission documents he carried on his person were registered with city authorities. But I was ready to make my own way as a free man, and perhaps even find where I came from.

There had to be people out there who knew who I was. Someone who cared that I'd gone missing thirteen years ago. The Sidonian traders had found me near a stream east of the Jordan in Gaddite territory. It was the only touchpoint I had, so that would be as good a place to start as any other. All I knew for certain was that soon I would officially no longer be a slave and wherever I went after that, the choice would be mine and mine alone.

"Yes," I said, solidifying the decision in my own mind as I spoke. "It's time."

Adin clapped his palm on my shoulder and squeezed. "You won't regret it, my friend. I have plenty of connections all over the territories. We'll find your people, I'm sure of it."

After so long, it was almost painful to hope, to root around in places I'd long buried, but I finally would have the freedom to do so.

The servant leading us through the maze-like palace turned into a Grand Hall, already full of chattering guests dressed in finery. Every surface of the cavernous room was a wonder. Scores of enormous pillars formed from clusters of unbelievably tall cedars held aloft a soaring roof three stories above us. Countless flickering oil lamps dangled from more cedar beams overhead, setting alight a wealth of gold and silver around the room. Beneath the wide skylight in the roof, the surface of a shimmering pool was dappled with blooming lotus and what remained of the dusky twilight hues overhead.

Once Raphad was seated on a reclining couch among his peers, Adin and I were sent to the periphery of the hall with the other servants—not a place of honor by any stretch of the imagination, but one that gave us a clear view of the massive columns, wrapped in garlands of vibrant blooms and green foliage, an army of ivory-inlaid reclining couches layered with lush fabrics and thick cushions, and a dazzling array of vibrant clothing and jewelry bedecking the guests of the king. Between the irritating buzz of overlapping voices echoing off the paneled ceiling, the acrid smoke of myriad oil lamps, and the clash of spices from incense burners, it was all rather overwhelming.

Wide-eyed, Adin pointed out a wooden apparatus made to look

like a stand of cedar trees set in one corner of the room, with four red-nosed baboons chained to the branches. Their beady eyes roved over the assembly with a menacing scrutiny that made my skin crawl. One stretched his mouth wide to let out a horrifying screech, which set off the others. It took three brave servants armed with long, pointed sticks to calm the animals.

I'd never understand the desire of the wealthy to trap wild animals and put them on display. During our travels, Raphad and I had seen crocodiles, giant apes, spotted wildcats, and even enormous pythons and cobras inside palaces. I'd never gotten used to being in proximity to things that wanted to kill me. In fact, I'd been quite glad that on Shardana, the most dangerous animals were the wild boars that roamed forested areas. And even so, my friend Torben had found it far too amusing when a pack of them dashed out of the brush across our path during my first hunting excursion and I'd climbed a nearby tree to get away.

A pair of silver trumpets sounded near the doorway and the room went silent. Abibaal, King of Tyre, was announced, everyone kneeling as the man himself entered. Adin and I scrambled to do the same, heads bowed, but I kept my eyes lifted just enough to watch the king stride across the room, draped in a golden lion skin, its stuffed head perched on one bulky royal shoulder and lifelike amber eyes glittering in the lamplight. An intricately carved club was gripped in Abibaal's hand, a symbol of the warrior-god Melqart and the king's unquestioned authority in this city and its surrounds. Atop his head sat an ornate crown of pure gold inlaid with polished amethyst to match his deep Tyrian purple robes.

I'd been in the presence of kings all over the world, and the pomp demanded by the king of Tyre was nearly equal to that of the Pharaohs. Once Abibaal was seated atop the wide dais at the far end of the hall, the queen took her seat of honor on his left, one graceful hand concealing a small mound beneath her flowing lavender gown.

A slow parade of Abibaal's wives and sons then entered the hall, led by Ahiram, the crown prince, who was perhaps a year or two older than me. Numerous concubines followed, each of them bowing with grand flourish while reciting lofty salutations before taking their seats on the opposite side of the dais from the royal wives. Then, the daughters of the king were summoned.

The first young woman was announced as Seriyah, daughter of Queen Khamera. She favored her mother heavily, with black hair, dark eyes, and innate grace that evidenced her royal heritage. After greeting her father with great respect, she took her place on a couch to the right of the dais, near Ahiram.

A second young woman entered the room, reddish-brown hair flowing over her shoulders in gleaming tawny waves. Her name was given as Elissa, daughter of Leyana, as she bowed low before her father to recite a greeting of honor in a melodious voice that reminded me of a skillful strum on a lyre. However, instead of joining her sister, she turned to the left to be seated near the concubines beside a sprawling three-tiered lampstand. Not a pure-blooded royal like Seriyah, then.

The next daughter, Melita, was shockingly tall for a female, with bright golden hair that stood apart from the rest. With her eyes downcast and a tinge of pink on her fair cheeks, she made her way up the center aisle, but only paces from the king, she stumbled, her slipper coming loose and flipping once in the air before landing near the dais. Her face flushed crimson at the same time as a horrid crash sounded and a few exclamations of surprise echoed through the room. My gaze was torn from Melita to where the lampstand near the concubines had toppled, leaving shattered pottery and oil all over the tile.

One hand pressed to her mouth, Elissa looked horrified by the catastrophe. Yet as servants scrambled to clean the mess and the guests whispered amongst themselves, the young woman's gaze went to Melita, who snatched up her wayward slipper, fled the king's presence with her face aflame, and scurried over to sit beside Elissa. When the next member of Abibaal's extensive brood entered the hall, pulling all eyes away from the two young women, Elissa stealthily wiped the tears from her sister's face and pulled her close to whisper in her ear. Realizing I was brazenly staring at members of the royal household in a private moment, I tore my eyes away to watch the remainder of the procession.

Once the entirety of Abibaal's household had entered the hall, the king raised his golden cup in the air and announced in a booming voice, "Welcome to my home, friends. We give thanks for the rebirth of our exalted lord, Melqart, and the blessing he shines upon our city year after year. May his eternal flame never be quenched and our ships be ever under his protection."

With their own cups lifted, every guest in the room echoed his salutations, drinking in honor of both king and deity.

"Enjoy the bounty of my table, my friends!" announced Abibaal.

As if released from a spell, the room came to life. Music from a chorus of lyres, drums, and pipes began as a bevy of servants swarmed the room carrying overladen serving tables to place near the guests or refilling silver drinking bowls with mixed wine drawn from large bronze kraters.

My belly snarled at the smell of roasted meat and heavily spiced dishes, but as we were relegated to the ranks of handservants, Adin and I had no choice but to stand watching from afar as the king and his guests devoured more food and wine than seemed possible. The many serving tables around the room held thick slabs of smoked whitefish and wild game, steaming pots of shellfish and tentacled sea creatures, cheeses of every variety, and endless baked goods that made my tongue water. Even the baboons were afforded baskets of fruit on their perches.

Adin leaned in. "Almost makes you wish you were back with the Shardan, doesn't it?"

On the island, I had eaten the same fare as everyone else in the village—simple, but fresh and plentiful. And yet even with all the liberties I'd enjoyed there, I'd still been considered Raphad's slave. For all the beauty of the place we'd lived for the past three years and the people I'd learned to call friends among the Shardan, I would far prefer true freedom.

Once the king finished his meal, a delegation from the northern city of Gebal was announced. The envoy offered fawning salutations and requisite gifts from his king. Then, with a flourish, he produced a stone tablet and handed it to the king's steward, who delivered the missive to his master. Sprawling back on his couch, Abibaal read the message intently before calling for Princess Seriyah.

All eyes moved to the daughter of the queen, her black hair shimmering in the light of a hundred oil lamps as she floated toward the dais.

"For the past few months," Abibaal said with a satisfied grin, "the king of Gebal and I have been negotiating a profitable trade agreement to include shared port access, safe passage for merchants, and the union of resources in our continued efforts to keep enemies far from our shores. I am pleased to say we are mutually satisfied with the terms. To solidify this special union between our two kingdoms, my daughter Seriyah will be joined in marriage to Ittobaal, heir to the throne."

Great celebration broke out in the hall, guests lifting their cups and shouting felicitations.

The king's daughter accepted the accolades and well-wishes with appropriate humility, bowing to her father before returning to her mother's side. The queen beamed at her daughter, obviously thrilled Seriyah would one day sit beside her future husband on the throne of Gebal, one of the most powerful and ancient Canaanite city-states.

"Preparations will begin immediately," said the king. "In two months' time, we shall accompany the princess to her new home and see her wed to the crown prince."

Seriyah flinched, the movement so slight I doubted anyone else noticed. But immediately she spread a serene smile across her face, smoothly wiping away the shock that had leaked through the mask. She may have been prepared to wed, but perhaps not quite so soon.

Unbidden, my gaze flicked back to Elissa. She watched Seriyah with a troubled expression while the king expounded on the profitable treaty he'd negotiated with Gebal. From my observations during the years of travel with Raphad, most royal households seethed with jealousies and competing ambitions. It seemed this one was no different.

Even Uvaldo's household on Shardana, humble though it was in comparison, had been rife with politics. His two wives were notorious for fits of hysteria when one or the other appeared to be granted more favors, and their children were vicious with one another, all vying for clout with their father and the loyalty of his subjects. Uvaldo had confided to me once that none of them deserved to inherit his leadership, and he planned to name his nephew Torben as heir, which would inevitably spark a firestorm amongst his offspring.

"Raphad looks even worse now than he did before," said Adin, dragging my attention away from Elissa and toward my master. Instead of visiting with the other wealthy merchants around him, he picked at his food and barely even touched his wine. In fact, once the king and a select group of guests withdrew to the gardens to escape the oppressive heat in the hall, Raphad seemed to retreat further into himself while the clamor around him rose. I was very nearly to the point of crossing the room to offer assistance when the king's steward approached him, bending low to speak in his ear.

Raphad went an alarming shade of gray but nodded. Then he lifted his chin to meet my eyes and gestured for us to follow as he was led from the room. Adin's curious gaze flew to mine, but I shook my head and lifted my heavy pack. There was nothing to do but obey.

A salty wind chilled my overheated skin as we walked through an open portico with an expansive view of the black sea and the starry sky overhead. We followed the steward down three sets of stairs to the bottom level of the palace and out into the gardens. A line of torches marked the winding pathway through abundant foliage and towering palms, past a chattering man-made stream that gushed into a tiered pool, fountains topped by winged lions, and toward the sound of voices and soft laughter.

We emerged into a small clearing lit with even more torches and flickering braziers, which illuminated small clusters of wealthy guests and royal family members reclining on soft cushions, talking amongst themselves. The king himself sprawled on a massive stone seat, wine cup in hand. Two enormous black panthers were chained to either side of his footstool, like shadowy specters guarding the throne. A chill raced up my back as they caught sight of us, their heads lifting and unblinking golden eyes reflecting the torches as they tracked our every step.

"Ah yes, there he is," the king called out as we approached, his own piercing gaze locked on my master. "Raphad, esteemed merchant of Tyre, has returned from sea after four long years. Come, my *friend*, tell us how you were resurrected from the dead!"

Raphad's step faltered, his sandal catching on something in the path. Unthinking, I reached to steady him and, for just a moment, he met my eyes. I'd been wrong before. My master was not ill at all. He was terrified.

4

My master bowed low before the king, pressing his forehead to the dirt. "Most exalted king. I have returned with a grateful heart, for I was not certain I would ever have the pleasure of setting foot in your beautiful city again."

Abibaal's bejeweled finger flicked a silent command for the merchant to rise. "I've been told you were shipwrecked?"

Raphad struggled to his feet but kept his chin low. "Yes, my lord. Off the coast of the island of Shardana."

The king's brows arched. "Indeed?"

"Uvaldo, king of the Shardan himself, invited us to remain in his city after we were found by fishermen and generously provided us with food and shelter while on his island. Having heard of your greatness, all the way across the Great Sea, he sends his salutations and hopes for friendship between our peoples."

Calling the village we'd lived in a city was a far stretch of the imagination. The watchtowers the Shardan built were impressive to be certain, but even after centuries of settlement, Shardana was nowhere near as advanced as Tyre. Yet I sensed the designation was a calculated one on Raphad's part.

Abibaal squinted, seemingly unimpressed with overtures from an unknown king. "I thought most of the Shardan were taken captive in Egypt after their failed invasion decades ago."

Raphad swallowed hard but nodded. "This is true, my lord. Only a remnant of their people remained on Shardana."

"Perhaps they should not have strayed so far from their island," the king sneered. "Nor cast their sights on Pharaoh's lands."

Raphad shifted foot to foot. "Too true, my king. The Shardan came to regret joining with the other sea peoples in their foolish attempt at conquest. Many ended up either enslaved or conscripted into the same army that humiliated them. However, after inheriting the throne at a young age, Uvaldo has spent most of his life reviving his people's proud heritage and rebuilding what was lost or neglected during those years of war."

"And what took you so long to return? If this *king* was so amenable?" Suspicion was thick in Abibaal's condescending tone.

"It took these three years before any seafaring vessel landed on their shores, then Uvaldo generously bartered our passage with goods from his own storehouse. And to express his great respect for my exalted king, he sent us with gifts—"

"I don't need gifts from some savage pirate," sneered Abibaal, causing Raphad to flinch. "I *need* the investment in the ship I commissioned for you repaid, since the cargo you owe me is at the bottom of the sea."

His accusation hushed every whisper in the clearing and made my blood go cold. Although I had been privy to many of Raphad's dealings, I'd not known the king had loaned the capital for the ship we'd nearly perished on. Raphad had often bragged of its construction by the king's own shipbuilders and declared it practically indestructible. The cost of such a ship would have been great indeed.

Raphad had been a wildly successful merchant, one whose holdings had grown exponentially since I'd been in his service. But there were times when he made foolish gambles for the sake of his reputation. And apparently he'd wagered much more than I knew on that last trip across the Great Sea. No wonder he looked practically green.

"My king, your generosity is legend—" My master's fawning words wavered.

Abibaal cut him off again. "When you came to plead for a loan, your business was thriving. There was little risk in such an investment, especially with a merchant whose reputation was so steadfast." His expression darkened, looking eerily similar to the sharp-toothed lion head on his shoulder as he leaned forward to pin Raphad in his sights. "But you've been *dead* for three years. Your creditors, of which there were far more than you led me to believe, have already eaten away at your holdings, including the five smaller ships you already owned and the vast majority of your lands. Your villa has not yet been seized out of respect for your wife, the daughter of my father's most favored adviser. But now that you've returned, that too will likely be auctioned to satisfy those lingering debts."

"I still have many contacts in this region," stuttered Raphad. "I'll rebuild my business—"

"Any trading partners you had before have replaced you with other profitable merchants, ones not languishing on an island. You have no ships. No goods to trade. You are finished." Abibaal slashed a bejeweled hand through the air, causing the panthers to flinch, then swish their tails restlessly.

No wonder the villa had seemed half empty when we arrived. I'd assumed Portea let go of most of their servants for simplicity's sake when her husband did not return. But the poor woman had been left behind to endure Raphad's debtors calling in their loans. With no sons to help her, it was a miracle she'd not been thrown into the streets.

Raphad sputtered, his face deadly pale. "My lord, please. There was a terrible storm . . . there was nothing . . ."

"You knew the risks of such a long journey. Had you returned with the cargo, this would be a different conversation. But the fact remains I have not been compensated." The king threw up his hands in a helpless gesture. "What choice do I have, Raphad? Shall I empty my treasury of silver for every beggar and let Tyre slip into the sea?"

Raphad fell to his knees, shaking palms uplifted. "Of course not, my king. But please, have mercy on your servant. I can and will find a way to build back my trading networks; it will just take some time to repay you."

"It would take a decade or more," Abibaal said, leaning back on his throne. "And I may be generous, but patient I am not. Guards . . ." He gestured to Raphad. "Take this man into custody. He can work off his debt to me in prison. If he lasts that long."

A choked sob came from Raphad on the ground, his bulky shoulders shaking as everything he had left was stripped away with one wave of the king's hand. No wonder he'd been so frightened tonight. This had not been an invitation. It had been an ambush.

My gut twisted as I watched the guards lift Raphad to his feet. He may have been my master for the past eleven years, but he'd never been cruel like the Sidonians. And he'd been true to his word, drawing up manumission documents on our return and telling Portea to treat Adin and me as honored guests in their home. But what could I do? The king had every right to throw him in debtor's prison.

As if my mouth had moved on its own accord, I heard myself speak, making a wager of my own. "My king, please, there is something you must know."

Abibaal's piercing gaze moved to me, the force of it hitting like a thousand bricks. Not only was it forbidden for a servant to speak out of turn, but addressing a king without permission was inexcusable. I, too, may very well die alongside Raphad in prison for my audacity. So, with nothing left to lose, I slid my pack off my shoulder and withdrew its contents.

The king's eyes went wide for only a fraction of a moment before narrowing. "What is this?"

I held aloft two hefty pieces of silver statuary: horn-helmeted warriors, both a full cubit tall. The well-polished disks between their long horns glittered like diamonds in the torchlight. "The island of Shardana is rich with silver, along with lead, zinc, and iron—even tin. There is untold wealth in its mines, untapped."

Abibaal shifted forward on his throne, attention snared. "Guards. Halt."

His men immediately froze in place, an ashen Raphad held between them.

"*Who* are *you*?" asked the king.

My mouth went dry. Abibaal of Tyre was famous for his violent overthrow of his own uncle, Ragembal, nearly three decades ago, and for his mercilessness with anyone who dared threaten his power. I was less than nothing in his eyes.

"This is Mattaniel," Raphad offered before I could formulate an answer. "My personal scribe who was with me on the island. He knows everything about the Shardan—*everything*. Speaks their language like a native, whereas I have only a rudimentary grasp on their strange words. He is telling the truth. Those mines have been kept secret for generations and are mostly used for local weaponry or tools. There is a massive supply of ore belowground, practically untouched."

"And I suppose you think this will satisfy your debt to me? The promise of a little silver on some obscure island across the sea?" Abibaal scoffed. "This pirate king of yours must be a fool to reveal such a thing. I could easily send my ships tomorrow to take it all."

Raphad blinked at me in desperation. Although he was a shrewd negotiator when he had the upper hand, he'd never been articulate when things were out of his control. I'd spent more than my fair share of time in foreign ports brokering deals on his behalf. So, I took a deep breath and once again addressed the king.

"Uvaldo knows it is far too costly for Tyre to maintain mines so far from your shores. And although, yes, your fleet is powerful, the Shardan are skilled at repelling invaders. Large vessels are no match for a flock of swift boats steered by native navigators who practically breathe seawater. Especially those determined to protect their people at any cost. They did not gain a reputation for piracy by accident."

The king's expression had gone stormy at the insinuation that his naval fleet might have a weakness, but there was no other way to convince him of the strength in Uvaldo's position.

"However." I paused to take a breath. "The Shardan are willing to negotiate."

Abibaal's chin tipped to the side. "How so?"

"I've seen these mines with my own eyes, my king," I said, encouraged he hadn't yet called for my own arrest. "While they are extensive, the Shardan do not have the resources to unearth the metals on a large scale, nor do they have your shipbuilding capabilities and extensive trading networks."

Raphad somehow pushed past the fear that had paralyzed his voice. "Uvaldo is eager to form a partnership, my king. One that will benefit both our peoples. Mattaniel was taken beneath the mountains by the king's nephew and told me the veins in those caves run as thick as tree limbs."

The king went quiet, his slitted gaze traveling from my master, to me, to the silver statues, and back to me. My belly churned as he took his time contemplating. But then he frowned as he leaned back into his throne, giving a quick shake of his head. "I know nothing of these Shardan, aside from their foolhardy attempt to take down the most powerful king on earth. I don't enter a battle unless I know who and what I am up against." He waved to the guards once more, who began dragging Raphad away.

"Please, my king." My master's voice pitched high. "Uvaldo is desperate to make an alliance!"

I scrambled for something, anything, that would capture Abibaal's interest. "He'll give you land. Your kingdom will stretch all the way across the Great Sea."

"Wait." Again the king's sharp command immediately halted the guards. Raphad stared at me, wide-eyed and trembling. Although not as portly as he'd been when we landed on the island, he was no small man, yet in this moment he looked a bit like a frightened child as he silently pleaded with me for rescue.

Abibaal narrowed his gaze on me, waiting for an explanation.

I swallowed hard against the burning lump in my throat. This was my last chance to keep Raphad from debtor's prison. "Aside from its abundant natural resources and plentiful mines, Shardana is perfectly positioned for Tyre to dominate not only the entirety of trade on the Great Sea but far beyond it, due to its proximity to the Straits. Even a small port on Shardan shores would give you a strong advantage over any other nation. Including Egypt."

There was a long pause as the king's jaw ticked back and forth while he considered. "And how would I be assured this pirate king would even fulfill his end of the bargain, *scribe*?"

I pulled in a sharp breath, sifting through a few ideas before remembering the announcement Abibaal had made earlier in the night regarding his agreement with Gebal. It was audacious, but it was all I could think of in the moment. "Above all else, Uvaldo desires status among the other rulers around the Great Sea, my king. He would value an alliance between his family and yours."

Abibaal tapped the rim of the silver cup on his knee. "A marriage?"

Blood thrumming at my temples, I nodded. Such political unions were common between kings, after all. It would not be a stretch that Uvaldo would accept such terms. I doubted he would have any interest in another wife. The two he had were already a handful, but his nephew was yet unmarried. Torben had confided in me that none of the women on Shardana held his interest. Perhaps a woman of Tyre would please him.

Abibaal gestured for his steward, then spoke to him in low tones. With a bow, the steward darted from the clearing, blue robes flapping at his heels.

"Do these Shardan speak our tongue?" the king asked.

"No, my king."

"But you speak theirs?"

"I do."

"Good. Then it seems you have a new master, scribe."

My body went numb, my jaw going slack.

To my shock, Raphad lifted his voice again. "No, please, my

king. I vowed to set Mattaniel free. He saved my life. I have the manumission documents here in my purse. I will go back myself and convince Uvaldo—"

"I thought you had little mastery over their tongue." Abibaal's flat tone was dismissive.

Raphad's mouth opened and closed a few times. But what could he say? He'd relied on me heavily to translate for him while we were on the island. Adin was more fluent, but I was not about to bring any attention to my young friend. I dared not even look his way now.

"Tell you what, scribe . . ." Abibaal scrutinized my face. "I am not without mercy. I'll let you go free."

Blood rushed in my disbelieving ears.

"But only when a treaty is in place that guarantees me both land and the rights to the Shardan mines. Until then, you will serve me."

There was no arguing with the king of Tyre. Besides, what were a few more months of slavery if it meant I could keep Raphad from dying in prison and his wife from the streets?

I bowed low. "I am grateful for your mercy, my king. It would be my pleasure to serve you."

"I thought as much," said Abibaal, waving to his guards. "Go on and take Raphad to a cell."

"But . . . but I thought—" Raphad stuttered, voice shaking.

"*You* still have a debt to pay," snapped the king, with a dismissive flick of his wrist. "And until your pirate king brings me enough silver to cover it—plus four years of double interest—you'll begin working it off in my shipyards."

Abibaal peered at me as the guards dragged Raphad from the garden. "We understand each other, scribe?"

I nodded. What choice did I have?

"Excellent." He lifted his gaze beyond me. "Oh, good, here she is."

Disoriented by the shift in his tone, I blinked in confusion as the king's steward approached the throne. And a few steps behind him, a black-robed eunuch escorted an obviously confused young woman toward her father. The three of them bowed low before the king.

"Raise your cups, my friends," the king said, lifting his own in the air with a grin, "and congratulate my beautiful daughter Elissa. She is to be married!"

5

Elissa

The stairs blurred as I climbed toward the top level of the palace. I missed a step and lunged forward, but before I cracked my head on the landing, Shamzur grabbed my arm, pulling me upright.

"Are you well, my lady?"

"Fine." I shrugged off the eunuch's hold. I'd been telling myself and everyone around me the same lie for the past three days.

What I really wanted to say was that I was tired of being shadowed by Crows everywhere I went. That the last thing I wanted to do was report to the Hall of Records today. And that, above all, I did *not* want to marry some savage pirate. But from the moment my father ambushed me with an announcement of my betrothal in a garden full of witnesses, I'd had no choice but to feign delight over his decision. I'd always known I would be a token in my father's political machinations but never dreamed I'd be sent to an island a world away from everything and everyone I loved.

"Lost, sister?"

I looked up to find Yarikh, my half-brother, jogging down the staircase to meet us, a wry expression on his handsome face. He, far more than Ahiram, favored the king in looks and form: dark brown hair, piercing, deep-set eyes, and broad shoulders that evidenced his years of training in the king's ranks before being appointed to high command.

"No. Are you?" I wasn't certain I'd ever seen Yarikh in this wing of the palace, which was for the most part the domain of scholars, scribes, and priests.

Greasy-haired and still dressed in sullied leather armor, Yarikh chuckled but gave no answer.

I screwed my face as his stale odor wafted on the breeze through the towering window beside us. "You smell awful."

He barked a laugh. "So I've been told."

"Where have you been?" His beard was as long as I'd ever seen it.

I'd not spoken with Yarikh for what seemed like months, which wasn't all that unusual, since most of my time was spent at the other end of this sprawling palace with the women. In fact, I'd lived my entire life under this roof and had never even stepped foot in the wing where the royal men held quarters. However, I had thought it strange when Yarikh did not make an appearance at the Awakening Feast. Our father usually insisted every one of his children make an appearance during such public displays—a reminder that the king enjoyed an abundance of wealth, enough to boast multiple wives and numerous concubines, along with nearly twenty children, several of them with ancient royal bloodlines.

"My unit was sent to patrol near Cyprus for the past three months. There has been a rash of pirate attacks on our trade vessels in that area recently. We returned this morning." As the commander of one of Tyre's celebrated naval units, known for their powerful warships, Yarikh was frequently out to sea but never for months at a time. No wonder he looked like a pirate himself after so long.

"So." Yarikh's eyes flicked to Shamzur and then back to me. "Where exactly *are* you headed?"

"The Hall of Records." I pulled a tight smile. "To be trained in the language and ways of my bridegroom."

His eyes flared. "You're betrothed?"

"Soon. The king wants to secure a treaty with the Shardan."

Yarikh's mouth parted. "The Shardan? I thought they scattered decades ago."

I shrugged. "You would know better than I. Before the Feast, I'd never even heard of them."

He frowned, his gaze assessing. Then he addressed Shamzur. "I'll escort my sister the rest of the way. You may return to your duties."

The eunuch looked slightly annoyed by the dismissal, a rarity for Shamzur, whose placid demeanor had been a constant for most of my life. But he bowed his head and then spun to obey, the knotted fringe on his richly embroidered black robes flapping at his heels as he descended the stairs. Regardless of his high status in the household, a command from a prince was nothing he could ignore.

Yarikh offered me his arm. "Come, sister. Tell me what I missed."

Relieved to have someone to talk freely with after three days of pretense, I accepted his support as I continued my climb toward the upper level of the palace.

"All I know is some merchant who was presumed dead years ago came back with tales of silver on some distant island. Apparently, my marriage will secure rights to those mines."

I'd heard little about the particulars of the agreement after my father made his shocking announcement. But it made no difference. Once the king of Tyre made a decision, it was as good as carved in stone.

"He's getting desperate, then," murmured Yarikh.

I halted as we reached the landing, where two red marble pillars framed the northern port and the sparkling sea in the distance. "What do you mean?"

He gestured toward the view. "Construction takes capital, sister. And Abibaal is determined to expand that port into the largest north of Avaris. Not to mention the extensive additions to the palace, the renovations to the temples, and the flumes his crews have been constructing for over a year to bring water down to the city. And building a naval force is no small investment either. His coffers are likely going a little dry."

No wonder he'd been so determined to make an alliance with the king of Gebal, a rival only superseded in my father's disdain by the king of Sidon. The negotiations for Seriyah's hand in marriage must have been extremely lucrative.

"Besides, I thought Father had already promised you to Elithan."

Heartsick, I shook my head, my gaze tracking out the window to the far horizon. I'd always wondered what lay beyond the place where sky met sea. Now that I was faced with the prospect of finally knowing the answer, I wished such mysteries would remain hidden forever. "Nothing had been decided. I only have a few months, at most, before I'm shipped off to an island I've never heard of before."

"And Leyana?"

"I haven't even told her yet. She won't . . ." My throat ached as hot tears stung my eyes. "She won't take it well."

It had been a mercy my mother was not well enough to attend the Feast. I'd forbidden Danice from revealing the truth for now, but I needed to tell her before someone else did. I dreaded revealing that I was being forced to break my vow to her. The revelation may send her back into the darkness, just like when my tiny brother took his one and only breath outside the womb and she'd refused to eat or drink for days. I shuddered at the thought of what she might do without me here to watch over her.

Yarikh's stormy expression indicated he understood perfectly. Although the son of Ulya, my father's second royal wife, my mother had been his sole comforter when the woman died from a stomach ailment when he was only seven. Even after he'd been deemed a man and moved to the other end of the palace, he still came to visit her often. And unlike Ahiram, who never so much as spoke to me anymore, Yarikh never treated me like a concubine's daughter, only a sister.

"This isn't right. I'll talk to Abibaal, persuade him to change his mind."

"When has our father ever changed his mind once he's set a course?" No one questioned the king's decisions, at least in his presence. Not even the second in line to the throne.

The fact that my mother had once been his favorite concubine was of little consequence. There was a time Abibaal had even doted on me, but when I was nine years old, something had broken deep inside my mother after my brother's death. The king had called in physicians and healers and priests to help her, and although there were times she seemed normal and even full of life, the cycles of sadness and frightening episodes of panic and rage always returned. Eventually, he lost interest in both of us. It was an inexplicable mercy he'd not sent us away, as was certainly his right.

"So you'll just capitulate? Let him send you off to some gods-forsaken island and leave her alone?"

I threw up my hands. "Not even you can defy the king, Yarikh."

Frowning, he scratched the scruff on his jaw and glared at the floor. "There has to be a way."

"Believe me, I've spent the last few days trying to figure out how *not* to be packed off by a horde of brutish marauders. But right now, I must go learn their language."

"From who?"

"Some scribe who was on the island with the merchant. I am to be presented to these pirates as the perfect bride, schooled in their ways and delighted to be a living sacrifice to our father's ambitions."

I'd not even noticed the man who'd apparently been there when my father called for me the other night, but Magin had stunned me this morning by explaining that the scribe, who apparently was now in service to my father, would be teaching me the ways of the Shardan over the next few months.

"What if you weren't?"

My brow furrowed. "Weren't what?"

"The perfect bride?" Yarikh smirked. "What if, when the

Shardan arrived, they discovered you could not speak their language? That you were too much of a dullard to learn it?"

"I am not an idiot."

He laughed. "Of course not, Elissa. You're more intelligent than most women I know. I mean pretend. Play along with these lessons, but when the Shardan come, feign ignorance. Perhaps even insult them. Abibaal will be angry, but what can he do if the bride he offers them is unacceptable? He'll have to come up with another way to procure rights to their mines."

I swallowed, contemplating the consequences of such a scheme. "What if it doesn't work?"

"Isn't it worth a try? And in the meantime, I'll work on my own plan." He squeezed my arm. "Leyana needs you."

"She's getting worse, Yarikh. I can't leave Tyre."

He slipped an arm around me, pulling me tight to his side. "I know. Play the game for now, little sister. I'll think of something."

I nodded, grateful I did not have to explain things to him. He'd seen her at her worst a few times over the years. "I need to get to the Hall of Records. Shamzur said this scribe is waiting for me there."

"All right, let's go." He pressed a kiss to the top of my head. "But make the old man's job as difficult as possible for the next few months."

"I'll do my best." I wafted a hand in front of my nose. "But *you* need to bathe. You smell like you've been marinating in sweat and seaweed for weeks."

He barked a laugh. "If you were out to sea for months, you'd reek as well."

If this idea failed, I'd find out soon enough.

The scribe in question was anything but an old man.

As soon as I stepped over the threshold into the dim Hall of Records, my gaze was drawn to the tall figure standing in a spill of sunlight from one of the high windows alongside Nolam, the elderly eunuch who was my very favorite among the Crows.

Wishing Yarikh had not left me at the door, I wrinkled my nose at the overpowering smell of old papyrus, dusty tablets, and stale parchment as I made my way across the cavernous room, past a few scribes and priests seated on stools, heads bowed as they studied texts in the miserly light of a few flickering oil lamps.

The moment he saw me approaching, Nolam shuffled over to offer me a kiss of greeting while the young man waited, a solemn expression on his downturned face. Most scribes trained for decades to earn a place in my father's employ, but this one could not be much older than Yarikh.

Perhaps my ruse would not be as difficult to maintain as I'd thought. I breathed a quiet sigh of relief before pressing my lips to the eunuch's papery cheek. "*Salmu Laki*, Nolam. If I'd known it was you waiting for me, I'd not have dragged my feet on the way here. I'd far rather you watch over me than endure Magin scowling at me for the next few months."

A dry laugh came from the eunuch. "Unfortunately, my dear, Magin scowls at everyone. In fact, I suspect his face may be permanently etched that way."

I giggled at the twinkle in his rheumy eyes. Although he must be somewhere in his seventh or eighth decade of life, Nolam's voice was unnaturally high, like many of the eunuchs. Yet there was a distinct warble in his words that, when paired with the worsening hunch in his back, made me worry he might soon be retired from service. I had few allies in this palace, but he'd been a steadfast one my entire life.

"This is Mattaniel, Elissa," said Nolam, with a gesture to the young scribe. "He'll be your tutor in the ways of the Shardan."

Mattaniel towered over Nolam and would top the height of most of the Crows, whose long limbs and lanky stature evidenced childhood castration. But although this young man was slender, he looked nothing like one of the smooth-skinned, round-faced eunuchs. His sharply defined features were striking, even in the dim sunlight, and whispered of some foreign heritage I could not immediately place. And his shoulders, bared by a sleeveless tunic, were chiseled like stone, as if he were accustomed to hard labor.

"My lady," he murmured, his voice a soft rumble as he pressed a hand to his heart in a gesture of respect. A strange patch of silver marked his close-cropped black hair just above one brow. It glimmered like polished metal as he bowed before me, eyes never meeting mine.

"From what he tells me," said Nolam, "Mattaniel is fluent not only in the Shardan language but several other tongues as well. I'm certain under his tutelage you'll become well-versed in their customs before the delegation arrives."

My stomach lurched. There was nothing I wanted less than to spend the next few months learning the ways of vicious pirates, but Yarikh's advice resounded in my mind. *"Play the game for now."*

If there was anything the Crows had taught me, it was how to feign serenity when my insides were roiling like the sea. The daughter of a king was expected to appear tranquil and composed in the presence of all men, no matter the circumstances. And Mattaniel, though a servant, was still a man.

So instead of fleeing from the dim room and the unnervingly handsome scribe, I affected a pleasant expression and willed a teasing lilt into my voice reminiscent of Ashabel, the most feather-brained and flirtatious of my father's concubines. "I look forward to hearing about this fascinating island. It sounds as though you are quite the expert."

For the first time since I'd entered the room, Mattaniel's eyes flashed up to meet mine. They were pale brown, almost gold in the light from the window, and brimming with what appeared to be curiosity. But then, as if a veil had dropped, his gaze went blank before it fell away.

"I am at your service, my lady." The scribe's quiet voice held a slight accent of some sort.

"Excellent." Nolam squeezed my arm reassuringly before releasing me. "I'll leave you to it, then."

I shot the eunuch a confused look. "You're leaving?"

"I'll be right over there, where the light is better." He gestured toward a well-cushioned chair under the far window. "The scribes have just acquired a large lot of ancient tablets from Aram, and I'm anxious to examine them. These old eyes don't do so well in lamplight, you know."

A strange buzz of nerves gathered under my breastbone at the idea of being alone with Mattaniel, even if Nolam was within sight. But perhaps it was best. The dear old man knew I was no addled fool. My ruse would be much easier to manage without him listening.

"There's nothing better than well-aged wine." I gave him a wink. "Enjoy your reading, my friend.

Nolam shuffled off with a chuckle, black robes dragging at his heels. If only all the Crows were as tenderhearted and good-natured. If I failed in this scheme, I'd miss him nearly as much as I would my mother and sisters. The thought sent a wave of excruciating pain careening through my chest but instead of crumpling, I drew a steadying breath.

Yarikh was right. I could do this. I could not let the king send me away from Tyre. How difficult could it be to feign stupidity with a servant? I mustered my most sparkling smile and fluttered my lashes.

"Shall we begin?"

6

Mattaniel

I dropped my eyes, disoriented by the unexpected, breathtaking smile the king's daughter directed my way, and gestured toward the table I'd been told was reserved for our lessons. "After you, my lady."

She swept past me, the smell of flowers and sweet spice lingering in her wake, and gracefully sank onto one of the stools, tapping the empty tabletop. "Where are the Shardan texts?"

I frowned, scrambling for a coherent answer. "Oh . . . there are none. They don't care much for writing. Their histories are oral."

"They do not have a written language?"

I cleared my throat. "They employ a few symbols. Mostly clan markings and such. Nothing like the collection in here." From what Nolam said, Abibaal was an avid collector of both local records and foreign texts. Curiosity had buzzed in my bones from the moment I stepped over the threshold of this wondrous place. The countless shelves stretching nearly to the high ceiling seemed to whisper my name. If only I had the freedom to answer the call.

Elissa blinked up at me for a moment with long, painted lashes. "Well, I'm glad to hear it. I can't imagine anything more tedious than studying crumbling old tablets for weeks on end." She rolled her eyes and brushed at some imagined speck of dust on her spotless sage-colored gown.

I settled on my own stool across from her, fumbling about for how to begin. I'd never formally tutored anyone before, although I'd taught Torben a good deal of the Tyrian language in exchange for lessons on defending myself—something he'd insisted upon when he discovered I'd never even held a sword, let alone used one in battle.

But I'd certainly never instructed a royal bride in the ways of an entirely foreign people. From what I'd gathered over the past three days, there were a variety of protocols and strict divisions in this palace I had no knowledge of. Chances were, if I offended her or stepped over some invisible line, I would be punished severely. I knew what a lash felt like. I had scars on my back to prove it and never wanted to endure anything like that again. Besides, I could do nothing to endanger the agreement I'd made with the king. Raphad's life and my freedom were at stake.

So, I began the only way I could think of and spoke a greeting in the language of the Shardan. "Peace to you. It is an honor to meet you."

Her brow furrowed. "What does that mean?"

I translated the phrase.

"The words are unknown to me." She tilted her chin curiously. "But they also seem familiar."

"If you've been in contact with Philistines, then I would guess the language might sound familiar. Their peoples have ancient connections."

"Ah. Yes. The king entertains Philistine nobles here on occasion. Though I've never cared much to listen to what they had to say." Her gaze tracked away from me and toward the scribes at the other end of the room, quietly debating a text, then up to the sundrenched windows, seeming far more interested in the gray dove that had roosted on one of the sills than anything I had to say.

"Please repeat after me, my lady." I spoke my introduction again at a slower pace.

She huffed a sigh, dragging her reluctant attention back to me. "I don't understand what you are saying. Can you not begin with something easier?"

I wasn't certain what I'd expected when I met the woman who'd so captured my attention at the banquet. From her well-timed distraction with the lampstand to save her sister from embarrassment, I'd assumed her to be both compassionate and intelligent, but so far, she seemed much more like the pampered daughter of a king she actually was.

I pushed down the odd sense of disappointment and tried again, stretching out the words. "*Sar-tee ba-lah*."

Her attempt at the simple phrase was so terrible that it was almost shocking. Instead of sounding like rolling waves in the manner of the Shardan, Elissa's tone was clipped and flat.

Afraid to embarrass her, I repeated the words again, this time allowing her time to respond after each one. There was a slight improvement, but her second attempt came out with a strangely exaggerated lilt that reminded me more of the goats on Shardana than the people. I pressed my lips tight, silently amused at the comparison, yet terrified to insult her.

Elissa frowned, sighing. "I'll never get it."

"We've only begun, my lady. It is no easy thing to learn a new language once past the age of a child. It takes diligent practice to become fluent."

She huffed, blowing an errant wave of red-gold hair from her cheek. "You seemed to have done just fine."

"Yes, but . . ." I cleared my throat, fidgeting in my seat. "It's much easier to absorb a new language when immersed in it for three years."

Not to mention, for some reason, new tongues came to me effortlessly. Before we'd even landed on their island the first day, I'd learned a few of the fishermen's words. It had always been that way, likely even before the hyena attack. I'd surprised both myself and the Sidonians by being able to speak numerous languages once I healed from my injuries. It was the only reason they'd not dumped me on the side of the road. I'd been profitable to their trade—at least, until I wasn't anymore.

Elissa lifted one tawny brow. Her eyes, as blue-green as Shardanian waters and twice as lovely, pierced me through as she waited for further explanation. Something deep inside twisted strangely. I let my gaze fall away, unsettled.

"How long were you in service to that merchant my father tossed in prison?"

"Eleven years."

"And who did you serve before?"

I hesitated, thrown by the probing question. "Sidonian traders."

"How long?"

"About two years."

"And before that? Where do you hail from?"

I wish I knew, I wanted to say. But that was a seal better left unbroken. I let my eyes track to the wall of texts behind her as I tried to form an answer that might satisfy her sudden curiosity.

"Never mind." She fluttered a dismissive hand. "I have things to do this afternoon. Let's get this over with."

This woman was nearly as confusing as she was beautiful. In the last hour, she'd swung from flirtatious to preoccupied, and then, inexplicably, to curious about me. It was clear she had little interest in these lessons, and I could not even imagine her married to Torben, who was my friend, but still as rough-edged and brutal as any of the Shardan men. She belonged here in this opulent palace, flouncing about in fine linens, not huddled barefoot in a rock hut wearing thick-spun wool, gutting fish, and scraping an existence from the ground.

Shardana was the most beautiful place I'd ever seen—with lush green forests, wild exotic blooms, and blue, blue waters—but there was no comparison between the two kingdoms. Yet, judging by the avaricious glint in Abibaal's eyes as I'd described the nearly virgin mines on the island, he cared far more about Shardan silver filling his coffers than his daughter's fate.

However, none of this was my affair. My task was to prepare

the woman for her new life and ensure the treaty with Uvaldo was a success. Not worry over a spoiled princess with the attention span of a fly.

I tried again with my original greeting, repeating it slowly. Yet, somehow, her next attempts were far worse than the first. She skipped over words and badly mangled the pronunciation. How would I ever teach her the entirety of a language brimming with subtle metaphors and cultural nuance if she could not even master a few simple phrases?

The longer we sat there, making little progress, and the more times Elissa became distracted by the cooing doves up on the windowsill or some overheard conversation between scribes, the farther away my freedom seemed. It took all my will not to drop my head into my hands and groan with frustration. She may be lovely to look at, but apparently my initial assumption of her intelligence had been woefully wrong.

If only Adin and I had left Tyre before the feast, ignoring Raphad's request that we help him carry the gifts from Uvaldo. We'd likely already be in Israelite territory by now. I'd not even had a chance to tell him good-bye before I was ushered out of the garden and assigned a bedroll in the servants' quarters at the back of the palace. I could only hope he knew how much his friendship had meant to me after a decade of loneliness and that he would find whatever he was searching for.

Elissa drummed her fingers on the table. "Who are these Shardan, anyhow? All I know is they are pirates."

Uvaldo would be thrilled to hear of his people's infamy across the sea. The king of the Shardan had purposely instigated that reputation for years by sending his swiftest boats and most audacious warriors to attack any vessels that dared come near the island, boarding and stripping them of all cargo. Although most sailors were either taken captive or executed, once in a while he sent a few back to their homelands with stories of the brutish pirates that controlled their waters. It was only because he'd shrewdly recognized the value of castaways from Tyre that we'd been allowed to live. Uvaldo was no fool. He knew the world had changed. Old nations had crumbled, and new kings held new ambitions. He'd guessed it would not be long before the ruse crumbled and someone made a true attempt at invasion. His proposal of an alliance with Abibaal was a way to protect his people from extinction.

"The Shardan do have a history of piracy," I conceded, "but that is not the whole of who they are. They are fishermen. Goatherders. Tower-builders. Farmers and vintners. They are skilled at reaping the bounty of their land and their waters to sustain themselves. They may be insular, but that is because their families are everything to them. They will do anything to protect their own."

A small ache throbbed in my chest. I'd come to respect the Shardan and counted many as friends. Adin and I had found it difficult to leave when the time came. Yet both of us felt a pull to return to these shores. And even more, dreams of some vague place my heart called home refused to let go.

Elissa tilted her chin, studying me again. I shifted in my seat under her renewed scrutiny, eyes darting over her shoulder to the old eunuch reading a scroll in the miserly light of the high windows.

Unlike Magin, the head eunuch who'd outlined my duties this morning with a haughty smirk on his rounded face and warned I would be watched *at all times* in Elissa's presence, Nolam seemed a kindly sort. I guessed Magin had assigned him to this duty only because there were plenty of scribes in the room to come to Elissa's aid in an emergency. He did not suspect that, thanks to Torben and the other Shardan men, such measures would be useless should I decide to do something to her.

A flash of something familiar niggled at my mind, as if I'd seen another man hunched over like Nolam, peering narrow-eyed at small text in dim light in the very same way. But instead of within a royal hall of learning, the man had been seated cross-legged on the ground of a richly outfitted tent, reading something foreign aloud. I could nearly feel the warmth of a nearby fire and hear the patter of raindrops on the roof. Was this a memory? A fragment of a dream? Or a figment of my imagination? I tried to hold on to the images, but they faded, disappearing like wisps of smoke.

"Mattaniel?"

I blinked, realizing the king's daughter had spoken my name. And from the confusion on her face, it was likely not the first time. How long had I been staring into nothing, trying to parse out the chaos inside my head? My face went hot. She must think me a madman.

"Please forgive my distraction, my lady. Let's continue."

She glanced over her shoulder at Nolam briefly, her brow furrowing. "Where did you go?"

I sucked in a breath and dropped my chin. "An errant thought. I beg your pardon, my lady. Shall we continue?"

She paused, staring at me for a few intense moments before rising to her feet. I scrambled to do so as well, my head bowed. "I've had enough," she announced, then swept from the room, her silken slippers barely whispering on the tile and the fragrance of honeyed jasmine and spice lingering in the air.

My stomach pitted as I sank back down on my stool and set my forehead on the table with a quiet groan. Only one day and I'd managed to insult the king's daughter. Abibaal may have me sent to haul stones alongside my former master before the sun set. And even if he didn't, I wasn't certain how I'd ever prepare Elissa to live among the rough-mannered fishermen and earthy villagers who made up Uvaldo's kingdom without endangering the treaty. If she knew what life on the island was truly like, she would never set foot on the ship. And if she didn't go, Raphad and I would both die in chains.

But the memory, if that's what it was, had sparked a kernel of hope I'd never dared entertain before. What if I could patch together some of the odd flashes of people and places I saw in my dreams and discover where I'd come from in the first place?

There were times such images were little more than gossamer threads, thin and fleeting, and other times when they were so clear and potent I mourned awakening. But once in a while, like today,

I was not asleep at all when visions seemed to take over my mind in a powerful way that could not be ignored. Perhaps I should stop pushing back against these dreams and visions—disturbing though they could be at times—and embrace them as stepping-stones to the past I could not remember. Because as soon as this treaty was signed and I was a free man, I needed to find where I belonged.

7

Elissa

"You'll look like a queen on your wedding day, Seri! I've never seen embroidery like this before." Melita leaned in to examine the golden threads hemming the spectacular linen mantle layered over a deep purple robe. More rich embroidery trimmed a pleated linen underskirt with tiny shimmering lotus blooms. The effect of such vibrant finery against Seriyah's black hair and bronze skin was beyond striking. She would be regal indeed as she stepped into her future.

"Take care," Shamzur said through the pinch of a threaded bone-needle between his lips, then slid between Melita and the small dais where Seri had been forced to stand while he scrutinized every stitch and seam. "The gown is a hundred years old. Utterly irreplaceable."

Flushing, Melita shrank back. "Forgive me."

Seriyah winced as Meli scuttled over to sit beside me on the cushions piled in the corner of the dressing room but said nothing. For a woman who would be a queen one day, she was far too easily cowed. She'd have to borrow a measure of her mother's arrogance to keep from being pushed around when she was married to the crown prince of Gebal.

Once satisfied with his alterations, Shamzur fiddled with the braided leather girdle wrapped around her middle, focused on making certain the wide belt was centered to highlight the graceful swoop of her curvy waist. No matter that the eunuch was the most solemn of the Crows, I had to admit he was skilled in dressing Abibaal's women and daughters to our best advantage.

There was no one in the palace who knew more about clothing than Shamzur nor was able to procure the most exotic fabric, leather, footwear, and accessories. He spent a great deal of time down at the market, making connections with traveling tradesmen and bartering with merchants who imported goods from across the sea. Always impeccably dressed himself, he wore an elegant floor-length black robe embroidered with intricate ebony motifs and trimmed with knotted fringe. An exquisite bronze toggle pin, inset with a deep crimson ruby, secured the garment at the top of his throat.

The gown he'd altered for Seriyah was the very same Queen Khamera had married our father in, and that her own mother and grandmother wore when they married princes of Egypt. It made my sister look like a daughter of Pharaoh himself.

"Meli is right. Your groom won't be able to tear his eyes away."

Seri unsuccessfully suppressed a grin at my tease. The heir of Gebal had come to Tyre with his father a few months ago to negotiate an agreement between our rival kingdoms. He'd not hidden how smitten he'd been with our older sister from the beginning. The first time I'd seen the two of them walking in the gardens, I'd known he would pressure his father to accept the treaty proposal regardless of Abibaal's demands and make a union between them. I hated that Seriyah was leaving us for a city far to the north but was glad she would be adored.

Unlike myself, who would soon be betrothed to an absolute stranger.

From what Mattaniel told me this morning during our fourth lesson, after I'd practically had to pry answers from his tight lips, the king of Shardana was elderly and did not desire more wives.

But my tutor would not reveal who Uvaldo might choose as my groom, even if I had a feeling he had more of an idea than he claimed.

Feigning ignorance while Mattaniel attempted to teach me their language had become almost embarrassing. Yet no matter how many times I interrupted him with questions about the island or its people, or how many times I made him repeat the same phrases over and over under the guise of inability to distinguish between sounds, he responded in a calm, even tone, never betraying a hint of annoyance or frustration. Either he was so well-trained in his duty he had perfect control over his reactions, or he was impossibly patient.

The man was a servant. It should not matter to me why he'd drifted into a distant universe during our first lesson, eyes unfocused and a deep frown on his intriguing face, nor why he'd looked so melancholy when I asked where he'd come from, but my voracious curiosity had been piqued nonetheless. So each time I sat across the table from him, I reminded myself that the enigma of Mattaniel was best left alone if I was to honor my vow to my mother.

I would squelch my instinctual need to delve into such mysteries and continue to play the role of empty-headed, spoiled king's daughter, whether or not my ridiculous behavior grated on my own nerves. Thank the gods I'd been trained to flatter and tease, and to skillfully drive conversations toward my own purposes while keeping my personal opinions quiet. At least something the eunuchs had drilled into me would be of use while Yarikh worked on changing our father's mind.

One of the younger eunuchs-in-training rushed into the room carrying a bundle, his softly rounded face full of apology.

"It's about time, Opher," sniped Shamzur as the harried young man handed over the burden.

"A thousand apologies." Opher bowed his head, cheeks aflame. "The ferry was late. I had to wait at the dock for the courier for over an hour."

Shamzur had already turned away, his attention focused on untying the knotted cords binding the woolen wrap around the parcel.

"Why was the ferry late, Opher?" I asked. The boats that carried water from the mainland were notoriously regular in their frequent crossings of the channel and routinely carried passengers to the port as well.

"A terrible wildfire," Opher said, eyes bright and voice pitched high with excitement to share what he knew. "The flumes that carry water down from the mountains have been heavily damaged, so the transports are delayed. Some of the ferries have been redirected north to fetch fresh water so the city doesn't run dry."

"Fires?" Melita mused. "But it's been so cold lately."

Opher shrugged. "All I know is that much of the king's brand-new waterworks have been destroyed. It will take months to repair them."

Under my eldest brother's supervision, crews had been working on those pipes for the past few seasons, a replacement for the crude wooden channels and natural streams that had once supplied Tyre with runoff from the forested peaks. The large flumes were a marvel, made segment by segment from hard-fired terracotta, their joints plastered with thick mortar. The fires must have been extensive to cause such destruction. No doubt my father was furious. They were one of his grandest achievements in his never-ending drive to make Tyre the glory of the world.

"I also heard—"

"Help me with this veil, Opher," said Shamzur, holding up a long length of filmy linen.

At the interruption, Opher blushed all the way to the top of his shaven head and spun to obey.

Frustrated that Shamzur had cut off the young man mid-sentence but wise enough not to undermine his training, which would one day see him in a similar position to Shamzur's, I slumped back into the pillows, leaning into Melita as the two eunuchs tucked the linen piece into the circlet on Seriyah's head. The band was formed from many golden strands studded with tiny flecks of amethyst, carnelian, and lapis lazuli, and the veil itself was a cascade of white trimmed with shining golden threads that trailed all the way to the floor.

"This is extraordinary, Shamzur," said Seriyah, her fingers gliding down the smooth fabric framing her face. "Where did it come from?"

"One of my connections in Sidon, my lady," he replied, stepping back to take stock of her, head to bare toes. "Your new sandals from Damascus will do fine, I think."

"Thank you," she said. "My mother will be pleased to see me in her own gown during my wedding." Seriyah had been anxious about the fit and, in a rare act of assertiveness, had asked Shamzur to alter the garment before the veil arrived so she could see it all together well in advance of the journey north. The polished copper mirror shimmered with her satisfied reflection.

"I'll make certain everything is packed and ready for your departure." He turned away to gather up the wool the veil had been wrapped in and tucked the knotted length of cord into some hidden pouch inside his robe.

"I can't believe you'll be gone so soon, Seri," said Melita, folding her long legs and propping her chin on her knees.

Seriyah gave her a sad smile. "Now that Tyre and Gebal are closer allies, I'm certain we'll see each other from time to time. It's only a few days' journey on one of Father's swift ships."

"If I'm not sent off to some faraway island like Lissi," she said, her brown eyes shimmering. She'd not taken the announcement of my upcoming marriage well and had been crying off and on for days.

My heart clenched painfully. I'd not been particularly enamored of Elithan, especially since he was at least twenty years my senior. But when he'd expressed interest in me, I'd encouraged it because his trading business was firmly anchored on this coast and he owned a lovely villa on the other end of this island. And no matter how alluring Mattaniel made the island of the Shardan sound, it was still weeks—perhaps even months—away from Tyre. In all likelihood, I would never see anyone I loved again.

"Oh! Seriyah, your mother will be so pleased!"

The very last person I expected to see at the door of Seriyah's dressing room was my own mother, with Danice hovering behind her shoulder.

My stomach dropped. I'd worked very hard to make certain no one told my mother anything about the king's decision, hoping Yarikh might somehow convince him to change his mind before she even knew it had been a possibility.

Danice's expression was full of apology. She had been sworn to silence—not that she would ever purposely hurt my mother, whom she'd been serving for the past few years with unfailing devotion.

"Ama, you look well today!" I surged to my feet to embrace her. It was true. I'd not seen this much color in her face since before the Awakening Feast. And it was the first time I'd seen her venture out of our room in a couple of weeks.

Her eyes sparkled as she took in Seri in her magnificent wedding garb. "How is it the messy-haired little girl who used to hide in Elissa's bed when she did not want to return to her own could now be getting married? And to a future king, no less!"

Seriyah lifted her arms as Shamzur untied the belt at her waist. "It does not feel real to me either, Leyana. I expect any moment, I'll awake to find myself hiding under the covers, giggling with Lissi and Meli."

My mother's grin lit the entire room, the sight of it nearly bringing tears to my eyes. *This* was the mother I remembered from my childhood. The smiling, singing, laughing woman I adored like a goddess on earth. There was a reason she'd been the king's favorite concubine for so many years. Khamera may be an exotic Egyptian beauty, but my mother had been a sparkling gem of life and humor in this household, until it had all been stripped away in one horrible day, leaving us only a shadow of her former self, one whose moods shifted quicker than the tides.

She turned to Melita and me, a mischievous tilt to her chin. "I suppose we must go to the temple soon and ask our Lady Astarte for similar favor in marriages for the both of you."

"Well, me at least, since Elissa is already spoken for," Melita quipped. I sucked in a quick breath, and she turned to me, wide-eyed, her face going pale.

My mother furrowed her brow. "What do you mean? Has Elithan finally convinced Abibaal to accept his suit?"

With her palm over her mouth, Melita looked as though she might perish from guilt. There was nothing to be done now but admit the truth.

"No . . ." I swallowed against the burning knot in my throat. "The king has promised me to someone else."

"Who?"

All I could think of was her gut-wrenching wails echoing through the women's wing. "It's . . . it's not written in stone yet. Not until the treaty is made. Besides, Yarikh is working on a plan to convince him to change his mind, and I have been—"

She cut me off, eyes narrowed. "*Tell me*, Elissa."

My mother was no fool and knew me as well as my sisters did. I should have told her sooner, let her react in private. But she was giving me no choice.

"The king desires a treaty with the Shardan." I pressed a palm to the center of my chest, where it hurt most to speak the truth aloud. "And I am to be the guarantee of their partnership in mining silver on their island."

"Where?" Her voice was flat.

I bit my lip, stomach churning.

"*Where* is this island?" she pressed.

"On the other side of the Great Sea. Toward Galicia."

She blinked at me wordlessly, and I stepped forward, ready to catch her if she collapsed. But instead, she pressed a kiss to my cheek, affection shimmering in her ocean-blue eyes. "I knew Abibaal would see your great worth, my precious daughter. You will bring great honor to Tyre. To all of us."

Stunned by her response, all I could do was slip my arms around her as she squeezed me tight. I inhaled her delicate floral fragrance, the one that never failed to give me comfort, even during the worst of her bouts with melancholy.

There was nothing but delight on her face as she pulled back from the embrace. "We must go to the temple and give thanks to Astarte for such favor. And we will pray the goddess brings you the perfect mate as well, Melita. How soon will this marriage take place?"

"The king has sent a messenger to propose a treaty. It could be months before an agreement is reached and a delegation arrives. In the meantime, I'm being tutored in their language and ways by a scribe who was shipwrecked on their island for three years."

"Are you?" Her smile dipped for a moment, but she recovered quickly. "Well, it sounds as though everything is quite in order. Shamzur, I assume you'll make certain my daughter has all the proper attire for her new life."

The eunuch gave her a small bow. "Yes, my lady."

"Excellent. And please let Abenasser know we plan to go to the temple in a day or two, so we will need an escort and the proper offerings."

He nodded. "Consider it done."

"Thank you." She gave him one of her most brilliant smiles, one I recognized as an expression the eunuchs had taught us to employ when our emotions were at their most unruly. I'd used the very same one as my father announced my upcoming betrothal to a gathering of lofty witnesses. My cheeks had ached from the effort of keeping it aloft the rest of the night. It was a reminder that just as I'd been trained in the ways of political marriages, my mother had as well. She was the daughter of a high-ranking general in Tyre's army, after all. My father had desired her upon their first meeting when she was only fourteen, but my grandfather had been canny enough to spend the next two years preparing her for life in this palace, drawing out Abibaal's yearning until he was willing to give him whatever he wanted for the privilege of bringing her into his household.

Without allowing the curve of her lips to waver, my mother turned to her maid. "I think I'll return to my room for a rest." With a brief, apologetic glance at me, Danice took her arm, and the two women left the room.

Immediately, Melita slumped, dropping her forehead to my shoulder with a groan. "I'm so sorry, Lissi. My mouth spoke before my mind caught up. I am such a fool."

I patted her cheek. "You're nothing of the sort. She had to find out sometime."

"At least she responded fairly well to the news," Seriyah said, arms stretched wide so Shamzur could remove the purple gown and pack it away for the journey to Gebal.

I gave a soft laugh, shaking my head as I stared at the empty doorway. My mother may have left here with a smile pinned firmly in place, but she would likely not leave the room again for days. It only made determination settle deeper in my bones.

I would *not* let my father send me away. I simply had to find a way to change his mind or, if all else failed, undermine the treaty, no matter how angry he would be. If there was anything I'd learned by watching the king's political machinations over the years, it was that they were much like any other game of strategy. One must always be a full step ahead of the other players. And this was a game I simply refused to lose.

8

Mattaniel

Trees rose like giants all around, the smell of green thick in the air. Two boys walked ahead of me on the trail, wooden swords dangling from their belts. I tried to lengthen my stride, frustrated I was so far behind. I called out, but they ignored my pleas to slow down, getting farther and farther away. My vision blurred and my chest ached as I stumbled to a stop on the leaf-covered path. Then, without warning, a huge gray body brushed past me, and I choked back a cry as a giant dog turned to face me, teeth glistening and drool dripping from its enormous jaws, a well-chewed stick clenched in its mouth. However, instead of being terrified of the fearsome creature, it somehow felt like . . . a friend? A hand landed on my shoulder, and I turned to find a boy of about thirteen with a light coating of scruff on his chin and serious dark brown eyes. "Don't worry," he said. "I'll walk with you."

The feeling of relief lasted for only a few moments as the sky twisted above me in a swirl of blue and green. I saw those three boys again, older now, but instead of loping through the woods, they were chained together, garments torn and faces bloodied as soldiers marched them through the city of Tyre. People screamed foul names at the young men, throwing rotten food or animal dung at them, or reaching out to rip the knotted blue tzitzit *from their tunics. Pain gripped my chest as I followed, trying to get a glimpse of the boys. Everything inside me screamed to do something.* Anything. *I had to get them free. Protect them from the naked hatred of the Tyrians. Panicked, I stumbled along as the crowd pressed through the streets, vile accusations of treachery spewing from their lips. But no matter how hard I tried to catch up, pushing my way through the many bodies, the boys were always ten paces ahead. I tripped, falling to my hands and knees as people streamed around me, calling for the blood of the innocents. I tried to cry out, plead for their lives, but my mouth refused to open, as if an iron hand clamped my jaw shut. I fought hard against the grip, willing my lips to part as the boys disappeared from sight. There was only one name I knew to call.*

"Yahweh!"

I gasped, sitting up on my bed as my heart pounded and sweat poured down my face. Blinking at the darkness all around me, I tried to make sense of where I was. *Who* I was. But panic had its claws in deep. The feeling was a familiar one; it had claimed me many times since I'd first awakened in the back of the Sidonian traders' wagon with no memory of how I'd gotten there or where I'd come from.

I scrubbed my hands down my face, trying to clear the terrifying images from my mind. I'd dreamed of those three boys many times over the past thirteen years and was certain they were people from my past—friends, even—but never had I seen them in chains or being ruthlessly mocked and tortured.

Even when I rose from my bedroll in the servants' quarters, washed and dressed myself, then made my way up the four flights of stairs to the Hall of Records before dawn, I could not shake the dread. I hadn't been so disturbed by a dream in years. Not since I'd been plagued by visions of Raphad's ship sinking to the bottom of the sea in the days before the storm ripped that very vessel to pieces. And before that, when I'd dreamed of a beautiful black-and-white horse screaming for help in the desert, and then, only a few days later, stumbled across the very same animal in a dry wadi, tied to a dead man.

It *had* to mean something. So, as I tended my duties in the Hall while waiting for the appointed time for Elissa's lesson, I alternated between rehashing everything I remembered from the dreams I'd had before about the boys and silently pleading with Yahweh for clarity about the nightmare that had plagued me last night. From the sacred stories inexplicably etched on my heart, I knew the God of Yaakov and Yosef was the Giver of Dreams, but I could not fathom why he would bother gifting such insights to a slave of no consequence.

Elissa was due to appear in the Hall just after her midmorning meal but was almost always late, so I took advantage of a few moments of relative privacy to remove the wrinkled sheet of stained papyrus I'd managed to salvage from a refuse bin from my belt. I'd never thought I would miss the days of serving Raphad, but he'd always made certain I had clean sheets of papyrus, reed pens and brushes, and all the jars of strong ink I'd needed to keep his business affairs in meticulous order. But although Tabnit, the elderly head scribe, had been kind so far, assigning me various tasks in the Hall of Records to keep me occupied between tutoring sessions with the king's daughter—mostly climbing ladders to fetch texts or tending to the dusty shelves—I wasn't comfortable asking for any favors.

I'd learned early in my first days of slavery to the Sidonians that my wishes, and the endless questions that filled my heart and mind, were much better left unspoken. Until I knew the expectations of me in this palace, it was best to keep to myself and avoid any undue attention.

Using a sharp sliver of charcoal I'd pilfered from one of the kitchen hearths, I recorded as many new details from my dreams as I could remember beneath the ones I'd already cataloged over the past couple of days. I wasn't certain how any of it could lead to a clear picture of where I'd come from, but it was a start.

"What are you doing?"

I startled at Elissa's voice, the charcoal smudging across the last three symbols I'd just written.

Feeling like a fool for not watching for her entrance to the Hall, I surged to my feet and dropped my gaze to her daintily beaded slippers as I bowed. "My lady. Forgive me. I did not realize you had arrived."

"What are they doing over there?" Elissa asked.

I followed her line of sight. A few scribes were gathered around a nearby table, arguing, as they had been most of the morning.

"From what I overheard, a messenger from Gebal delivered a missive written on a clay tablet, and before it could be given to the king, the young man dropped it. The pieces were brought here to be reassembled by the scribes."

The messenger himself had been pale as death as he was led away, likely to be punished for his carelessness. Abibaal was universally feared in this palace. The merciless coup he'd accomplished decades ago still echoed through its colonnades.

Glad Elissa was distracted for the moment, I quickly slipped the wrinkled piece of papyrus and the charcoal shard into my belt, hoping she'd forget she'd seen my haphazard scribblings.

"Shall we begin, my lady?"

Turning back to me, she let out an exasperated huff. "My *name* is Elissa."

"My lady?"

"You have my leave to call me by my name." She waved a hand at the table between us. "At least when we are doing . . . this. I always look for the queen when others address me like that." Her sour expression made clear her opinion of the woman who sat on the throne beside her own father.

I nodded, obligated to obey. Yet, it would be no simple command to fulfill. I'd never even spoken Raphad's name to his face in all the years I'd served him. The Sidonians had beaten that instinct out of me many years ago, until I'd not even thought of any of the traders as anything other than *Master*.

Elissa pressed her lips together, brow furrowed as she stared at the scribes for a few more moments but eventually settled at the table. Once I was seated, she stared intently at me, questions swimming in those ocean-water eyes. My pulse raced. She had every right to demand I show her anything she wished. But how could I explain what I'd been doing without revealing the brokenness inside my head? If she told the king, he might rescind the bargain we'd made.

To my great relief, Elissa did not argue when I began the lesson, starting with a repetition of the things I'd taught her over the past few sessions. But just as every time before, she fumbled the phrases, asked me to repeat things continuously, and spent more time looking over her shoulder at the scribes than listening to me. She seemed to have even forgotten most of the simple greeting phrases we'd begun with, and those she did remember were so badly mangled that it sounded nothing like the melodic tones of the Shardan.

At this rate of progress, there was little hope Elissa would be ready for their arrival. It was fortunate I'd taught Torben enough of the Tyrian language to communicate with his bride in simple terms. If, that was, Uvaldo did as I guessed and chose his nephew to marry her. It was entirely possible he could decide to give her to another of his inner circle.

Pain spiked in my right temple, causing my vision to blur for a moment. Closing my eyes, I rubbed at the ache that was as familiar as it was unwelcome. Thankfully, over the years, the bouts of searing pain were less frequent and not quite as debilitating as they had been in the first months after I'd been found. But once in a while, I would still see swirling colors and flashing light for hours. After so long, I had little hope such reoccurrences would ever fully go away.

Blinking, I looked up to see that Elissa had disappeared. Panicked that I'd once again offended her by losing my sense of place and time, I searched the room. Nolam was already asleep in his preferred chair under the windows, unaware his charge was now leaning over the table where the scribes had seemingly given up on the impossible task of reassembling the message. Only Tabnit, the head scribe, remained, looking baffled that Elissa seemed intent on taking up where his well-trained scribes had left off. Unsettled at remaining seated but not knowing what else to do, I made my way over to the table as Elissa reached for one of the larger pieces, turning it over to examine the other side.

"There's too much missing, my lady," Tabnit was saying to Elissa. "We've been trying for hours."

"Does the messenger not know what it said?"

"Men chosen for delivering sensitive missives usually cannot read," said Tabnit.

Elissa hummed, her eyes on the many pieces of clay scattered across the table. The scribes had managed to organize about six of the larger ones together, but the rest of the shards were the size of a thumbnail or smaller, a few no bigger than a melon seed. Fully assembled, the tablet would be only the length of my wrist to forearm, a handspan wide, and was impressed with common Aramean symbols.

Biting the corner of her lower lip, Elissa set down the piece in her hand but reached for another, sliding it across the surface to line it up beside a different shard. She frowned when it did not fully align.

"My lady, it's quite useless. Another messenger will be sent to Gebal to fetch a replacement, anyhow."

She ignored him, twisting the piece and moving it flush with one of the larger shards. It fit perfectly. Grinning to herself at the victory, she bonded the two pieces together with a dab of sticky bitumen from the little pot on the table.

Once she was satisfied it was secure, the woman who'd seemed unable to grasp the concepts of a new language or hold the sounds of the tongue in her mind, remained astonishingly fixated on methodically aligning a host of small pieces, one by one, until over half of the message was reassembled, revealing that it was little more than a request for a full accounting of all persons who would be traveling to Gebal for Seriyah's wedding. Hardly sensitive information after all.

Regardless, I'd learned quite a bit by watching the king's daughter. She may struggle to emulate the foreign sounds—although I was beginning to doubt her ineptitude in that respect as well—but perhaps I'd been going about these lessons entirely the wrong way.

"Please forgive the intrusion, Master Tabnit," said a young servant. "But Prince Ahiram is asking for tomorrow's lumber shipment manifest right away."

The head scribe grimaced, running ink-stained fingers through his frizzled gray curls. "Oh yes. I'd quite forgotten in all the chaos this morning. I'll send someone to deliver them shortly. Please convey my apologies for the oversight."

The young man nodded and strode from the room, the knotted blue fringe on the corners of his simple tunic denoting him as Hebrew. He was not the first of my countrymen I'd come across in this palace, but most labored in the kitchens or the gardens. From what I'd learned by talking to them at mealtimes, almost all were from the tribe of Asher, which inhabited numerous enclaves in valleys between here and Akko, and in the foothills to the east, and all paid regular tribute to Abibaal in exchange for peace and security. More than a few Hebrews had been forced by the demand of rising taxes to sell themselves into service, or watch their families go hungry.

Leaning on his walking stick, Tabnit limped away to organize the requested shipping manifest. Elissa stood with a sigh, arching her back, then lifted her arms over her head and stood on tiptoe for a moment, as graceful as one of her father's famed swans stretching their lovely wings. Seeing me watching, she went stiff, dropping her hands to her sides, eyes wide.

I bit the inside of my cheek to control the smile that threatened. She looked very much like a little girl caught with a pilfered honeycake. And she'd never looked more beautiful than she did now, with a smudge of bitumen across one slightly flushed cheekbone and dust on her chin.

She blinked a few times, then lifted that pointed chin and wiped the guilty expression from her face. "I'm done with this for the day." She waved a flippant hand at our empty table. "I have other things to do."

"Of course." I gave a bow. "Until tomorrow, my lady."

She pursed her lips, giving the half-constructed tablet one last, longing glance. "I'll be going to the Temple of Astarte with my sisters tomorrow. In fact, I doubt I'll have time for any lessons for at least a couple of days."

"I am at your service," I replied, a palm pressed to my heart.

Her ocean-water eyes turned up to meet mine, one perfectly groomed brow arched imperially. "Good. Then, when I return, you will tell me what you were so furiously scribbling earlier that you did not even notice my arrival."

I froze. She had not forgotten. Because although for some reason she had been hiding behind a vapid mask during our lessons, she was indeed an extraordinarily intelligent and perceptive woman.

There was nothing to do but nod in agreement before she walked away, leaving behind her now-familiar, sweetly spiced fragrance—one that was far too intriguing for my comfort.

From across the room, Tabnit called my name, waving me over to his cluttered worktable. Setting aside the question of how to allay Elissa's curiosity, I quickly obeyed.

"I need to make use of those long legs of yours," he said. "Haldon will be gone for a few days or I'd have him make this delivery."

I'd wondered why I hadn't seen Tabnit's apprentice lately. He was only a few years older than me and in his sixth year of serving under the head scribe. He was a quiet sort, rarely conversing with the other scribes, aside from issues relating to his daily tasks. But he'd been nothing but kind to me since my arrival, even taking the time to explain the complicated and oftentimes arbitrary method Tabnit used to organize the royal records.

"He's not unwell, is he?"

"No. He was notified in the middle of the night of an emergency at home, from what I understand. His family lives up in the foothills, so it may be a week or two before he returns."

Tabnit handed me a sealed roll of papyrus. "Take this to Prince Ahiram's chambers in the royal wing, right away. And once again convey my apologies to his steward for my tardiness. I quite forgot to finish compiling this document when that destroyed message was brought in." He sighed, gesturing to the mess splayed over his worktable. "Without my apprentice here to keep me organized, it's a wonder I've not forgotten my own head lately. Haldon is usually the one making certain the daily cargo manifests are duplicated and delivered on time."

After promising to help in whatever capacity Tabnit required, I headed for the royal wing of the palace, a place I'd never set foot before this, but when I arrived at the chambers of the crown prince, I discovered the receiving room empty of his steward and the door to the prince's quarters closed.

Since it was unwise not to hand the document directly to the steward, I stood inside the entrance with my back against the wall to wait for his return. Staring at the floor, I let my mind wander back to Elissa and the startled look on her lovely face when she realized she'd given herself away. I could only guess at her reasons for such pretenses. Perhaps she was not thrilled with her father's decision to send her across the sea. However, my duty was to teach her their language, not concern myself with her feelings on the arrangement. There had to be some way I could stir her interest in the lessons. She'd been brilliant at seeing the patterns in the broken message, able to line up fractured symbols by recreating their order in her mind . . .

I jerked up my chin as an idea sparked, one that would take a fair amount of work and ingenuity but might just pique Elissa's curiosity enough to destroy her ruse. It would take some time to create a method that would tap into her obvious strengths, but there was simply too much at stake to fail.

Prince Ahiram strode into the receiving room with another

richly dressed man, the two so engaged in heated conversation that neither noticed me.

"What is your point, Yarikh?" snapped the prince as he pushed through the door into his quarters, leaving it ajar as they disappeared inside. I stepped away from the wall, meaning to wait out in the courtyard for the steward's return, but the man I now knew was his younger brother spoke words that immediately halted my escape.

"My point is that the Hebrews had to have started those fires. Why else would jars of bitumen be found at the source with Asherite symbols? There's no other explanation."

My entire body went cold. I'd heard about fires up in the hills causing a shortage of water after the flumes were damaged. But not that those fires had been intentionally set.

"What reason would they have for doing that?" Ahiram protested. "Their people need water just as much as our own."

"We've had problems with them in the past."

"Decades ago," retorted Ahiram with a scoff. "And it was nothing more than a few zealots clinging to myths anyhow. But they were dealt with. The rest of the Hebrews pay their tribute with no complaint."

"Abibaal raised taxes three times over the past couple of years to fund the harbor projects. It wouldn't take much to stir another generation of religious fanatics who think this land is theirs by some divine right."

Deep in the hidden caverns in my head, I had somehow retained the knowledge that Yehoshua, an ancient commander of the Hebrews, delegated this region to the tribe of Asher as their portion of the land promised to Avraham. It did not surprise me that some Asherites still held out hope they would someday take hold of that inheritance. But without an army, what could they possibly hope to accomplish other than bringing the ire of a powerful king down on their heads?

"What do you expect me to do?" asked Ahiram with an edge of frustration. "Asherites live all over this region. Plenty within the city walls too. Even if your accusation is true, it's impossible to know who among them is responsible. Besides, I have my hands full with the renovations to the temples and the new docks we're adding to the southern harbor, not to mention organizing water distribution until the flumes are repaired. Take this up with Father."

"He's too busy making deals to fill his coffers to care what's happening on his own shores. You've heard he's selling Elissa off to a horde of pirates?"

Ahiram sighed. "He's making an advantageous treaty to gain access to silver mines. We need the capital."

"He's sending our sister to some backward island, Ram. I promised I would help get her out of this mess."

"You aren't going to change his mind."

"You're his heir. He'll listen to you." Yarikh's tone softened. "Leyana is getting worse, Ram, much worse. You know how much she relies on Elissa."

There were a few beats of silence as Ahiram contemplated.

"There's nothing I can do, Yarikh. Elissa knows her role. We all do."

"Ah yes." Yarikh gave a sardonic laugh. "Our divine duty to scrape the floor with our chins and kiss the royal sandals."

"He's made you a commander in his naval force. Perhaps you should have a bit more respect."

"Perhaps you should stop acting like one of his precious pets and remember *you'll* be on the throne someday."

"How dare you." Ahiram's voice was deadly even. "I know you're too busy drinking and whoring to care about this kingdom, but Tyre is the most powerful city in this region for a reason."

"It won't be for long."

"What do you mean?"

"Look. The Asherites aren't the only problem. We've lost three ships to pirates between here and Cyprus over the past few months. And you know there have been a rash of attacks on our trade caravans."

"And?"

"We're already stretching our resources far too thin. He's pouring silver into his building projects instead of his army. And if these Asherites rebel further, maybe even instigate the rest of the Hebrew tribes to come north, I'm not certain we could withstand a prolonged attack."

Ahiram laughed. "The Hebrews can barely keep the Philistines at bay. They're not coming north any time soon."

"You laugh now. But I've heard stories about those people that would singe your beard. They are dangerous, brother. You would be wise not to ignore the threat within our own city."

"And what would you have me do?"

"They need a reminder of Tyre's strength to keep them in order."

"Meaning?"

"They burn our water supply? We burn a couple of their villages. Simple."

My stomach clenched hard. Attacking villages meant innocent women and children would suffer, along with many others who'd had nothing to do with destroying the water supply. And although I'd not lived among them since my memories had been knocked from my head, they were still my people.

Unbidden, the images from the nightmares I'd endured last night arose: those three Hebrew boys being dragged through the streets of Tyre, bleeding as they were mocked and tortured. And the feeling of utter helplessness as I stumbled along behind.

"Who are you?"

Flinching, I turned to find Ahiram's steward in the doorway, scowling at me over the large tray of fruit and cheese in his hands.

Bowing, I held out the roll of papyrus. "Tabnit sent me to deliver this shipping manifest, with his apologies for its tardiness."

"About time." The man gestured with his chin. "Put it over there on my worktable."

I obeyed and took my leave, wishing I could hear more of the conversation between the two princes, or maybe that I'd left the room before it began. Because not only did I fear I'd been somehow given a warning of another deadly storm, but once again, I was helpless to keep others from perishing. Whatever was coming for the Hebrews in this city, there was nothing at all I could do to stop it.

9

Elissa

A cacophony greeted us as we approached the temple of Astarte, escorted by Abenasser, a couple of younger eunuchs who carried our offerings, and six of the king's guard. It had been years since I'd come here, preferring to bring my tributes to the private sanctuary on the palace grounds.

But as I'd anticipated, my mother had not left our room since my revelation, alternating between silent tears, prostrating herself on the floor before her gods for hours on end, and staring blank-eyed at the flickering lamp. My promise to bring a sacrifice directly to the temple on her behalf was the only thing that made her finally relent to Danice tucking her into bed.

Melita, too, was anxious to come, hoping to consult the oracle about her own uncertain future. Khamera had refused to allow Seriyah to accompany us, insisting she was far too busy with preparations for her upcoming wedding. I wasn't certain why that barred her from asking a blessing from a goddess of marriage and fertility, but there was no questioning the queen.

Regardless of my lack of enthusiasm for this outing, at least it helped me avoid yet another interminable lesson with Mattaniel. It was becoming almost excruciating to continue my ruse of stupidity around the man, especially when he studied me with honey-brown eyes I was certain saw far more than I wished.

I'd made a mistake by giving in to my compulsion to piece together that shattered message. I'd known it the moment I peeled myself away from the half-reconstructed tablet to find my tutor staring at me with the barest hint of a knowing smile on his lips. The glimpse of humor in a man who'd been unerringly stoic in my presence had been jarring, as if he'd dropped a veil to reveal his true self for only a moment. I'd been so stunned, I'd practically run from the room, but not before daring him to reveal just a little bit more. Whatever he'd been writing on that scrap of papyrus was nearly as intriguing as the broken tablet.

The line to enter the temple courtyard wound around the corner and down the street, a multitude of feet shifting restlessly in the dust. Most of the worshipers carried baskets of fruit or pots of grain, some cages of doves or geese, or jars of oil or wine. A few—those who could afford more—led a sheep or a goat by a tether. Abenasser led us past the crowd, making certain we avoided refuse in the street to protect our costly footwear. But as we neared the gate, a few of the people in the crowd began to scowl at us.

"Why do *they* get to go in?" cried a girl of about ten as we approached the head of the line. "We've been waiting too long!"

The girl's mother hissed for her silence but glared at us as well, her face pinched with loathing. She held nothing in her hands but a sleeping baby wrapped in a threadbare brown cloth.

A pang of guilt twinged as Melita pressed closer to my side. I'd never thought too much about the privilege of being escorted to crowded places like these, since it was a familiar occurrence, but these people looked as though they'd been waiting for hours with no shade.

"Keep calm," hollered one of the temple guards. "Only twenty in at a time. You'll get your chance!"

Abenasser pushed past those bold enough to attempt to force their way inside and addressed one of the guardsmen. "The royal household requires entrance."

The guard's eyes tracked over our fine clothing and leather slippers, then to the soldiers behind us before unlocking the gate. While the people in line complained loudly, a few even shouting surprisingly foul curses about us and our father, he ushered us into the temple courtyard.

"Apologies," said the guard to Abenasser. "These people don't understand that until renovations are finished, we can only allow a limited number of worshipers in at a time. Next time we'll bring you through the private entrance now under construction."

The outer court of the temple was enormous and, when renovations were complete, would hold all the people outside the gate and more. Teams of workers stood on scaffolding, painting designs on the lime-white walls all around, while others perched on precarious ladders, brushing dark resin up and down the enormous cedar columns that lined the porticoes.

"How much longer until it will be done?" asked Abenasser.

"Another week. It was supposed to be finished before the Awakening Feast," said the guard, then lowered his tone in an aside. "I even heard Prince Ahiram threatened the foreman with a month in the dungeon should he delay the reopening any longer."

Abenasser glared at the man. "It's not your place to spread gossip about the crown prince."

The guard went crimson from his receding hairline to the neck of his tunic. "Of course, my lord. Please forgive my rudeness."

The eunuch let haughty silence linger, a rarity for Abenasser, who was usually mild-mannered, especially in comparison to Magin. But neither would he let any slight to the royal family go unanswered. The man was loyal to his very bones. He'd told me once that he'd served in Abibaal's court since he was a boy of seven, one of the few holdovers from the previous king's household after my father overthrew his own uncle. His gratitude for sparing his life, when so many others died that day, had made taking the vow of lifelong service to Abibaal an easy one.

The now-somber guard led us through the center of the courtyard, the only place not actively under construction, and past a huge two-horned altar piled high with bloody carcasses. I held my breath against the stink of sun-drenched flesh as we passed.

Once we'd climbed up to the expansive stone porch, a group of priestesses greeted us with deep, respectful bows and placid smiles on their heavily painted faces. All of them wore plunging linen gowns trimmed with deep purple fringe, long strings of colorful beads and shells around their necks, tinkling bells on their ankles, and scrolling designs on their arms and chests that marked them as consecrated priestesses to Astarte. I remembered as a child being so fascinated by their distinctive markings that I drew with charcoal on my skin and wished that my own feet jingled prettily with every step.

Melita and I removed our slippers, then followed the priestesses inside while Abenasser ordered the king's guard to remain by the entrance. As we entered the sanctuary, a waft of strong incense caused Melita to sneeze three times, the sound echoing through the holy place. Both priestesses glared over their shoulders at the noise, and Melita's cheeks went pink.

I slipped my hand into hers and gave her an encouraging wink. "Are you ready? This is your chance to ask the goddess for favor in love."

My distraction worked. "Do you think she will hear my plea?"

"You're just as deserving as any other supplicant here today. More, in my opinion. In fact"—I patted the linen bag slung over my shoulder—"I brought an extra jar of lotus perfume to offer on your behalf."

Her brilliant blue eyes sparkled with delight. "You did?"

"I know how anxious you've been about the king choosing the right man for you. I don't want you to worry, so I brought the most expensive thing I had."

"That is so kind of you, Lissa."

"You're my sister," I said, nudging her. "There's nothing I would not do for you."

We approached the Queen of Heaven, who stood two-and-a-half times the height of a man under a wide skylight, her polished crescent-moon crown sparkling beneath the sun. Part of the renovations must have included a fresh coating of gold over her exaggerated nude form. In one outstretched palm sat an ivory dove and in the other a curled wooden snake with jeweled eyes. Beneath her, the dais was painted with sharp-toothed lionesses and fearsome sea creatures. Hundreds of food and drink offerings lay around Astarte's gilded feet, along with scores of votives of all shapes and sizes.

A group of worshipers knelt in front of the goddess, some with arms held high as they chanted traditional blessings to Astarte and others prostrate before her, pleading for fertility, for prosperity, for protection over loved ones. Their voices reverberated off the limestone walls, a droning din that seemed to meld with the fragrant smoke of the many incense burners.

Across the room, three young priestesses in nearly sheer garments led a few well-dressed worshipers to a private section of the temple. I was no fool; I knew what occurred in those hidden places both here and on the mountaintop sanctuaries. Such rituals ensured the fertility of our land and our people. But still, I averted my eyes from the curtained doorways at the back of the temple.

We laid our own offerings on the dais and lit two oil lamps, chanting routine prayers of supplication. I even included a whispered plea for the gods to release my mother from whatever held her captive, even though I'd been asking the same thing of every deity I knew of for years, to no avail. Either the gods of Tyre were unsatisfied with my sacrifices or simply deaf to me. If prayers to the gods of our people were enough to heal her, she would have been released from torment many years ago.

Our guides ushered Melita and me to the side of the sanctuary into a dimly lit alcove containing another stone altar. Another priestess waited there in the shadowy corner, giving us a regal nod as we approached. Abenasser handed her a small cage holding two gray doves as well as a purse that undoubtedly contained a good measure of silver.

"Excellent. And whose fortune shall we divine first?"

The deep voice of what I'd assumed to be a priestess startled me. The priest wore identical garments and cosmetics to his female counterparts, his long white hair twisted into a complicated upsweep of braids and copper beads, topped with a similar headpiece to the goddess at our backs. For some reason I'd assumed all Astarte's attendants were female since she was the goddess of motherhood, but she was also a divinity of war, so a male priest should not have surprised me. It took me a few moments to reframe my perception before I pulled Melita forward.

"My sister first," I said, knowing she would never volunteer herself, nor speak the truth of her all-consuming worries to a stranger. Melita tended to ruminate obsessively, sometimes even marking the anxieties on her beautiful skin. I hated the furious pink marks streaking down her pale forearms and over her shoulders many mornings, evidence of sleepless nights. Perhaps a promising word from the oracle would assuage her fears over what Abibaal might decide for her future.

With a quick press of crimson-stained lips and a dip of his smooth chin, the priest reached into the cage and withdrew one of the doves by the legs, then held the fluttering bird atop the altar with one hand while slipping a shiny copper blade from his ornate leather belt with the other.

My stomach swooped. I'd seen sacrifices performed before, many times, but never quite so close. I felt a sting of pain in my own chest as the priest plunged the blade directly into the center of the little bird's breast, then held my breath until a last desperate flutter of its wings preceded the life leaving its eyes. As the priest used his long, hennaed nails to tear into the gaping wound and yanked out the soft innards of the innocent animal, my stomach lurched. I pressed a hand to my mouth, vowing to never bear witness to such a thing again.

Once the entrails were splayed across the stone altar, the priest leaned close, his painted face contorting as he divined whatever shape or configuration he found in the glistening gore. I held my breath, swallowing against the nausea swelling in my throat.

"You seek knowledge of your future?" he asked Melita.

She pushed in even closer to me, her nails digging into my arm, but she nodded. "About whom my father will choose for my husband. And whether he will be kind and good. And also, will I be sent away from Tyre? I don't want to have to go someplace far away like Elissa." She paused to give me an apologetic glance. "I just . . . I just need to know . . ."

The priest stared at her for a moment, condescension in his kohl-darkened eyes. Then, as if he'd suddenly remembered she was a daughter of the king, his demeanor shifted, his red-lipped smile ingratiating.

"Of course, my dear." He took one of those long, painted nails and prodded the entrails, humming to himself. "Yes. Well, as you can see from the shape of the liver, portents are very good." He pointed to the bloody viscera. "The gods look on you with favor, my lady. All indications are that you will make an excellent match with a man of both great wealth and sway among the elite of Tyre."

"But will he be kind? Will he cherish me?"

The priest batted his lashes at her, smirking as if she were a simple-minded child. "If you continue to venerate our goddess with devotion and regularly bring her tokens of your gratitude, there is no reason she will not give you every desire of your heart."

Melita squeaked happily, gripping my arm so hard my fingers went numb. But I'd take the abuse if it meant her mind was eased. This was, of course, the exact outcome we'd hoped for. Yet, for some reason, the exchange left me oddly unsettled.

The priest reached for the second dove in the cage and my stomach revolted at the idea of watching another bird being slaughtered, so I held my breath and averted my eyes as the priest plunged the knife into its flesh, trying not to imagine the swell of crimson that would mar its pristine white chest.

A shout, a scream, and a horrific crash drew our attention back toward the main sanctuary. I darted over to the doorway to see what had happened. Melita followed, gasping at the terrible scene before us.

One of the workers had fallen from the scaffolding while painting resin on one of the enormous columns. He was on the ground on the opposite side of the sanctuary among the remains of what used to be a towering lampstand, a few of his fellow laborers already gathering around his unmoving figure.

He must have broken a few bones in such a fall, if he survived at all. Yet none of the temple attendants or priestesses came to the man's aid, or even took more than a second look, too busy with their duties to care about one of the swarm of laborers rebuilding their holy sanctuary.

"The oracle is ready for your reading, Elissa," called Abenasser.

I peered over my shoulder at the altar in the dim alcove, glad I could not see the eviscerated bird from here. Instead of returning, I leaned into what was expected of me as a daughter of the king.

"I'm no longer in the mood for oracles." I flitted a hand through the air dismissively. "We got what we came for. Abenasser, let's go."

"Are you certain?" asked Melita. "Don't you want to know your future?"

I laughed, hoping there were no sharp edges on the sound. "Actually, I'd rather spend some time shopping in the market at the docks, wouldn't you?"

Melita brightened. "Could we? I heard Shamzur say a ship from Athens just arrived. I'm certain the stalls are full of new goods. Perhaps we can find a gift for Seriyah?"

"Excellent plan." Glad she was so easily swayed, I told Abenasser to take us to the market before we returned to the palace. To my relief, he did not argue like Magin or Shamzur would have done and simply led us past the giant statue where a few young attendants were tossing some of the offerings from around Astarte's feet into a handcart. Food, cakes, sacks of grain, even jars of oil and wine were roughly tossed into the cart. My eye was drawn to one of the offerings placed among the rest.

A small bundle, wrapped in a threadbare brown cloth.

Halting for a moment, I stared at the bundle, wondering if perhaps I was misremembering what I'd seen earlier. Then, ignoring

Melita's questions, I slipped my hand from hers and strode ahead to the porch of the temple, hoping I was wrong. But there, just near the gates, was the little girl who'd been upset we'd entered the sanctuary before her. Her mother walked beside her, striding away from the temple with empty arms.

My gut clenched tight. Surely a mother would not simply drop her babe at the feet of Astarte, would she? Even though I'd been only eight years old at the time, I would never forget the inhuman wails that came from my mother's soul when my tiny little brother perished in his first and only moments of life. Nor would I forget the months of painful silence that followed the day that stole the vibrant, cheerful mother from before.

"What is wrong?" Melita searched the courtyard for whatever had made me dash off, but the mother and her daughter had already slipped through the outer gates. I glanced back at the towering golden goddess, seeking the brown bundle that had been at her feet. It was gone. My stomach dropped. Had it been thrown into the cart with the other offerings?

"We should go," interrupted Abenasser before I could respond, his round face glistening with sweat. "The ceremony is beginning soon."

"Which ceremony?" asked Melita.

"A dedication," replied one of the nearby priestesses, gesturing toward the group gathered near the horned altar. "Those who wish to give their children into Astarte's service will bring them before the goddess today, in hopes theirs will be chosen. It is quite a coveted honor."

As we walked past the line of parents, some with toddlers in hand and others standing beside boys and girls of around six or seven, my tongue tasted of bile.

I'd always thought the priestesses glamorous with their brightly dyed gowns, glittering jewels, and intriguing tattoos, but I could see now that their eyes were dull and lifeless as they went about their duties in this place. To think that these children might one day look the same made me slightly ill.

My mother may trust the gods on her altar to listen, even after nearly ten years of daily supplication and countless offerings. But she'd only grown more despairing and erratic as time went on. I wasn't certain how she would ever be free from the darkness that seemed to consume more of her each day, but I was fairly certain the answers were not found in this temple.

10

Mattaniel

The spindly ladder shuddered under my feet as I climbed another three rungs, but I could not pass up the chance to read one of the tablets I was supposed to be reshelving while Tabnit argued with a few other scribes across the room.

I also did not expect to see Elissa for at least a couple more hours, if at all, since she'd not appeared in the Hall of Records for nearly a week. Nolam had told me she was occupied with other duties, but I couldn't help but wonder if there was something else keeping her away. At least I'd had a few extra days to prepare for our next lesson. I could only hope my efforts would not be in vain.

I skimmed the palm-sized clay tablet with greedy eyes. Written in an early form of the Canaanite language, the text was a letter from a chieftain informing Tyre of Hebrew invasions in the valley of Megiddo. He begged for the thousands displaced by the invaders to be given refuge in the coastlands in this region. The letter also warned that should Akko, Tyre, and Sidon not take precautions to fortify their own defenses, the Hebrews would swarm over them like locusts as well.

As with many of the Israelite histories, details about this very time period were etched deep in my mind. I could clearly recall a number of battles fought by the Hebrew forces under the famed Yehoshua, along with what seemed like scroll after scroll of information about the next four hundred years: cycles of prosperity and subjugation, victories and losses, reconciliation and rebellion, enemies and champions. During my two lonely years with the Sidonian traders, I'd spent endless hours of travel recalling stories of Yahweh and Hebrew histories in my head, clinging to every morsel of hope within them—especially those regarding my ancestors' victory over their slave masters in Egypt. I had no explanation for why the words, ones I must have learned as a boy, had stuck with me when my own history had been wiped away.

Reading the accounts of those same battles now, from the perspective of Israel's enemies, filled in a few of the gaps. I'd known the people who'd settled this coastal region were Canaanite, but not that a great number had come north because of Yehoshua's forces. Why so many from the tribe of Asher and Naftali would settle here among their ancient enemies was a mystery. Even after hundreds of years enmeshed with the Tyrians, it sounded as though they'd not fully assimilated and old grievances were still held on both sides.

The ladder trembled beneath me, and I nearly dropped the tablet. Tabnit frowned up at me, his hand on one of the lower rungs, which he'd shaken to get my attention. "Are you afraid to come back down? You've been up there for a while now."

I settled the tablet atop the pile on the wooden shelf, noting that I needed to dust again soon, before descending to stand in front of the head scribe.

"Forgive me," I said. "I must have been lost in thought."

Tabnit peered at me, his lips pursing. "A common occurrence, I fear."

Guilt twisted in my gut. I'd hoped none of the scribes had noticed my tendency to get waylaid by some blurry memory I needed to write down later or when an overheard discussion triggered a passage of Hebrew history to suddenly unroll in my mind. But apparently, I'd fooled no one but myself. I'd selfishly given in to my voracious curiosity, endangering my bargain with the king and therefore Raphad's freedom.

"Please forgive me, my lord. I am exceedingly grateful for this position and enjoy my work here in the Hall of Records."

He frowned, looking perplexed. "I'm not sending you away, Mattaniel."

"You're not?"

He shook his head. "Merely calling out your deception."

"What . . . what do you mean?"

"You were reading that tablet, weren't you?" He tipped his chin toward the top shelf. "And you read those reports from Egypt that were on my worktable the other day. As well as the missive the Hittite envoy delivered last week."

Dread washed through me, but there was no use lying. I braced myself and nodded.

"How many languages do you read, young man?"

I swallowed hard. "Fluently? At least nine or ten. Others I can muddle my way through when necessary."

"Impressive. I know you worked as a scribe for your former master but was not informed about your skill with reading and writing foreign tongues." He barked a rusty laugh. "You are wasted dusting these shelves, aren't you?"

"You aren't angry?"

"With a fellow student of the written word? Of course not." He put a warm hand on my shoulder. "In fact, I need your help."

I opened and closed my mouth a couple of times. "Anything."

He gestured toward the other side of the room, where a few scribes were gathered around the table where I usually taught Elissa. "We've been arguing over this text all morning. We need fresh eyes."

Stunned, I followed Tabnit to the gathering. He pushed aside two of his fellow scribes to reveal a clay tablet missing its top half.

"It appears to be Babylonian in origin," he said, "but a dialect none of us can fully decipher. According to the trader who brought it to Tyre, it was discovered in the ruins of an ancient

Elamite stronghold near Susa, but we don't know anything else about its origins."

I bent to take in the symbols, many of which had faded with time. "I don't think it's Elamite either, although there are a few similarities." From somewhere in the recesses of my dim and tangled memories, I dredged up the knowledge that the dynasty of Elam only held Babylon for a short time and was conquered a little over a century ago by an exceedingly strong king determined to revive the traditions of his ancestors. But who came before? This text was far too ancient to be from the Elamite period. The answer seemed to hang from my tongue as I studied the marks.

One of the lines of text, not nearly as worn as the others, caught my eye.

. . . of the ancient ways, he speaks no more . . . for five hundred years past the waters' receding, he has resided in the same valley where the Ark came to rest . . .

I knew this story well. It was another of those inscribed on my heart from before my memories began: a flood sent by Yahweh to drown every living thing and wipe out an ancient evil, and of the righteous man called Noach, who endured mocking to build a boat on dry land. But I also had the strangest feeling that I'd even seen this same tablet before, or perhaps its missing half . . . I shook my head to clear the ridiculous thought.

"I don't know what dialect this is, but I'm fairly certain this is an account of the ancient floodwaters."

"Ah yes. We've found a number of similar accounts in the texts we've collected for the king, from several different nations," said Tabnit.

"This one seems to be a secondhand account of someone who survived."

Tabnit's mouth parted, surprise in his dark brown eyes. "Is it indeed? Extraordinary." He grinned at the other scribes. "Didn't I tell you?"

Then he turned to me again. "Mattaniel, I'd like you to translate whatever you can onto papyrus so we can add it to the other records we've compiled for the king. He's especially interested in knowing more about the dimensions of the fabled ship. For a vessel to weather such a disaster, it must have been perfectly crafted."

Three hundred cubits by fifty cubits and thirty cubits high. The answer whispered from some well-etched place in my soul. But out loud, I said, "I'd be happy to do so."

"Once you're done, I have a few other texts I'd like you to take a look at. Since Abibaal is set on collecting every text ever written, visitors bring him scrolls and tablets from all over the world, some engraved with markings we've never seen before and on stone we have no name for. But perhaps you'll have some insight."

"It would be my honor." I did my best to keep the excitement from my voice, but from the moment I'd entered this cavernous room, I'd been desperate to delve into the mysteries on these shelves. I could barely believe I'd been offered the opportunity to do so.

However, when I'd only halfway completed the task of transcribing the flood account onto a blessedly pristine sheet of papyrus with impossibly smooth black ink, the king's daughter walked into the Hall of Records on the arm of Nolam.

I scrambled to my feet, reed pen still in hand as the two approached, then bowed low to the king's daughter. "My lady."

When I lifted my eyes, she was scowling at me, a reminder of her demand that I call her by name. But I could not do so in front of Nolam. As kind as the old man was, he was still one of the eunuchs—or Crows, as I'd heard them called by other servants—and it would be considered a great impertinence. Regardless that I'd been given the opportunity to read and decipher ancient texts, I was still a servant.

A hint of shadow lingered within the deep aquamarine of her eyes today, as if she were drained of her usual vibrancy. She sighed heavily, running her fingers through her thick hair, and the movement released a waft of spicy-sweet fragrance into the air. Out of pure self-defense, I held my breath and shifted backward a half step.

"Could we not do this lesson somewhere else? This room is so dreary, and it stinks of must and stale leather." She wrinkled her nose.

"I don't see why not," said Nolam, his cheer sounding a bit forced. He, too, must sense something was not quite right with his charge. "Perhaps we can find another empty chamber."

Elissa hummed thoughtfully, gaze going to the windows. "What about the gardens? We'll find some shade under the trees."

"That's an excellent plan, my dear," said the eunuch, taking her arm again and heading for the doorway. "A bit of sunlight would do us all some good."

I gave my unfinished translation a longing glance, though I had no choice but to follow. I retrieved my satchel from under the table, informed Tabnit I would return to the task as soon as possible, then jogged to catch up.

The elderly eunuch shuffled along painfully slowly, so as I followed them down three flights of stone stairs and into one of the outer courtyards on the far side of the palace grounds, I silently rehearsed how I would introduce the new method I'd devised without explicitly calling out her duplicity. Whatever Elissa's reasons were for trying to avoid this arrangement, I could only hope she'd be intrigued enough by what I'd created that she would let me teach her what she needed to know. My freedom, and Raphad's, depended on it.

Passing through the open gates of the gardens, we continued along what I guessed to be the same winding path I'd walked with Adin the night of the feast. In the daylight, the gardens were breathtaking. Explosions of colorful blooms lined both edges of the crushed-shell walkway, which was dappled by shade from plentiful date palms rustling softly in the sea breeze. We turned toward the towering limestone wall that marked the perimeter of the fortress. In the distance, seagulls chattered as waves crashed against the rocky foundations of the island.

A piercing cry cut through the quiet afternoon that I recognized as belonging to the baboons from the feast. Thankfully, it came from the southern end of the royal compound, where I hoped the horrible things were contained behind iron bars. From what I'd heard from the other servants, the king was famous for his collection of exotic animals from far-flung places. As with the black leopards chained to his throne that night, I was certain the frightening display was as much to entertain Abibaal's honored guests as it was to intimidate them.

The path spilled into the same clearing as before, surrounded by well-manicured flower beds and ornamental grasses whispering in the salty air. I waited near the fountain—now dry since there was still a lack of water in Tyre—while Elissa led Nolam to the wide stone seat situated at the base of the largest palm in the garden. She pressed a kiss to his cheek, and he smiled up at her like a doting grandfather but frowned once she'd turned away, concern evident on his round face. I'd assumed Elissa had only been avoiding our lessons out of disinterest, but perhaps whatever had kept her away was more serious than I thought.

When she reached the fountain, her usual veneer was firmly in place. She turned one of her practiced smiles my way. "Shall we begin?"

It didn't matter that it was entirely false; the flirtatious look on her stunning face barreled into me full force. Since the first time I'd met her, I'd done my best to ignore the way Elissa affected me, reminding myself over and over that she was the daughter of a king and in no way meant for me. But I was still a man, and the woman had just stolen the breath from my lungs.

She peered at me strangely. "Mattaniel?"

I cleared my throat, giving my muddled head a shake. "Yes . . . yes."

"Shall we walk around the garden? You can teach me how the Shardan name the trees and flowers."

"No. We'll need to sit."

Elissa arched her brows.

I put up a palm, horrified I'd spoken so freely. My unwelcome attraction to her had knocked me sideways. "I only mean that I've brought something with me for our lesson, and I'll need somewhere to lay out the materials."

Genuine interest sparked in her eyes. "Well, then . . ." She perched on the wide ledge surrounding the dry fountain, arranging her flowing gown as she angled herself toward me. "By all means, let's sit."

Her expectant expression and proximity caused a foolish hum to buzz in my veins. I inhaled deeply, willing my pulse to calm as I sat an arm's length away from her, then dumped the contents of my pack on the limestone between us.

Her blue-green eyes flew up to meet mine. "What . . . what is this?"

"I created a written language to help you learn Shardan."

11

Elissa

He'd written me a *language*.

I stared in wonder as Mattaniel explained the markings he'd drawn on shards of pottery, each corresponding to a sound in the Shardan language. I recognized a few of the symbols, since he'd employed a few Tyrian ones, but borrowed from other tongues as well. For sounds that were unique to Shardan, he'd created completely new symbols.

"Your ingenuity in reconstructing the broken tablet gave me the idea," he said, eyes down. "I thought connecting what you see with what you hear might help you remember the new words more easily. Much like you pieced together that message, we can use these symbols to form words and phrases."

I *did* remember much of what he'd taught me, even if I'd been pretending to ignore him and feigning distraction during our lessons. The Shardan language was a beautiful and melodic tongue and especially captivating in Mattaniel's deep voice, and he was extraordinarily patient and careful not to shame me when I purposely mangled the words he taught me.

Guilt speared me between the ribs. Not only had I made his job terribly difficult for weeks, I'd gone missing for the past few days with no explanation. But after I'd gone to the temple, my mother had only sunk deeper into despair. I'd remained near her bedside since then, worried what she might do if I left her for any longer than a couple of hours.

Danice and I had taken turns making certain the flame remained lit and setting fresh offerings on the altar. But she'd only grown more agitated over the past few days, swinging from gut-wrenching wails of supplication to shrill curses at the gods themselves for taking first her son and now her daughter. After six nights of vigilance, I was beyond exhausted, so Danice gently insisted I escape the suffocating chamber for a few hours. I'd gone to the Hall of Records, never dreaming that while I'd been missing, Mattaniel had created an entirely new written language for my sake.

I'd been served by a multitude of slaves my entire life—even the eunuchs were bound by an oath of lifelong service to the king—but never had I been so intrigued by one of them. Not only was he perhaps the most striking man I'd ever met, as if he were some sort of Egyptian royal in disguise, but he was as brilliant as he was kind.

Who *was* this man?

"How many languages do you speak, Mattaniel?"

Eyes still down, he shifted a couple of the pieces on the ledge between us. "A few."

His reticence intrigued me further. "Which ones?"

He pressed his lips together, looking abashed. "Hebrew. Canaanite. Shardan, of course. A fair bit of Egyptian. Aramean. Hittite. Amurru. Philistine. And I am familiar with at least a dozen dialects among those languages—and those spoken by Kenites, Midianites, and Ammonites, along with a smattering of phrases from Babylon and Mesopotamia, and a few other places we traveled over the years."

I blinked at him in astonishment. "How did you have time to learn all of those tongues? You cannot be more than twenty-five years of age."

He scratched at the thin scar bisecting his right eyebrow, something I'd noticed him do before when he was uncomfortable.

"A little older than that," he said, then muttered, "I think."

Mattaniel was as much a puzzle as the broken tablet had been. Each tiny piece he revealed made me want to turn over another. From the beginning, his reticence had only served to pique my interest. I'd spent far too much time mulling over the few crumbs of information he'd offered about himself, and just as much time thinking about his rare half-smiles or the accidental glimmers of amusement that sparked in his beautiful eyes when I took my pretenses a little too far.

I was weary of feigning stupidity with this man. So at least for today, I would set aside the plan Yarikh and I had made and let Mattaniel teach me the symbols he'd painstakingly created. If anything, trying to slide past his defenses would keep my mind off my mother.

"Well, then." I smiled and leaned in. "Since I have an *expert* to teach me, I should not waste any more time." I picked up one of the pottery shards with an unfamiliar symbol on its face. "What is the sound of this one?"

He blinked a couple of times, as if clearing his head of confusion, then made a noise like waves rushing over a stony beach and spoke a word that employed the sound. I repeated it, emulating his pronunciation easily.

Mattaniel's golden-brown eyes met mine, his lips twitching as if he were holding back a comment, but instead of calling out my deception, he simply picked up another shard and demonstrated the next sound, and then the one after that. Once I had mastered most of the symbols, he arranged the shards into different variations to teach me simple words. By the time the sun touched the top of the wall, I was already reading short phrases.

Mattaniel had relaxed a great deal over the course of the afternoon, the tight formality and stiff posture that characterized our every interaction thus far softening into a gentle familiarity that left me almost giddy.

As engrossed as I was in our lesson, I'd quite forgotten Nolam was waiting on me. Yet there he was, still seated on the stone chair under the largest of the palms in the garden, head slumped forward and chin on his broad chest.

"Is he well?" Mattaniel asked, following my line of sight.

I waved my hand absently. "Only sleeping."

His brows pinched. "Doesn't look very comfortable."

"Nolam has a rare talent for dropping into sleep anytime, anywhere. At meals. During religious rites. One time, when I was about ten, he fell asleep in the middle of giving a history lesson." I laughed to myself, remembering how Melita, Seriyah, and I had each placed a kiss on his forehead before stealing out of the room while he snored away, cheek pressed to the table before him.

When I turned back to Mattaniel, his lips were curved in a faint reflection of my own smile. Sunlight illuminated the gold in his eyes and turned them translucent, like faceted amber held to lamplight. Pulse fluttering, I held his gaze for three whole breaths before he blinked and looked away, as if embarrassed to have been caught looking.

I was used to men staring. Had been taught to make certain they did. So it never unsettled me to have male attention directed my way, like it did Melita. But those short-but-intense moments of Mattaniel's close scrutiny rattled me.

"What were you writing on that scrap of papyrus the other day?" I blurted, needing a distraction. "When you didn't notice me come into the room?"

He winced. "Apologies, my lady . . ."

"*Elissa.*"

He scratched at that scar on his brow again, pausing for so long I didn't think he would answer. But of course, as a servant, he had little choice. He took a deep breath. "My apologies, Elissa. I should have been paying better attention."

"I was not offended." I leaned back on my palms, tilting my chin as I peered at him. "But I am curious what had you so occupied."

He hesitated, gaze darting around the clearing as he ran his fingers through his short black curls and that fascinating silver patch. But I refused to speak until he gave in.

"You asked about the years before I was a slave to the Sidonian traders. The truth is . . . I don't remember."

I shifted closer, enthralled. "How can that be?"

"They found me in the wilderness. Apparently, I was under attack by hyenas."

I caught my breath. "You were alone?"

"The traders threw rocks to run the pack off. They said it looked as though I'd fallen from a short cliff nearby and hit my head on a rock. It took days before I was fully conscious, and even then, I made little sense. I don't remember anything from before I woke up in the back of their wagon. Where I am from. Why I was out there by myself. Or even my real name."

My jaw went slack. "*That's* why you don't know your true age."

"I was young, likely around fourteen or fifteen, but there's no way to know."

I blinked, equally fascinated and horrified. "So your family . . . ?"

He shrugged. "There were no towns or villages for hours in all directions. And no clue as to where I'd come from. All I know is that I am Hebrew, because of my language and the garments I was wearing. But from what tribe, I could not tell you."

A thousand questions flooded my mind, but I returned to my original one. "And the writing?"

He sighed, rubbing his temple. "I have dreams sometimes. Memories, I think. I've been writing down images that reoccur, hoping perhaps I could piece together some idea of where I came from. So that once I am free . . ."

"You can go home," I finished for him.

"If I have one left," he murmured.

My chest ached at the sadness in his low voice. "You said 'once you are free.' What did you mean?"

His eyes flared. "You don't know?"

I shook my head.

"The night of the feast, I promised the king I would teach you to speak the language of the Shardan and ensure a successful treaty, hoping he might have mercy on my former master . . ." His words drifted off, as if he were reluctant to finish.

"And?"

"And once they arrive and treaty is sealed, I will no longer be a slave."

I flinched, stunned by the revelation. I'd been so focused on the way my father had shaken my world to pieces that night, I'd never considered what happened before I stepped foot into this very garden.

I opened my mouth to ask another question, but Mattaniel frowned, his brows pinching as he looked past me. Then he dropped his gaze, posture stiffening as all semblance of familiarity melted away. Confused by the sudden shift, I turned to find Yarikh coming around the bend on the path, in the company of two men I did not recognize.

"What are you doing out here, Elissa?" he asked, his eyes tracking to Mattaniel, then to Nolam still asleep on the stone seat, and then back to me.

"Being tutored in the language of the Shardan," I said, gesturing to the shards scattered between us on the ledge. "So I can please my new *husband*."

He winced at my pointed emphasis. Obviously his attempts to sway our father had not gone well. I'd already guessed he'd been avoiding me, but I certainly could not press him about it in front of strangers.

"Who might this lovely young woman be?" asked the tallest of the men in a strongly accented voice, icy gray eyes focused on me. Although his expression was friendly, there was something faintly menacing behind the polished veneer.

"This is my half-sister," said Yarikh. "Elissa, this is Zandar, the eldest son of King Enesidu of Gaza, and his brother, Ruel."

I gave them a nod but did not bother to stand. It annoyed me that Mattaniel had transformed back into a silent servant, and I wished the three of them would simply leave us to our lesson.

"I did not know the king was on friendly terms with the Shardan," said Zandar.

Yarikh shrugged one shoulder. "A new development. They are negotiating a treaty."

"Your king negotiates with pirates?" asked Ruel, a subtle sneer in his deeply accented voice. His disdain surprised me, especially when the coalition of sea peoples who had long ago attempted to overtake Egypt had included Philistines. It seemed they were no longer allies.

"When it serves his purposes," said my brother. "Elissa's marriage will be the seal on their trade agreement."

"Even after the attack?" Zandar sounded incredulous.

"What attack?" I asked, reeling from the realization that Yarikh must have actually given up on convincing the king not to give me to the Shardan.

"I told you. That wasn't pirates," Yarikh said, ignoring me. "At least not Shardan ones. It was Hebrews who overtook that lumber barge near Akko."

In the corner of my eye, I saw Mattaniel stiffen. Thankfully, Yarikh did not even glance at the man who was, to him, only one of the inconsequential, nameless slaves in this palace. I feared even dismissing my tutor would draw unwanted attention his way.

The Philistine heir snorted. "All the more reason to listen to our proposal. The Hebrews need to be sent back out into the desert where they belong."

"I have no sway over my father," said Yarikh, bitterness practically dripping from his tongue. He gestured to the dry fountain behind me. "I tried to get him to do something after Asherites burned the flumes up in the mountains. Even Ahiram ignored me."

We'd gone over a week without a steady flow of water, but I'd not heard anything about the waterworks being destroyed on purpose, and certainly not that Hebrews were involved.

I was surprised my brother would discuss any of this openly with these Philistines, let alone in front of me and a slave. However, Yarikh had never been one for protocol. He was the opposite of Ahiram, who took his role as successor to our father's throne deadly serious. Yarikh far preferred the freedom of life on the sea to what he deemed the suffocatingly luxurious atmosphere of the palace.

"Maybe now he will finally ally with us to rid our lands of the invaders," said Zandar.

"Perhaps," said Yarikh. "Although I have a feeling it will take more than a couple of small-scale attacks to convince Abibaal to go to war with Israel."

"If he's not careful, war will come to him," said Zandar. "The Hebrews think their invisible god gave them all the territory from Sidon to Egypt. And even if we have mostly kept them in their place, they've multiplied like roaches over these past decades. It is time to stamp them out once and for all."

I knew little about the animosity between Israel and Philistia, but I hated that Mattaniel was trapped listening to these men discuss his people with such vitriol.

I stood, aggressively brushing nonexistent dust from my skirts, and affected a flippant tone. "I've had enough of this war talk, and I'm famished. Mattaniel," I said, without looking at him, "go fetch Nolam. It's time to go inside."

"Yes, my lady," he murmured before striding away to obey my command. Because even if I'd managed to forget for a short while that there was an insurmountable wall between us, he was still a slave—one whose freedom I now knew depended solely on the marriage I still refused to accept as inevitable.

12

Mattaniel

I shivered in the darkness, the smell of rotting leaves and dust clogging my nose. Thirst scratched insistently at my throat, my tongue clinging to the roof of my mouth. But the empty waterskin beside me lay in a shallow puddle of mud from where I'd accidentally dropped it on the floor of the cave before even taking one drink. I'd been told to stay, but how could I when I was so, so thirsty? The stream wasn't so far away. It wouldn't take me long. I scrambled out of the cave on hands and knees, glad I was small enough to easily slither through the narrow opening. Sunlight blinded me the moment I emerged, and I tried to blink away the violent glare, but lights flashed purple, white, and blue across my vision as I pushed myself to standing. My head swam, dull pain throbbing in my temples. A low, grating sound came from my left. I turned toward it, blinking harder against the glare as I tried to discern its source. Another deep sound came from only a few paces away, raising the hair on the back of my neck. As my vision finally began to clear of the floating lights, I saw only dark-spotted fur, sharp black eyes, and glistening yellow teeth. Gasping, I tried to step away, but the sun was so bright and everything seemed to swirl around me. More growls echoed off the stone. Disoriented and heart galloping, I retreated from the sound, wishing for the safety of the cave, and then I was falling, falling, falling . . .

I startled awake at the sensation of horrifying weightlessness, my head feeling as though it had been drilled through with an awl. I wasn't certain if it had been revealing the hyena attack to Elissa this afternoon or hearing her brother and the Philistines discuss my people with such naked hatred that had stoked the recurrent nightmare to life, but I doubted I would be able to go back to sleep.

Eyes on the black ceiling and surrounded by the heavy breaths and snores of the other male servants, I began silently reciting one of the stories etched deep in my soul, just as I used to do during my loneliest nights in the Sidonian caravan.

For months after my injury, my head had been so muddled and the conjured images of Yosef, Yaakov, and Avraham so vivid in my mind, I'd thought some of them were my own memories. Now, as I told myself the story of Yaakov and his ladder reaching to the heavens, one of my favorites, I took comfort in the reminder of Yahweh's unbreakable covenant with the line of Avraham. There was nothing I could do to protect my people from whatever their enemies had planned, but the God who promised to always walk beside Yaakov that night—and rescued his descendants from slavery hundreds of years later—certainly could.

Although the pain in my head lessened and the swirling lights dimmed, it felt like I was still in that tiny cave from my dream, unable to catch a full breath. I rose from my bedroll, then carefully padded barefoot through the dark, past my sleeping roommates, and out the door. The brisk night lifted gooseflesh on my arms, but I welcomed the bite. Leaning against the wall outside the servants' quarters, I inhaled a deep, cleansing breath and let it out slowly, my eyes dropping closed.

Unbidden, the image of Elissa's sunlit smile rose up. As soon as she'd repeated that first word yesterday, with near-perfect inflection, an almost visible wave of relief came over her, as if the pretense had been a burden. Not only did she easily memorize the words I spelled out in symbols, but she knew many from our earlier lessons too. She'd hidden her keen mind behind that vacuous facade, but once she gave herself permission to drop the mask, she excelled in learning Shardan.

When those ocean-water eyes met mine, brimming with compassion and curiosity as I'd revealed a few of my own secrets, I'd been so entranced I'd nearly forgotten the impossible divide between us. For a few elusive moments, she had not been the daughter of a king and I had not been a slave. Yet as soon as her brother and the two Philistines came around the bend in the path, I'd been violently thrown back down to earth, the illusion shattered at my feet.

There was no margin for such foolish notions. I must keep a much tighter rein on myself in her presence.

Something white fluttered on the edge of my vision. At first, I thought it was just another swirl of light flashing behind my eyes, but then it moved crosswise across the servants' courtyard and toward the gate leading through the palace kitchens. It was a person—a woman, if I had to guess from the slender build. Probably some brazen maid on her way to meet a lover. It would certainly not be the first time I'd witnessed servants trysting in this palace.

Just before the woman reached the gate, she glanced back over her shoulder. Recognition hit me square in the chest.

Elissa was stealing through the shadows, alone.

I'd never once seen her, or any of the other royal daughters, without at least one eunuch nearby. Nolam was present for all of our lessons, even if he did fall asleep from time to time, and the rare occasions I'd seen Elissa from afar with her sisters or the king's concubines, there were usually at least two guarding them. From the way they hovered about, black-robed, sharp eyes always on their charges, the Crows were aptly named. But right now, none were watching over the vulnerable young woman stealing through the night.

I pushed away from the wall and dashed after her, darting across the empty courtyard under a star-filled sky. I stretched my gait, keeping light on the balls of my feet, just as Torben had taught me during predawn hunts on Shardana. I kept to the shadows as I followed her through the kitchens, out the side gate, and into the gardens. Whenever she paused to peer around a corner, I sank to my haunches, holding my body and breath still until she continued on. She seemed to know exactly how to avoid the guards posted around the palace entrances and when to crouch to avoid being seen by anyone who might happen to be gazing out a window. She even kept to the side of the path, just as I did, to avoid the crunch of shells beneath her sandals.

My gut clenched. Did she regularly meet someone out here in the shadowy gardens?

I tensed at the idea of witnessing Elissa embracing a lover under the stars, even as I chastised myself for caring. I'd followed to make certain she was safe, nothing else.

My eyes were trained on her white-clad form ahead of me, so when the path passed through a dense hedge of juniper and cypress into the far reaches of the royal grounds, I had no idea where we were. This far from the palace, darkness reigned. No flickering torches, no illuminated windows or porticoes, only dense shadows and the gentle rustle of the breeze through the trees overhead.

Elissa paused her steps, going stiff. Holding my breath, I slid into the blackness beneath a sprawling cedar, then dropped to one knee near the trunk to meld my form with its wide shadow. The last thing I meant to do was frighten her. Chin down, I peered at her still form but did not hold my stare long. *"Heavy eyes are like arrows to both man and beast, Salpa,"* Torben had once told me while we stalked a deer. *"Keep your gaze soft as feathers on the wind."*

I never became any great hunter, but Uvaldo's nephew and his friends had taught Adin and me a good deal in those years. I had certainly come to understand how they'd earned their fearsome reputation.

After a few tense moments, Elissa took off into the night again, her white garments fluttering at her heels as she slipped through moonlight-dappled shadows. I stepped from under the canopy of the cedar to follow when a howl split the night.

Dropping again into a crouch, I felt my pulse thunder. Nothing moved, aside from leaves shivering in the breeze, but an answering call, this one higher-pitched and closer, resounded.

My earlier nightmare hovered on the edge of my mind—sharp-toothed grins and chilling laughter, rancid fur and hot breath circling, circling, circling . . .

I shoved the terrifying vision aside and willed my thudding heartbeat to quiet as I took off after Elissa. If something was hunting me out here, chances were it had scented her as well.

Striding alongside the curving path in the soft grasses, I kept my gaze roving back and forth, alert for any twitch in the darkness. I turned the corner where I'd last seen Elissa and slammed to a halt when I came face-to-face with a wall of eyes—at least a dozen or more pairs blinked back at me for a breathless moment. And then the horrific screeching began.

All the hair on my neck standing on end, I took a stunned step backward as the caged monkeys I'd stumbled across sneered, yipped, hooted, and hissed with bone-chilling fury, needlelike teeth bared and spindly arms grasping for me between narrow iron bars.

When a hand grasped my arm, I grabbed without thinking, twisting my body while sweeping my leg back to take them off their feet the way Torben had drilled into me. My attacker grunted in surprise, falling, but I spun, reaching around to bar my forearm across their neck, then yanking them in a tight chokehold against my chest, both of us breathing heavily as the animals continued screaming.

Far too slowly, I realized the form pressed against me was not clad in armor like a guard, nor even the angular build of a man. Instead, the body was soft and warm, and the hands gripping my forearm small and delicate. I pulled in a sharp breath and a familiar spicy-sweetness flooded my senses.

"Mattaniel?" The sound of my name rasped by lips I'd caught myself staring at several times yesterday melted the rest of my confusion in one horrified moment.

I had the daughter of the king locked in an iron grip, my forearm pressed tight to her graceful neck. I dropped my hold and tripped back, all the blood in my body rushing to my feet. I'd *attacked* a royal family member. If she screamed right now, I could very well be strung on the walls of Tyre before the sun rose.

I dropped to my knees, head down. "Please, my lady, forgive me."

She tugged at my arm. "What are you *doing*? Stand up. We need to go!"

Stunned, I looked up into her face, illuminated by moonlight. Her eyes were wide as she glanced back toward the palace, then she tugged again, harder. "The guards will hear these awful things screaming and come looking! Get up! Now!"

The desperation in her voice jolted me into motion. I surged to my feet, and she took off down the path, fingers wrapped tight around my wrist.

"Hurry," she hissed but was forced to take two steps to my every stride as we plowed through the darkness past other caged beasts that hissed, growled, and clicked their teeth at us. Once we were at the base of the towering limestone wall that marked the edge of the royal compound, Elissa dropped my arm but gestured for me to follow as she slithered behind a huge, flowering oleander.

I paused to survey the darkness, ensuring we'd not been followed before pushing through the oleander. Just behind the sprawling bush was a hidden alcove at the base of the wall, and within it, a wooden door standing slightly ajar. Confused but intrigued about where she'd led me, I pressed through the door and halted in the pitch-blackness just past the threshold.

"My lady?"

A huff came out of the dark. "*Elissa*."

I ignored the implicit command. "Where are we?"

"First, tell me why you followed me."

"I saw you run through the servants' courtyard alone and wanted to make sure you were safe. Please forgive me for grabbing you. I was startled."

"I grabbed you first. You didn't hear me call your name?"

"No. Did I hurt you?"

"I'm fine."

"Are you certain?"

"You only knocked the wind from my lungs for a moment, I promise."

Even that made me feel ill. "I vow I only meant to ensure your safety. I would never dream of hurting a woman—"

"Mattaniel." Her voice softened. "I am all right. I am not angry."

Relief poured through my limbs. "How did you know it was me?"

"I didn't. Not until I moved off the path and waited for you to pass me."

Clever woman.

"Where are your usual escorts?"

She went silent for a moment. "Sleeping, I would guess. I came out the window."

I shook my head, glad she couldn't see my amusement in the dark. "You've done this before, haven't you?"

I could practically hear the mischievous smile curving her lips. "My sisters and I have used this passageway for years."

"I find it hard to believe the guards would ignore such a vulnerability in the wall."

She jingled something in her other hand. "I have the key. The *only* key."

"Oh?"

Her sly snicker nearly made me lose hold of my composure. "And how did you come across that?"

"Will you think less of me if I say I stole it?"

"Does it matter?"

She hummed, sidestepping my question. "In my defense, Seriyah challenged me to do so when we were twelve. And I rarely say no to a dare."

Somehow that did not surprise me. “They never replaced it? Or changed the lock?”

“There are plenty of other ways for the guards to get outside of the wall for their rotations. I would guess that after spending a few weeks looking for the key, they gave up and simply forgot about this passage altogether, especially since it’s only usable when the tide is low. I doubt most of the younger guards even know it’s here. Once the oleander grew large enough to fully cover the alcove, the three of us stopped worrying.”

“Where are they tonight?”

“I needed time alone. Somewhere quiet.”

The palpable sadness in her voice made my chest ache. I had no right to question her reasons but could at least offer a reprieve from whatever was causing her pain.

“I’ll wait here. Make sure no one bothers you. When you’re ready, I’ll escort you back.”

She caught her breath. “That’s . . . that’s very kind of you.” She paused. “Would you . . . would you like to come with me? See why this is where I go when I need to breathe?”

In truth, if she asked me to follow her under that wall and directly into the heart of the sea, I would do it without hesitation.

“All right.”

“There is a stairway here. Take my hand, and I’ll show you.”

With my pulse rushing like a wellspring, I reached out, and somehow she found my hand in the dark, the feel of her fingers sliding into mine pure bliss. Since I’d met Elissa, I’d tried to block errant thoughts about her, remind myself that she lived in an entirely different universe than I did, but it took only one touch of her soft skin to destroy weeks’ worth of defenses. I swallowed hard and focused on my feet as she guided me onto the first stair.

“There’s a wall on your right,” she said, releasing my hand. “I’ll go a couple of steps ahead and count aloud.”

Quelling foolish disappointment, I placed a palm on the frigid stone as she began a measured count. With every downward step, the air and the limestone beneath my bare soles grew colder, as if we were descending into the very heart of the rock Tyre was built upon.

"How did you even discover this passage?" My voice echoed off the walls.

"Melita and I were playing in the gardens one day . . . twenty-two . . . twenty-three . . . and we saw two of the guards unlock and then disappear behind the door. We were curious so we followed them. Twenty-four . . . twenty-five. We didn't get too far down before we heard them coming back up, talking about how the tide was still too high. So we ran to the top before they caught us. After that, it became something of an obsession to discover what was at the bottom. We asked one of the gardeners, who said the passage was used long ago to bring cargo to the back entrance of the palace, but once the expanded sea breaks around the northern harbor and new docks were constructed, it was no longer needed, especially since it was only accessible when the tide was low. We think perhaps it may have been constructed as an escape route, should the island be invaded. Thirty-two . . ."

It would take a mighty force with impossible determination to breach the walls of this city. Now that Abibaal boasted the largest naval fleet on the Great Sea, it was doubtful anyone would try.

"We spent weeks wasting afternoons in the Garden of Beasts waiting for another opportunity, and when it came, it was almost ridiculously easy. Forty-five . . . forty-six . . . The guards left the key hanging from the lock when they entered. Seriyah dared me to run over and steal it." Her low laugh echoed all around us on the stone walls. "I took the key off the ring, leaving behind the others, and dropped them on the ground near the entrance. When the guards returned, they argued over why none of the keys would lock the door and one of them said it was the only key they had. Once they left, Seri and I ran down the stairs to finally satiate our curiosity before the tide came in."

"And it was worth the wait?"

"Sixty-two . . . Absolutely. Sixty-three. You only have two more, then there is a path through a cave. It's uneven and slippery since much of this is underwater most of the time. But I know every step by heart. Where are you . . . ?"

Her soft hand landed on my upper arm, causing both an unbidden flex of muscle and a spike of liquid heat to radiate through my veins. She slid her palm past my elbow and down my forearm in an inadvertent caress until her fingers again slipped into mine.

There had been many lovely Shardan women on the island, some who'd made their interest overtly clear, but never had the simple touch of a woman's hand caused my heart to stutter. I let myself be led through the dark, over slippery stone and wet sand, and through shallow puddles of seawater left behind by the outgoing tide.

The crash of distant waves ahead grew louder, and soon dim light at the end of the path outlined Elissa's form as we made our way toward the narrow opening of the cave. We emerged into the cool night, and after winding our way through a narrow valley between huge boulders slick with seaweed and encrusted with barnacles, we came to the edge of the water, our feet sinking in the soft, wet sand. When she released my hand, I felt the loss at the center of my being.

Moonlight highlighted the wide beach and a host of shells left behind by the retreating tide. Water sparkled in tide pools, reflecting the glimmer of stars overhead. To the north and the south, limestone cliffs embraced the sandy cove, shielding it from view from everything but the sky above and sea stretched out before us. No wonder this was a place of respite for her. If she had the only key to the passage and the entrance to the cave was below sea level most of the time, no one else would bother her and her sisters here during low tide.

At my side, Elissa searched the starry sky, and for the first time, I let myself study her profile at length. She was radiant, her skin made alabaster by moonlight and her tawny hair braided away from her face, affording me a view of the gentle curve of her cheek. My fingers ached to sweep down that curve, trace the line of her jaw and over the full lips that, at times, twitched with secret amusement during our lessons. Yet there was a gulf as wide as this sea between us, one that could never be crossed. For my own sake, I needed to keep my walls intact. So although everything in me wanted to reach out to her, I kept my invisibly shackled hands firmly at my sides and dropped my greedy eyes to the ground where they belonged.

"Who gave you the name Mattaniel?"

Surprised by the question, I gave a soft, humorless laugh. "One of the traders. He said I was a gift from El, because I made them so much silver."

The ancient, white-bearded god the Canaanites revered as the father of the other gods was said to live in a tent on a mountain at the edge of the world, far away from the humankind he supposedly created. For so long, Yahweh felt just as distant to me, just as unreachable. After all, I'd been left with nothing but tortured dreams of places I didn't remember, blurred faces I did not recognize, and disembodied voices that whispered of peace at night but offered me none during the day—no matter how much I'd pled for the healing of whatever was broken inside my head.

But something had changed after the shipwreck. It began when Adin divulged to Uvaldo during a fishing excursion that I knew a multitude of stories, and the chieftain insisted I tell a few as we waited for the nets to fill with fish. It had been a challenge to find the language to express the ways of Yahweh to the Shardan, especially since I was still learning theirs, but the more I spoke aloud the stories I'd only told myself for so long, the more I felt their power. I recounted to them of Mosheh, of Avraham, of Yosef and Yaakov, and gradually I stopped thinking of them as simply legends and instead as Yahweh revealing his very nature to not just his people, but to me personally. They'd also been a reminder that once I'd had a home and people who cared enough about me to teach me the ways of the Holy One.

"Do you think the gods can see us down here? Or are we simply all alone is this life?" Elissa asked, her gaze still on the sprawling heavens overhead.

I weighed my answer carefully before I spoke, reciting a passage from the Song of Mosheh that I had clung to, even during the loneliest of my days with the Sidonians.

"'He found him in a desolate land,
in a barren, howling wilderness;
He surrounded him, cared for him,
and protected him as the pupil of His eye.
He watches over His nest like an eagle
and hovers over His young; He spreads His wings, catches him,
and lifts him up on His pinions.'"

"What does that mean?" she half-whispered, as if afraid to disturb the quiet shush of the waves rolling into the shore.

"I cannot speak to the gods of Tyre or Sidon," I said. "But the God of my people, Yahweh, does not keep himself separated from the world he made."

We both went silent for a long while, cocooned by the night, the sea, and the cliffs.

"My mother is . . . unwell," she said, though she kept her eyes on the shimmering water ahead of us.

"I'm sorry to hear that."

"She's been that way for a long time. Since I was a girl. I've pleaded with these stars for many years that she would be restored to the mother I remember from my childhood. Pleaded with every god I know to take away the darkness that consumes her at times." She inhaled a shuddering breath. "And yet here I am once again . . ."

I did not speak, sensing she needed the quiet in a way few could understand. I certainly did.

"Tell me about this Yahweh of yours," she whispered, her eyes still fixed on the starry tapestry above us. "He is a God I do not know."

Something deep stirred inside me, warm and welcome. "What would you like to hear?"

"Anything. Everything."

So, as the waves lapped quietly against the rocky shore, I started from the beginning. I spoke of the Creator's words bringing everything into being. Of the first breath of life given to Adam in the paradise of Eden and how he and his wife were driven from the garden after pride tempted them to lust after equality with the Eternal One who'd made them. Of Avraham and the Promise and how Yahweh rescued Yaakov's descendants from slavery.

And when I finally paused, Elissa's glittering gaze was pinned to me, her face limned in light and more beautiful than the shimmering reflection of the moon on the water. Silence hovered between us, thick and intoxicating as we stared at each other, breathing in tandem while the sea kissed the shore, again and again. I longed to breach the short distance between us, suspected that perhaps she did too, but there was nothing in this world that would ever set my feet on even ground with Elissa's. I took a step backward.

An eerie, high-pitched wail floated toward us on the salty breeze.

"What is that?" Elissa spun toward the sound, but it was swallowed up by the crash of a large wave against the rocky shoreline.

We waited silently as the sea receded and the night went quiet again.

"Perhaps it was only—"

She lifted a palm. "Hush. There it is again."

Before I could respond, she took off running.

"Elissa!" I dashed after her. "The tide is coming in."

She ignored me, too focused on winding around tide pools and climbing over slick rocks and around boulders to care about the slow creep of seawater toward the exposed base of the island. I gave up what was obviously a futile protest, glad my feet were thick-soled from three years of barefooted life on Shardana as we scrambled over rocky ground studded with broken seashells.

The cry lifted again, much closer this time and higher-pitched. Elissa came to a halt with a gasp, wide eyes searching the darkness ahead of us. "Is that a *baby*?"

13

I had no chance to react before she was on the move again toward the cry, which beckoned us up a rocky slope, slick with seaweed. Scrambling behind her as she doggedly climbed to the top, I was not surprised when she darted forward to snatch up a tiny naked body that lay atop a flat boulder.

"Oh, little one!" she breathed as she held the infant in front of her. "Why are you here all by yourself?"

The child looked to be only a few weeks old, dark eyes wide as he cried again, head lolling as he squirmed against Elissa's hold.

"Look," I said, pointing to the boy's flailing right arm. "That is probably why."

The infant's hand was splayed wide, revealing two missing digits and a twisted thumb in the moonlight.

"No, it can't be," said Elissa, her tone full of disgust.

I was not surprised by the abandonment of a disfigured child on the rocky shoreline of Tyre, nor even of her disdain for an infant whose parents likely considered him cursed by the gods, but I was shocked by the depth of my disappointment in a woman I'd thought compassionate.

"It's quite common for unwanted infants to be left on the shore," I said, trying to hide my dismay with a flat tone. "To be taken by the sea."

Elissa pulled the baby close to her chest, brow furrowing as she glared at me. "How can you be so cold?"

My mouth opened and then shut again. Did she not know this was a usual practice with her people? It was the least of the barbaric practices I'd been horrified to witness over the years. The Shardan would not have even let this child live past his first day of life, considering such a deformity a foul omen and a dangerous portent of empty nets the next time their boats headed out to sea.

"I don't care what you do," she snapped, "but I'm not leaving this little one to drown."

She wasn't upset by the baby's malformed hand; she was *angry* that he'd been left to die. Affection for this lovely, kindhearted woman welled up.

I glanced back over my shoulder. "The tide is coming in fast. We'd better get going or none of us will survive."

Her eyes flared. "You're going to help me?"

"I don't know what we'll do with the babe once we are back inside the palace walls, but we cannot just leave him here to perish."

The delighted smile she gave me made my chest swell to an almost painful degree. "All right. Let's go."

The climb down from the outcropping was complicated by Elissa's determination to hold the child tight against her chest, but she let me grasp her arm as we slid down the slick rocks toward what remained of the beach. Once back on the sand, we headed south, our path narrow along the water that hedged us close to the limestone cliff on our left and the many tide pools that lay between us and our destination. But Elissa refused to turn back and did not pull away whenever I reached for her hand. The baby had gone quiet as we ran, either sensing our goal was to save him or lulled into calm by the warmth of Elissa's embrace, blissfully unaware that the sea was still eagerly trying to claim him.

By the time we were within sight of the boulders near the cave entrance, the water was already crashing against the backs of our knees as it surged toward the island, turning the sand liquid beneath our feet.

"We're not going to make it!" Elissa's voice warbled with exhaustion as she took another labored step against the retreating waves.

"Give me the babe," I said, reaching for him.

She yanked him closer with a firm shake of her head.

"I won't let him drown. I promise. But if you don't let me help, you certainly will." I came closer. "Please, Elissa."

She looked up at me, her eyes full of worry. "You'll make sure he is safe?"

"I'll make sure both of you are safe."

A wave smashed into us, throwing her off-balance. I gripped her by the waist to keep her from toppling into the water with her charge, and the moment she regained her footing, she pressed the baby into my arms.

I'd never held an infant before, at least that I could remember, but somehow I instinctively knew how best to secure him against me. His dark eyes peered up at me curiously.

"It's all right, little friend," I said. "I've got you."

I strode through the water, following Elissa as she pressed against the insistent roll of the waves, now waist-high. Once we reached the boulders lining the way to the cave entrance, our progress was slowed even more by the sea's determination to dash us against the enormous rocks. With my free hand, I grabbed the back of Elissa's dress, refusing to let her be pulled under the surface, and with the other I held the small, shivering body of the baby high on my shoulder. His little chin quivered as he made his discomfort loudly known.

"What do we do?" Elissa cried when we finally made it to the entrance of the cave and discovered only about a cubit of the opening remained above water. Both of us clung to the closest boulder as the force of the waves lifted us off our feet.

"Can you swim well?"

She nodded, her teeth chattering.

"You go first," I said, gripping the slippery rock with icy fingers. "Get through the opening and onto firm ground. I'll follow with the baby."

Elissa's eyes were wide, full of terror. "Are you sure?"

"I've been living on an island for three years and much of that time was spent on the water with Shardan fishermen. I'm probably part fish after so much time in the sea." Not to mention those memories of learning to swim from a boy with laughing, forest-green eyes. "Go. We'll be all right."

She obeyed, taking a deep breath before she dove for the opening, which was now barely a handspan above the water.

After a few moments, her voice echoed through the narrowing gap. "I'm through. Hurry!"

I held the little boy in front of me as I moved us closer to the cave opening, wishing for his sake I did not have to put what I'd learned on Shardana to the test, but I had no choice. I took a deep breath and dropped down below the surface, praying the babe's instincts would take over. Even with my eyes open, everything was pitch-black as I kicked my feet hard. Glad for the swift momentum of the waves, after a few moments, I took a chance that the sea had propelled us through the entrance of the cave and swam upward.

My head broke free of the surface and I gasped for breath, the sound echoing around me in the cave. I lifted the infant out of the water and held him over my head as I kicked to keep us afloat. He was far too silent, his little body limp as I searched about with my bare feet for somewhere to land. Had I killed the child in my attempt to save him?

"Mattaniel? Are you all right? Where's the baby?"

I had no chance to respond before a sharp wail pierced the darkness, echoing off the walls and making me nearly giddy with relief. The infant squirmed in my hands as I moved toward where I'd heard Elissa's voice.

My feet found purchase on the rocky ground, just as the king's daughter practically ripped the baby from my grasp. I wasn't sure how she'd even been able to do so when I could see nothing but black all around me.

"Is he all right? I thought the both of you had drowned."

Blindly, I crawled out of the water and then lay on the ground panting as Elissa cooed comforting nonsense to the baby until he calmed.

"I told you, I'm part fish."

"Perhaps so, but this little one is not." Her chiding tone echoed off the limestone.

"Shardan mothers teach their infants to swim long before they walk. When I was shocked to see them carry their newborns with them into the waves, they told me babes will reflexively hold their breath underwater. Every Shardan child is fearless in the sea. It's why they make excellent pirates when grown."

I immediately wished I could reel the words back in. She was destined to marry one of those pirates, after all. I scrambled for a way to deflect from my mistake. "What should we do with the baby?"

Obviously his mother did not want him, and it may be difficult to find someone in Tyre willing to take in a child with a deformed hand since most would see the infirmity as a curse from the gods.

"I know just the place for him."

"You do?" I sat up, wishing I could see her face.

"But thank you, Mattaniel. For helping me tonight." Her voice trembled. "I trust you'll say nothing about this place or what we found here."

"Of course not." However, I'd probably visit this night over and over in my dreams, especially the elusive moments I'd had the privilege of touching her. Moments I'd likely never have again.

"Ready?" she asked, her voice floating in front of me like a disembodied shadow. "We have sixty-five stairs to climb."

14

Elissa

For the first time since we'd begun language lessons, I entered the Hall of Records and Mattaniel was nowhere to be seen. Nolam, however, was seated in his favorite cushioned chair under the windows, studying a text with his narrowed eyes only three fingers away from the parchment.

I greeted him with a kiss to his papery cheek, and he startled, then laughed when he realized it was me.

He patted his chest, sighing theatrically. "I thought one of the scribes was playing a trick on me."

I perched on the seat beside him. "What are you studying so intently?"

"Oh, nothing that would interest you, I'm afraid. I was trying to remember the name of one of the former king's concubines, but I've looked through scrolls spanning the past four decades and there's nothing about her at all."

"What made you think of such a thing?" Any concubine who'd not been brought into Abibaal's household after the overthrow of Ragembal would likely have been sent away, if she'd survived the coup at all.

He waved a gnarled hand. "Oh, something reminded me of her.

It's not all that important. But there's simply nothing about her in any written record that survived the . . . transition."

Meaning those my father did not burn when he wrested the throne from his uncle.

"Poor Mattaniel has been up and down the ladders a multitude of times over the past days retrieving documents for me."

The mention of my tutor caused a tremble in my belly. After our unexpected adventure the other night, I'd been so anxious to see him. Not only because I wanted to tell him about the baby but because I was desperate to thank him again. Without his steady presence, his strong arm holding me upright as I pressed through the waves, and his soothing voice keeping me calm, I'd never have made it back to the cave entrance with the child.

"Where is he? For once I am here on time."

Nolam frowned, looking around the room. "He was here earlier. He must have been sent on an errand by Tabnit. I'm certain he'll be back soon . . . Oh! Well, there he is now."

My heartbeat picked up as Mattaniel entered the room. I'd always thought my tutor handsome—distractingly so. But before the other night, I'd been able to ignore his finely chiseled features by reminding myself that he was only a servant, albeit one who resembled the Egyptian gods in human form depicted on the plastered walls of the banquet hall. But now I constantly found myself dwelling on the sensation of his long arm wrapping around my waist, the compassionate way he listened to me speak of my mother, and his melodious voice as he told me of the God his people revered. It did not matter that it was dangerous to entertain such notions about a servant in my father's household. The more I learned about Mattaniel, the more I wanted to know.

His black brows were furrowed as he entered the room and his full lips drawn into a frown, but the moment he saw me watching his approach, his features went instantly blank.

"Forgive my tardiness, my lady," he said, with a bow, his voice empty of the gentle humor I'd caught glimpses of over the last couple of days. "I was tasked with an errand from Tabnit."

Before the other night, I'd have attributed his coldness to subservience, but I sensed his detachment went deeper than adherence to his expected role. Something had slammed closed the gate that had just begun to swing open between us on that beach. Questions piled up in my mind that I could not ask in front of Nolam. For as tolerant as the elderly eunuch was with me, he was still steeped in royal protocol and would not look kindly on familiar interactions between myself and a servant.

"Let's not waste any more time, then," I said with a haughty tone.

Though there was a flash of something in his eyes, Mattaniel's expression did not change as he led me to our usual table and laid out the pottery shards inscribed with the symbols he'd devised. "Let's review some of the words I taught you last time before we begin with new ones."

He arranged the pieces into the word *nuraghe*, which he'd told me were distinctive stone towers built by the Shardan all over their island for rituals, storage, and protection.

I glanced over at Nolam, who'd returned the scroll he'd been studying, and lowered my voice. "What has you so upset?"

Mattaniel's eyes flicked up to meet mine, his one scarred brow lifting slightly before he wiped the surprise from his face and returned his attention to the pottery before us. "Nothing. Do you remember this word?"

Frustration sparked. Nolam was nearby, true, but his hearing was no longer sharp, and he was completely engrossed in his search for some long-dead woman's name. Still, I gritted my teeth as I feigned a smile. "Nuraghe. Now tell me why you're gnawing on your tongue."

His lips pulled taut, his eyes darting to three priests across the room arguing over an ancient Babylonian astrological text. Although their voices were mostly hushed, their furious whispers bounced around the plastered curves high above us.

Mattaniel's silent point was made. It did not matter how quietly we spoke. Even with the shelves of scrolls and tablets lining the walls, this room was a chamber of echoes. I let out a sigh, which did, in fact, whisper back at me from the star maps painted on the ceiling.

Mattaniel shifted the symbols around on the tabletop. “And this word?”

I narrowed my eyes, but he refused to look up, so I grabbed one of the pottery shards from the word he’d formed and hid it in my palm. He frowned at the incomplete word and then met my gaze again, clearly frustrated with my refusal to let him dodge my curiosity.

An idea flashed into my mind.

I took the piece I’d stolen and set it back down, then shifted a few of the others into one of the words he’d taught me in the garden.

child

I stared at him pointedly. He frowned, his brows bunching, but said nothing.

With a huff, I leaned in and selected a few more symbols, then slid them into order on the table.

safe

His golden eyes flared at the word, and a little thrill of victory zinged through me. He was beginning to understand.

Again, I shifted the pottery symbols around, borrowing a couple from my other two words.

mistake

I pursed my lips, hoping he understood what I was asking. When he gave a quick shake of his head in answer, I let out a breath of relief. Whatever had been bothering him earlier was not that he regretted saving the child.

I’d been shocked when he’d offered to do so. Just being there with me on the beach—without a eunuch as an escort—had been dangerous enough. If we’d been seen, accusations would have been made. But risking his own life to rescue a deformed child had shown him to be a man of extraordinary kindness.

With my still-limited grasp on the Shardan language and the

small number of symbols on the table, I wasn't certain how to proceed with this coded conversation. But I tried again.

man

angry

Mattaniel frowned again as he tried to discern my meaning.

I shifted a few more pieces, then tapped on the table with my brows arched to indicate I was asking a question about who he was upset with.

woman

angry

His golden eyes lifted to mine and held, causing a flip of my stomach as he shook his head.

He was not angry with anyone.

I pointed at myself.

Another shake of his head.

The relief was instant, and truthfully, a little foolish. I should not care so much what a servant thought of me, but after the other night, his status mattered little to me.

However, at the pace of this game of guessing, it would probably be hours before I figured out what was wrong.

Mattaniel stood suddenly and strode across the room to speak to Tabnit, then returned with one of the flat limestone tiles the scribes used for tallying sums, a thick piece of charcoal, and a scrap of wool.

"Perhaps it would help to write out some of the words I've been teaching you." His tone was casual, but after he'd written a few symbols on the slate and slid it across the table, my heart flipped. He was playing along with my subterfuge.

child home

I read the Shardan words aloud. Then nodded. The child did have a home. "How do you say 'my mother's servant'?"

Mattaniel's lips twitched as he wrote the symbols down and then spoke the words. I repeated them a few times, wishing I could easily write down everything I wanted to tell him. Danice had not hesitated for even a moment when I asked for help with the child and had immediately gone to the kitchens in search of goats' milk. And my mother . . . she'd sobbed at the sight of the tiny boy. The deformity of his hand meant nothing to either woman. Danice had once confided that she'd lost a child many years ago, before she'd become a servant in this household, which was why she'd always been so understanding of my mother's pain. What may have been considered a curse to one woman was now a blessing to two others.

All I could do was ask, "How do you say, 'The child is loved'?"

He met my eyes, a flicker of something new crossing his face before he wrote the symbols and repeated the phrase.

Although I wanted to push him about why he had been so upset when he arrived, instead I took a chance on revealing what I'd been contemplating since he'd told me of the injury that stole his memory and the dreams that hinted at clues to his past.

"How would I write, 'I want to help you'?"

His brows pinched, but he wrote the words.

"May I see the papyrus you were writing on the other day?" I asked in a low tone, since the priests had finally left. Tabnit and the other scribes were busy at their work across the room and Nolam, as usual, had fallen asleep.

Mattaniel sat back, clearly shocked.

"That is not a command," I whispered. "You've helped me. I only want to help you figure out where you came from."

He swallowed hard, rubbing at his scar as he contemplated.

I tapped my own brow. "The hyenas?"

He shook his head. "I don't remember. However . . ." He looked around, then whispered, "I do have dreams sometimes about falling out of a tree. Perhaps it's not a real memory. But who knows . . ."

Anticipation fluttered in my gut. "What else do you remember from the dream?"

He pressed his lips together, taking a deep breath, but to my absolute delight, he continued. "It's murky, as if I am seeing the images from underwater, but there are three boys who find me on the ground. In fact . . . I dream about them quite often."

I leaned forward, captivated. "Tell me about them."

One of the scribes knocked over a stool across the room, which clattered loudly to the floor, making Mattaniel stiffen once again. So I pushed the writing tile toward him.

It took a great deal of effort, but through writing back and forth, he told me one of the boys had green eyes and taught him to swim; one seemed to always carry a wooden sword, pretending to be a soldier; and the other was quiet but protective. Most telling was that many of these dreams took place in a forest atop a mountain.

"Weren't you found in an open wilderness?"

"I was. On the east side of the Jordan River."

"Not a thick-forested mountain, then," I mused, wishing I knew more about the territory the Israelite tribes inhabited.

"No. It was a dry place, rocky and full of caves, near a stream."

"You remember?"

He winced. "Not exactly. But sometimes I dream of the hyenas."

My stomach pinched. I hated to imagine a boy left to his own defenses against such vicious creatures. How could his family abandon him like that?

The last thing I wanted to do was add to his pain by voicing such thoughts, so instead I pushed to my feet and strode over to ask Tabnit if he knew of any record that might speak about the terrain of ancient Canaanite lands. Although the elderly scribe was confused by the odd request, he fetched a couple of scrolls from a nearby shelf and told me he'd seek out more. Which probably meant he'd have Mattaniel climb the ladder and search the shelves as soon as I left.

When I returned with the scrolls and unrolled them on the table, Mattaniel's jaw practically unhinged.

"What is this?"

"We may not be able to find exactly where you came from, but perhaps we can rule out a few areas."

He stared at me, looking stunned. "You don't have to do this, my la—" He cleared his throat and dropped his voice, "Elissa. It very well could be a road that leads nowhere, and I'm certain you have far better things to do."

"Don't you remember the broken tablet? I adore a delicious mystery. Besides, you can teach me more Shardan words as we search."

Mattaniel blinked for a few long moments, as if he could not remember how to formulate speech, then shook his head and let out a sigh as he tugged the open scroll a little closer. "If that is what you wish."

"I do."

For the next hour, perhaps even two, we bent over the texts, which turned out to be a series of letters between Canaanite chieftains from before the Israelites left Egypt. None of them were particularly descriptive of the land itself, but Mattaniel and I managed to sift out a few important details. From missives about timber harvests over difficult terrain, we decided there must be forested hills in the central area of ancient Canaan stretching from Har Hermon all the way down past a valley called Elah, while the Philistine-held lowlands on the coast between Akko and Gaza were rich with sprawling farms, vineyards, and orchards. The area across the Jordan River was a great deal more difficult to determine, since the Ammonites, Moabites, Arameans, and other tribes who'd once dominated those lands had not been friendly with Tyre. But there was one account of a battle near a city called Jericho that spoke of the barrenness in the region around the Salt Sea.

I was so caught up building a vivid map in my mind of these places, many I'd never heard of, that I nearly missed Mattaniel finally answering the question I'd asked hours ago.

"Tabnit sent me to deliver some shipping documents down at the docks," he said, voice low and eyes still on the text in front of us, "since his apprentice is still with his family. And I heard some disturbing news. That's why I was preoccupied when I returned."

"What news?" I breathed.

"The other day, Prince Yarikh said Asherites were responsible for the burning of the water flumes." He frowned. "I don't know if that's true. But either way, word has spread in Tyre. I heard some sailors discussing the expulsion of a few Asherite men on their crew, saying many Tyrians are refusing to do business with *any* Hebrew."

I was not surprised to hear tensions were rising. Fresh water was still in short supply all over the city.

"I fear it will only get worse," he said. "Desperation oftentimes overrides common decency. Especially between those who used to be bitter enemies."

His people and mine were certainly that, even if there'd been a certain tolerance of the other's presence here over the past few hundred years. It sounded as if the Philistines were stirring ancient pots for their own purposes.

I must have been frowning as I contemplated whether to speak to my brother about these rumors because Mattaniel suddenly looked stricken.

"I apologize," he began, eyes wide. "It's not my place to speak of anything your brother discussed with—"

I reached across the table to place my hand on his forearm. "No. I am not angry. I promise. I was only thinking about how I might help. Whether or not a few Asherites were involved in the fires, the rest should not suffer."

Mattaniel's body was perfectly still as he stared at me with those luminous golden-brown eyes, as if he were holding his breath. Then he blinked and leaned back, sliding his arm away from my touch. My palm tingled from the brush with his skin, so I set it in my lap.

"You are very kind," he said. "But I doubt there's anything that can be done. Hopefully the perpetrators will be caught and the furor will die down."

I did not like that his voice had gone formal again, but perhaps I'd pushed him too far today. Seriyah and Melita did always tease me about being more curious than a stray cat. And he'd indulged my prodding for nearly the entire afternoon.

I sat tall, stretching my arms above my head. "I should probably go or my sisters will come looking for me. I was supposed to join them for a swim."

Mattaniel nodded as he rolled up the ancient scrolls.

Remembering how adept he'd been in the water, I could not resist asking just one more question. "Did you swim often on Shardana?"

"I did. I spent many hours diving for shellfish and urchin near the shore, but also fishing with them in open waters, which sometimes meant diving down to untangle nets."

"That didn't frighten you after the shipwreck?"

He contemplated for a moment. "For a while it was a little unnerving, especially when we were far from land in the predawn hours, but much like Tyre, Shardan life revolves around the sea. I had little choice."

I'd grown up swimming in the waters around this island but could not imagine diving into a bottomless sea in the dark. My skin prickled. "Are there sea monsters in the waters around Shardana?"

With his lips pressed tight, he reached over to scribble a short phrase on the writing slate and slid it toward me.

"What does it say?"

He paused a couple of moments, looking grim. "Yes. There are only three toes on my right foot."

I gasped and bent to peer under the table at his sandaled feet, both of which were completely intact.

Stunned, I sat back up in my chair, jaw agape. "You—"

Mattaniel's golden eyes shimmered with mirth. When I glared at him for playing such a horrible trick on me, he lost his tight control for the first time since I'd met him and let out a short huff before slipping a palm over his mouth.

Laughter bubbled up my throat. I had to bite my bottom lip to keep it from bursting free. With the exception of the night on the beach, Mattaniel had been unfailingly reserved since I'd met him a month ago. The glimpse of irreverence in him was like one bite of an indulgent cake. I immediately wanted more.

15

Mattaniel

Ribs exposed to the gray sky, the hulls of three half-built vessels loomed over the shipyard. Bitumen lingered in the air, sharp and acrid, as a swarm of laborers scurried about the worksite. The din was overwhelming. Hundreds of mallets pounded asynchronous beats to the incessant rasp of saws and chisels and augers, while sharp cries from overseers rose above it all.

I could not help but search among the workers for the familiar form of Raphad as I trailed after the king's steward and Tabnit, who'd insisted I come with him today. I always looked for my former master on the docks and among work crews in the city whenever Tabnit sent me to deliver messages around Tyre, but I had yet to glimpse him anywhere.

After three years on Shardana, Raphad had grown accustomed to hard work since everyone—including Uvaldo—was expected to take part in fishing, harvesting, and other daily labors. Even so, he relied on me much of the time to carry heavy loads and tend to the most grueling tasks in his stead. I could not imagine he would be up to the backbreaking work of shipbuilding and saw no one resembling him among the laborers.

Had he been imprisoned in some dank cell this whole time while I ate regular portions and slept on a soft bedroll each night? Every time I remembered his ghostly face as he was dragged away the night of the Awakening Feast, guilt pressed in a little deeper. I'd asked a few of the servants around the palace if they'd heard anything about Portea, but no one knew what had happened to the merchant's wife. She'd been so kind to Adin and me and had endured so much in the years she'd thought her husband dead. How much heartache could one small woman shoulder? I simply *had* to succeed in teaching Elissa, even if the idea of her marrying a Shardan was becoming more disconcerting by the day. Raphad and Portea were depending on me.

We neared the shoreline, where a smaller boat perched atop sturdy scaffolding within a deep pit, much closer to completion than the hulking skeletons behind us. With their hands and clothing coated in tarry resin, a group of slaves brushed a thick coating of the sticky sludge over the hull, cabin, and decking, while others climbed tall ladders or shimmied up masts to string rigging in place.

And near the lion-headed prow of the ship, the king of Tyre himself, with Prince Ahiram at his side, spoke with a few rough-clad men I assumed oversaw this massive shipbuilding operation, for which Tyre was famous all over the world.

What Uvaldo would not do to be here in my place. Of all the ways the king of Shardan obsessed over Tyre, it was her ships he coveted more than anything. Although his people built smaller vessels that were more than seaworthy and nimble in rough waters, there were no trees on the Shardan island to equal the towering cedars of Lebanon, and therefore nothing they could do to match the ships that Abibaal's vast crews and expert builders could produce.

"It must be complete and well-tested by the time we depart for Gebal," Abibaal was saying to the overseers. "It should have been done weeks ago."

The eldest of the three men shifted from foot to foot, looking pale and unsettled by the king's presence. "Yes, my king, the work will not stop day or night until it is finished, I vow it upon the name of Melqart. If the shipment of bitumen had not been waylaid, it would have been done on time, I assure you."

"Why do you not have enough resin in the first place?" snapped Abibaal. "I was assured you had all the necessary materials well in hand before I commissioned this ship months ago."

"We did, my king," the shipbuilder sputtered. "But unfortunately the frigid weather ruined all we had in storage. It became brittle and refused to soften evenly because of the way it had crystallized. It was far too inferior for a ship meant for your own fleet, so we sent for a new batch from the eastern shore of the Salt Sea with instructions for quick delivery."

"What is the problem, then? The Moabites have always been a good source of bitumen before now."

"They are, my king, and the best price for such, but the caravan was overtaken just past Akko by some Hebrew brigands, the wagons overturned and the bitumen spilled in the dirt. It took weeks for another shipment to be procured—under heavier escort this time. It arrived only yesterday."

"The Asherites have never been an issue before this," the king replied with a scowl. "I've been generous in letting them live in my territories. What reason do they have for sabotaging my shipbuilding operations?"

"I wasn't convinced before either," said Ahiram. "But like I told you, Yarikh is certain they destroyed the water supply as well. And now this . . . There *is* a large population of Asherites just north of Akko."

The king's face had gone as dark as the storm clouds gathering on the western horizon. "I don't abide treachery. They should be grateful I let them live here. Especially when their king has been so hostile to our southern neighbors in Philistia."

"We've never had an issue with the Asherites on our labor crews," said the shipbuilder.

Abibaal frowned. "You have Hebrews working here?"

"At least a couple of dozen."

"Dismiss them. Right now," Abibaal bellowed. "And get this ship finished before we depart for Gebal or you'll find yourself slathering pitch in their place."

The overseer's face was ashen as he scurried to comply with the king's orders. Tabnit likely regretted his haste in coming here to share his news, shifting uncomfortably beside me while Abibaal ranted and cursed.

"Komar, what are you doing here?" Abibaal's tone was sharp from his interaction with the shipbuilders as he turned to his steward.

"Apologies, my king," said the steward as the three of us bowed low. "Tabnit brings urgent news regarding the Amurri."

Abibaal turned his gaze on the head scribe, and I felt Tabnit stiffen beside me. Yes, I'd made a discovery that might help negotiations with the northern tribe, but it was nothing that could not have waited.

Tabnit again bowed before the king, and I dutifully followed suit. "A thousand pardons, my lord, but the information you seek regarding the Amurri has been discovered in the archives."

Abibaal pursed his mouth and folded his thick-muscled arms across his broad chest, making him appear very much the warrior who'd led a merciless coup against his own uncle. The assessing rise of one dark brow was familiar; I'd seen it across the table from me for weeks now.

"You've found something I can use as leverage?"

"Yes, we have, my lord. Or rather, this young man has done so."

My stomach flipped as Tabnit's gesture caused the full force of the royal gaze to turn on me. Even without his sharp-toothed beasts and ornate throne, Abibaal's power and presence were imposing.

"Mattaniel has been diligent in tutoring your daughter Elissa in the language and customs of the Shardan," said Tabnit. "But I've since discovered he is uniquely gifted in understanding a considerable number of other foreign tongues. Among them, that of the Amurri."

The king's mouth pursed thoughtfully. "Is that so?"

"While I, and the other royal scribes, have only a limited understanding of the northern Amurri dialect, which differs greatly from that of other Amorite tribes, Mattaniel spent time in Arwad, where an offshoot tribe resides."

"You speak their language well?" Abibaal asked me.

"Yes, my king," I replied, eyes downcast. "My former master regularly traded in Arwad, and we spent a full season there a few years ago when his ship required repairs. A large group of Amurri live on the outskirts of the city."

"And you acquired their language in one season?"

"As I said, he is particularly skilled in—" Tabnit interjected, but the king spoke over him.

"What did you find that will ensure I have rights to their timber?"

I took a deep breath, willing my voice to remain even. "Three decades ago, Hittites invaded Amurri lands. They managed to repel them, being more familiar with the region's difficult terrain and because Hittite chariots could not navigate the mountain passes and thick forests. But still, many of their settlements were destroyed."

"Yes. Yes, I know all this." He circled two fingers in the air impatiently. "But how does any of this equal an upper hand in my negotiations?"

"From what I read, the main center of worship for their god, Martu, was destroyed during the invasion. The complex had been atop a high mountain, incorporating sanctuaries and altars that took centuries to complete, and matching some that were there long before records note who built them. The texts spoke of how vast supplies of materials had to be hauled up steep inclines and from distant quarries within what is now Hamathite territory. The Amurri still mourn the loss because it has never been rebuilt. In fact, during my time there, I witnessed the yearly lament of the loss, when the people mark the destruction with communal wailing and self-flagellation." I'd been horrified at the sight of hundreds in the streets whipping themselves bloody for the sin of allowing Martu's temple to lie in ruins. "They have neither the materials nor the resources to bring it back to its former grandeur."

The king's eyes lit with understanding. "But I have *both* at my disposal—including a friendship with the king of the Hamathites."

I nodded. "If you come to their aid and help rebuild the mountaintop temple, they would be beholden to you. They may be an insular people, deeply suspicious of outsiders, but they revere Martu too much to ignore such a generous offering."

Abibaal rubbed his thick, well-manicured beard. "And they would have no choice but to reward my kindness by making a trade agreement."

"Yes, my lord. If care is taken to respect their ways, you have the opportunity to create a long-lasting pact that would benefit both Tyre and the Amurri."

"I like it," said Abibaal. "We've sent plenty of envoys up there, yet they ignore every overture we make. But this could work . . ." He looked at me. "What's your name again?"

"Mattaniel, my lord."

"And you hail from?"

I shifted on my feet. Whether or not I'd been enslaved to men from Sidon and then Tyre for more than a decade, my accent was still distinctly Hebrew. There was little point in trying to hide the truth.

"Israel, my king."

His eyes narrowed, but Ahiram spoke first. "You are a Hebrew?"

I held back a flinch at the sharp tone but nodded.

"Are you Asherite?" Ahiram demanded.

My stomach pitched and roiled. "No . . . not that I am aware."

The king blinked at me, thrown by the vague answer. "How can you not know? Aren't all you Hebrews obsessed with tribal affiliations? I've been told half of you still refuse to bow the knee to your own king due to squabbles among the tribes."

"I . . . don't know," I stuttered. "I have been a slave since I was a boy. I haven't lived among Israelites of any tribal heritage for many years."

"You cannot tell me you are unaware which tribe you hail from, regardless of your enslavement."

I had no choice but to reveal the truth, or at least part of it. "Many years ago, Sidonian traders found me in a wilderness across the Jordan River, bleeding from the head and unable to tell them where I came from or why I was there by myself in the first place. They enslaved me, and I served them until Raphad took me on eleven years ago in Ashdod. I have never recovered my memories. I could be from anywhere. Of any tribe."

"You have no memory of your origin yet somehow are an expert in languages?"

If only he knew that I barely believed it myself. "Although I have no idea where I came from, or even my true name, somehow I retained the ability to speak and read several tongues—something I must have been taught as a child. I have no explanation for my ability to absorb and decode new languages, other than a natural talent for such things."

"So you have nothing to do with these Asherites?" Ahiram asked, suspicion coloring his own tone.

"No, my lord. I've come into little contact with any Hebrews, other than one of the men on Raphad's ship. He was of the tribe of Benjamin and left after the Feast to return to his people."

Adin must have been home for weeks now. I could only pray he'd finally found the peace he'd been looking for all these years.

The king was silent as he stared at me, as if by studying my face he could discern the truth of my words. I kept my eyes downcast and my expression bland.

"All right," he said. "You'll go with us."

I lifted my chin, confused. "My king?"

"You'll come with us to Gebal, be my translator while I negotiate with the Amurri leaders who've been invited at my request to the wedding of my daughter. Thankfully, the king of Gebal has a good relationship with his northern neighbors but, like us, has been hampered by an inability to converse freely in their language. They refuse to speak our common tongue. I like your plan, and it sounds as though you can give me additional insight into their ways."

Wordlessly, I bowed. There was nothing I could do but comply when the king gave an order, unless I wanted my head separated from my shoulders like the corpses I'd glimpsed hanging near the entrance to the city—thieves, Tabnit had informed me.

"Besides, Elissa needs to continue her lessons. She's intelligent enough, but I doubt the girl is ready to represent me fully with the Shardan, and that treaty is too important to chance her failing to make a good impression."

Frustration flared in my chest. I did not like how dismissive he was of his daughter. "She will be a credit to you, I am certain. Her progress has been excellent, my lord."

"Then it's settled. You'll go with us," said the king, gesturing toward the ship that would carry the royal household north to Gebal. "In the meantime, dig further into the Amurri texts and find me more leverage. I want that timber. There's nothing better for ship masts than lumber from northern cedars. I want *all* of it at my disposal."

I nodded, no choice but to submit.

He pointed one of his bejeweled fingers at my face. "But if you are lying and are in league with these Asherite zealots who think your invisible God gave them *my* land, I will have you cut to pieces slowly—beginning with your fingers and toes—and feed them to my beasts while you watch, just as I will do to whoever has been attacking our water supply and undermining my interests. Do you understand me?"

Years of well-rehearsed control served me well as I bowed low before the man who held my life, and Raphad's, in his powerful hands. "I am your servant alone, my king."

"Good. That glorified farmer you Israelites call a king does not deserve your loyalty. He cannot even control his own people."

I had no personal opinion of King Saul, who'd apparently been in power since a year before I was enslaved. As a fellow Benjamite, Adin felt an obligatory loyalty to the man and said he'd been quite successful in battle over the years of his reign, keeping the Philistines and surrounding nations mostly at bay. But my friend also admitted that opinions about the king of Israel were deeply divided and growing more fractured by the year.

"Now that I think of it, Ahiram, perhaps we *should* deal with them now, before they can cause further damage." He paused, his gaze tracking back to the workers slathering waterproofing resin over the hull of his new ship even as a soft rain began to fall. "What did Yarikh suggest . . . ?"

As the two of them walked away scheming about punishing the Asherites, a vision of those three terrified boys being dragged through the streets of Tyre rose up in startling detail. I'd suspected the dream had been a warning, but now I was certain of it. Conviction began to thrum deep in my bones, a deep and familiar compulsion to do *something*, even if I wasn't quite sure how.

Tabnit's hand landed on my shoulder, startling me from my thoughts. "It seems you'll be going to Gebal with the king's family, young man." There was an unexpected twinkle of pride in his ebony eyes.

"You did not have to give me credit for that discovery."

He shrugged. "I did not. But your success will reflect well on me, anyhow. And anything you can do to make the king more favorable toward you will bring you closer to being a free man."

I was shocked he would even care. "I appreciate your faith in me."

"I've worked with scores of scribes over these past decades, Mattaniel, but rarely have I come across anyone with a mind like yours. You are gifted by the gods. Perhaps one day you'll even take my place in the Hall of Records."

Stunned, I could only stare at him. There was little I'd desired over the years as much as the luxury of exploring the histories of the nations and their varied languages at my leisure. And yet, although I'd never felt more at home than I did in the Hall of Records, with the soft drone of scribes and priests discussing their studies in the background, I wasn't certain I could bear to remain once Elissa was gone. In truth, every time she left the room after our lessons now, the room felt almost achingly empty.

"However," Tabnit continued, his knowing gaze pinned to me, "pleasing the king first means success in preparing his daughter for marriage. So take care to keep that duty ever in your sights, especially while you travel to Gebal with the king and his family. Plenty more eyes will be watching—ones that don't drop closed the moment someone sits in a well-cushioned chair. Yes?"

The warning was stark. Tabnit may have seemed occupied during our lessons, but he'd been much more attentive than I'd guessed.

I nodded, knowing he was right. I must take more care to shore up my defenses when in Elissa's presence. I'd been a fool to let her slip through the cracks in my walls. There was too much at stake, especially after Abibaal's vivid threats. If I wanted to help Raphad and to be a free man myself, I had to make sure she got on that ship to Shardana. Anything else was not only foolish but dangerous.

"Excellent." Tabnit patted my shoulder affectionately. "Let's go see about arranging suitable garments for you to attend a royal wedding."

16

"There is simply not enough time to purchase anything adequate," said Tabnit. "This young man will be traveling with the royal family to act as translator for the king during the celebrations. He must be outfitted appropriately."

Pausing as he folded a shimmering length of golden fabric, the eunuch named Shamzur glared at Tabnit. "I have six royal women to prepare garments for, not to mention the concubines and their daughters to dress over the course of the voyage. Take this up with the king's steward."

"I did," said Tabnit, unbending. "And he sent me to you."

"My apprentices are already working from sunrise to sunset. We do not have time to prepare a completely new set of clothing."

"There is no use arguing, Shamzur." Without his usual black cone cap, for once, Magin reclined on a luxurious couch. This communal chamber, near the entrance of the women's court, was solely for the Crows' use and was nearly as well-appointed as the royal rooms. He lifted a finger, gesturing for one of the servants to refill his wine cup. "If the king wishes this slave to accompany him, he must be dressed well. There will be royalty and ambassadors from all over the region in attendance. Abibaal expects his household to represent him well. Even the slaves. And these negotiations with the Amurri are invaluable."

Aside from Nolam, I'd not had much contact with the black-clad eunuchs who ghosted about this palace in almost eerie silence and watched over Elissa as if they were indeed sharp-eyed crows. These three men, especially, seemed not only to wield a great deal of power but enjoyed a surprisingly lush lifestyle, with a bevy of servants to tend their needs and a host of underlings and apprentice eunuchs to delegate. They may, for all intents and purposes, be bound in service to the throne, but the lifelong vow they'd taken, and the physical sacrifice they'd made to earn the king's trust with his wealth, women, and reputation, set them above the rest of us.

"The young man is tall and slim. Perhaps something from one of the princes' wardrobes can be altered?" Although his towering bulk was intimidating, Abenasser's voice was soft and high like a timid boy of ten—likely why I'd never even heard him speak before now.

"Excellent plan, Abenasser," said Magin as he reached for a roasted oyster on the serving table at his knee. "Shamzur, take his measurements. The princes have plenty of clothing they'll never use again. It should be fairly simple to alter a few items before we set sail."

The scowl passed over Shamzur's face so quickly, I nearly missed it as he turned away from Magin to fetch a long linen cord. Then, with his usual blank expression back in place, he gestured for me to spread my arms wide as he used the cord to measure my wingspan.

"I've heard the Philistines will be sailing with us," said Abenasser as he took a seat near Magin in a chair that seemed it might barely hold him, then silently invited Tabnit to sit nearby and partake of the food on his own serving table.

Magin nodded. "Enesidu and his sons will be attending the wedding, along with the lords of Ashkelon."

I held myself very still at the mention of Gaza's king, whom I remembered well from four years before. I doubted Enesidu would remember me, nor Adin, who'd helped a talented female goldsmith escape his royal fortress with a priceless crown, but I was glad my friend was not here to find out. The Philistine king's strange obsession with that crown had likely not ended when he thought it sank to the bottom of the sea with Adin's friend Zahava.

"Surely not everyone will fit on the king's new vessel," said Abenasser. "It's made for speed, not so many passengers."

Magin hummed, chewing his mouthful of urchin and swallowing before answering. "Prince Yarikh's ship will carry the Philistines while we go with the royal family. The king may be keen on maintaining a close relationship with Enesidu, but his sons are notorious. I doubt he'll want the lechers anywhere near his daughters."

Shamzur wrapped the cord around my waist, then swiftly tied a small knot to mark the length. I'd never seen anyone other than sailors utilize such complicated knots, and each set of my measurements seemed to have their own designated shape. I was tempted to ask about his method, but he did not seem the type to welcome questions.

"Will there be a naval escort?" Abenasser asked. "There have been quite a few attacks on our trade ships lately."

Magin waved his concern away. "I know you abhor the sea, my friend, but not only is this new vessel to be the fastest in Abibaal's fleet, we'll be escorted by Yarikh's ship and his company. Besides, we'll likely cling close to the coast most of the way. It's the open ocean closer to Cyprus that is dangerous right now."

"I'll stay down in the hold, all the same," said Abenasser, already looking a little seasick. "That way I can pretend my feet are on dry land."

Magin's sharp laugh cracked through the room. "Not to worry. I'm certain you can find a corner of the king's private chambers down below to sleep in."

"I'll gladly take a corner over an open deck and a bottomless ocean." Abenasser shook his head. "My grandfather told me far too many stories about monsters inhabiting the Great Sea when I was a boy."

Once Shamzur finished my measurements, he finished wrapping in wool the golden garment he'd been altering when Tabnit led me into the room, then tied it with another of his long, knotted cords before trimming the ends with one sharp edge of his ruby-headed toggle pin.

"Where is Opher?" he asked. "I need him to make a delivery."

"I sent him on an errand to the mainland earlier," said Magin. "He'll be back this afternoon."

"Mattaniel can make your delivery," offered Tabnit. "I can spare him for a while."

Shamzur frowned. "I'll wait."

"He's quite trustworthy, I assure you," said Tabnit. "He's been delivering messages and documents for me since Haldon left. And look at those long legs. He's quick." The elderly scribe gave me a wink. I wasn't certain how I had earned his trust so easily, but I was grateful for it.

"What happened to your apprentice?" asked Abenasser.

"Oh, it's quite tragic," said Tabnit with a click of his tongue. "I just received a message from him. His father and both older brothers were killed in those awful fires up in the foothills. He had to see to his mother and younger sisters. He'll be responsible for them now, you know, so his position here is even more important than before. He'll return soon."

I could not imagine the pain Haldon must be enduring with such a terrible loss and now to have the additional worry of caring for his mother and sisters on his own. I determined to do all I could to aid him when he came back to the Hall of Records.

Shamzur pushed the wool-wrapped parcel into my hands. "Fine, then. You will go directly to the laundress. No detours. Understand?"

"You can't use the palace launderers?" asked Tabnit.

The eunuch shook his head. "This is a delicate fabric from the Far East. Must be handled by someone who knows how to care for it correctly. It cannot simply be tossed into a vat of hot water and scrubbed with rocks. It's irreplaceable. *Especially* in the short time before we depart for Gebal." His narrowed eyes told me that should I fail to protect the expensive gown, there would be a steep price to pay.

So, as I followed his detailed directions to a building on the other side of the island not far from the southern docks, I held the parcel close. The last thing I wanted was for a dress to be the downfall of my efforts these past weeks.

The laundress was located in a second-story apartment, above a tavern that seemed to be frequented by off-duty guards, judging by the many palace uniforms on the men inside. The veiled woman who answered my knock refused to open the door more than a handsbreadth.

"Who are you?" she snapped, her kohl-lined eyes full of suspicion.

"I have a delivery from Shamzur the eunuch." I held up the wool-wrapped parcel. "A dress to launder."

She slipped her arm through the gap in the door and snatched the package from me. "Wait here."

The door slammed in my face before I could respond. An odd woman, to be certain. I'd never seen a woman veiled so completely before. Apart from her eyes, only her hands were uncovered, the skin of which was mottled with white and brown patches. Perhaps it was for that very reason she covered herself. I doubted the people of Tyre accepted her deformity any more than they had the babe Elissa and I had found.

Grateful for a few moments of solitude before I ran back to the palace, I leaned my elbows on the parapet and peered down into the small courtyard behind the tavern. The space was full of off-duty guards and soldiers eating and drinking, their loud laughter and chatter floating upward. I recognized a few from the palace but did not know their names, since they were trained not to speak to anyone while they stood guard. Abibaal expected those who served him to be seen but not heard, unless expressly commanded to respond.

I wondered whether Adin had found his own place among the soldiers of Israel. He'd said his older brothers held high positions in Saul's personal guard, yet Adin was determined to serve within the ranks of a different company and away from his family in Gibeah. During our years on Shardana, Torben and his companions had honed my young friend from a slender, untried youth into a well-built and stealthy warrior, so I knew he'd have little difficulty proving his worth. Hopefully Adin had found his friends and secured a position far away from his murderer of a father.

Down below, one of the men among the guards tilted his head back to take a drink of his beer and caught me watching. His dark eyes flared, and he nudged the man next to him, who was too busy talking to someone across the table to notice. Embarrassed to have been caught staring while lost in my thoughts, I quickly took a step back. Within moments, the laundress returned to press a similar parcel to the one I'd delivered into my hands, then once again slammed the door before I could speak. I shook off my confusion at her rude behavior and descended the stairway, anxious to return to the palace in case Elissa happened to come to the Hall of Records today.

However, as I passed by the gate to the tavern courtyard, I noticed *both* the guards from before were now staring at me intently. The hair on the back of my neck prickled. I did not wait to find out why I'd seemed to have snared their notice. The moment I set foot into the street, I held Shamzur's parcel tight under my arm and ran all the way back to the palace.

17

Elissa

Stars winked and flickered on the surface of the black sea in the distance, the reflection of the full moon dappling the waters and illuminating the rooftop around me. I bent forward with a sigh to lean on the parapet, peering down at the empty roof of the palace below. I was skilled in evading both eunuchs and guards after years of spiriting around the building, so no one had seen me sneak up the winding stairs to the Celestial Tower.

And to my favor, Shamzur had been distracted talking with one of the scribes in the courtyard and missed me stealing through the shadows just fifteen paces away. But perhaps Mattaniel had not been so fortunate. Or maybe he'd not yet seen the note in the basket I'd had delivered to him.

"You don't mean to jump, do you?"

Shock and delight collided in my chest, but I held still, composing a relaxed expression before I slowly turned to find Mattaniel's lanky form at the top of the stairway.

"I wasn't planning to."

"Glad to hear it." He came to look over the stone parapet. "It's quite far down."

"I wasn't certain you'd come."

He shrugged. "It took a while to decipher the note."

"What do you mean? I told you to meet me at the Celestial Tower tonight, three hours after sunset."

"No, you wrote 'Come to the sky building three days after the sun is in the underworld.'"

My face heated. "Surely it wasn't as bad as that."

He huffed a soft laugh. "Thank you . . . for the gifts."

"I needed a way to get a message to you without garnering suspicion. Sending a stack of papyrus and a set of inks to a scribe seemed fitting."

"Clever. But also"—he gave a little nod—"greatly appreciated."

"You were running out of room on your first sheet of notes." Also, I hated to see him using cast-off materials and a lump of charcoal from a hearth fire in his quest to determine where his roots lie.

"Is there something I can do for you?"

The formality in his voice set my teeth on edge. "To begin with, you can cease speaking to me like that."

His brow furrowed. "In what way?"

"As if I am Seriyah or Khamera. I am a *concubine's* daughter, Mattaniel. And while yes, that sets me apart in this household, I am not considered on the same level as true royalty."

He was quiet for a few long moments. "That may be true, but *I* am still a slave."

"Not to me."

He flinched.

"After what happened on the beach, I'd hoped you and I were friends."

"Are we?" The question was barely above a whisper.

I nodded. "And as I said before, I want to help find where you came from. Which is why I sent that note. I think perhaps I've figured something out."

"You have?"

"Do you know what this tower is for?"

"To observe the stars?"

"Yes. But it is more than that." I gestured to the carving on the stone where I'd been leaning. "These are directional markers for finding the sacred constellations. There—" I pointed to the southeastern sky—"are the Kotharat, the Seven Stars."

I moved to the next carving, Mattaniel trailing me. "And there, farther east, is the Great Bull of Heaven. If it were closer to dawn, we might even catch a glimpse of Shahar, the morning star."

Turning away from the parapet, I gestured to the tall standing stone in the center of the round rooftop. "The priests use this tower for rituals at solstices and to track the movement of the sacred stars above us. We revere the ancient gods and goddesses who rule from their places in the heavens. Their stories, like the ones you told me the other night, have been passed down through the centuries via our holy ones."

Mattaniel stared at me in palpable confusion.

"I think you are a priest," I clarified.

He blinked rapidly. "A . . . priest?"

I leaned back on the parapet. "Who else would know so much about the God your people worship? You told me the other day that you somehow retained many of their sacred texts in your memory."

"I did, though it makes little sense why, when everything else was erased."

This was exactly what I'd been contemplating when the idea had occurred to me. "It all must have been taught to you when you were very small. You said it's usually difficult to learn a new language when someone is older, but children absorb new things easily."

"True."

"Do the Hebrews consecrate children as priests and priestesses like my people do?" The memory of those little ones being given to Astarte still left a bad taste in my mouth. I did not want to think about Mattaniel being left by his parents as a small boy in some temple. The thought had even occurred to me that he'd run away from just such a situation when he'd been found by the Sidonians.

He folded his arms, dropping his chin as he contemplated, then shook his head. "It is not the same. Centuries ago, there was an entire tribe set aside for priestly service. The men of Levi."

"Where do these Levites reside?"

He went quiet again for a while, as if he were searching deep inside his mind for the answer. "From what I remember of the records, they were not allowed a portion of land like the rest of the tribes when our ancestors came into Canaan."

My hopes that I had deduced his origins deflated. "Why not?"

"The Levites were consecrated for sacred duties: maintaining the Mishkan, the Holy Dwelling Place; making the offerings and leading worship; and teaching the Hebrew people the Words of Yahweh and his ways. They were allotted a host of dedicated cities scattered all over the territories."

Which meant Mattaniel could have been from anywhere. "Where is this Mishkan?"

"I don't know. All I remember is that it was an enormous tent my ancestors built in the wilderness after escaping Egypt and then carried with them for forty years of wandering."

I sighed, disappointed that what I thought had been a breakthrough had yielded little in the way of answers.

"However . . . I think perhaps you might be right about my lineage."

My eyes flared. "Truly?"

"I do have an extraordinary number of sacred Hebrew stories locked inside my head. Adin told me a great deal of it is word-for-word from his own memories. And not only do I remember the Hebrew histories, but their laws and ceremonies as well—in great detail. And sometimes I do have dreams of sitting among a group of young men listening to a tall, thick-bearded man speak about Yahweh."

"Dreams like the ones about the boys in the woods?"

"I've been plagued by vivid dreams for as long as I can remember. Sometimes they make no sense at all, merely a jumble of strange and unrelated images from my current life. And then—like the ones with the boys—I am certain they must contain memories because they feel so . . . *familiar*, as if my heart remembers my home and my loved ones, even if I do not."

My chest ached for him. I could not imagine losing the memory of my mother, my sisters, my home. He must feel so alone in this world.

"But then there are other dreams that linger long after my eyes are open . . ." His words trailed off as he tilted his chin up to look at the sky. "Ones I cannot explain."

Gooseflesh rippled up my arms. "What do you mean?"

He gave me a wry look. "You would think me mad if I told you."

"I will not."

He went quiet, eyes traveling across the black horizon, then took a deep breath. "One of the stories I remember is about a man named Yosef . . ."

He told me the tale of a young man, brash and arrogant, who dreamed that his entire family would bow down before him and how even after his own brothers had sold him into slavery in Egypt, Yahweh had given him dreams and foreknowledge that guided him along a path he could never have imagined.

The implications were fascinating, especially in light of my guess that Mattaniel may have been born into the priestly line of Levites he'd spoken of.

"Do you think Yahweh is giving you dreams like Yosef?"

"I know it sounds unbelievable. But how else can I explain that some of the things I have dreamed have come to pass?"

My eyes flew wide. "Which ones?"

"The first I remember was when I was traveling with the Sidonians. I dreamed the caravan would be attacked, and two days later, a group of Midianites robbed us. Thankfully, no one was killed, but it rattled me that I'd somehow *known* it would happen."

He shook his head, as if disbelieving his own story. "It also happened a few days before the shipwreck. I dreamed my friend Adin and I were locked in the cargo hold as the ship sank. It was horrifying and vivid, just like the dream of the attack. So I insisted we sleep on the deck, even though the sea was perfectly calm for days on end. The storm appeared out of nowhere, and he and I, along with Raphad, were the only ones to survive—although I did try to warn the crew beforehand, but they only laughed at me." He swallowed hard, his voice pinched as he spoke. "I should have tried harder."

"You did all you could. It would be difficult to explain a dream warning you of danger."

"Perhaps. But I still have no answer why Yahweh would warn me in the first place. No matter where my roots lie, I am a slave. Not a high priest."

"All I know about this God of yours is what you've told me." I turned my own eyes back to the heavens, where all the legends I knew spoke of cosmic struggles between distant gods and goddesses who cared little for mankind unless persuaded to intervene by costly gifts and bloody sacrifices. "But if some ancient deity were talking to me, I'd certainly listen *all* the time for his voice—whether I was asleep or awake."

He flinched, his body going stiff next to me. "What did you say?"

I repeated myself, confused by his snappish tone.

His gaze went hazy for a couple of moments, his mouth opening and closing twice before he finally spoke. "Someone told me that before. . . a long time ago. An old woman . . . I can see her face so clearly in my mind."

His eyes turned upward as if the memory were written in the stars above us. "'Awake or asleep, keep seeking truth, and listen for the voice of the Ancient One. . . .'"

The hair on the back of my neck lifted. "You have a memory?"

"It's nothing distinct, just the woman's face and her words—" Mattaniel's eyes flew to the top of the stairway, then back to me as I, too, registered the sound of voices.

My pulse took flight. We both would be in trouble if found alone together, unchaperoned, but he far more than I. I grabbed his hand, pulling him along as I ran behind the towering standing stone in the center of the rooftop. We pressed our backs to the cold granite, breaths coming quickly as footsteps scraped the rooftop on the other side.

"See?" said a man. "There's no one here. You were seeing things. Let's get back to our rounds."

"Stop trying to make me think I am losing my mind," replied the other guard. "I *know* I saw something up here."

"Probably a bird or something."

"At night?"

"Some birds fly at night." He sounded offended. "Owls. Nightjars. Could even have been a bat."

The voices came closer as the guards began to walk around the perimeter of the rooftop. Mattaniel and I moved in silent tandem, keeping the large stone between ourselves and the men. I thanked the glittering stars above that my slippers were made of softest calfskin, and Mattaniel was barefoot. Three-quarters of the way, the guards stopped their circuit to argue more about ghosts and then about which of the new cooks was the prettiest and the easiest to persuade into their beds once their weekly rotations were complete. The fools had unknowingly trapped us on the opposite side of the roof from the exit.

There was nothing to do but wait until they left. I could not chance even a whisper to the man pressed close to my side. He took a deep inhale, and I looked up to find him staring at me, the high cut of his cheekbone limned in moonlight. I'd caught those golden-brown eyes on me a few times during our lessons, when he turned his searching gaze away one breath too late, and then for a few heady moments on the beach, but never had the space between us been so laden with intensity. Gazes locked, we watched each other as something new and intoxicating hummed between us.

Slave or not, Mattaniel was a beautiful man, and especially so beneath the stars. But beyond that, he was both brilliant and kind, and I was drawn to him in a way I'd never experienced before with anyone. And judging by the way his gaze suddenly dropped to my mouth, I was not the only one affected.

My body swayed closer of its own volition, my lips tingling

with anticipation as I lifted my chin in invitation. To my delight, his head bowed and our breath mingled. I let my eyes fall closed, trembling as I waited for the touch of his soft lips to mine.

Instead, his warmth disappeared entirely. Startled, my eyes flew open. Mattaniel stood a couple of paces away, fists clenched at his sides.

"They're gone."

I blinked at him until my mind began to clear. The guards. I'd been so caught up, I'd forgotten their presence. The rooftop was silent again, the two of us alone.

"I'm going with you to Gebal," Mattaniel rasped. "For the wedding."

"You are?"

"Your father wants me to translate his negotiations with the Amurri."

My reckless heart should not be glad to learn he was coming with us to Seriyah's wedding, but the thrill in my chest was undeniable. For as much as I'd dreaded the lessons at first, now I practically counted the hours between them.

"Also, he does not want your lessons interrupted." Mattaniel finally lifted his gaze to mine, sounding pained. "Because it will likely not be that much longer before the Shardan come to Tyre."

The reminder erased whatever remained of my foolish notions, leaving behind the truth I'd been trying to ignore: Even if I somehow found a way to extricate myself from this particular arranged marriage, I would still be expected to marry a man of the king's choosing. And, if the treaty was not brokered with the Shardan, Mattaniel would not earn his freedom—because of me.

Chest hollow, I let my eyes linger on him for only a few moments more, not trusting my voice to speak. Then I nodded once and turned away from him, heading for the stairs with my eyes burning.

I'd been unfair to both of us by pretending we could have anything beyond a stolen night under the stars. Because I may be the daughter of king and he a slave, but both of us wore chains. His were made of iron and mine of pure gold.

18

Mattaniel

Salt stung my nose and eyes as the ship shifted slightly northwest, gaining speed with the cool winds sweeping down from the thick-forested mountains. After a full day of rain, which I'd spent huddled beneath my woolen mantle on deck, I was grateful to have found a dry place near the stern to spread my bedroll.

Hidden behind a stack of baggage crates tied to the deck, I lay with my hands folded behind my head and stared up at the starless sky. Yet all I could see was *her* face.

Elissa would never know how much of a temptation she had been that night on the tower, her beauty bathed in moonlight and her lips only a whisper away. But no matter how much it had pained me to pull away while everything in me was screaming to accept her silent invitation, I could not dishonor her.

I refused to give in to desires that could never result in a true and lasting union between us. She was far too valuable to tarnish in such a way, and I'd break my own heart a hundred times over before treating her as anything less than precious, even if she hated me for it now.

She'd not spoken to me since we'd boarded her father's ship. I would not be surprised if she refused to acknowledge my existence this entire journey, nor would I blame her. I'd embarrassed her; I saw it on her face as she fled the tower, but I'd been too near the boundary of my restraint to chase after her and apologize.

One of the sailors perched high in the front rigging called out an assurance that all was well, which was echoed by another man near the rear. This close to the coast, there was more danger from rocky shoals than marauders, and we'd passed a few firelit watchtowers on shore that marked the presence of sandbars and jagged reefs.

The king's new ship was impressive, with the sleek lines of a war vessel yet the girth of a merchant ship. We easily outpaced Prince Yarikh's ship shortly after we left port. I suspected our speed had more to do with impressing the Philistines than necessity, since the wedding was still a few days away. With forty men rowing down below and the voluminous purple sails pushing us northward at a fast clip throughout the night, Abibaal would have plenty of time to negotiate with the Amurri before the weeklong wedding festivities even began. I dreaded wearing the princes' castoffs—no matter how skillfully Shamzur had altered them—while watching Elissa celebrate her sister's marriage alongside the wealthy and the royal. But it would be a good reminder that the divide between us was as vast as the Great Sea itself.

A strong gust of wind billowed the sails, causing the deck to tilt slightly just as a dark form stumbled around the crates and fell into me. I barely had time to throw my arms around the body and cushion their fall while both of us grunted in surprise.

With one inhale of spicy-sweetness, I knew the soft form I held was the woman who'd occupied the better part of my thoughts for months now.

"Are you well?" I murmured.

She caught her breath but did not move as she whispered, "Mattaniel?"

"Yes. Are you hurt?"

"No. I just tripped over something."

For as much as I wanted to pull her closer, savor the feel of her in my embrace, the moment she twitched, I released my hold. I was almost grateful the moon was hidden behind thick clouds so I could not see her lovely face as she slid out of my arms.

"My bedroll, I'm afraid," I said, sitting up. "I apologize that it was in your way, my lady."

She paused, and I could almost hear her teeth grinding at the formality, but I needed a wall between us so I did not reach for her again.

"Shall I escort you back to the cabin?" I wasn't certain why she was wandering the deck at night by herself, but with the ship's crew around, it was not safe. Where were the Crows?

"No. It's too suffocating in there. So many women packed into one small room is miserable. And the queen has the only comfortable bed, so I am squashed between my sisters on a bedroll. It's fortunate they both sleep like the dead."

It seemed strange to me that Abibaal would insist on dragging half of his family on this voyage, including wives, concubines, and his older children—especially with the queen a few months pregnant. But the king of Tyre was nothing if not extravagant in his show of wealth and virility, and held little regard for anyone else's comfort. After all, he slept peacefully belowdecks in a small but lushly appointed room. Only Ahiram was afforded similar luxury in his own private quarters below. There was so little room aboard by the time all the crates of clothing, necessities, and accoutrements were loaded that Shamzur and a few other servants boarded Yarikh's much larger ship instead.

"You must forgive me for the other night, Mattaniel," Elissa whispered in a rush. "It was late, and I was not thinking clearly. I did not mean to throw myself at you like that. I don't blame you for refusing to be pulled into my foolishness. Can we please forget that it happened?"

The desperation in her voice shocked me. As if she feared she'd insulted me by offering me something I wanted more than my next breath.

"There is nothing to forgive. Truly."

"So, we are still friends?"

"Of course." It was all I could have of her, so I was determined to be satisfied.

She exhaled, slumping back against the crates. "I'm glad to hear it."

Apparently, she had no intention of leaving, so I shifted to sit an arm's length away with my own back to the crates, the shush of the waves against the hull the only sound as I tilted my chin up to peer at the black sky.

"I don't have many, you know, friends. Aside from Melita, and Seriyah, but now she is leaving . . ." Her voice trailed away, as if it was too painful to continue the thought.

"I've only had one, at least that I can remember. Adin."

"You spoke of him before. He was with you on the island?"

"Yes. He was desperate to flee Gaza, where he'd been taken captive, and eager to see the world. So I asked Raphad to give him a position on the ship. Although, to be honest, it was more of a selfish decision than anything."

"Selfish to help him escape?"

"I knew the journey to the far north would be treacherous, but I'd been alone for so long and it was good to finally have someone to talk to, since Raphad's crew mostly ignored me. There had been other slaves in the Sidonian caravan, but most considered me either far beneath them or touched in the head."

"Why?"

"Because for many months after the attack, I was a jumbled mess. Not only did I not know who I was, but sometimes I could not tell what was real and what was a dream. It was as if I was walking around half-awake much of the time."

"Did the Sidonians mistreat you?"

A host of lonely nights, sleeping under a wagon in the cold with an empty belly, flickered through my memory. "I survived" was all I could manage to choke out.

She went quiet and the wind shifted again, wafting her alluring scent my way. I closed my eyes, greedily drawing it into my lungs.

"Why did they sell you? If you made them so much silver?"

Phantom wounds on my back throbbed at the question. I'd never told anyone of that day, not even Adin. But after what she'd revealed on the beach about her mother's long illness, I sensed she understood pain in a way few others of her status did.

"I'd been with the Sidonians' caravan for a couple years, mostly traveling along the King's Highway up past Damascus, but also down into Egypt and Midian. We even spent an entire year east of the Euphrates River, which is where I discovered I somehow spoke a bit of the Elamite language."

"You have seen much of the world," she murmured. "Those are places I've only been told about by the eunuchs. Gebal will be the farthest I've ever traveled in my life."

Before now, I'd not considered how sheltered Elissa was. She'd lived her entire existence on the island of Tyre, most of it within the palace walls, never experiencing the delight of discovering new people, new lands, new cultures. Unbidden, an impossible vision arose of the two of us traveling to some of the places I'd been, but I pushed it away before it could take root.

"After so long, my masters' wives grew tired of their travels and demanded to return home to Sidon. It took many months, but we made our way west along the trade roads and happened through a town in Hebrew territory called Beit Shemesh, just north of the Philistine city of Gath."

Elissa shivered, so I offered her my woolen mantle.

"Thank you. Go on," she urged as she wrapped it around her shoulders.

"Are you certain you don't want to go back inside?"

"I'd rather be here . . . with you." The last two words were barely a whisper.

My heart clenched tight at the quiet admission. She'd not simply been escaping the suffocating cabin tonight. She'd been looking for *me*. I forced myself not to react, swallowing hard before I continued.

"There was a boy in the marketplace of Beit Shemesh looking for work, whose father had been injured. The Sidonians took advantage of his desperation, telling him they knew of a farmer looking for field hands and offered to take him to the next town. But over the years, I'd seen too much. I knew they meant to sell him to Philistine slavers."

She was leaning close now, enthralled by my story. "You helped him escape?"

"Before we'd even departed Beit Shemesh, I told him they were lying and to run all the way back to his home. Then I caused a diversion so he could get away. My masters were furious, as you'd expect. They whipped me senseless."

She caught her breath, a hand to her mouth. "Oh, Mattaniel . . ."

I shrugged. "It wasn't the first time. It is a fact of life for many slaves." *Even some in your own father's house*, I thought, but kept that to myself. "I'd not even healed from my wounds when we arrived in Ashdod where Raphad overheard me bartering with an Egyptian merchant at the port. He convinced the Sidonians to sell me, and the next day, I boarded a ship for the first time."

On Shardana, Raphad had told me that he'd not even realized how talented I was then but could see that I'd been abused. *"It was as if something* compelled *me to get you away from them,"* he'd said. *"I would likely have offered twice as much if they'd not capitulated easily in negotiations."*

I hated to think that he may now be enduring similar treatment and prayed continually for Yahweh's protection over my former master. The fact that his freedom was dependent on Elissa being sent away was a conflict that had led to many a restless night of late.

The ship shuddered, then lurched hard as a horrible cracking sound split the night. Elissa gasped as both of us were jolted sideways. I grabbed for her with one arm and the crate behind me with the other to stop us from sliding along the deck. She dug her fingernails into my forearm, breathing heavily. "What *was* that?"

"We've hit something. A reef, maybe." Had the watchmen missed a signal fire on shore?

There was a sharp cry and then something slammed to the deck with a sickening thud, so hard the wood beneath us vibrated. My stomach hollowed. I feared the man who'd been up in the rigging must have lost his footing. A few other shouts and cries went up around the ship.

"Are we sinking?" Elissa trembled, burrowing closer to me.

Unlike three years ago, this ship was not far out to sea. There was no storm, and both of us were strong swimmers. Yet we were not the only ones in danger. I could almost hear the faint echo of Raphad's crew pleading to their deaf gods.

"I'll make sure you are—"

"*Pirates!*"

My blood went cold at the horrified scream. We'd not simply hit a reef. We were under attack.

Thankfully, the two of us were well hidden here among the baggage for the moment, and the thick ropes holding the crates to the deck had kept them from shifting. I pulled Elissa closer so I could whisper in her ear. "Stay behind the crates. I'll go look—"

She grabbed my tunic with shaking hands. "No, don't leave me."

Too afraid for her to care that I was crossing boundaries, I stroked a reassuring hand down her silken hair. "I need to see what's happening. I'll be right back, I promise."

Her fingers clenched tight for a moment, but she nodded and released my tunic.

"Don't move," I whispered as I got to my feet. "And hold tight to the rope behind you."

The ship lurched again, as if we'd struck the reef a second time, and I barely kept myself from tumbling back down. More cries, followed by the sound of pounding feet on the deck, made my stomach curdle. I had no idea what I was up against and was completely unarmed. No matter what Torben had taught me, I was at a terrible disadvantage. But as much as I wanted to simply grab Elissa and jump overboard, there were dozens of other souls aboard this ship.

Glad for my bare feet, I slipped around the corner, toward the sounds of fighting and the growing cries of the vulnerable women in the cabin Elissa had fled.

"Be a ghost," whispered Torben's instructions from my memories. *"No shadow. No form. Don't let your enemy see you coming."*

I obeyed, measuring my breaths as I hunched to creep along the deck, pressing close to the solid railing on my right. A few grunts up ahead halted my movements, and the black outline of two men struggling came into view. Metal clanged as they fought, and I searched around for something to defend myself with. Not far from my feet, an empty wooden bucket sat upside down on the deck, attached to a length of rope. It was better than nothing, so I grabbed it by the handle and moved toward the fight. However, before I'd gone another few steps, I came across a body sprawled on the deck.

From the way his limbs were splayed, it had to be the man who'd fallen from the rigging, but he also had two arrows jutting from his chest.

I stepped over him, heartbeat flying as I came closer to the chaos near the middle of the ship. A torch held aloft by one of the attackers at the railing illuminated my worst fear. At least twelve men were engaged in battle near the cabin, including Magin and another younger eunuch whose name I did not know, along with a couple of guards and crewmen. But where was everyone else? There were forty rowers in the belly of this ship, not to mention the king, the crown prince, and a handful of servants and guards. I peered past the melee to see two unfamiliar men guarding the hatchway, swords in hand. I had the awful feeling everyone below was locked down there. And from the way we were now beginning to list, there was a break in the hull. The hold would be filling with water.

Having struck down the young eunuch, one of the attackers now headed in my direction. Toward the back of the ship, and Elissa.

I pressed deeper into the shadows. *"Let the enemy come to you, Salpa. Patience . . ."*

Breathing softly through my nose as Torben had taught me, I waited until the pirate was almost on me before striking. I swung the bucket, hitting him square in the jaw. With a grunt of surprise, he tripped backward, slashing his knife aimlessly. Taking advantage of the darkness, and my long limbs, I swept his leg out from under him, a thrill of victory going through me as he toppled sideways, his knife clattering to the deck and sliding toward me. But before I could reach for the weapon, he was up again and barreling toward me. We collided, instantly twisted in a desperate struggle.

"Control the head, control the body."

The words came from nowhere and were nothing that I ever remembered Torben saying, but I did not question the wisdom of whatever long-buried memory they stemmed from.

My attacker was sturdy but a good two hands shorter than me, so once I was able to lock one arm around his neck, I twisted, then punched him repeatedly with the other until he was so dazed I was able to easily shuffle him toward the edge of the ship. I pressed his back to the railing while his feet scrambled to catch hold.

"Who are you?" I demanded.

He gritted his teeth, trying to buck against my hold and snarling foul curses. But I'd spent three years on Shardana doing hard labor alongside men who lived by the sweat of their brows and sparring with pirates.

Besides, I had no more time to waste. Elissa needed me. I swung my fist upward, striking his chin with such force that his teeth clacked together. Eyes rolled into the back of his head, he toppled over the railing into the sea. Before I even heard the splash, I spun, grabbed the knife from the deck, and headed for Elissa.

To my dismay, before I'd even taken more than a few steps, I heard her voice rasping my name. I searched the darkness, finding her crouched behind a rack of wine jugs where I guessed she'd watched the entire struggle. "Are you well?"

"Are you?" She skimmed a palm over my cheek, her hand coming back dark with blood. I'd not even noticed the injury. "I thought he was going to *kill* you."

"We need to get you to shore."

"But my sisters—"

"Magin and the guards are protecting them," I lied, certain it was the only way to get her off this ship.

She shuddered, her teeth chattering. "We can't just leave them."

I cupped her soft face in my hands. "Listen to me. This ship is going down—soon. I will come back and help your family, I promise. But first, I must get *you* to safety."

"But—"

I pulled her close enough to taste her sweet breath on my lips. "Elissa. Please trust me."

With a deep inhale, she nodded. I took her hand, pulling her behind me. We fought the slant of the deck until we both clung to the rail near the stern. Perhaps fifty paces away lay the black outline of land. No wonder we'd hit a reef.

"It won't take long to swim there—" I began, then bloodcurdling screams split the night. With a start, we spun to find the forward sail aflame.

"My sisters!" Elissa cried, twisting from my hold.

I lunged for her, dragging her back by the waist. "No. Swim for shore. I'll get them."

"I can't leave them! They're going to die!" She struggled against my hold.

With no other choice but to startle her, I jerked her against me and bent to stare into her wide eyes. "Every moment you argue with me is one less moment I have to save them."

She pulled in a shuddering breath, her eyes darting back and forth between the spreading fire and my face, but she turned back to the rail, visibly collecting herself to jump into the black sea.

I braced her as she climbed and then perched atop the handrail, feet dangling over the water. "Don't linger on the shore. Find a place to hide."

She nodded, body shaking with terror as she gripped the rail with white knuckles. Knowing it was more than likely the last time I would see her beautiful face in this life, I let my eyes linger for a few breathless moments and dreamed about what could have been, had I not been a slave and she'd not been the daughter of a king.

And then, without pausing long enough to talk myself out of the most foolish thing I would ever do, I surged forward and pressed my lips to hers for three blissful heartbeats.

"Just in case," I whispered against her mouth, then peeled myself away to head for the fire.

19

Elissa

I'd never been so cold. My whole body shook, jaw aching from the futile effort to clench my teeth, but they'd not stopped chattering since I hit the surface of the frigid sea. Huddled behind a rotted tree stump on the edge of the wide jetty where I'd come ashore, with my arms fruitlessly wrapped around myself, I peered through the tall seagrass as my father's new ship burned with nearly everyone I loved trapped aboard. None of it seemed real. Not the attack. The fire. Not even the shock of Mattaniel kissing me before dashing off to what was likely his death.

But no matter how many times I blinked my eyes, the ship, now half-submerged, still burned atop the black sea. Not long after I'd begun my bone-chilling swim toward the shore, a small vessel rowed off into the darkness, the shadowy outlines of four men stark against the flames consuming two of the three sails. How could such a small group of pirates bring down an entire ship so easily? And why hadn't Yarikh's crew come to our rescue? We'd left the port in Tyre together, but his ship was nowhere to be seen. None of this made any sense.

Something fluttered on the edge of the water, barely illuminated by starlight. I blinked hard, thinking perhaps I was imagining three white-clad forms emerging from the sea, but then two more rose up, supporting each other as they pressed through the rolling waves toward the shore. I surged to my feet and ran across the rocky beach, past a dazed Khamera and the maids half-carrying their mistress to safety, and plowed into the surf to throw my arms around my sisters, all of us sobbing in relief.

"You're alive!" said Melita, squeezing me so tightly my chest ached.

"Where did you go?" Seriyah demanded, shaking me a little. "We thought they'd killed you!"

"I left the cabin before the attack. Mattaniel made me jump overboard."

"Thank the stars," said Meli, shivering. "Your tutor saved us too. If he hadn't broken the lock on the cabin door when he did, we'd all have burned to death."

Thalassa and her mother, along with three more maids, had also escaped and emerged from the sea thirty paces away, but there was no other sign of survivors along the glimmering shoreline. My bones went cold as I realized the flames had vanished, along with the remains of the ship. My father, Ahiram, Mattaniel, and so many others had been swallowed by the black abyss. My knees wobbled as a sob built in my throat.

Melita pulled me close, her arms alone keeping me from collapse. "He went to try and help those down below. The hatch was chained shut. He must not have been able to—"

Seriyah gasped, cutting her off. "Father!"

I twisted around to see the king, bedraggled and half-naked, trudging toward us from the opposite end of the beach. He must have been swept north by the sea current.

The moment Khamera saw her husband, she yanked free of her maids and, with one protective hand cradling her rounded belly, ran for him. "Where's Ahiram?"

Her cry was piercing and desperate, but he only stared at her, hollow-eyed and ashen.

"Abibaal!" she shouted. "Where is my *son*?"

His answer came out strangled and raw. "The rocks broke through the hull. Water rushed in so fast. He was . . ." He ran a shaking hand over his chalky face. "He's . . . he's gone."

The tortured scream that came from the queen's mouth as she collapsed into the sand was like nothing I'd ever heard before. The sound of a mother's heart being torn in two. Seriyah ran to her side, throwing her arms around Khamera.

"It can't be," the queen sobbed on her shoulder. "No! Who did this? Who killed our child?"

"Asherites," the king ground out through gritted teeth, chest heaving as he stared at the glittering black waters stretching endlessly toward the distant horizon while Seriyah and Khamera keened for Ahiram. "And they will regret what they have done. *All of them* will pay for this."

Melita inhaled sharply, then nudged my side. "Lissi. Look."

Two figures emerged from the chest-high grasses at the far end of the beach. Heart pounding, I held my breath as their shadowy forms came closer, the broader one leaning heavily on the other.

Relief tore through my body almost painfully. Pressing into me, Melita tangled her fingers with mine, squeezing them tightly as Mattaniel and Abenasser slowly limped toward us. Apparently, my sister understood my heart more clearly than I'd ever guessed. Perhaps even better than I knew it myself.

When the two men finally came within ten paces of those of us who'd survived, Mattaniel's eyes flashed up to meet mine. A look of palpable relief came over his too-pale face, and it took every bit of will left in my grief-battered heart not to recklessly run to the last man on this earth I should ever have fallen deeply in love with.

And from the desperation in his eyes as he held my gaze, it seemed I was not the only one.

20

Mattaniel

Seven days passed with the entire palace in required mourning for Prince Ahiram. Seven eternal days since I'd seen her. I'd not even been called to the Hall of Records since our return. Aside from quick and somber meals in the courtyard alongside a household of grief-stricken servants, I'd spent most of the time staring up at the ceiling from my bedroll, either dreaming of that kiss, reliving the horrors of the attack, or pleading with Yahweh for wisdom about how to help my people.

Only a third of the dozen pirates who'd boarded Abibaal's doomed vessel had escaped. But they'd managed to kill most of the crewmen on deck, along with the lookouts and guards, before I returned from sending Elissa to shore. I'd found only Magin left standing, valiantly fending off two attackers as the sails and masts burned. I'd dealt with one pirate, but even though Magin killed the other, the head eunuch succumbed to a strike in the chest. As he lay bleeding out on the deck, he'd managed to choke out two final words that haunted me: *"They knew."*

Some of the crewmen on that ship *had* to have been involved. I could think of no other explanation for the ease with which we were boarded, for what seemed an intentional ramming on a rocky reef, nor for the thick chains on both the door of the deck cabin and the hatchway. But I was certain that those who'd attacked the vessel were not Israelite, even if they'd been dressed in Hebrew garments fringed with blue and white tzitzit. I'd known it from the moment the first attacker cursed me in the name of Eshmun. They were the same foul words I'd had flung at me for two years by the traders who revered that particular Sidonian god.

And yet I had no way to prove what I suspected to the king. He'd seen the attackers' clothing that night with his own eyes and immediately bellowed threats against the Asherites, vowing to avenge his son.

So for the past seven days, since Yarikh's ship had returned us to Tyre, I remained trapped in the servants' quarters, helpless to do anything more than pray for the innocent to be spared Abibaal's wrath. Yet so far, not even my dreams had yielded answers for how to convince the king he'd been deceived into blaming the wrong people. Nor how to determine who exactly had been involved in the plot to murder the royal family.

The only comfort I had was the memory of holding Elissa for those brief moments of recklessness, ones I knew would never be repeated, but proved worth every risk when she'd met my gaze on the beach with an expression of matching longing. I both yearned for and dreaded the next time I saw her, because before that night, I'd been able to keep my foolish desire for her locked away inside a secret place in my heart. Now that I'd brazenly kicked that door open, I wasn't certain how I would ever keep it latched again.

"Mattaniel?"

My eyes flew open to find the last person I'd expected to see frowning down at me on my bedroll—Komar, the king's personal steward.

Stunned, I lurched to my feet. "My lord?"

"You're to come with me. Bring your belongings."

"My . . . my belongings?"

"Yes," snapped the steward. "Make haste."

Head swimming, I gathered my meager possessions, including

the papyrus and inks Elissa had given me, and followed Komar through the maze of the palace, dread rising with every step as we neared the royal wing.

He led me across a lavish courtyard overflowing with exotic flowers and manicured trees I had no names for and past a fountain cascading from some invisible cistern atop the roof. Then we entered what I guessed was one of the king's chambers, judging by the extravagant furnishings, lush carpets, and the familiar lion skin draped over a gilded throne in one corner.

Dazzled by the wealth on display, it took me too long to realize the king himself was lounging on a thick-cushioned couch on the other side of the room, eating from a silver plate. And on either side of him, the two panthers lay on the floor, polished bronze shackles at their necks gleaming in a spill of sunlight. As their golden eyes tracked Komar and me across the room, the hair on my neck prickled.

"I will have you cut to pieces slowly—beginning with your fingers and toes—and feed them to my beasts while you watch . . ."

Had I been saved from wild animals in my youth only to be ripped apart as a man? It was entirely possible Abibaal had decided that I had been involved in what appeared to be a Hebrew attack on his family.

Komar and I both bowed low ten paces from the king and his terrifying pets. Once permitted to rise, Komar excused himself from the room while I stood, head down and bracing for the king's fury.

"I was told you are a man of words, a uniquely talented translator and scribe," said the king as he gnawed on a meaty rib bone dripping with thick sauce. He swiped at the mess on his chin absently, then pointed the bone at me. "But that was not the entire truth, was it?"

My gut twisted. "My king?"

Abibaal ripped another hunk of flesh from the rib, even as he put out his hand to one of the panthers, allowing her to lick the mess from his fingers. "My daughter Elissa told me what you did."

All my blood seemed to drain into my feet. She'd told her father about the *kiss*?

"You helped her escape and fought those cowards who murdered my son. And then saved my queen and the other women from burning to death." I gaped at the king as he continued. "And if you hadn't broken that hatch open, I'd be at the bottom of the sea as well."

He'd never know how close I'd come to giving up that night. I'd been able to kick in the door to free the women before flames consumed the cabin, but nothing I'd tried would break the chains on the hatch. Thankfully, in my frantic search of the deck, while choking on smoke and ash, I discovered one of the slain pirates still gripping an ax and used every bit of strength I'd had left to pound the latch until it splintered—fully expecting to find no one alive. For the rest of my life, I'd never forget the sight of a white-faced Abibaal and a severely injured Abenasser clinging to the ladder, surrounded by floating bodies. Both men appeared to have been fighting off desperate survivors for the only pocket of air remaining in the hold. Only the two of them, out of the many men who'd been down there, had lived. Fifteen souls alone had made it onto that beach.

"So, the question is . . ." said Abibaal. "How do I reward you?"

Stunned, all I could do was stare as he tossed the bone to the second panther, which snatched the prize in midair with a growl. "With the wedding now delayed, negotiations with the Amurri have been waylaid. You'll prepare a missive for their chief, extending my generous offer to rebuild their sanctuary. I would send you up there to initiate talks in my stead, but there's too much to deal with here. I'll need your pen at my disposal."

I blinked at him in abject confusion. "My pen?"

"Komar!"

His steward seemed to appear from nowhere. "Yes, my king?"

"Show my new personal scribe to his quarters and have Shamzur outfit him properly. Then bring him to my council chambers so he can begin transcribing orders immediately. There's no more time to waste. I need all my ships back in port, and my armies prepared to march south by the new moon."

The hair on the back of my neck prickled with intuition.

"Oh, and Komar," Abibaal said, "did you order the guards to get those traitors out of my palace?"

"I did, my king. They've assured me they'll see to it."

"Good," he snapped. "I want *every* Asherite out of Tyre by the end of the week. After that, any Hebrew found within two thousand cubits of my city is to be arrested."

My stomach wrenched hard at the threat. *Hundreds* of people were being displaced for a lie.

The king turned his potent stare back on me. "Except for my new personal scribe, of course, who saved my life."

The threat was implicit. Remain loyal or suffer the same consequences. Or perhaps, worse ones.

I had no choice but to bow low, offer thanks for his extravagant generosity, and pledge to serve him with excellence.

"I doubt you'll have much time to tutor Elissa now." He waved a flippant hand. "Hopefully you've taught her enough to impress the Shardan. My envoy sent confirmation they've accepted our invitation and will arrive within the next month."

Pain sparked in my chest as the first flaming arrow hit before he re-aimed to shoot another.

"It's even more imperative this treaty is successful, now that we're going to war with Israel."

21

Elissa

Eyes closed, my mother turned her face up to the sun. I'd not seen this much color in her skin for months, perhaps years. I'd been so delighted she'd agreed to come to the gardens with Melita and me today, after eight days of being pent up inside mourning Ahiram, that I'd asked Abenasser to arrange for a large woolen blanket to be laid near the fountain, along with a spread of food and drink.

Little Otzar squawked, squirming on the blanket, and my mother's eyes flew open. She scooped him up, placing him on her shoulder to rub circles on his tiny back. "Hush now," she whispered. "Danice will be here soon with your milk."

The baby had plumped significantly since Mattaniel and I had rescued him, his appetite voracious for one so small. I had the feeling the woman who gave birth to him had neglected his feedings for the first few weeks of his life.

Although Danice had assumed most of his care, it was my mother who was his champion. When Magin had found out about the child, she'd lied, saying the babe was her maid's and therefore under her personal protection. He'd threatened to go to Abibaal, but she'd dared him to do so with such adamant zeal that it had shocked the head eunuch into backing down.

"Have you girls heard how the queen is? Has the bleeding stopped?" my mother asked. A curl of warmth filled my chest as she rocked the baby back and forth, humming a soothing melody. It was as if the little one had given me back the vibrant and lovely mother of my youth.

"I think so," said Melita, "but my mother said the midwives told her she must stay abed until the birth."

The queen had lost several pregnancies since Seriyah had been born, so I was not surprised to hear they were taking extra precautions, especially considering her horrible grief. For as harsh as Khamera could be with those of us beneath her, I did not wish such pain on her. She'd not stopped weeping the entirety of the journey back to Tyre, and Seriyah hadn't left her mother's side since Yarikh's ship had found us on the beach at dawn.

I still could not believe Ahiram was actually gone. He had never been particularly kind to me, keeping aloof from the rest of us even when he lived in the women's wing as a boy. He'd spent his entire life being groomed to inherit the throne, after all. But my heart hurt for Seriyah, and I wished I had the freedom to go comfort her.

"Has Yarikh returned?" my mother asked.

"I don't think so," I said, plucking a slice of melon from the tray at my knee.

My brother's ship had delivered us to the port and then departed immediately, returning north to search for the pirates. A futile effort, in my opinion, but the king had demanded it. The one time I'd seen Yarikh while aboard his ship, he'd been deep in conversation with our father, both of them looking somber and resolved. Now the heir to the throne in Ahiram's place, whether he liked it or not, his duty was first and foremost to Tyre. His days of escaping what he deemed "frivolous palace life" were over. I hoped that also meant the Gazan princes would leave. I did not like the way they stared at Melita and me with a predatory gleam in their eyes.

"Ah!" Melita cried out. "Get away!"

Two monkeys had crept up on us, one brazenly snatching my sister's half-eaten fig right from her hand.

"I hate those things!" My sister flailed her arms at the animal, but it only grinned and chattered cheekily before taking a juicy bite of his plunder. "Why are they allowed out of their cages?"

One of the three eunuchs who'd been watching over us from a short distance strode up to the monkeys and bellowed at them, flapping his long billowing sleeves menacingly. The awful things scampered off, screaming what sounded very much like obscenities at the Crow in their animal language.

"Are you well, my lady?" the eunuch asked, concern pressed between his plucked brows. "Did it bite you?"

"No. Thank you, Rahej. He only stole my fig."

The man bobbed his bald head but remained much closer than he had before. As his first order since being elevated to Magin's empty post, Abenasser had ordered twice as many eunuchs to keep watch over us, even inside the women's court. An overreaction, since we were perfectly safe inside the walls of this palace, but one I did not see ending any time soon. There were far too many unanswered questions about how those Asherites had been able to bring down that ship, and to my knowledge, no one had yet been arrested for Ahiram's murder.

The baby fussed again, flailing his poor deformed hand in the air, and regardless of my mother's consolation, he refused to quiet. Instead, his insistent cries grew louder, startling a long-legged crane nearby. The bird fluttered off in a rush of white, which in turn set the monkeys screeching again.

"Here, let me try." I stretched out my arms for the child. My mother handed him over, and I stood to pace back and forth, bouncing his tiny body in time to my tuneless humming. But nothing calmed his angry demands.

As if summoned by his cries from inside the palace, Danice walked through the garden gate, her face paler than normal as she strode past the eunuchs, carrying a small ceramic juglet shaped roughly like an elephant.

"There now, sweet boy," I murmured as he hiccupped a gasp for air between piercing cries. "Here she is. Time to fill your belly."

Wordlessly, Danice took the child and folded herself down to the blanket. Blessed silence filled the garden the moment he latched on to the leather-wrapped spout of the juglet, sucking down the goats' milk greedily.

"I'm so glad you came," said my mother. "He was having none of our soothing."

"Forgive me for being gone so long," said Danice, her eyes pinned to the child's face.

"Oh, not to worry," said my mother with a flick of her hand. "No one ever perished from a baby's cry."

Danice nodded, her mouth set in a firm line as she held Otzar a little closer. For a woman who was unfailingly polite, her behavior was oddly taciturn.

Melita and I met eyes across the blanket, and I was certain she noticed the same thing. My mother, too, was frowning at her maid in confusion.

Finally, my curiosity bubbled over. "Are you well, Danice? You don't seem quite yourself."

Her eyes fluttered as she looked up at me, as if I'd dragged her out of some deep pit into the light. "Pardon, my lady?"

"Is something wrong?"

Danice's face blanched, her expression pinching. "I don't know . . ." She shook her head, seemingly unable to continue. In all the years Danice had served my mother, I'd never seen her so unsettled.

My mother reached to place her hand gently on Danice's arm. "Tell us, my friend. Maybe we can help."

Tears glittered in the maid's eyes at my mother's words. For as faithful a servant as Danice had been over the years, I'd never heard my mother refer to her as a friend.

Danice stared down at the child, utter devastation on her face as she whispered, "I must leave."

"What are you talking about?" said my mother.

The maid took a deep, shuddering breath. "I am Hebrew. Of the tribe of Asher."

Although this surprised me, since I'd never asked about her origins, it did not seem to shock my mother.

"And?" she pressed.

Danice swallowed hard as if to keep her voice from wobbling. "The king has ordered every Asherite from the palace. Out of the entire city."

My stomach hollowed as the memory of his oath on the beach rang through my mind: *"All of them will pay for this."* At the time, I assumed he meant to find all those responsible for the attack and mete out justice, but apparently my father had meant *every* Asherite would suffer the consequences of his heir's death.

"That's ridiculous." My mother scoffed. "You've done nothing wrong. You aren't going anywhere."

"I have no choice but to leave by nightfall or face arrest. We have been deemed traitors to the kingdom and co-conspirators in the death of Prince Ahiram. In fact, *any* Hebrew found in the city after three days will be thrown in prison. Perhaps worse."

The three of us stared at the poor woman as she lost her valiant fight with tears. "I have—" She choked, voice cracking as she pulled the baby close. "I have nowhere to go."

"Do you have no kin?" I asked.

She shook her head. "Everyone is gone. My husband died from an illness, along with my little daughter. My family left the region shortly after I married to escape the crushing taxes. They went east into Naftali territory, but I don't know where. I was forced to sell myself into service to survive. I was fortunate Magin came across me in the marketplace as I was seeking work, or who knows what might have happened to me."

Another surprise. I'd never have dreamed it was the ill-tempered head eunuch who'd brought Danice to my mother. She'd simply appeared one day, shortly after the tragic birth that had changed everything, and it hadn't taken long before my mother relied on her completely. Perhaps I'd not given Magin enough credit while he'd lived. He'd certainly proved himself unerringly loyal by his death.

"And even if I had somewhere to go . . . what about Otzar? I have no way to provide for him on my own." She pressed her fingers to her mouth to muffle a sob.

My mother scooted close to put her arm around Danice. "I will speak to the king myself. I may no longer be his favorite, but perhaps I can convince him to make an exception."

"You said he would be angry if he discovered the baby was not mine," Danice said. "Perhaps even accuse you like he did Olythia."

I winced. A few years ago, a young concubine had fallen pregnant during a season when my father had not called her once to his bed. She'd been sent away in disgrace; some even said she'd been executed. For as generous as he was with his wives and concubines, affording them every luxury, he demanded *absolute* loyalty.

My mother frowned down at the child, her face going pale. "He might."

Danice shook her head. "It's too risky. And as far as anyone knows the babe is Hebrew as well. And with his little hand . . ."

Nausea flared in my throat at the implications, along with fear for what losing both Danice *and* the baby would do to my mother's state of mind. There had to be a solution.

Close on the heels of those worries came one more. There was another Hebrew in this palace I'd come to care for, deeply. I'd been forced to pretend Mattaniel was nothing to me aboard Yarikh's ship, barely acknowledging his existence so as not to put him in danger, and had not seen him since we returned. Was he, too, to be sent away from Tyre?

Panic pushed me to my feet. "I have to go."

Shading her eyes with one hand, Melita frowned up at me. "Where?"

I looked around the garden for a few scattered moments, trying to reorder my thoughts into a semblance of a plan. "Melita. You escort my mother and Danice back inside. Then tell everyone my mother has refused to see anyone because she is devastated her maid has been sent away. Keep the Crows out of our room, by whatever means you can. Can you do that?"

"Of course."

"Ama, you and Danice will have to keep the baby quiet until I can find a way to get them out of the city safely."

I wasn't certain how I could do so, but if anyone could help me think of a solution, it was Mattaniel. I refused to believe that he was already gone.

"But *where* are you going?" asked my mother, eyes glittering with tears.

There was no use hiding the truth. "To find my tutor."

22

Mattaniel

With a boar-bristle brush and gritty natron powder, I scrubbed at the ink stains on my fingers. After an entire day of writing letters to the king's commanders and various officials, I wondered if my hands would ever be completely clean again. As I rinsed the mess from my palms in the washing pot, the small crosswise scar at the base of my right thumb caught my eye, the only one of the many scars marking my body that seemed purposefully cut, though I could not fathom why. I had no memory of digging a blade into my own hand and none of the traders doing so. I ran my opposite thumb over the lightly ridged scar, wondering why it seemed almost . . . important.

"You *are* here."

I spun at the voice, hands dripping, to find the subject of my unwise affections standing in the open doorway with Nolam at her side and another eunuch standing guard in the hallway.

My pulse raced at the memory of holding her in my arms and the taste of her soft lips. I'd been right to dread seeing her after taking such a liberty—it was pure torture. I swallowed hard, bowing. "My lady. Forgive me, I did not hear you enter."

"I went looking for you in the Hall of Records. Tabnit says you've been *promoted*?"

I nodded, still just as astounded as she was. "To the king's personal scribe."

Her eyes flared. "No wonder your chamber is in the royal wing."

When Komar had led me here, I thought for certain he'd been mistaken. The room was stocked with every scribal tool I could ever imagine needing, and was so lavish I was still afraid to touch anything. An expansive worktable under the window held stacks of crisp papyrus and countless new reed pens, along with fresh ink palettes in a variety of hues. And on the shelves in the corner, sealed pots of prepared wet clay waited beside various wooden forms for making official tablets. Astonishingly, I'd even been entrusted with a royal seal, which hung now on a leather cord around my neck.

"Well deserved," she murmured, her gaze traveling around the room.

"Indeed," said Nolam with a kind smile. "Tabnit is quite proud. Said there is no one more deserving."

My chest warmed to hear the head scribe approve of my elevation. Especially when I doubted it was normal for a slave to fill such a high and trusted position.

"I am honored to serve in whatever capacity I am needed." I gave a little nod. "How can I be of service to you, my lady?"

I expected a scowl for my formality, but she only gestured to a well-cushioned couch beneath the window that I'd yet to sit on.

"That looks quite comfortable, Nolam," she said. "Why don't you rest your bones while Mattaniel and I have our lesson?"

"Gladly. Why there must be so many stairs in this palace is beyond me," he groused as he shuffled over to the chair. "Of course, it was much easier when my knees didn't creak so loudly."

Although I was confused by her mention of a lesson, I gestured for Elissa to sit at my worktable, then fetched a stool for myself.

"Excuse the mess," I said, tidying the area of my scribing tools. "It's been a busy day."

"I truly am glad for you," she said, although her blue-green eyes shimmered with a sadness I attributed to the loss of the prince. "After what you did for us on that ship, we all owe you a great debt."

"I am sorry about your brother," I said, forcing away the terrible image of so many bodies floating in the water belowdecks. "May his memory be a blessing to you."

She blinked at me absently for a couple of moments. "Oh . . . yes, thank you."

"Did I miss a message from Tabnit? I wasn't aware we were to have a lesson."

Her eyes darted to Nolam, who'd produced a scroll from somewhere in his billowing robes and was happily reading in the brilliant sunlight pouring through the window.

"I need some refreshing," she said, her eyes telling me a different story, "on some of the words you taught me to write last time."

Bewildered, I slid a clean sheet of papyrus toward her, then a reed and a palette of black ink.

With a deep inhale, she took up the reed and began to write, not in our Shardan symbols but in her own language.

I thought you'd been sent away with the other Hebrews.

My eyes flashed to hers as she offered me the pen to respond.

Your father believes in my loyalty.

I did not want you to leave

She paused, meeting my eyes with a weighty glance that spoke louder than the words on the page. It seemed I was not the only one deeply affected by that kiss.

at least not without saying good-bye.

One way or the other, we would eventually have to say good-bye. No matter what had passed between us, she was still marrying someone else, and once she did, I would leave Tyre for good.

My mother's maid is being forced to leave. With the baby.

Asherite?

She nodded sadly, biting her lip.

She has no family. No friends outside of the palace. And nowhere to go. My mother is distraught. I don't know what to do other than keep Danice and the child hidden in my mother's room until I find a way to get her out of the city.

I had no idea how to help her. Any Hebrews I'd met in the palace had already left. Elissa's eyes flashed to Nolam, who'd predictably fallen asleep with his scroll pressed to his chest. She breathed a sigh of relief.

"Finally," she said, voice low. "I had to argue with Abenasser to let Nolam escort me here, and only then with the additional guard."

Although far enough away he would not hear our quiet conversation, the black-robed eunuch was watching us carefully through the doorway. After witnessing Magin take on the pirates that night, I had no doubt all Crows who guarded the women were highly trained fighters, even if their soft facial features were deceiving. Though it was difficult to imagine Nolam, with his crooked, hunched back, as anything but harmless.

"Are we really going to war with Israel?" she whispered.

I gestured to the stack of identical messages I'd been working on all day. "The king is ordering his commanders to rally their troops and march south within two weeks. Ships too."

"Why did they do this, Mattaniel? Don't they know that your people will suffer for their actions?"

"The Asherites?"

"Yes. Burning the waterworks. Attacking caravans and barges. Sinking the king's ship. Are they fools? Do they not remember who my father is?"

I did not doubt that everyone in this region knew exactly who Abibaal was and how ruthlessly he'd wrested power from his own uncle. Nor that he would go to war with those he blamed for the death of his son. In fact, I was certain some had counted on it.

"The Asherites did not attack our ship," I said, dropping my voice low.

She leaned closer. "But Melita said they were dressed in Hebrew garb."

"They were. Yet the one I fought used a curse only a Sidonian would employ. Certainly not a Torah-abiding son of Yaakov with sacred tzitzit tied to the corners of his garment. I am convinced they were Sidonians dressed like Hebrews, in hopes blame would be cast on the men of Asher."

"But we're at peace with Sidon. Have been for decades. We may be rivals but we still trade freely and often."

"That may be true. However, the pirates on that ship deck were not Hebrew, and I've lived among enough Sidonians to recognize their accents and speech patterns." I rubbed at the scar on my brow. "Besides, it never sat right with me that Asherites would burn waterworks that supply their own farms and orchards with water. Or attack trade caravans in areas so near their own villages. Only fools would bring destruction to their own doorstep when they are so far outnumbered in this region." I folded my arms, frowning. "Something is not right."

"My father won't stop, Mattaniel. Not after what happened to Ahiram."

"I know. I suspect that may have been the goal all along."

"Whose?"

"The Philistines, perhaps? They've not hidden their intention to drag Abibaal into the conflict between Israel and Philistia. Or maybe it *is* Sidon. Tyre has overshadowed them in trade and status for decades now. There is bound to be some resentment, no matter how calm the waters between the two cities may seem."

No matter who was at the center of this plot, things were becoming more and more dangerous. If there were traitors on that ship, as I guessed, they'd had a concerning level of access to Elissa and her family. It had been a swift and well-coordinated attack by men who'd known exactly where the ship would be and when. They'd doused the signal fire so the ship would founder. Boarded with little effort. And then, there was the question of why Yarikh's ship had gotten so far behind that night. There *had* to be someone within the king's court feeding the attackers information and possibly orchestrating sabotage.

She leaned forward. "You think this is a conspiracy fueled by jealousy?"

"I wish I knew. And I wish I knew how to help your mother's maid."

"I'll find a way. I *have* to." She slumped back in her chair, brows drawn. "My mother relies on Danice so much. And the baby . . . you should see how much joy he brings her." She shook her head, her eyes glistening. "She's been so tortured all these years, Mattaniel. Going weeks trapped in the depths of sorrow or flying into furies no one can calm, not even me. At times, she'll prostrate herself before the gods until her knees bleed, begging for relief from the pain and for the voices inside her head to cease. No amount of prayer or sacrifice has done any good. Until you and I found that baby, and somehow everything changed . . ." She sighed, the sound full of pain. "I thought the gods had finally heard me. But perhaps they were only toying with me."

"What makes you think that?"

She threw her arms wide. "My father is sending me off to marry a pirate, Mattaniel. And after losing hope that I'll find some way to avoid it, my only consolation lately was that my mother might finally be getting better on account of the baby. That perhaps she would not become even more broken when I'm dragged off to the ends of the earth. And now the only maid she trusts *and* the child are being stripped away. And then there's you—" She dropped her eyes closed, shaking her head. "I never expected you."

I swallowed hard against the tightness in my throat and all the foolish words that begged to be set free. What I needed to tell her instead was that the true God of the Universe did not play games with humankind like Tyre's perverse, capricious gods.

Just as I opened my mouth to explain, Komar strode into the room, the sparse hair atop his balding head sticking out in all directions, as if the steward had just removed his usual conical cap.

"Are those letters finished? They must be sent out this afternoon—oh . . . Lady Elissa." He dropped into a bow. "I did not know you were here."

She stood, giving him a regal nod. "Just came by for a short language lesson."

"The king was quite pleased to hear of your progress. I am certain when the Shardan arrive next month, you'll dazzle them with your mastery of their language."

Her own smile dipped, just a little, at the reminder that her time here was swiftly coming to an end, but Komar seemed not to notice.

"Are the orders ready, then?" he repeated, turning away from Elissa.

"They are."

"Excellent. I am short a couple of messengers this afternoon. I'll need you to deliver missives to Prince Yarikh at the docks and also to Commander Hanno, who lives on the mainland."

While Komar gave me directions to the home of the naval commander, Elissa gently shook Nolam awake. Eyelids fluttering open, he smiled up at her like a doting grandfather. But when he registered her troubled expression, he lifted a gnarled hand to cup her cheek comfortingly, swiping a tear with his thumb.

As ridiculous as it was, I'd never been so jealous of an old man in my entire life. I'd give anything to be the one to wipe away her tears. And yet nothing had changed. My freedom—and Raphad's—still meant the end of hers.

I fidgeted with the king's seal at my neck, wishing I could at least do something to ease her mind about the Asherite maid, when an idea sparked in my mind. It may prove to be a foolish one, but worth the risk if it would give Elissa, and her mother, a small measure of relief before she left all of us behind.

The moment I left the house of Abibaal's commander, I ran, determined not to waste the narrow window of freedom I was stealing to carry out my plan. If all went well, perhaps I'd even have time to send Elissa a note before the sun went down.

I found Raphad's villa easily, situated only a short distance from the commander's abode. But when I knocked on the freshly painted door, I was greeted by an unfamiliar house steward.

Portea, it seemed, no longer lived there.

Although he was suspicious at first, when I told him I was delivering a message from the palace, the steward gave me directions to a small hamlet in the foothills just outside of Tyre. Raphad's creditors must have called in the last of his debt after all.

Now concerned that his wife may be in trouble after being forced from her home, I pushed my stride even further on the run to the foothills. She'd been so kind to Adin and me upon our arrival from Shardana, fussing over filling our bellies while she clucked over our wild appearance and asked a thousand questions about our time with the Shardan.

Once I arrived in the hamlet, a neighbor sent me to a ramshackle home on a hillside, where I found Portea on her knees in the dirt, a silver-threaded black braid trailing down her back. Dressed in simple woolen garments as she tended an ailing vineyard, she only vaguely resembled the bejeweled, wealthy woman who came to the docks to greet Raphad on my first trip to Tyre. Even then, she'd been one of the few people to speak to me as a man, not chattel.

Fearing I would startle her, I called out her name, and she pushed to her feet, hand shading her eyes, then came forward with a wide smile. "Mattaniel! Welcome!"

Out of sheer force of habit, I bowed as she approached.

"That's enough of that, young man," she said as she clapped dirt from her hands. "Why do you look as if you've been chasing down a chariot?"

"It took a while to find you." I wiped the sweat from my brow, my palm coming away muddy from the road dust coating my skin. "I ran most of the way."

"I suppose you went to the villa first? It's been a few weeks since I moved out here, thanks to the king."

"Abibaal forced you from your home?"

"Oh, not at all. In fact, he made certain this vineyard was

protected from the creditors by having it registered in my name, since it was part of my dowry in the first place. And he even had my belongings delivered to the door."

Extraordinarily generous for a man who'd had her husband imprisoned for many weeks now over a debt. She must have seen the disbelief on my face.

"I know." She waved a hand. "It sounds impossible after what happened with Raphad. But my father was quite loyal to Abibaal, and a large part of the reason his coup was successful. The king vowed upon my father's death to make certain I was well cared for. If it were not for him, I'd have been out in the streets long ago. And truly, I am quite grateful I have this little plot of land to tend. The villa was lovely, but with only a couple of servants, the task of keeping it up were increasingly a burden." She smiled, her cheeks rosy from the sun. "I've taken it as a personal challenge to get these vines producing again. Sadly, the man Raphad employed to care for the vineyard disappeared after your shipwreck, and it's been deteriorating all this time."

Although the vineyard sprawled over most of the hillside, the overgrown vines around us covered the ground in wild tangles, the once-neat rows of wooden fences either broken or rotted away. It must have been profitable years ago, but without a team of workers trimming vines, plucking weeds, and harvesting grapes, it would be an enormous undertaking to unravel the mess. Although Portea had become a strong and capable woman in the years she thought her husband dead, I did not know how she could resurrect such a desolate patch of earth alone.

But perhaps with Danice's help . . .

"You look famished," she said, taking me by the arm to guide me toward her little house. "Let me fill your belly. There's no more wine, since the tenant farmer either stole it or drank it all before he left, but I fetched some water from the spring this morning, and it's still cold."

"Oh no, that's not necessary, my lady. I merely have something I'd like to speak with you about—"

She halted to glare at me. "You would deny me the pleasure of feeding the first guest I've had in my new home?" She clucked her tongue. "I've never known you to be so heartless, Mattaniel."

Appropriately shamed, I dropped my chin. She was no doubt incredibly lonely. The wealthy friends she'd once entertained in her sprawling villa would have nothing to do with her now. I flicked a gaze back toward the city, swiftly calculating how much time I had left. There was one more message to deliver to Prince Yarikh, but if I ran all the way back to the ferry dock, I'd make it back well before sundown. "Forgive me, my lady. Your kindness is most appreciated."

"Excellent!" Her satisfied grin was pure delight as she pulled me forward. "I have plenty of barley stew since I'd prepared extra for my neighbors—an elderly couple whose sons are both up in the mountains with the labor crews fixing the water lines. Now, tell me why you've come all the way out here. I thought you were busy tutoring Elissa. That girl is lovely, just like her mother. I haven't seen Leyana in years, not since she took ill, which I've heard was more than just a malady of the body but perhaps the mind. Poor thing. I don't care much for gossip, of course, especially when it's malicious, but she was always such a sweet thing and I did hear she lost a babe when Elissa was small. A difficult thing when one has her heart set on holding a child in her arms . . ." Her flurry of words trailed off, and I knew she was speaking from experience.

Something Portea had said to me before the Feast of Awakening had given me hope she might be willing to help the Hebrew servant. When I'd tried to refuse her kind offer of a haircut that morning, thinking it far beneath a woman of status to take up shears and trim the wild mess on a slave's head, she'd insisted.

"After all you've done to bring my husband back from the dead, I will always think of you and Adin as my own sons," she'd said, a pinch of emotion in her voice. *"The gods did not bless my womb, so I think it's only fair they've afforded me two kind young men to dote upon. And someday perhaps you'll bring me little ones to spoil as well. If there's anything I grieve most about barrenness,*

it's not having grandchildren." The memory of the tremulous smile she'd given me then, as she'd revealed the desire of her broken heart, gave me courage now to speak.

"Actually, it is on behalf of Elissa's mother that I've come to see you." As Portea led me inside her tiny home, no bigger than four small rooms atop a stable that held three speckled goats and one weary donkey, I told her of the edict Abibaal had ordered and why Danice and the child needed refuge.

"Bring them! Of course!" Portea interjected before I'd even finished explaining the dangers of harboring an Asherite fugitive. Then she directed me to sit on a cushion near her open hearth where a stew pot crouched among glowing embers. My stomach snarled at the delicious aroma wafting through the cozy room. As Portea collected a jar of spring water from a small floor cellar under a board in the corner, I settled onto the cushion and lifted a silent prayer that Portea's innate compassion might extend to the child as well.

"There are . . . special circumstances you must consider. The baby is not Danice's own. He was found abandoned on a beach because he is deformed. Missing a few fingers from one hand."

She frowned, her black brows pinching tight with disgust. "That's awful."

"If that changes your decision, I understand—"

"Why would it?" she interrupted. "There are plenty of cruel people in Tyre who would throw aside a child for a variety of reasons, including foolish superstitions, but I am *not* one of them."

I let out a long breath. "Elissa will be so relieved."

A flicker of something knowing shifted over her features. I'd given myself away. "And of course Danice will be so grateful." I rushed to add. "I don't know her, but I'm certain she'll be glad to help you with the vineyard in payment for her keep."

A smile teased the corner of Portea's mouth, but she kindly allowed me to skim over my mistake. "You just bring the two of them here, and we'll get along fine. My neighbors have been generous with their gardens. And I learned to be quite resourceful while the three of you were with the Shardan."

“I cannot thank you enough, Portea.”

She patted my hand. “I told you one day you’d bring me little ones to dote upon, didn’t I? The first of many, I hope.” She winked and turned away to ladle stew from the hearth pot into a bowl. “And besides, when he returns to Tyre,” she continued, “Raphad will be thrilled to hear that I’ve not been alone here. He was worried about how I would manage the vineyard without help. But of course, I told him I’d survived in that great big ridiculous villa with only two servants for three years and would be just fine.”

“Returns from where?” I asked, scrambling to understand.

She’d frowned at me. “From Shardana. Don’t you know the king sent him there to negotiate the treaty?”

My jaw went slack. “I . . . I thought he was in prison. Or on a labor crew somewhere.”

She set the bowl in my hands. “Oh no. He was only locked in a cell for a few days. You know my Raphad, he found a way to negotiate an alternative to debtor’s prison. Something about a colony . . . ? I’m not certain of the particulars. He was allowed to visit me once, chained and under guard, to arrange for the sale of the villa and what little remained of our holdings. Then two days later he was back on a ship headed for Shardana.”

I stared at her in utter bewilderment. “But he was terrified of the sea after the wreck. Even boarding the ferry was difficult. Why would he offer to go back?”

She folded herself down across from me, her own bowl of stew in hand. “He was. He’d vowed he would never set foot on a ship again when you all returned. But he did it—for you.”

“What?” I breathed out, the blood rushing from my head.

“He owes you his life, Mattaniel. Not only did you rescue him from certain death in the Great Sea, he told me how loyal you were to him on the island and that you helped him survive when he was so inept at fishing and hunting. He was grieved that you sacrificed yourself to the king before he could free you. And, in truth, he was terribly ashamed he did not fight harder for you that night. He told me the least he could do was set aside his fears and personally negotiate with the Shardan king." She shrugged. "I am not the only one who considers you like a son."

I was at an absolute loss for words as I stared at her open-mouthed.

Her soft smile was full of understanding for my confusion. "He also said that the stories you told the Shardan about your God made quite the impression on him. There was something . . . *changed* about him when he returned. Perhaps you can explain to me why that might be?"

An hour later, I left Portea's home with an overstuffed stomach, still reeling from the revelations about my former master. I knew he was grateful to Adin and me for saving his life after the shipwreck, but I could not fully wrap my mind around the idea that he'd gotten back on a ship for my sake. Nor that he'd been so affected by my stories of Yahweh.

I spent the entire run back to Tyre and down to the wharf mulling the incongruity of a master willing to step past his own fears on behalf of a slave, but as soon as the ferry bumped against the dock, I was on the move toward the other end of the bustling harbor, focused on swiftly delivering my message to Prince Yarikh. It was entirely possible that my detour to the outskirts of the city would already result in discipline when I returned to the palace, but it had indeed been worth the risk.

For some reason, the prince eschewed his luxurious quarters in the palace to stay in a portside inn, not far from where his warship was docked at the far end of a long wooden causeway. Once I found the establishment, the innkeeper sent me to the flat rooftop where Yarikh was entertaining a group of rowdy men, including the two Philistine princes, three Egyptians, and others I recognized as crewmen from his ship. Instantly, I regretted not coming here first before going to the mainland. The prince was already inebriated when I handed him the message and immediately laughed at the contents.

"It's about time the king does something about the Hebrews," he sneered, waving the message in the air. "Too bad it took my brother ending up at the bottom of the sea for him to finally take action."

Unsettled as I was by the callous statement about his own flesh and blood, I had not been excused by the prince. I had no choice but to wait for his permission to go.

"What's that about?" asked one of Enesidu's sons.

"I've got less than two weeks to prepare my company for war."

The Philistine grinned at his brother, then back at the prince. "Tyre is coming south after all?"

Yarikh lifted his overfull cup. "We'll run the cowards all the way back to the Red Sea together."

A shiver feathered up my spine.

"What do you think, Bayek?" The other Gazan prince elbowed a man at his side. "Want your slaves back?"

The Egyptian spat on the ground. "Let them rot in that *sea* alongside the ancient bones of our people."

The alliance between these three ancient enemies was a terrifying prospect. The Philistines had not been able to rout us from the Land of Avraham's promise alone, but if they were joined by Tyre and Egypt, I wasn't certain how Israel would fend them off. Adin said the standing army of Saul had grown significantly since his crowning, but it was still minuscule compared to those of Egypt and Philistia, and dependent on the cooperation of fractious tribal militias with negligible training.

As Yarikh turned to speak to one of his crewmen, the elder Philistine leaned over to his brother and dropped his voice low, speaking in his native tongue. "What did I tell you? One last push was all it took."

Being only two paces behind them, I doubted anyone else had heard the exchange. Mind spinning with the possible implications, I held my breath in case they said more.

Instead, the younger Gazan lifted his voice to address Yarikh again. "And what of the fair Elissa, my friend? Have you convinced Abibaal to give her to me yet?"

My blood went still, my fists clenching.

"Not yet," replied Yarikh. "He's still set on sending her off to some backwards island."

"Now that you're the heir," said the Philistine, "I'm sure you'll make him see reason."

Frowning, Yarikh took a long draft of his wine, as if stalling his answer. "I told you, she's valuable to him. The child of his first, and *favorite*, concubine."

"If the mother is anything like the daughter, I can certainly see why." The Gazan prince grinned lasciviously.

I walked away before he said anything else and I lost hold of my tenuous control. Yarikh was too drunk to care that I'd not waited for his dismissal anyhow.

In my haste to escape the rooftop without attacking a lecherous Philistine prince in front of the future king of Tyre, I nearly collided with someone halfway down the stairs.

"Whoa there," said the man, who was nearly as tall as I was and twice as wide. "What's your rush?"

"Forgive me." Head down, I pressed myself to the wall but noticed a distinctive, familiar tattoo on his forearm as he and three more rough-looking men passed by me.

When I looked up, I was stunned to see Haldon, Tabnit's apprentice, coming up the stairway as well. I had not seen him since his return after the tragedy that had befallen his family. What possible reason would the young scribe have for being here tonight, especially in the company of such rough men? Had Tabnit sent him?

Haldon's gaze snagged on the king's seal around my neck, which must have slipped out of my tunic during my run. "Ah yes. I heard you were *promoted*. My congratulations." The way he spat the word made it sound more like a curse than a blessing. Odd, since the last time I'd worked with him, he'd been nothing but cordial.

"I was sorry to hear about your father and brothers," I said, tucking the seal away. "May their memories be—"

"What do you know of it?" he snapped, his eyes darting up to the three men, who'd stopped to stare at us from a few steps above.

"Tabnit only told me there was an accident," I said, astounded by his hostility.

"The king is a fool to let you so near his court." Haldon narrowed his eyes, hatred dripping from his tongue. "*All* of you need to be run out of this city. And out of our lands. If he'd done so years ago, my family never would have burned to death in the first place."

Shocked by the vitriol, I remained pinned in place until Haldon had joined the others on the rooftop—including the one with an eerily similar tattoo to one of the men I'd fought on the ship.

Night had fallen by the time I hit the bottom stair, but with so many torches flickering beside doorways as invitations to drink and gamble, among other darker vices, it was easy to find my way up the street toward the palace, which sat at the highest point on the island.

I wondered if Tabnit knew his apprentice was here right now, in the company of at least one Sidonian. It was too farfetched to imagine that Haldon had something to do with the sinking of the king's ship. He was a *scribe*. A man of dusty texts and reed pens scratching across papyrus. And one who was responsible for caring for what remained of his family. Would he jeopardize his coveted position to get mixed up in a plot against the throne?

And yet . . . hadn't Haldon been the one Tabnit usually relied on to deliver freshly copied cargo manifests?

Embroiled in my thoughts, I turned onto a darker street, hoping to cut my return to the palace a bit shorter, when the back of my neck began to prickle. Soft footsteps a few paces behind me quickened as I picked up my pace.

A dark form took shape against the blackness up ahead, coming toward me, and my stomach hollowed. What kind of fool was I? Torben would slap the side of my head if he knew I'd let down my guard, especially after running into Haldon and those Sidonians. I was alone. Unarmed. And in unfamiliar territory.

A third man turned onto the narrow street from an adjacent alley.

I wasn't just being followed. I'd been surrounded.

The man approaching emerged from the shadows, past a row of dimly lit windows. Recognition hit. It was one of the guards who'd caught me staring in the tavern courtyard. Cold crept up my spine as I halted in front of the only well-lit window on the street. I closed my left eye, a technique Torben had taught me to preserve my sight when light was sparse, and braced myself as the second man joined the other, just as tall as me but built like a cedar.

Blood pounded in my ears. Even during the attack on the ship, I'd only fought one man at a time. I had little hope of succeeding against three.

"It *is* you." The tallest man strode forward, palms spread to show he was unarmed. But I was not *that* much of a fool. I rushed forward, slamming into him with my shoulder, then twisted as he grunted and threw my elbow hard into his lower back. He crumpled forward, wheezing.

"Whoa!" The other man grabbed for me, but I pulled back my fist and hit him square in the jaw. He stumbled back, a palm cupped over his cheek, and blinked disbelievingly. "Ow, Shay. Was that necessary?"

Stunned by his lack of retaliation, and the unexpected familiarity in his tone, I froze in place just as the third man grabbed me from behind, locking his arms around my chest to pin my arms to my sides.

"Enough!" he rasped into my ear as I struggled against him. "We aren't here to hurt you Sh—Mattaniel. Adin sent us."

The name of my friend sent a wave of shock through my body, and I went stiff in his iron hold, mind reeling. "Who are you? Where's Adin?"

He paused, almost as if he were collecting himself before he spoke, while his two companions stared at me, eyes wide in the meager light.

Then, removing one arm from around me, he lifted his palm in front of my face, tilting it toward the light spilling from the window above us. At the base of his thumb was a small crosswise scar—a perfect match to the one on my own.

"We're your cousins, Shalem. We've come to take you home."

23

Can I let go?" the man asked.

Mind whirling and body rigid from shock, I gave a sharp nod.

Instead of releasing me immediately, he strengthened his hold on me. "I can't believe—" His voice cracked. He paused and cleared his throat. "I can't believe we actually found you." He let go, then went to stand beside his companions. He was the shortest among them but certainly no less of a threat. No matter what they claimed, I was not about to let my guard down again.

The one whose cheek I'd struck huffed a wry laugh, rubbing the reddened side of his face. "I'm going to have quite the bruise. Where'd you learn to fight like that, Shay?"

I frowned at the moniker but answered simply. "Pirates."

The tallest one chuckled at my response. "Not quite the answer I expected."

My ears were still ringing and my head ached as if I'd been the one hit with a fist. "What did you call me?"

"Shay." The tall one cleared his throat. "That's your name. Shalem ben Iyov."

Shalem? After thirteen years of wondering . . . finally I knew my real name. And that I had a father named Iyov.

"I'm Avi," he said, then gestured to the one I'd struck in the jaw. "This is Gavi, and that"—he pointed at the man who'd first seen me in the tavern courtyard—"is Zevi."

I stared at them, waiting for a flash of recognition or some indication that they were my relations. But they were simply strangers who looked nothing at all like me.

"Your *ima* is going to faint dead away when she sees you, my friend." Avi stepped forward to clap his large palm on my shoulder. "I think you can even look *me* in the eye now."

"My . . . my ima?" I rasped through a knot in my throat.

"Give him a few moments to adjust, Avi," said Zevi. "He's in shock."

There was an air of authority in Zevi's voice that made me think he might be the eldest among them, so I addressed him.

"You said Adin sent you. Where is he?"

"His commander refused to release him to come with us. I tried to persuade him, but the Philistines are raiding again now that the rains are over. Every man was needed to guard the foothills around Lachish."

So my friend had joined the army of Israel after all. "How did he even find you? When he left here, neither of us knew where I came from."

"I was in Gibeah delivering weapons," said Gavi, "and stumbled across him training with his company at the fortress. He told me where you two have been for the past few years and where to find you."

I blinked at him. "I don't understand. Why would he think we were related?"

"I barely missed you in Gaza, Shay. If it weren't for Zahava, I would have gotten on a ship myself to find you."

"Zahava? The goldsmith?"

"My wife."

My jaw went slack. "You are *that* Gavriel?"

He grinned, spreading his arms wide. "In the flesh."

I rubbed at my scarred eyebrow, the beginnings of a splitting headache forming. How was it that the fearless and celebrated soldier Adin spoke of so often—a man he seemed to practically worship—was my own cousin? I did not even know where to begin with the hundreds of questions that sprang to mind. "None of this makes any sense."

"I know this is difficult to believe," said Zevi. "But we *are* your cousins. We've been searching for you for thirteen long years."

My chest squeezed painfully. "You have?"

He gave a solemn nod.

"How did I even get lost in the first place?"

"That is a very long story, one we don't have time for now," said Zevi. "We need to get moving. It'll be difficult enough to find a boat to take us across the channel this late."

I blinked at him, confused. "A boat . . . where are you going?"

"*Home*, Shay," said Avi. "Your mother and father have spent all this time mourning their son. Your sisters too."

I have sisters?

"I know all of this is confusing," said Zevi. "I can't even begin to imagine what a shock this is—"

"I can't go anywhere with you," I interrupted as some of my sense returned. "I need to get back to the palace. If anyone realizes I've not yet returned, they'll send the guard after me."

"You're safe with us," said Gavi. "I promise."

"No. You don't understand. I am a *servant*. And not only that, I am a slave to the king of Tyre. One who has recently been entrusted with highly privileged information. If I ran, I'd be considered a traitor, and Abibaal would stop at nothing to put me to death."

Avi's jaw dropped. "I thought you were a scribe."

"I am. The personal scribe to the king."

All three looked stunned.

"I have to get back. Now. It will be difficult enough as it is to explain my absence, and there's too much at stake—"

"What's at stake?" Zevi folded his arms across his chest, brow furrowing.

I paused, uncertain how much to tell them. They may claim to be my cousins, but how did I know it was true? What if they were spies sent to trick me into divulging information?

"That scar on your eyebrow," said Gavi, tapping his own. "You got it falling out of a tree when you were seven. We thought you were dead when we found you. Your ima threatened to make stew out of us if we ever let you climb higher than three cubits off the ground again."

My pulse thudded hard. That memory *had* been real after all . . .

"And that patch of silver on your head," said Avi. "Your ima said it was the touch of Yahweh, a special blessing on you from birth. She called you her special treasure—even though your sisters hated it when she did. She has grieved deeply for you, Shay. Everyone has."

I swallowed hard, emotion clogging my throat.

Zevi raised his palm, pointing to the mark there. "And this is from when we were boys and made a pact that we would always take care of one another, like brothers."

Gavi and Avi stretched out their own palms, where identical old scars marked their skin.

"We did a terrible job of that when we were younger," said Zevi. "But we have never stopped hoping and praying for this day. And we are *not* leaving this city without you, cousin."

My throat burned at the designation. Over the years, I'd been a slave, a translator, a tutor, a scribe, and even a friend, but I'd never had anyone call me family. I wanted it to be true. Wanted to remember who these men were to me and what they knew of who I was before my injuries.

I turned up my own palm, rubbing at the little mark that had always been such a curiosity. It testified that I'd once trusted these men. Had known them well enough to ensure the reminder of that friendship was permanent.

I took a shuddering breath, shoved aside my lingering trepidations, and told them about the Asherites. About the shipwreck and the fires and the king's decision to go to war with Israel.

"I can't go anywhere," I said. "At least not right now. I don't know how to prove it was not Hebrews on that ship, but I can't just walk away."

"We heard about the Asherites being sent out of Tyre," said Gavi. "In fact, from what I gathered at the tavern the other day, things are getting dangerous for our people here."

Zevi nodded, his expression somber. "One of the guards told me they've been given free rein to beat any Hebrew they come across. As a warning for what will happen if they don't leave."

"You see?" I said, sickened to hear things were worse than I knew. "Even the Hebrews serving the royal family have been told to leave. I *have* to do something. Not only because many innocent people are in danger but also because I suspect there may be traitors in the palace itself."

And I was *not* leaving until I knew for certain Elissa was safe.

Zevi, Avi, and Gavi exchanged another of their mutual speaking looks, as if they knew each other so well that words were unnecessary. Jealously hit me, swift and powerful. What would my life have been like had I not been separated from them?

"All right, then," said Zevi abruptly. "Let's make a plan."

I blinked at him in confusion. "A plan?"

"How are we going to get the proof you need?"

My mouth opened and closed a few times before I could form a response. "You're going to help me?"

Avi spread his long arms wide. "We've been looking for you since you were fifteen years old, Shay. You didn't think we would just leave, did you?"

I cleared my throat, eyes burning. All this time I'd wondered whether anyone even missed me and here these men—*my cousins*—had been searching for me.

Gavi grinned mischievously, reminding me of Torben, who loved nothing more than a good brawl. "It's been far too long since the four of us had an adventure together. We're not going anywhere without you."

24

Elissa

I read the note again for at least the fiftieth time since it had been delivered to my door at dawn.

Bring the maid and baby to the hidden door tonight. I found help. Be careful.

I traced my fingers over the neatly aligned Shardan symbols, wishing I could have immediately gone to the royal wing to ask about the plan or, preferably, run into his arms and thank him profusely. After I'd spent most of last night worrying instead of sleeping, the prospect of relief was overwhelming.

My mother peered over my shoulder. "Are you certain this man is trustworthy?"

Startling at the intrusion, I refolded the note and tucked it into my belt. Even if she could not read the symbols, I wanted his words all for myself.

"I told you, Ama, without Mattaniel, I'd never have made it back here with the baby in the first place. And he saved all of us on that ship. He is a good man. One of the best I've ever known."

She peered at me. "Take care, my darling girl."

For many years, my mother had been so lost to her heavy grief that I wasn't certain she saw me much of the time. Yet, since I'd returned after the shipwreck, she was not only more present but far more observant. Perhaps *too* observant.

I schooled my features, as I'd been trained to do. "I know my place, Ama. And my duty."

She frowned, her blue-green eyes traveling slowly over my face. "I have missed so much. Please forgive me, Elissa."

My heart squeezed. "I am just glad you are feeling better."

I wasn't certain how to explain it, but even the air in the room seemed less heavy. She kept the curtain flung wide every day now to let sunshine pour in and only rarely remained in bed past sunrise. And when I'd come to tell her that Mattaniel had found a way to help her maid, she'd wept—but from relief, not from fear.

"Do you have everything you need?" I asked Danice.

She patted Otzar's back as he slept blissfully, tied to her chest. "I think so. Poloma made certain I had a skin of goat milk in case we have far to travel."

My mother withdrew a jingling neck-purse from her jewelry box and pressed it into Danice's hands. "This should be enough to last you a good, long while."

Her maid's mouth parted. "Oh, no, Leyana. I could not take—"

"You *will* take it. It will comfort me to know you and Otzar are provided for. Besides"—she curled Danice's fingers around the purse—"you have given me a gift that is far more dear, my friend. One that has changed everything. And there is no amount of silver or gold to equal your compassion and patience with my brokenness all these years."

"We need to go," I said. "Mattaniel will be waiting."

Nerves fluttered in my stomach. Thankfully, none of the guards had come for Danice yet, but I dreaded what might happen if Mattaniel's plan failed.

My mother wrapped a fine black woolen cloak around Danice, who this time accepted the gift without complaint, then stopped to press her lips to Otzar's bald head. She inhaled deeply, as if memorizing the scent. Then she pressed a kiss to her maid's cheek as well. "I will miss you both."

Danice's eyes filled with tears. "Are you certain—?"

My mother shook her head and squeezed Danice's hand. "You are his ama now."

The maid took a shuddering inhale. "I will protect him with my life."

"I know." My mother smiled through her own tears. "Which is why you are exactly who he needs."

"Give us a quarter of an hour to get across the courtyard," I said to my mother as I snuffed out the lamp closest to the doorway, "and then do whatever you can to create a diversion."

"If there's anything I'm skilled at, it's making a commotion." She winked, then waved her hands. "Now, *go*."

Grateful for the many times I'd slipped out of this chamber undetected, I led Danice out into the courtyard. Dressed as we were in dark clothing, we blended easily with the deep shadows beneath the eaves. Pausing behind an enormous blooming rock rose, we listened for footsteps. Years of tracking the eunuchs' nightly rotations had taught me to wait until they'd passed through the gate at the other end of the women's wing before attempting to steal through the courtyard.

I grabbed Danice's hand, squeezing as I breathed out, "Ready?"

"I don't want to leave her," she whispered back. "Especially with you being married soon. If I had a choice . . ."

My stomach wrenched at the reminder that my time in Tyre was far too short. "I know."

"But I have faith Yahweh will finish what he has begun."

I had no chance to ask what she meant before Rahej walked through the gate at the far end of the courtyard, whistling softly as he approached the large fountain at the center. He paused there, bending to swish his fingers in the burbling water, which was finally flowing again after weeks of the rooftop cisterns being dry. And then, to my dismay, he folded his arms and turned up his chin to study the night sky.

I went rigid. We had no time to wait while this eunuch gazed at the stars. The guard rotation outside the gardens would be changing soon. And even if Danice had fed Otzar well earlier, he could wake at any moment. My pulse thrummed as my mind spun in circles, seeking a solution.

But then my mother began to scream.

I winced, hating the distressing cry after weeks of calm, but at least this time the sound of shattering grief had a purpose.

"No! No!" she wailed. "Why did he send her away? *Why?*"

Rahej ran through the courtyard, black robes flying. Since he'd only been promoted to this wing of the palace after Magin's death, he'd never experienced one of my mother's episodes and likely thought she was under attack.

The moment he plowed through the door, Danice and I dashed across the courtyard and through the gate leading into a narrow corridor that bridged the women's wing with the rest of the palace. The sound of booted footsteps approaching halted us, and I pressed Danice into a dark corner before running forward to meet the three guards, hands splayed wide.

"Thank the stars!" I cried out, leaning into desperation. "My mother needs help! Please hurry!"

"What is wrong, my lady?" said one of the shocked guards.

"I don't know. She's screaming in her room—please, go see what is happening. What if those people who attacked our ship have come for us?"

Fooled by the terror in my plea, the three men dashed away. As soon as they were out of sight, I grabbed Danice's arm, helped her to her feet, and we were off again, down a flight of stairs and through the servants' courtyard, where two gossiping female cooks stared at us with open mouths as we passed by.

"Say nothing!" I rasped, hoping my status was enough to keep them quiet. Or at least if they were questioned, Danice and I would already be safe behind the door.

The baby squawked, awakened from being jostled. We only slowed long enough for Danice to press the twisted end of a milk-soaked rag into his little mouth, which he greedily began to suckle before we were off again. By the time we'd made it to the Garden of Beasts, both of us were panting. There were rarely guards in this area of the palace grounds, so I slowed our pace on the winding path.

A canine howl echoed off in the darkness, raising gooseflesh on my arms. No wonder Mattaniel had been so on edge when he'd been following me that night. I had been sneaking through here in the dark so long, I had forgotten how eerie it was to pass by cage after cage of wild animals gnashing their teeth, shrieking, or staring at us with voracious yellow eyes.

When we finally pushed past the sprawling oleander near the wall, every muscle in my body was strung like a bow. I came to a halt in front of the wooden door, which I could barely see in the few shafts of moonlight that slipped through the thick branches.

My stomach sank. *He's not here.*

Perhaps we'd only arrived before him but what if something had gone awry? What would I do with Danice and the baby if he never came? Even if we made it onto the beach below, I had no idea where to take her from there.

A horrible realization struck me square in the chest. "Oh no!"

"What is it?" Danice whispered.

I pressed my fingers to my temples with a groan. "I forgot the key."

"What key?"

"This door has a lock. I was in such a rush, I forgot to retrieve the key from its hiding place."

As if he sensed the precarious situation I'd put us in, Otzar let out a sharp cry that cut through the night like a blade. Danice hushed him, fumbling to replace the suckling rag before he alerted the entire palace where we were.

"Elissa?"

The voice on the other side of the door was muffled. I pressed my face near the hinge. "Mattaniel? Is that you?"

"Yes." His voice was closer now. "Why haven't you opened the lock?"

"I forgot the key."

He went silent for a moment, likely as frustrated with me as I was with myself. "Back away from the door."

Danice and I obeyed, pressing ourselves back into the oleander bush.

Boom.

Boom.

The door shivered with each strike. Then there was a long pause. Mattaniel was strong for certain; I'd seen him take on the pirate, but that door was thick and made of—

BOOM!

The door swung open with a horrible crack, slamming into the stone as a large body flew across the threshold, falling with a pained grunt and a thud that shook the ground under our feet.

Mattaniel appeared in the doorway, holding a small torch. "Elissa?" he whispered.

"We're here," I said but did not move since the other man was still sprawled on the ground in front of us. As he pushed back to his feet, groaning and stretching to his full height, Danice leaned into me. Whoever he was, he was enormous, even taller than Mattaniel and with a hulking form. One of my father's guard, perhaps?

"It's all right." Mattaniel came forward and I could barely see his face in the meager moonlight. "I promise you are safe. This is Avidan." He paused, then shocked me to my bones when he said, "My cousin."

25

Mattaniel

While Avidan led Danice and the baby down the stairs, Elissa held me back by the arm.

"You are certain these men are your cousins?"

"I am fairly convinced." I told her of the scars on their palms that matched my own. "And you were right. I *was* raised as a priest. Or at least, I was born a Levite, the tribe set aside to perform sacred duties along with the *kohanim*. I am from a small community called Naioth, which was founded by a famed prophet to teach the things of Yahweh. My father is one of the instructors, which is why I have memories about sitting with a group of students. My cousins said that even as a tiny boy, I begged to go listen as he explained the Torah."

For as desperate as I'd been to have answers, the flood of information my cousins had offered was almost overwhelming. When we'd parted ways last night, my head was spinning. Most surprising of all had been that they'd been in Tyre for weeks trying to find a way to get close to me. Avidan had spent day after day talking with people in the market, trying to discover how to steal inside the royal compound, with no success. Zevi and Gavi had made contacts among the guard, which was why they'd been at the tavern the day I'd delivered the parcel to Shamzur's laundress. They'd chased after me then but hadn't been able to catch up before I reached the palace gates. Gavi had even told me how impressed he was with my long-legged stride, saying that when I was a boy I'd always been frustrated when I could not keep up.

Yet, after all that time and effort, the three of them had merely stumbled across my path last night. Gavi had seen me pass by him in the street while I'd been too preoccupied to notice I was being followed and alerted the others. They'd wisely encircled me, knowing I would otherwise have fled without hesitation.

"My name is Shalem," I told her, saying it aloud for the first time. "Shalem ben Iyov."

She inhaled, wide-eyed, pausing before she spoke. Then, even though I could not see her face, the smile in her voice was evident as she said, "It is very good to meet you, *Shalem*."

The sound of my name, my real name, on her lips nearly undid the resolve I'd made to not repeat my brazen actions on the ship.

Down below, the baby let out a sharp cry, which echoed around the cave and broke me out of my Elissa-induced stupor. "The tide will be coming in soon. We'd better hurry."

"Are you certain she will be safe with this woman?"

After we'd closed the door Avidan had plowed through like an ox, I'd swiftly explained the plans we'd made to transport Danice and the baby to the hamlet.

"Raphad's wife is a kind woman, I assure you. And they'll be well beyond the boundary your father set for the Asherites."

"And what about you?" Elissa asked, her voice soft. "Are you returning with your cousins?"

There was an edge of pain in her tone, an echo of the ache in my chest when I thought of watching her leave with the Shardan.

"Not yet. Not until I know for certain you are safe."

"Why wouldn't I be?"

"I think someone within the palace may have been involved in the attacks."

"Who?"

I dare not accuse her brother of treason when I had no proof, but his involvement with the Philistines pushing for war with Saul, the fact that his ship had tarried behind the king's, and both Haldon and the Sidonians arriving at the same tavern all added up to suspicious circumstances.

"I am not certain," I hedged. "Which is why I am not going anywhere . . . for now."

Since Avidan had taken our only light, Elissa once again led me down the stairway, counting aloud each of the sixty-five steps in the blackness. Once we emerged from the cave, I guided her to where we'd landed in a small, well-protected inlet where guards up on the wall could not see our boat.

It had taken only a note from the king, impressed with the royal seal, for me to leave the palace grounds on a purported official errand before meeting my cousins at the docks just before nightfall. I hated to abuse the freedom I was afforded by Komar, but in this instance, it was warranted.

Avidan had already settled Danice and the baby in the boat. He and Zevi stood thigh-deep in the waves, holding onto the vessel he'd borrowed from some local fisherman he'd befriended, while Gavi met Elissa and me at the edge of the water.

"Took you long enough, little cousin," he said, a note of humor in his voice. I still had trouble accepting that all the stories Adin had told me about this fearless warrior, brilliant spy, and talented metalsmith were about my own cousin. "Although, I can't call you *little* anymore, now, can I?" He scrubbed at his bearded jaw with a grin. "Still no facial hair, though."

I ignored his teasing. The three of them had made much of my height last night, saying I'd been small and slight even as a youth, which had apparently been quite a sore point for me then. Besides, my beard had been just as full as his while I'd been on Shardana. I'd let it grow as soon as I was free to do so.

I fished a folded sheet of papyrus from my belt. "Here are the false caravans I planted in the documents. One for tomorrow and another the next day. I made it seem as though they were both carrying costly materials meant for a replacement of the king's vessel. If the pattern holds, they'll attack near the crossroads south of the city."

The humor dropped from Gavi's face as he received the list, replaced by the deadly seriousness I would expect of a seasoned spy. "Excellent work."

"And you remember where I told you Portea's home is?"

He nodded. "We'll find it."

"Don't scare the poor woman. She was only expecting me to escort Danice to her door."

"Noted." His brows arched. "You certain you aren't coming?"

I shook my head. "I have work to do."

Gavi's eyes tracked to Elissa, who was looking back and forth between us, probably confused by talk of the plan we'd conjured to entrap whoever was attacking caravans. If Haldon was involved, as I guessed, then the false shipping documents I'd given Tabnit earlier for his apprentice to deliver would be irresistible bait.

"Will they be safe?" Elissa asked him.

"I vow to protect them with the same care I do my own wife and children, my lady," said Gavi, right hand pressed to his heart. As irreverent as he seemed to be much of the time, his sincerity in this was unmistakable.

Elissa thanked him and then he joined the others to climb into the boat. Avidan pushed the vessel out into the water and was pulled aboard by Zevi. As they rowed into the night, Danice waved to the woman at my side, who silently slipped her cold hand into mine.

"I cannot thank you enough," she said. "My mother is so relieved."

"Portea will take good care of them."

"My mother sent a fortune in silver with Danice, so she'll be able to pay for her keep."

"Did she?" I chuckled. I could only imagine Portea's surprise when the woman she'd agreed to rescue out of the goodness of her heart ended up rescuing her as well. It seemed Yahweh had smoothed the path for both women in a way I'd never anticipated.

Elissa's eyes were still trained on where the boat had disappeared from sight. "They must really love you to have come so far to find you."

"I don't remember them." I frowned, rubbing at the scar on my brow that I now knew for certain I'd received falling from a cedar tree while trying to keep up with my older cousins in the woods around our grandfather's house. "They must be the three boys from my dreams. But they are still strangers to me. I guess I hoped . . ."

"That your memory would come flooding back if you discovered who you were?"

I released a deep sigh. "Yes, exactly. I may have been born Shalem, the son of a Levite, but I only know how to be Mattaniel, the slave."

She was quiet for a while. "You are both. But then . . . perhaps, also neither."

"What do you mean?"

"Sometimes I wonder what it would have been like had my infant brother not died. Perhaps my mother would still be Abibaal's favorite and my life wouldn't be defined by constant worry and fear. But I think, maybe, I am stronger than I would have been if I'd lived carefree. I may not see the world in the same way."

She bent down, digging in the sand for a moment. When she stood again, she held a broken mussel shell in her hand. "This once held a creature out there in the sea but at some point was separated from its original purpose. It was tossed about by the waves, shattered and dragged across the sea floor for who knows how long." She turned it over, the opalescent shine of its underside gleaming in the moonlight. "And yet what remains was made smooth by sand and polished by seawater. Now it's so beautiful it could find new life as a piece of jewelry on some wealthy woman's neck or finger."

She handed me the shell. "No matter where you came from Mattan—" She paused and smiled. "Shalem. The things you've endured have shaped you into someone new. Someone who is selfless enough to risk his own life for others, repeatedly. Someone I am very grateful to know."

I clutched the shell in my fist, throat tight. "My years in slavery have been difficult, sometimes painfully so. But I think I would go through it all over again to have met you. If only . . ." I took a deep breath. "If only I were free . . ."

"Perhaps, just for now," she said, coming so close that all I could see was her beautiful face, "we could pretend we *both* were free."

"I like that idea very much." I lost the fight against what remained of my good sense to slide my hands around her waist and pull her even closer.

I bent my head, whispering words of adoration in a language I was certain she did not know before pressing my lips to hers once again.

The kiss on the ship had been hurried and desperate, one I'd been convinced was not only my first but my last. Now I took the time to explore her soft, sweet lips, to let myself pretend that this was the second of thousands of kisses with the woman I loved and there was nothing in the world to keep us apart.

However, Elissa quickly seemed to lose patience with my leisurely pace and, on a hum I felt in my bones, tangled her fingers in the curls at the nape of my neck and pressed herself into me. The very last thread of my restraint snapped, and I gave in to her silent urge for more.

How would I ever let her go now? I wasn't certain I could survive watching her sail away with Torben or whoever would have the privilege of holding her this way for the rest of his life.

She pulled back, breaths short and quick against my mouth. "Let's go, Shalem. *Now*."

My head was far too muddled by desire to parse her meaning. "Where?"

"Anywhere. Away from here. I don't care if we swim to the mainland. The idea of never seeing you again . . ." She shook her head, frowning. "Let's be free together. We'll go with your cousins to Naioth. Make a new life there where no one knows who I am."

She stood on tiptoe, and as she pressed her mouth to mine again, I dreamed of what it would be like to run. To snatch her away from this place and refuse to let the king of Tyre sell her for the sake of expanding his kingdom. And yet it did not take long for reality to sneak through the cracks.

"Wait." I pulled back but did not release my grip on her waist. "What about your mother? Your sisters?"

Her swollen lips parted as she blinked up at me, then frowned as if she, like me, had suddenly remembered the high cost of our escape. Too many lives were at stake to give in to our selfish desires.

Wordlessly, I pressed the shell back into her hand.

A light flashed across Elissa's face, illuminating pain in those gorgeous eyes at the same time a shout echoed off the rocks nearby. I twisted, pushing Elissa behind my back. A group of men barreled toward us across the rocky beach, a few with torches in hand and two with black robes fluttering around their long legs.

"Let her go!" Abenasser snapped as he outpaced the rest of the men, a long, thin blade pointed at me.

"No!" Elissa yanked out of my hold to throw herself in front of me. The eunuch practically snarled at her to get out of the way, but she stood fast, arms outstretched. "Leave him alone. He's done nothing wrong!"

He ignored her pleas and grabbed her by the wrists, yanking so hard she fell into him with a cry. I darted forward, but the other eunuch had slipped around me while I was distracted, hooking his arm around my neck to jerk me away while the other one dragged Elissa farther from my reach.

"You should have kept your hands off the king's daughter, *Hebrew*," the man snarled into my ear as he held a blade to my throat.

"Stop this, please!" Elissa cried. "He is innocent."

Abenasser's scowl seemed wrong on such a softly rounded face. "Then he can explain to the king why he was spotted sneaking onto this beach with a boat full of men in the middle of the night."

My gut wrenched. We'd been so careful to avoid being seen. I could only hope my cousins were far away with Danice and the baby.

"I vow to you, Abenasser, all he was doing was helping me!" Elissa argued.

"Yes, I know all about your maid's escape. Let's go."

She fought against him.. "You do? How?"

He swung around on her, and I went rigid at the fury on his face. "Do you think me a *fool*, Elissa? As soon as Rahej said you'd been spotted running into the gardens, I knew you were heading for that door. Yes, yes . . . I've always known about the door. Why do you think you were never bothered when you and your sisters stole down here to swim?"

Elissa stared at him with her mouth gaping wide. "You knew?"

"Believe me, I regret the indulgence now. Because I will have to explain this all to the king, who will be furious when he discovers you've been hiding a Hebrew. Especially when he hears you were tangled up with this traitor while his docks burn."

"What are you talking about?" She dug her feet into the sand, refusing to let him pull her away easily.

He jerked her so hard she cried out in pain, and if the eunuch at my back didn't have the point of his dagger pressed into the side of my neck, I'd already have broken Abenasser's jaw for hurting her. But his next words stopped me short. "The harbor is on fire, Elissa. Your brother's ship was among the first to burn."

"What?" she gasped, going limp with shock.

"Yarikh is dead," the eunuch spat out as he dragged her away. "And I suspect *your lover* is to blame."

26

Elissa

I hadn't slept all night. I could only stare at the ceiling, seeing Shalem being hauled off by the guards over and over, wondering if it was the last time I'd ever see him alive.

I'd begged to see my father last night, demanded it even, but Abenasser insisted he was far too busy dealing with the raging fire down at the harbor and directing the search for those responsible to listen to my protests about his scribe's innocence. Instead, I was escorted to our room, where two eunuchs were stationed by the door and one at the window. It seemed Abenasser was taking no more chances with me.

My mother had been devastated when I told her of Yarikh's death, saying she'd always remember him as that scared little boy who begged her for songs after his own mother died. She'd cried herself to sleep beside me, grieving both for him and for the loss of Danice and the babe. I feared all of this would throw her back into the deep valley she'd finally climbed out of after so long.

An hour after dawn, I slid out of the bed, trying not to jostle my mother, and began to dress myself in the finest of my gowns, preparing to once again beg for an audience with the king, but then Melita flew into the room, golden hair unbound and blue eyes unlined by her usual kohl. She was followed by a solemn-looking Seriyah, whom I'd not seen since the shipwreck.

"Lissi! What *happened* last night?" said Meli. "My maid says there are horrible rumors flying about. And why are they guarding your door?"

"I got caught helping Danice escape."

Melita's eyes went wide. "She's gone?"

I nodded. "Mattaniel's . . . friends took her to a safe place on the mainland. But Abenasser caught us down on the beach. He also said someone set fire to the docks and that Yarikh was killed."

Melita gasped, hand on her mouth. "Oh no! Are we under attack?"

"I don't know, but they are accusing Mattaniel of being involved. They dragged him off somewhere. And all he was doing was helping *me*."

"Why didn't you tell me what was happening? I would have helped you."

"I didn't want to worry you."

Her mouth flattened. "You mean you didn't trust me."

"That's not why—"

"We both would have helped," said Seriyah. "Why didn't you come to us?"

"You have far more important things to deal with, Seri. Your wedding, your brother, your mother—"

"Is sitting in bed, content to be served her every whim," she said. "She is grieving, to be sure, but every indication is that the babe is fine. I'm reeling over Ahiram's loss, but that doesn't mean I have forgotten my sisters." She folded her arms. "And as for the wedding, I don't think that's the most important thing right now, do you?"

"There was no need to burden either of you with this situation. Nor for you to have to answer for my actions."

"This is my fault," said my mother. She sat up in the bed, remnants of yesterday's kohl still streaked down her cheeks.

"It was my decision to help Danice, Ama."

"No. I mean, it's because of me that you try to carry the entire world on your shoulders." She shook her head. "I'm so sorry, Elissa. Now that my eyes are clear, I can see what is right in front of me."

"What is that?"

"You. My precious daughter. I've been in such a thick fog for so long that I could barely see my own hand in front of my face, let alone the innocent girl who grew into a capable woman with very little help from me. Who had to shoulder the burden of a mother so consumed by grief and pain that she lost herself in it. *You* had to bear the weight of my fits of sadness and bitterness and watch me prostrate myself before powerless gods, begging for help they could not provide."

She gestured to the corner. For as long as I could remember, the ivory-inland table there had been inhabited by a gathering of statuary. Astarte had been the largest of the assembly, her golden arms outstretched and usually holding fresh garlands of flowers or blooming branches as offerings. Over the years, other gods had joined the throng: various depictions of Ba'al, one of a lion-headed Melqart, even Eshmun—the Sidonian god of healing—among lesser gods. And at the center of it all, that lone oil lamp used to flicker day and night among the daily food and drink offerings. Now all that remained on the table in that once-sacred corner was a vase of wilting flowers.

"Where are they? And the lamp?"

"Gone. I had one of the servants take the last of them back to the sanctuary yesterday."

I frowned at her in bewilderment. How had I not noticed? "But . . . why?"

"Because there is only one God who had the power to bring me back to life. Yahweh, the God of the Hebrews."

My jaw gaped. "What . . . ? How . . . ?"

She shrugged. "Danice stopped being afraid."

"I don't understand."

"It was she who had to fetch those daily offerings for my gods.

Gods that, according to her people, are not only false but evil. It was not until Yahweh gave her another child—through you, my love—that she finally gathered the courage to tell me no."

She explained that Danice had trembled from head to foot as she told my mother she would no longer take any part in laying offerings before graven images Yahweh called abominations. It had so shocked my mother that she agreed to ask another servant to attend the duty. Over the next few days, she asked her maid questions about this mysterious God and became fascinated by stories of a deity who rescued his people from slavery, shook entire cities to the ground, fought impossible battles *for* them against powerful enemies, and called himself "The God Who Heals."

"One night, I decided that if the gods of Tyre and Sidon were deaf to my pleas, perhaps I ought to try calling out to Danice's God instead. I asked that, if he was a God who heals, then to show himself to me. To *free* me." A slow grin grew on her face. "The very next morning, I woke with such a burning desire to go outside and bathe in the sunlight, I could do nothing but obey it. It was, as I said, like a fog had lifted. After so many years of heaviness, of terrible whispers that harassed me day and night, the weight—the oppression—was gone."

"But we aren't Hebrew," said Melita. "Why would their God heal you?"

"Danice said he is the God above all gods. The King of the Universe, not only the tribes of Israel. So, I had the servants take away the idols. And the lamp too."

I understood the implication. She'd finally let go of the obsession with keeping that flame alive in my infant brother's place.

"You still believe this Yahweh is God over all, even though your maid had to leave with the baby?" Seriyah asked.

My mother took a deep breath. "I questioned that too, but Danice told me the story of a woman named Hagar. A concubine who endured much heartache as well. But when she was cast out of her home and her only child lay dying in the wilderness, she cried out to Yahweh in the midst of that pain and he heard her.

Provided for her. Promised a future she never could have imagined. That didn't mean all her suffering was gone, but she clung to that hope, and it sustained her.

"And yes, I am heartbroken over losing my friend and Otzar, and the death of Yarikh. And yes—" she came close, curving her warm hands around my face as she stared into my eyes—"I hate to think of my daughter leaving. But I have *hope* now. Hope that something good will come of all this sorrow. And for the first time in my entire life, I finally feel free."

27

Mattaniel

Every breath hurt.

I lay crumpled in the same place the guards left me when they threw me into a dark, frigid cell somewhere in the bowels of Abibaal's fortress. The thrashing the Sidonian traders had given me before they sold me in Ashdod was nothing compared to what the king's men had inflicted tonight. And no matter that I protested my innocence in the plot against the throne of Tyre, insisting it was not Asherites who'd killed the princes, but men from Sidon, the guards in charge of my torturous interrogation refused to listen.

At least when I died here on this cold stone floor, I would do so finally knowing who I was and where I came from.

"You alive?" croaked a voice nearby.

Loath to move my swollen jaw, I moaned in response.

"You didn't tell them where anyone is, did you?"

The man was speaking a Hebrew dialect, not that of the Tyrians. "Who's . . . there?"

Instead of answering, two men gently lifted me from the floor, then helped me lean against the frigid wall of the cell. It felt like paradise against the bruises on my back.

Through the narrow slit of my swollen right eye, I peered at the seven shadowy figures gathered around me. From what I could see by the dim flicker of a torch outside the cell, they too had bruises and bloodied faces, torn garments, and crimson slashes across their limbs. Tortured like me.

"Who are you?" I mumbled, regardless of the searing pain in my jaw.

"Ithiel," said the man beside me. "Son of Baruch, an elder of Asher. Who are you, son?"

I inhaled, then regretted it from the way pain lashed around my torso. But for the first time, I could speak with knowledge of my true parentage. "I am Shalem ben Iyov, a Levite of Naioth. And, until this morning, personal scribe to the king of Tyre."

"A Levite in the house of Abibaal?" Ithiel's shock was echoed by murmurs of disbelief from his companions. "How did that come about?"

I huffed a sardonic laugh through painfully gritted teeth. "A long story."

"Seems we have plenty of time," said another man.

I let my head tip back against the wall and took a few more deep breaths before telling them how I was lost, enslaved, and eventually ended up in service to Abibaal, only to be caught helping an Asherite maid escape and then blamed for the fire on the docks.

"Why are our people being held responsible for all of this?" asked the youngest of the group, who could not be more than fifteen—the same age I'd been when I'd been lost. "We've done nothing. We pay our taxes like everyone else and live in peace with Tyre. Sidon, too, for that matter. It is our olive groves that supply most of the oil in this region. Our grain that fills the storehouses of the king."

"Because," said Ithiel, "long before you were born, Zimri, a few zealots thought they could succeed where Yehoshua and our ancestors failed—by driving the rest of the Canaanites out of the land given to us by Yahweh. The only thing they accomplished was getting themselves killed. Whoever is behind this plot must have decided that history made us an easy scapegoat."

"Why did you not flee the city as soon as Abibaal sent out that edict?" I asked.

"Hundreds did. Some have taken refuge in the territory of Naftali," said another man. "But many are in hiding in the hills, hoping Abibaal will relent."

"Then why are you here?"

"That is my fault," said Ithiel, his voice cracking. "I asked my brothers to help me."

"We all agreed it was worth the risk," said Zimri.

"What was?"

"The Torah scrolls," replied Ithiel. "Gifted by Samuel the Seer to the elders of Asher decades ago. They have been protected by our family since then, kept hidden beneath our uncle's home. He was one of the shipbuilders driven from the city weeks ago after the king accused them of sabotage. There was no time to take the scrolls then, so we were attempting to retrieve them. Unfortunately, we made our attempt just before the docks were set on fire, and we were arrested. They burned the priceless scrolls in front of us. Now, unless those who are guilty of these attacks are found, *we* will die in their place."

The prison cell went quiet after the dire pronouncement. Shortly, a few of the men began breathing heavily as exhaustion overtook them. But I could not find a comfortable position for my body, nor could I keep my mind from reliving the moment Elissa was dragged away by Abenasser, weeping over her brother's death but also pleading my innocence. I'd felt powerless for many years, but never as much as I had last night.

"I still cannot believe a Levite has been living in the court of Abibaal," Ithiel said, his voice low.

"As I said, I only discovered I was a Levite a couple of days ago."

"Still. It has to be significant that of all the places you could have ended up, it was the house of a king."

"Why would that matter? I don't remember my youth in Naioth. I have never trained as a priest or a prophet. I am no one of consequence. A slave."

"You were not born a slave. You are a descendant of Levi and therefore called to a holy purpose."

The hair on the back of my neck prickled. "What purpose is that?"

"To protect and preserve the Word of Yahweh. To remind Israel of her holiness and the terms of the covenant we made with Almighty God at the foot of the Mountain. To proclaim and uphold truth."

"Even if that is the case, what use is such a calling in this prison cell?"

"I certainly do not know the mind of Yahweh, Shalem, nor can I understand his ways. But if He allowed your path to diverge from that of your cousins all those years ago, perhaps it was so that you would be here now, in the house of a foreign king, when truth needs most to be proclaimed."

"But how can I do that if Abibaal won't listen to me?"

He let out a slow breath. "You'll have to take that up with the only one who can answer it for you."

Ithiel went silent then, his soft snores soon joining those of his brothers, and I was left alone in the darkness with his words. *"You are a descendant of Levi and therefore called to a holy purpose."*

Even after what seemed like hours of pleading with the King of the Universe to give me the opportunity to help my cousins and my people, I felt little comfort and endured a restless, troubled sleep.

And when I woke to the foreboding sound of a key clanking inside the iron lock, I was certain that day would be my last.

28

Elissa

My father flatly refused to see me, although I'd pleaded with his steward for only a few moments of his time. And my mother's attempt to claim an audience with him had been thwarted as well. Increasingly fearful for Shalem's safety, I considered trying to send a message to his cousins through Raphad's wife, but since Rahej said no one was allowed to pass in or out of the gates today, all I could do was pace the room, worrying.

Seriyah and Melita appeared at our door that afternoon to offer a small measure of reprieve from my imprisonment. They'd talked Abenasser into letting the three of us walk together in the gardens until sunset—accompanied by Rahej and another eunuch, along with a couple of guards. We invited my mother to join us, but she said she planned to join the other concubines and their children out in the courtyard pool for a swim, something she'd not done in years that I could recall.

The difference in her was truly remarkable. All day long, I expected her to fall to pieces over Yarikh's death and Danice's departure. But instead of wailing or raging or disappearing into blank-eyed paralysis, she'd gently probed me about Shalem for a while, then stared out the window, watching the birds in the trees, once in a while quietly wiping tears from her cheeks. I must have been blind not to see how drastically she'd changed over the past few weeks. Even though she was grieving, her skin was no longer pale, her cheeks and lips were full of color, and even her hair seemed to shine as it once did when I was young. I wasn't certain what it all meant, but I was so very grateful to the God of the Hebrews for bringing her back to life and wished I had asked Shalem more about him when I had the chance.

"Do you know where he's being held?" asked Melita once we'd walked far enough ahead of our guard not to be overheard.

I shook my head. "Not that it would do any good even if I did."

"I don't understand why you did not tell us how you felt about this man," said Seriyah. "We vowed to always tell each other everything."

"There was not much to tell you, Seri. He was my tutor. A servant. I was trying not to be caught up in impossible fantasies. The last thing I wanted to do was distract you from your own wedding plans."

One black brow arched imperiously. "It wasn't as if we did not notice you went from avoiding those lessons to counting the hours until the next one."

"I saw how you looked at him as we boarded the ship," said Melita. "As if it were painful to stay away."

I gave her a helpless shrug. "It seems I am much more transparent than I thought. Not that it matters when I have no control over my own future."

Without discussion, we turned onto the path leading to the Garden of Beasts. In the daylight, there was none of the skin-prickling foreboding as animals watched us pass from behind the bars of secure cages. However, for the first time, I realized how much I had in common with these prized beasts of my father. I, too, lived in a gilded cage, well cared for and celebrated for my beauty, the walls that protected me from danger impossibly thick with foundations deep in the bedrock of Tyre. Going to

Shardana would only change the location of my prison, not set me free.

"I have hope *now . . ."* my mother had said this morning. *"And for the first time in my entire life, I finally feel free."*

Could it be that she'd found the key that might unlock my own cage too?

"Are you certain there's nothing to be done about the treaty? It's not signed yet, after all," Seriyah said, while Melita pressed her fingers through the bars of an enclosure and wiggled them to beckon the striped sand cats. The tiny felines froze at the intrusion, huge ears twitching and tails bushed, then disappeared into a hole in the ground.

"Believe me, I tried."

My sisters chuckled as I told them how I'd feigned ignorance for the first few lessons, hoping Yarikh would have success convincing Abibaal not to send me away. "Once Shalem saw through my ruse and came up with the written Shardan language, I could no longer play the fool, so I figured I'd use the knowledge to my advantage instead. From what he told me, the king of the Shardan is enthralled with Tyre, so I hoped to negotiate with him myself before the treaty was cut."

"Negotiate for what?"

"Ships," I said. "Above anything else, Shalem says the king wants vessels like ours, ones that can not only sail long distances for trade but can protect his shores from invaders. I hoped to convince him to ask Abibaal for ships instead of a bride, and possibly even timber, along with the chance to learn our techniques so they could build their own vessels on Shardana. The king wants those silver mines; I doubt he cares how he procures them. But even if I avoid marriage to a Shardan man, Abibaal will choose another."

"Perhaps if your Shalem can get free, we can find a way to—"

Melita's words halted when shouts echoed across the palace grounds, followed by one sharp blast of a signal horn. The three of us stared wide-eyed as high atop the wall, a few guards ran in the direction of the gates. Were we under attack by whomever burned the docks and killed Yarikh? Another guard had joined those charged with watching over us, waving his hands as he spoke with Rahej. Curious, I strode back along the path, my sisters in my wake.

"What is happening?" I asked as the guard ran back toward the palace.

"Nothing to worry about," Rahej said. "You're safe here."

"Are we being invaded?"

"No, my lady," the eunuch said. "It's only a couple of Hebrews causing a commotion at the gates. The guards have it in hand."

The hair on the back of my neck rose. "Are you ready to return to the palace?" Rahej asked.

"No," I replied a little too quickly, then cleared my throat. "I am enjoying the air after being cooped up all day. And Melita wants to see the lions before we go inside."

Meli frowned at me curiously but then Seriyah slid her arm through mine and Meli's to guide us back the way we'd come. "Me too. And the monkeys. I wish we'd brought some fruit to entice them . . ."

After fifteen paces, Seriyah dropped her voice. "It's your tutor's cousins, isn't it?"

I hoped the crown prince of Gebal knew what a canny woman he was gaining as his future queen. It would be to his own detriment if he underestimated her.

"That's my guess," I said. "But what can I do? There are four men watching our every move."

"We need a distraction of some sort, so you can go find out." Melita bent over a low stone fence to pet a stout hyrax. "Oh, you are sweet." She cooed as it leaned into the caress, groaning with pleasure. "I wish you could come back with me."

Seri and I met gazes.

"Meli, you are brilliant," I said.

"I am?"

I grinned. "I think you should absolutely let the hyrax out of their enclosure."

"I'll see to the monkeys," said Seri, already striding away.

I glanced around, my eyes landing on another enclosure housing two brown bear cubs just weaned from their mother. They were too distracted rolling about in the dirt together to notice as I unlatched the handle of their cage, but when I clicked my tongue a few times, their attention swung to the open gate.

Within moments, they'd bumbled out of the enclosure, tripping happily over their own paws as they loped down the path toward the palace.

A few monkeys dashed by, squawking in joy at their freedom, the rest already screaming from nearby trees.

"Go!" Seriyah waved us toward the two eunuchs who stood in the pathway, looking utterly bewildered at the sudden chaos. The guards had already taken off after the bear cubs.

"Help!" Meli shouted as she ran toward Rahej, sounding genuinely terrified. The startled eunuch caught her in his arms as Seriyah barreled toward the other wide-eyed Crow, a squealing hyrax passing by them on the way.

I did not wait for either of the men to catch their bearings but turned and ran, glad I knew these garden paths like the lines on my own palm. I pressed through a row of thick hedges, then yanked up my skirt to climb over a stone fence and cross through another enclosure, startling three red-tailed foxes that scurried into their den. Once on the other side, I followed the path past lions, an elephant, and black-and-white-striped horses before climbing over the garden fence and landing with a grunt on the path once again. I ignored the shouts from behind me and sped toward the gates.

When I came around the corner of the palace and saw what had caused the guards to come running, I'd whispered a prayer of thanks to Shalem's God for my sisters, because we'd been right. His cousins *had* come for him.

Sword drawn, Zevi stood confidently in front of the well-armed guard alongside two tied and gagged men in Hebrew garb. In the other hand, he gripped a lead rope knotted around their bound wrists and necks. Avidan had two others secured, and Gavriel stood beside yet another man, the biggest of the pack, a gleaming bronze knife held to his throat. All the captives looked to have been thrashed thoroughly, their faces a mass of bruises and cuts.

". . . not until we see our cousin," Zevi was saying to the head of the guard. "If the king wants to know who is responsible for the death of his sons, he'll release him."

"What is the meaning of this?" My father bounded down the front steps of the palace, fury on his face and robes flying.

"These men claim to have captured Hebrew traitors," said the captain of the guard. "But they refuse to talk to anyone but you."

"Take them all into custody," said Abibaal with a wave of his hand. "It's a trick."

"No!" I shouted, bolting forward. "They are telling the truth!"

The king startled, scowling as I flew up the stairs to meet him. "Elissa? What are you doing? Get inside."

"You have to listen! These are Mattaniel's cousins!"

"I thought the scribe did not know who he was or where he came from."

There was no way to explain the situation easily, so instead I challenged him. "If you arrest them now, you'll never know who killed Ahiram and Yarikh."

His jaw worked back and forth as he scrutinized my face. "Fine. But you stay right here." He pointed to the step beneath my feet, then looked at someone behind me. "*Watch* her."

Abenasser appeared at my side, his long fingers wrapping around my arm. "Of course, my king."

I glanced up at the eunuch, but he would not meet my eyes. He looked nearly as livid as my father. I wondered if he would ever let me out of the women's wing after this.

Abibaal descended the rest of the stairs, standing ten paces from Zevi, his arms folded over his wide chest. "Speak."

Shalem's elder cousin did not seem intimidated in the least by my father. "We have proof of not only our cousin's innocence but a plot against your throne. One from *inside* your own house."

My father scoffed. "You bring me more Hebrews? What proof

is that, other than your king means to topple me and claim my territory?"

"All is not as it seems. Gavriel, show the king who these men actually are."

Gavriel jerked the rope tied to his captive, dragging the struggling man closer to the king. Swords raised, the palace guards crowded toward him, but Gavriel's knife flashed as he stuck the tip of it into the captive's neckline and ripped his tunic from sternum to navel. Then, with one foot, he kicked the man in the back of the knee, making him fall to the ground. Behind his gag, the crimson-faced man growled muffled curses.

"Look for yourself," he said, knife already sheathed.

Scowling, the captain of the guard started toward Gavriel, but my father raised a staying palm. "It's fine."

Abibaal approached and tugged the torn neckline to the side, revealing a large tattoo on the man's chest. *Eshmun*. Just as Shalem had said. This was a man devoted to the god of Sidon.

Relief flooded through me as my father yanked the gag from the captive's mouth. "Who are you?"

The man sneered and spat at the king.

Before my father could even recoil, Gavriel moved like lightning, wrestling the captive to the ground and pressing his elbow into the man's neck to grind his face into the dirt.

"Show the king of Tyre *respect*," he said through gritted teeth.

The Sidonian refused to relent, spitting foul curses at Gavriel and trying to twist from his iron grip.

"Perhaps he needs more incentive," Zevi said, his tone terrifyingly flat.

"With pleasure," Gavriel ground out, once again drawing that long, jagged bronze knife from his belt. I watched in fascinated horror as Shalem's cousin hacked the man's smallest finger from his hand.

The scream that came out of the Sidonian's mouth was echoed by the loosed monkeys in the distant trees while his blood soaked the dirt.

"Now," Gavriel said, voice lifted over the man's redoubled curses, "tell the king who you are and why you were lying in wait by the crossroads south of the city."

The man shook his head, his face white with pain.

"All right," said Gavriel almost gleefully as he lifted his bloodied knife, "you have nine more—"

"No! Please!" the Sidonian cried. "I'll tell you, stop!"

Gavriel halted, a satisfied smirk on his face. "I thought as much."

I caught Avidan's eye behind the others, surprised to note his face was nearly as pale as the man who'd lost a finger.

"Tell me, then," demanded my father. "Who sent you? Why are you dressed as men of Asher?"

"I don't know," said the man, wincing as the stump of his finger continued soaking the ground crimson. "All I know is we were paid well to do so."

"How can you not know? Are you not King Hannibel's soldiers?"

When the man did not respond fast enough, Gavriel stepped on his wounded hand.

"No!" the Sidonian screamed. "Stop! We're dock workers! We were recruited in a tavern."

"By whom?" asked the king.

"I don't know his name. He told me to round up thirty men willing to attack a few caravans and timber barges while wearing these garments. Said we could keep whatever spoils we wanted."

My father stared down at the man, unmoving and blank-faced. "And my ship too?"

"He paid double for that. Said to make sure everyone went down."

"Were some of you embedded with my crew when we left port?"

"Yes."

"But none of you are Hebrew?"

The man shook his head, looking faint.

The king gritted his teeth. "So the fires on my water lines? And the docks?"

"The water lines, yes. But we haven't been near your harbor. We were busy going after the caravans we were told to ambush."

"Caravans that didn't exist this time," said Zevi with a smirk. "Thanks to our cousin."

My father folded his arms, assessing the bleeding man on the ground. Then he lifted his gaze to the others. "Is he telling the truth?"

No one answered.

"This young man's blade looks quite wicked. Perhaps you should reconsider."

After a tense few moments, all four capitulated. None wanted to endure Gavi's form of questioning.

"All right. It seems I need to deal with Sidon. But what is this about a conspirator in my house?"

"That is an answer only Shalem—I mean, Mattaniel can give you," said Zevi flatly.

Abibaal narrowed his eyes, seeming to recognize a shrewd negotiator in the Hebrew.

"Go fetch the scribe," he said to his head guard, who, along with three others, scurried away to do his bidding while I once again thanked the God of the Hebrews that Shalem was in fact still breathing. I hadn't let myself consider anything else.

Gavriel wiped his knife on his hip and tucked it back in his belt, giving me a covert wink as he did so. Poor Avidan still looked a little sallow. Whether or not the man was built like a cedar tree, I began to wonder if he was not a soldier like the others.

Zevi, however, remained in place, arms crossed and jaw set, plainly unwilling to speak again until he saw Shalem with his own eyes and seeming completely unafraid of the powerful king standing before him, equally unmoving.

Only my horrified gasp pulled their attention toward the guards dragging a bruised and bloodied Shalem between them.

I pressed my hand to my mouth as they brought him before

the king, his beautiful face so battered it barely looked like the man who held my heart. Slumped against the guard on his right, as if his own leg would barely hold him, Shalem peered up at me with the one eye not swollen shut. Hot tears spilled down my cheeks. How could they have been so vicious to this kind and tenderhearted man?

Out of the habit born of thirteen years of slavery, Shalem gingerly sank to his knees and bowed his head to my father.

All three of his cousins appeared on the verge of murder. Even Avidan had lost his ghostly pallor. His face was flushed, enormous fists white-knuckled at his sides, and his chest heaved. Gavi's knife was back in his hand, eyes black as midnight, and Zevi's razor-sharp gaze was locked menacingly on the head guard. I suspected that, were the king of Tyre not standing ten paces away, half the guardsmen in this courtyard would already be dead.

"Your cousins say you have proof of a conspiracy in my household," said my father without preamble. "Who is it?"

Shalem's one-eyed gaze turned to Zevi, then Avi, and then Gavi. "You caught them?" One side of his face was so battered his mouth barely moved, his words muffled.

Zevi gave a sharp nod. "Just where you said they would be."

Shalem took a labored breath, and I felt the echo of his pain in my own chest. "I planted false information in shipping documents three days ago. I'd already suspected Haldon, Tabnit's apprentice, was passing details about caravan routes and cargo to someone outside the palace but needed to be certain, so I sent my cousins to the crossroads to catch the brigands in the act of attacking. But of course, the caravans never existed."

"Abenasser. Fetch this Haldon," said my father without turning. With one pointed glance, the eunuch gave me a silent warning to remain still before obeying in a swirl of black robes.

"Who else is involved in this conspiracy? Or would you have me believe an apprentice scribe coordinated all of this on his own for some reason?"

Shalem dropped his chin, as if gathering courage before he

spoke again. "Two nights ago, I delivered your orders to Prince Yarikh at an inn near the docks. With him were the two sons of Enesidu of Gaza."

"Are you accusing—" My father's face went crimson.

Shalem shook his head. "I am not accusing, my king, only reporting what I saw."

Abibaal's mouth pursed into a tight line, but he waited for Shalem to continue.

"There was some talk between the Gazan princes that made me think they knew about the attack on your ship in advance. And then . . . there was discussion of giving Lady Elissa to the Philistines."

Nausea flamed at the base of my throat. The idea of being turned over to either of the lecherous Gazan princes made me ill. Had Yarikh actually been entertaining such a thing?

The king glared at Shalem wordlessly, the tension stretching so long that a few of the guards began to fidget restlessly. I recognized the tactic as a familiar one my father employed: The fool speaks first.

And Shalem was no fool.

A rush of air swept past me. Abenasser bowed before my father, holding up a small stack of papyri.

Abibaal received the offering with a frown. "What is this? Where's the man I sent you to retrieve?"

"Dead, my king."

"What do you mean, dead?"

"By his own hand, it seems. He must have anticipated the accusation. The body is not yet cold. From those messages, it seems he was indeed involved in this conspiracy. He'd been extorted to pass information on threat of harm to his family."

My father lifted one sheet, turning it toward a nearby torch as he read the message.

"I suspect Haldon's father and brothers were killed as a warning against betrayal," said Shalem. "Tabnit said his mother and younger siblings were left vulnerable and in his care."

It seemed now the poor woman would be left to fend for herself.

"I want those Gazans brought to my chambers for questioning," my father said, his tone deadly even. "*Now!*" he snapped when the bewildered guardsmen didn't move fast enough. "And take these brigands into custody."

He turned to Abenasser as a few of the guards dragged the bound thieves from the courtyard. "*Everyone* is to be questioned. Every scribe. Every servant. Every water carrier. Every maid and groundskeeper. There will be *no* traitors in my house. Anyone involved will regret crossing me, whether my blood flows in their veins or not."

The threat raised the hair on the back of my neck. If Yarikh had indeed been a part of a conspiracy against the throne, it was likely better for him that he was already dead. Abibaal had shown no mercy to his uncle, nor the people of his court, and I doubted even his own heir would have escaped his wrath.

One thing was for certain: If Sidon was behind all of this, our peaceful coexistence with our neighbors was over.

The king turned to go back up the stairs, expression stormy, the men behind him already forgotten as he pursued answers.

I darted after him. "Aba?"

My voice halted him. I hadn't called him by that name since I was a little girl. He turned his gaze on me.

Refusing to be cowed for Shalem's sake, I gestured toward him and his cousins. "Are they free to go?"

He scowled, eyes darting toward Shalem for a moment and then back to me. He stared at me for so long, my heart began to pound and my palms to sweat.

"I meant what I said, *daughter*." He leaned into the word, lowering his voice to a dangerous rasp. "Disloyalty will not be tolerated."

"Yes, but I—"

"And if *you* aren't on that ship to Shardana in the next few weeks, Melita will be."

My blood stilled. "What?"

"The Shardan won't care which of my concubines' offspring they collect. What's important is the treaty."

The thought of my fragile-hearted sister being sent off with pirates sent terror buzzing through my veins.

"Am I *clear*?"

A glut of hot tears welled in my throat as I nodded.

He glanced back at Shalem, raising his voice again. "Get out of my palace. And do *not* return."

Shalem surprised me by responding to the king. "What of the Asherites in your prison? They are innocent."

My father swung back around, his expression fierce. "You may have proved that Hebrews were not involved in the attacks on the caravans and my ship, but *nothing* has been confirmed with regard to the fire. You saved my life and that of my queen; otherwise, you'd be back in that cell with them. So take the mercy and *go*. You're free."

Shalem flinched as the declaration reverberated through the courtyard. Then, eyes closed, he took a deep and shuddering breath.

"Do you still mean to send your army south?" asked Zevi.

Abibaal's eyes narrowed. "Do you take me for a fool? Why would I reveal war plans to an enemy?"

"Israel has no connection to the conspiracy in your kingdom," he replied.

"That remains to be seen," said the king, then pointed at the gates. "Now get *out* of my city."

Just as he turned to go, a voice rang out through the courtyard. "Abibaal, King of Tyre, I have been given a message for you . . ."

Shalem lifted his head to stare at my father, then slowly rose to his feet with strength that belied his obvious injuries. *What is he doing?*

"Fool," hissed Abibaal. "What did I—?"

To my utter amazement, Shalem simply spoke over the king. "This is the Word of Yahweh to Israel: Cursed be those who curse you and blessed be those who bless you."

The king's complexion mottled in anger. "How dare you—"

"I dreamed of a clearing on a high mountaintop," Shalem continued, "a vast forest spread all around me . . ."

Gooseflesh spread up my arms as he spoke, now standing at his full, impressive height. No longer bent in submission, the quiet, humble man I'd come to know seemed to transform before my eyes. He lifted his gaze, and though only one golden-brown eye was open, it was pinned on my father with precision. The king seemed so stunned by the audacity that he said nothing as Shalem continued.

"As I watched, a sapling of cedar burst from the stony ground, dislodging a diseased stump as it came. Growing to a lofty height, the mighty cedar spread its branches in many directions. Soon, another offshoot of that cedar broke through the surface, and then another, both stretching tall beside the first. But, alas, men came and cut down the first offshoot, tossing its remains into the sea. And then fire fell from the heavens, and the second toppled with a mighty crash."

"I've heard enough of this," snarled the king. "Guards, take him back—"

Shalem only raised his voice until it echoed from the limestone walls of the palace at my back. "But then, even as the mountains themselves trembled from the impact, another sapling sprang from the dust . . . in the very place the first offshoot had once been. And this sapling was far sturdier than the first two. On its crown, a bright red flame flickered. The sapling grew swiftly, overtaking the height of all the others, *including* its rootstock, which eventually withered into obscurity. And this towering cedar, crowned in fire, spread branches far and wide, over hills and valleys and even across oceans, spreading seed that took root in foreign places without name."

Something in the strange description of Shalem's dream must have sparked Abibaal's interest. He lifted a palm to hold off the guards. "What does any of that mean?"

"I do not know," Shalem admitted. "That is where the dream

ended. Yet, I had the dream a second time: Three cedars, one by one disappearing, all replaced by the one with the flame atop its crown. I awoke confused and disturbed. And then, once again, I fell back to sleep and dreamed of the three cedars coming up from the ground. But this time, the roots of the first stretched toward the south, destroying everything in their path and when those grasping tendrils reached a valley called Jezreel, an earthquake shook the Land, so fierce that the foundations of the earth itself were shaken. Every stone was thrown down into the sea until nothing remained of this island but barren rock, forever."

Abibaal's eyes narrowed to slits, his fists white-knuckled. "You dare threaten me with curses from your invisible God?"

"Pharaoh shook his fist at the Most High once before too."

The challenge was unmistakable. That night in the tower, Shalem had told me about how Yahweh had destroyed Egypt to redeem his people from slavery—and even generations later, Egypt was a shadow of what it had once been. Would Tyre, too, be swept away because of my father's stubborn refusal to listen to such a warning?

Shalem took a deep breath, as if collecting himself, then spoke again with a softer tone. "As Yahweh once told his people at Shechem: 'I call heaven and earth as witnesses against you today that I have set before you life and death, blessing and curse. Choose life so that you and your descendants may live.'"

My knees trembled so badly as the silence stretched taut, I could barely stand. Would my father rescind his mercy and have him killed right here, in front of me?

Every eye was on Shalem, no longer a slave who cowered before his master, but a man who stood tall and unflinching as he spoke truth to the king. To my utter amazement, instead of lifting his royal finger to condemn Shalem and his cousins, my father simply turned and climbed the stairs, disappearing through the enormous cedar doors of the palace. No one moved for a few breathless moments, all just as confused by the king's actions—or lack thereof.

But then Shalem's weighty gaze turned to me and nothing else mattered. It was as if the thick and impenetrable wall that had been between us all these months had crumbled to pieces. He was no longer a slave, by decree of the king. And I was certain that if I descended these stairs and ran to him, threw myself into his arms the way I wanted to, he and his cousins would fight anyone who dared try to stop me from leaving with them now.

Everything inside me screamed to go. To succumb to the bone-deep urge to follow him on the next leg of the journey that would finally take him home to those who'd ached for his return for so long. To help him discover where he'd come from and who he was now.

But my father's warning still echoed in my heart. No matter how much I'd come to care for Shalem, I could not sacrifice Melita. Nor could I simply walk away from my mother without even a farewell. Besides, it was entirely possible my father would send a battalion after me if I dared run.

Shalem took one step toward me, determination written all over his battered face, but I threw up a shaking palm. Immediately, he halted. Searing pain tore through my chest as I let my eyes flutter closed and shook my head.

I held still for a few moments, a deep fracture forming in my heart. Hot tears streaking down my face, I lifted my chin and looked at him one last time.

Then I turned away, forcing my unwilling feet to climb the palace stairs and feeling the weight of my golden shackles like never before.

29

Mattaniel

It took three days before I could see clearly out of my left eye, but my vision blurred now as I stared at the firelight while Avidan detailed another of the adventures we'd had as boys, this one involving a buried arm bone and a hidden cave in the heart of a mountain. My cousin was wildly expressive as he unfurled story after story with descriptions so vivid I could practically see the four of us tromping through the woods with Zevi's enormous gray dog bounding along, tongue lolling out the side of his huge maw.

I squinted. "You mean to tell me that dog was *real*?"

"Igo? Of course. Although you were a little frightened of him when he and Zevi first came to Kiryat-Yearim. But he protected you like one of his own pups."

"I dreamed of him," I said with a chuckle. "Often. I could never understand why such a terrifying creature seemed like a friend to me."

Avi set a palm on Zevi's shoulder and squeezed. "We all mourned Igo's passing like he was a family member. But some of his children and grandchildren are still beloved pets in both Kiryat-Yearim and Naioth, and a good number protect flocks in the surrounding valleys."

"To Igo." Gavi lifted the glistening rib bone of the small fallow deer he'd trapped earlier. "May he have an abundance of squirrels to chase in the *olam ha'ba*."

This blessing was echoed by Zevi and Avidan as they lifted their own bones.

Now that we were well into Israelite-held territory, my cousins had begun to relax. Zevi's punishing pace slowed a little, and we'd found a small hollow near a river to camp for the night. Surrounded by whispering pines and stately oaks, and with no enemy tribes in the vicinity, I hoped to finally claim a full night's sleep.

If only I could close my eyes without a vision of Elissa's silent tears as she turned to walk away from me forever.

Since the moment she'd disappeared from sight, I'd been arguing with myself over whether I should have fought for her in that courtyard. But she'd waged a mighty battle in those final moments, and from the resignation on her face as she'd walked away, I knew her decision was set in stone.

Besides, if she had left behind her mother with no one to care for her, for the sake of my selfish desires, she would not be the generous and devoted woman I'd come to love. So, for as much as I'd loathed walking out of those palace gates knowing I'd never see her again, I did it—for her.

"So that dream you revealed to Abibaal . . ." said Avi from beside me, bringing me back to the fireside, where he and I were now alone. I'd been so lost in the flicker of the flames and my ache for Elissa, I'd not even noticed Gavi and Zevi had disappeared, probably off to gather more kindling or wash in the river. "Does that sort of thing happen often?"

"Dreams . . . yes. For as long as I can remember, I've been plagued by vibrant images when I sleep. Much of the time it's nonsense, but over the years, many of them remained with me long after I'd awakened." I gave a soft laugh. "As I said, I often dreamed of that dog, Igo. I dreamed of you too."

"You did?"

"In the woods with the others, mostly. But there was one that recurred, of you teaching me to swim. I didn't know who you were, of course, only that it was an older boy with green eyes. But it was you, wasn't it?"

Avi's grin was so wide I could see all of his teeth as he grabbed my knee and shook it affectionately. "Yes! Yes, that was me! You had to have been five, maybe six. You were a little nervous at first, but finally—"

"You told me to stop struggling so hard, relax my body, and let the water carry me."

His mouth dropped open. "That's it, exactly."

My throat went tight. "You saved my life, Avi." I told him of those moments of panic after the shipwreck and how it had been his voice that calmed me, even in the middle of the Great Sea.

Rubbing his hand over his mouth, he shook his head as if at a loss for words. When they did come, they were choked. "Please forgive me, Shay." He pressed his lips tight for a moment, his jaw ticking while he collected himself.

"There's no need—"

He lifted his palm. "No. I have waited for thirteen years to say this. Please let me."

Chest tight, I nodded.

"I will never forget the awful moment I crawled into that cave and realized you were gone. It haunts me. You were only there because I was a selfish fool. I wanted to be a soldier. Show myself to be a man. When, really, I was barely more than a child. If I had turned back when you appeared on the road to Bezek that night, none of this would ever have happened."

One of the logs in the fire popped, sparks spiraling into the air. I watched the flare of light until it floated back down to earth as ash.

"But you said you met your wife across the river. Isn't that right?"

He'd briefly told me the story of Keziah masquerading as a boy to escape marriage to a monster, but I suspected he'd only scratched the surface of the tale because he knew it would press into my fresh wounds. None of them had said anything about Elissa, but I sensed they understood all the same.

"Yes." He smiled ruefully. "Without your disappearance, I'd never have found her that day, thinking she was you being thrashed by those little beasts who'd robbed her. But regardless, I still regret leaving you out there unprotected."

"I don't remember that day, although I've had plenty of nightmares about those hyenas. But it sounds like I was insistent on going with you."

He laughed, the rich sound echoing off the trees across the river. "Oh yes. And among your many talents as a boy was your ability to coerce the rest of us into letting you have your way. Your mother, most of all."

"Quite the pampered child, then, I gather."

"Your sisters used to seethe with jealousy over the way she coddled and adored you."

Talk of my mother caused a painful tightness in my chest. Would I remember the woman who'd cherished me so dearly? It did not seem real that in only a matter of days, I would find out.

Avi sobered. "Back to the dreams. The words you spoke to the king of Tyre were powerful, Shay. Has Yahweh given you visions like that before?"

I sighed, shifting my seat. "All I can say is that I've had dreams and then things happened that I cannot explain. It's very rare, but it's as if I am *compelled* to listen. And usually those types of dreams reoccur two or three times." I spread my hands, palms up. "Does that mean I am some sort of seer?"

"I wish I could tell you, cousin," he said. "Although I have had a few brushes with similar deep impressions on my soul that I am certain were the voice of the Ancient One. We grew up in the community of Naioth, after all, which was created by Samuel as a school for prophets. Torah knowledge is buried deep in you, so it does not surprise me that Yahweh would use you to speak truth in a way only he can do. Yosef had dreams and visions. Samuel too. And now you'll have the rest of your life to discover what it all means."

For so many years, I'd dreamed of being free, of determining my own path without answering to any master. But somehow, thinking of the unwritten future ahead of me, endlessly sprawled before me like an uncharted sea, it was almost terrifying in its sheer vastness. I had no idea what my next step should be, only that I wished Elissa were beside me to help decide.

"That is the mount of Gilboa," said Zevi, pointing to the slope just east of the trade road. "And on the other side, a little to the north, is the valley of Bezek, where we rallied with the army before the battle at Yavesh."

We'd just crossed over the Jezreel River south of Megiddo, where endless fields of barley and wheat, along with countless olive and fruit orchards, grew from some of the richest earth I'd ever seen. The slope of Gilboa was just as green as the valley and dotted with thick patches of deep purple iris swaying in the gentle breeze. I was certain I'd traversed this same road with the Sidonians, perhaps more than once, since we'd traded in Megiddo at least twice, but I'd been far too entangled in confusion and sadness to notice just how beautiful this valley was back then. Freedom had given me new eyes.

"It only took me thirteen years to circle back," I said on a chuckle.

Ahead of us, Gavi and Avi were arguing over whose son was the wildest, trading escalating stories about their headstrong offspring, but Zevi had slackened his swift pace to walk beside me.

"It should have been only a couple of days," he said, his expression grim. "That's my fault."

"As I told Avi, what happened was meant to be. I do not hold any of you responsible for choices you made when we were young. Especially when I don't remember any of it in the first place."

"Well, I do," he replied, stopping in place to press a palm to his heart. "You were *my* responsibility. And I failed you."

I went quiet as the clouds slid lazily across the horizon. "For so long I thought I'd been forgotten. Either I'd gotten lost out there in the wilderness and no one bothered to come looking, or maybe I'd been left behind on purpose because I was not wanted. But whenever I began to wallow in those thoughts, the story of Yosef inevitably came to mind. Granted, I had not been betrayed by my brothers like he was, although I did not know that. But I remembered how he said that what they'd meant for evil, Yahweh meant for good. I didn't know why I'd been lost, but somehow, I knew there had to be a reason for it." I shrugged. "Maybe it was to help the Asherites in Tyre. Or so Avi could rescue Keziah. I doubt I'll ever know . . ."

"Perhaps there are reasons only Yahweh knows. He certainly directed our paths to cross in strange ways."

"What do you mean?"

"After Avi returned from across the river with the news he'd found proof you were still alive, I did not believe him. The evidence at the cave was fairly damning. There was quite a bit of blood on the waterskin we'd left with you and all those hyena prints. Packs like that usually hunt at night, so I assumed they'd been so desperate for food that they'd dragged your body off." He took a breath, then let it out slowly. "But then Avi handed me this . . ."

He dug around in his belt pouch and produced a white shell, which reminded me of the sea-polished one Elissa had handed me on the beach. "I'd given this to you when we were boys. A reminder to be brave because it gave me courage when I was alone and afraid."

I held the shell in my palm, and although I didn't exactly remember it, there was something about its weight that was familiar. I turned it over. Scratched into the underside was a childish drawing of a dog. "Igo?"

He smiled, something he rarely did. "Yes. He was a source of comfort for me after my father rescued me in Ashdod."

A couple of days ago, Avi had told me the incredible story of Zevi's father, a Philistine champion adopted by our grandparents, and how he'd purchased Zevi's freedom, keeping him from enduring slavery like me, and possibly far worse.

"Avi found this in the road, and it pointed him in the right direction to discover your knife in a nearby village. It was as if Yahweh himself arranged for these clues to tell him not to give up the hunt for you."

The idea that the God of the Universe would bother to do so was overwhelming.

"And two years later, when I stumbled across a woman in the market of Lachish who remembered you, I realized I'd been a fool not to believe Avi in the first place."

"What woman?"

"A weaver. Apparently, you knew some words in her language."

"I remember her," I said, eyes going wide at the connection. "The wife of one of my Sidonian masters came from some small island up near Athens. She sometimes spoke in that tongue, so I asked her to teach me her words. I was surprised to stumble across a woman in Lachish who spoke the same tongue." How could I have ever guessed such a small exchange could have meant so much?

"I pursued you hard north after that. Dragged my whole company with me, actually, along with Yochana." He smiled again, his gaze tracking southwest for a few moments, as if he could see his wife there in the distance. "If things had not gone awry, I may have even caught up to you in Beit Shemesh."

I winced at the name of the town and the horrible memories it evoked. I'd not told any of my cousins the entire story of how I'd come to be sold to Raphad.

"I thought I had, actually," continued Zevi, "when I came across a boy who looked a little like you, walking south. I chased the poor young man down and scared the life from him. But he was returning home after looking for work—"

"Because his father had been severely injured," I spoke over him, as a current of something ghostly feathered over my skin.

Zevi blinked at me in bewilderment, coming to a halt. "Yes. How did you know?"

I wiped a hand down my face, trying to order my thoughts before I told him about how I'd helped the boy escape from the Sidonians before they sold him, and the beating that followed just before Raphad came across me in Ashdod.

He stared at the ground for a long while, likely just as astounded as I was. Then he murmured, "'What you meant for evil, God meant for good.'" When he looked back up at me, tears were swimming in his brown eyes. "You saved my life, Shalem."

"What?"

He then explained how that same boy had come across him a few days later, lying in a stream after being struck down by a man he trusted.

"If you hadn't sent Osi back to Azeka, I might have died from my wounds that day. His family nursed me until Yochana came and took me home to Kiryat-Yearim so I could heal."

I could do nothing but stare at him in utter astonishment. For all the years I'd felt helpless and worthless, the knowledge that Yahweh had used me to preserve my own cousin's life, without even realizing it, was almost incomprehensible. And yet, why not? A God who could speak the universe into existence and part the Red Sea to rescue his people could certainly arrange such a divine appointment, couldn't he? And yes, the Sidonians had mercilessly beaten me that day, but now that I knew the good that had come of it, it was worth every lash.

Mind still reeling, I held out the shell to Zevi. "Thank you for not giving up."

He threw up a palm. "No, I gave it to you. I'm only returning it."

I shook my head, insistent. "It served its purpose. You miss him. Keep it as a reminder of your friend."

Zevi pressed his lips tight as he accepted the shell and placed it back in his pouch. "He was yours too."

"I know." Dreams of Igo and my cousins had brought me plenty of comfort over the years. They had been the only thing that felt anything like a home to me—at least until I'd met Elissa.

"What are you two doing?" Gavi called out. "Your legs getting tired?"

Avi barked a laugh, stretching his long arms wide. "Need us to carry you the rest of the way?"

"Fools," Zevi muttered, shaking his head and grinning to himself as we walked on. "They never change."

Warmth gathered in my chest. For as devastating as it had been to leave my love behind, I was grateful these men had never given up on finding me and that somehow, even without our knowledge, Yahweh had directed our paths to cross time and again.

After seven days of Avi's stories about my childhood, my family, and all that had happened while I'd been enslaved, I did not think I could be surprised anymore. But as we began to climb the final slope that would take us to Naioth, Gavi shocked me to my bones when he casually mentioned Adin was married.

I stumbled to a halt, jaw unhinged. "Married? What do you mean? He only left Tyre a couple of months ago."

He chuckled. "It's quite the story. I'll let him tell you when you see him. But that's yet another reason why he could not come with us. Although he certainly wanted to."

"I still cannot believe you and I came within hours of each other in Gaza," I said. "And that you are married to Zahava."

The young woman who'd been held in Enesidu's palace had been enormously talented with gold and other precious metals. I'd never seen the legendary crown the Philistine king had forced her to repair, but I'd seen the ceremonial armor she'd made for him and had been in awe.

"My little dove is without equal. I cannot wait to see her," he said, his voice going soft. "She's only a couple of months from the birth of our third child, but she refuses to stop working in the metal shop. She's teaching our oldest to carve wax molds already—when she can get him to sit still. He's just like I was at that age." The pride in his voice was unmistakable.

"You are blessed."

He inhaled deeply. "Far, *far* more than I deserve. If you only knew what an irresponsible drunkard I was when she found me."

Again, my cousin had surprised me. "That's not what I heard. Adin spoke as if the famous Gavriel were some sort of legend, able to take on whole armies by himself with both wrists tied together."

He barked a loud laugh, shaking his head. "He gave me far too much credit. And, in truth, he only got to know me well after I'd stopped drowning myself in wine."

"He did say you battled a few demons, and that both of you had monsters for fathers. But also that he aspired to be like you because of how you'd overcome all of it."

Gavi nodded. "And thankfully that worthless father of his is in the ground, just like mine."

"When did that happen?"

"A couple of years ago." He bent to pick up a fat stick from the ground, then began to snap off twigs as we wound through the thick trees on a well-used hunting trail. "I'm not certain what happened, but Adin said the beast got what he deserved in the end."

He swung the sturdy stick back and forth, as if testing a sword. "This is perfect. I promised Avi's boys I'd make them practice weapons."

A flash of what felt like a memory came over me, where a much younger version of Gavi exclaimed what a perfect stick he'd found on the forest floor. But then it was gone, like mist at sunrise. Such fleeting moments had become much more prevalent since we'd left Tyre, likely because Avidan spent many hours of the day telling stories from when we were children, but it made me wonder if, little by little, my memories might eventually come back to me.

"Do you want to go back?" he asked.

"Go back where?"

"For Elissa. I'll need to wait until Zahava gives birth, but if you want me to help, I will."

I stared at him in wonder. "You'd do that?"

"I went back to Gaza for my little dove. I know how it is."

My throat went tight. If only I *could* go back for her. "She's getting married."

"To whom?"

"One of the Shardan men," I said. "My first job in the palace was to tutor her in their language so she could be a treaty bride. Within the month she'll be on a ship to their island."

He let out a slow breath. "I'm sorry to hear that. But if you change your mind . . ."

"I appreciate the offer," I said, "even though it's impossible."

"I owe you, Shay."

"No—"

"Yes," he interrupted. "For all the things I had to reconcile when I took my head out of the jug, it was my selfishness regarding you I regretted most. I chose my sword over my cousin. There's no way to coat that bitter truth in honey. If I'd listened to Avi—"

"Then you probably both would have missed me in that village," I said. "I'm fairly certain the Sidonians hid me in the wagon until we were far away from that area. I remember being kept in the dark for a long time while I healed. Regardless of what decision you made, we obviously weren't meant to cross paths at that time."

"Perhaps that's true, but I should have tried. And it will be to my eternal shame that I didn't. Though I have to say . . ." He turned a crooked grin my way. "Your time with those pirates certainly taught you to fight well. I thought you were going to pummel poor Avi in that alleyway."

I laughed. "He didn't fight back."

"Of course not. He's no soldier, but Uncle Natan taught him to wrestle, and the man once known as the Champion of Ashdod is a beast. He taught you, too, even if you don't remember it."

Another of those strange feelings rushed over me. "*Control the head, control the body."* Had it been Natan's voice I'd heard in my head while I was fighting the attacker on Abibaal's ship?

I opened my mouth to ask, but the pounding of hooves in the distance halted me. Gavi had also paused, his sword already drawn and eyes sharp on the trail ahead. The ground vibrated as the thundering came closer and closer. And then an enormous black-and-white horse came up over a rise, mane flying, with what looked to be a woman on its back.

I blinked. And then blinked again. *Surely it can't be.*

The woman yanked on the reins, the majestic horse skidding to a stop in front of us in a cloud of dust.

Distracted by the impossible coincidence of a horse that looked identical to the one I'd found half-dead in a wadi worlds away from here, I hadn't realized Avi was running until the woman was leaping off the horse and into his arms with a cry of delight.

"Abba!"

"Abba!"

Little voices drew my attention back to the horse, where two girls bounced up and down on the saddle, screaming for their father while he kissed their mother as if the two were alone in the forest.

Once the girls had been greeted with hugs and kisses and Avi introduced me to Keziah, who was still red-faced from her husband's unabashed affection, I approached the horse, hand extended to let him sniff my fingers.

"This is Sarru," said Keziah. "He's not too fond of men, so be careful."

As the animal brushed his whiskered chin against my palm, I smiled at his mistress. "I know. We've met."

My cousins stared at me open-mouthed as I told them how I'd encountered Sarru in the wilderness. Although he was a good deal older now and his coat shiny and healthy, the distinct markings on his face and legs were unmistakable.

With a gasp, Keziah slammed into me, throwing her arms

around my waist and sobbing into my chest. "Thank you! *Thank you*, Shalem."

My throat swelled as I patted her back awkwardly. "I couldn't just let him die out there."

She turned up her face, tears streaking through the dust on her lightly freckled cheeks, smiling. "You will always and forever be my favorite cousin."

Gavi loudly protested this statement while Zevi swung one of the girls onto his shoulders and Avi set the older one on Sarru's back. Then we continued up the hill together while the girls chattered to their father about everything that had happened while he was off finding "*Dod* Shalem."

I was an *uncle*. I'd always tried not to imagine who my family was, mostly because I feared they'd abandoned me purposely. But now I was a cousin, an uncle, a brother—a son.

As we crested the summit, the little community of Naioth came into view. Tucked into a wooded area, there were several small homes, a few larger buildings where Avi said the unmarried students lived communally, and even some tents pitched around the area. One narrow street led through the center of the village, which meant plenty of people, young and old, cheerfully greeted my cousins along the way. Although I received many curious glances and a few pointed stares, no one asked who I was. I wondered how many would have known me as a boy. Did I really look all that different?

I'd at least grown back a thick scruff of beard along my jaw, which for some reason entertained my cousins greatly. Perhaps, now that I was free, I'd grow my hair long again as well. Would Elissa approve of such a change?

I flinched internally at the thought. It did not matter, did it? She would never see my beard or sink her fingers into my hair ever again. *What was the purpose of meeting her, Yahweh? To offer me a glimpse of something I could never have before snatching it away?*

I brushed the irreverent thought away as Zevi led us to a small home on the far edge of Naioth. It looked to be among the oldest in the village, two stories tall and with an abundant garden on the side. On the sill of the open window, a pot of something swirled steam into the air, releasing the delicious smell of rich spices. My stomach snarled and my mouth watered.

Zevi glanced over his shoulder at me, lifting his brows with a silent question. *Ready?*

A wave of nerves came over me, washing through my limbs to set them abuzz. But I took a deep breath, braced my body, and nodded. His knock rattled the wooden door on its hinges.

I swallowed hard, feeling off-kilter as the door swung open.

A woman with black hair and striking silver at her temples stood at the threshold with a wine jug in one hand, frowning up at Zevi. A fan of lines crinkled at the corners of her eyes as she squinted, her lovely face screwing up in confusion. "Zevi? I did not know you were in Naioth. Where is Yoch—"

Her words cut off the moment he shifted to the left, giving her a clear view of me.

She blinked her eyes rapidly as she studied my face, then widened them when her gaze landed on the crown of my head—on the silver patch of hair Avi said she'd called a special blessing from Yahweh. Her mouth dropped open at the same time the jar fell to the ground with a crash, shattering on the stone threshold. Both her hands flew to her mouth as tears poured from golden-brown eyes the very same color as my own.

"Shalom, Ima." I stepped toward her with upturned palms. "I am home."

Without warning, my mother's eyes rolled back into her head as she fainted, falling into my arms.

30

Shalem

Naioth, Israel
Six weeks later

Dust motes swirled in the sunlight pouring through the window as I dipped my reed pen in the ink pot, then began the next line of my careful transcription.

> *. . . And when he sits on the throne of his kingdom, he shall write for himself in a book a copy of this law, approved by the Levitical priests. And it shall be with him, and he shall read in it all the days of his life, that he may learn to fear the Lord his God by keeping all the words of this law and these statutes, and doing them, that his heart may not be lifted up above his brothers, and that he may not turn aside from the commandment, either to the right hand or to the left, so that he may continue long in his kingdom, he and his children, in Israel.*

For so long, passages like this one would come to me at the oddest times, sparked by a word someone said or sometimes simply without a reason. To finally read the Torah for myself—written in Samuel's own hand, nonetheless—was extraordinary. Though he'd not said as much, I was certain the old prophet alone knew the secret location of the originals, composed by Mosheh and Yehoshua hundreds of years ago and spirited away from Shiloh before the Miskhan was destroyed and the Ark stolen by the Philistines.

"Did King Saul actually write an entire copy of the Torah for himself?" I asked Samuel, who was sitting across from me at the wide table in his main room. Although he wrote a few letters of his own earlier, he'd been silently staring out the window at the treetops for the past half hour, arms folded across his barrel chest.

With a deep sigh, the elderly man shook his head. "He began the project soon after I anointed him. But within a few months, he was too entangled in tribal politics and border defense to come to Naioth and finish. It is a painstaking process, as you are learning, and Saul was a farmer before he was king, not a trained scribe."

The care taken by the Levitical scribes was remarkable. Not one tiny *yod* was to be out of place, and any accidental mark rendered the whole text unusable. Samuel was fiercely dedicated to ensuring each word of the original text was preserved.

Frowning, he lifted his gaze to the window. "I had my students finish it for him and deliver the scrolls to the palace. But I do not know whether he ever actually read it for himself."

"From what my cousins have told me, these commands are increasingly being ignored in Gibeah."

After so many years of imagining who Yahweh had chosen to elevate to such a sacred office, I'd assumed Saul was a man without reproach, righteous and wise, much like Mosheh had been. Yet even the great Mosheh had stumbled, so I should not have been surprised to hear that Saul's reign had been marked by inconsistency. He was only a man, after all. But I'd been truly shocked when I'd learned that years ago Yahweh had removed his divine blessing from Saul, who would be replaced by another yet unrevealed.

Samuel let out a mournful sigh, stroking his long silver beard. "Unfortunately, that is all too true. If he had obeyed from the beginning, the anointing of Yahweh would not have been taken from him. And what has filled the void will do great damage." He paused, frowning as he stared out the window once again at the gently swaying oak trees.

Though he'd walked this earth for many decades, there was nothing feeble about Samuel. It was not difficult to imagine him as the commander of Israel's armies, a feared judge of the tribes, and, according to Gavi, a righteous warrior who'd hacked the king of the Amalekites to pieces only a few years ago. The knee-length, silver Nazirite braid and barely tamed beard gave him an oddly wild appearance as well. Even so, there was something almost broken about the man, a spirit of heaviness he seemed to carry on his capable shoulders.

"I hoped for so long the Almighty One would cause Saul to bend his knee," he said, "and thereby become the king he was meant to be. Instead, the more power he has gained, the more willful he has become."

Four years ago, Gavi and Zahava had witnessed Samuel's public declaration that Yahweh had rejected Saul for his rebellion, but the man still sat on the throne. And from what Samuel had told me over the last few weeks, the tribes of Israel only grew more idolatrous and more fractured the longer time went on. My cousins had said that before Saul's crowning, we'd all been excited at the prospect of a strong and capable king to lead us, someone to make our enemies scatter and bring glory to our people.

Instead, our enemies still encircled us, growing ever more audacious in their attacks, and although Saul's power and wealth had grown exponentially, it was at the expense of his people. Just like Abibaal, Saul demanded more and more tribute each year, and more from those whose skill or resources he coveted. And most upsetting to my father, particularly, was that although the fortress at Gibeah was well-fortified and lavish, the Mishkan, or what remained of it, was in a shameful state. He'd confided that each time he'd traveled to Nob for his allotted service, where the ancient tent had been raised after the destruction of Shiloh, he returned home angrier.

"When will another king be chosen?" I asked Samuel.

The prophet nodded. "It is not quite time for the anointed one to be revealed."

It sounded as if he already knew who that might be, but I was sure it would be fruitless to ask for confirmation. I was learning that each of Samuel's words was carefully weighed and measured long before he opened his mouth. He had no cause to reveal such a weighty secret to me. I was fortunate he took the time to answer my questions at all. Regardless of the large portions of the law and histories that had inexplicably stuck with me throughout my slavery, I still had so much to learn about my role as Levite, but also about the Ruler of the Universe himself. At times, I felt very much like the youths who sat at my father's feet every day, hungry for knowledge and uncertain of what lay ahead.

When Avi told me my father was one of the first Levites to join this community, which was dedicated to the preservation and teaching of the Torah, I had not understood how integral he'd been to its creation. As young men, he and Avi's father, Ronen, had helped build the first permanent structures for students who traveled from all over the territories to live and study Torah. My father was now the leader of all Levitical teachers here and among those Samuel considered his council. When my father had taken me to meet Samuel shortly after I'd returned, I'd found the man of God endlessly fascinating.

"I remember you well, young man," Samuel had said, *"always begging to listen in on your father's lessons, reciting long passages from memory, and asking questions far beyond your tender years. I suspect the questions you have now, after so long, will be even more challenging."*

He'd said then that the best way to internalize the sacred words of Torah was to write them for myself, just like Saul should have done. So, in light of my father's status and long friendship with the man of Yahweh, I was allowed to do so from Samuel's personal copies, in his *own* home. It was an honor I did not take lightly.

It was also a welcome distraction from the ache that had grown with each day apart from Elissa. Now that more than a month had passed, she was likely aboard the ship to Shardana. I'd done my best not to imagine her as Torben's wife but failed often. Every time I did so, the pain in the center of my chest sharpened. All I could do was plead with Yahweh to watch over her.

I peered out the window, noting the low angle of the sunlight. "I should probably go home."

It was easy to lose myself in transcription, especially on days when Samuel had time to indulge my questions. But I hated to think of my mother worrying. I'd walked out the door one day as her doted-upon fifteen-year-old boy and returned a grown man with no memory of her love for him. I could see the effort she was making in trying to reconcile the two versions of me, but there was always a hint of fear in her eyes whenever I left the house.

"I'll walk with you," Samuel said as I rolled up the parchment and placed it back in its clay jar. "I have a question for your father."

After informing his wife he would return soon, Samuel and I began the short walk through Naioth. I'd come to enjoy life here in the community just up the hill from Ramah. There was no market here, since it was so close to the city, but there was plenty of life in the streets. Not only were there students gathered about in circles with their Levitical teachers, but also clumps of musicians and singers practicing songs, and plenty of children playing spirited games of chase or helping their mothers carry water from the nearby stream.

Since returning, I'd had flashes of doing the same thing for my own mother, along with a few other small memories in her garden or kitchen. But most potent had been the smell of my mother herself, almond oil and fresh bread. The moment she'd fainted into my arms, the familiarity of it had hit me like a tidal wave.

"Are you settling back into life with your family?" Samuel asked as if he'd known the direction of my thoughts.

"In some ways," I replied. "My mother and father have made me feel welcome, though I do not remember much about my life here before."

It had been difficult, at first, for them to understand just how completely my memories had been stripped away. But even if they were upset by the truth, they were incredibly patient. My sisters, both married and with eight children between them, had come to me separately to ask forgiveness for the way they'd treated me. I, of course, did not remember their jealousy nor the spitefulness they'd admitted to, but appreciated the gesture nonetheless. Besides, from the things my cousins told me about myself, I'd reveled in being a pampered and favored child, so they'd likely been justified in some of their frustrations. But any sense of entitlement or high opinion of my talents had been quite literally beaten out of me by the Sidonians.

"And yet you feel out of place, don't you?" said Samuel. "As if you are a stranger in the home you were born in."

I blinked at Samuel, who was too busy waving at a group of little boys to see how much he'd shocked me. "Yes. Exactly."

His brown eyes were full of compassion when he stopped walking and turned to me. "When I was only a few years old, I was taken to live in Shiloh, to serve in the Mishkan until I was grown."

My eyes flew wide. I'd known nothing about his history, other than his decades of serving as judge of the tribes and prophet of the Most High. "But why?"

"This is a long story I'll tell another day. But I understand what it's like to be separated from my family in my youth and to be ill at ease in the place I once called home. And then, of course, to feel guilty for doing so." I marveled that I had anything at all in common with this famed prophet, anointer of kings, and the man who'd led Israel for decades without the benefit of a crown.

"My feet hang off the end of the bed," I revealed, "but I don't want to say anything for fear of wounding my mother and father more than I already have."

He nodded, murmuring, "The man you are now does not fit the shape of the boy they knew."

"There are things I endured that I can never share with my family. It would hurt them too much, especially after all the grief they suffered." As Elissa had said, I was a broken shell tossed about by the sea, scarred from being dragged by the current along the gritty ocean floor, certainly not the wide-eyed innocent I'd been when I'd followed my cousins to Bezak.

"There was nothing easy about Avraham's many years of sojourn. Nor of Yitzhak's exile, Yaakov's struggle, Mosheh's banishment, and certainly not the enslavement and imprisonment Yosef endured. And yet these were the men used as foundation stones for the nation of Israel. Your suffering, difficult though it was, shaped you into someone new. Someone prepared to walk a path few are called to. It is not comfort or safety that forms us into vessels for his purposes, after all, but suffering and trial."

"Are you saying Yahweh has some sort of grand purpose for me?"

"Not necessarily. Although that might depend on what one considers grand. I doubt any of us will know the fullness of the impact we make during this life. One small act of obedience may have eternal repercussions, completely unbeknownst to us. Perhaps, one day, no one at all will remember the name of Samuel ben Elkhanah. And perhaps the name Shalem ben Iyov will be etched in stone for generations. But that is not what is important. Of far greater value is willingness to bow your knee to the King of all Kings and follow his ways for all the days of your life. Some of us will walk deeper, darker valleys than the rest, but that only means the light is much clearer, and far brighter, on the other side."

I stared at him in disbelief. "I have *dreamed* something like this. Every night for the past three nights."

"Tell me." He furrowed his bushy brows, his light brown eyes intense on me.

Eyes closed, I took a deep breath as I recalled the images I'd seen. "I dreamed a terrifying creature was following me down a long and treacherous winding road. I thought it was a hyena, like the ones that attacked me, so I ran. But the beast matched my pace, step for step. In my terror, I did not watch where I was going and blindly entered a deep valley, so dark I could not see my hand in front of my face. And yet I knew the creature was there in the blackness, breathing hot on my neck and sharp claws scraping on stones as it stalked me. I fell, tumbling head over foot into a rocky crevasse. I lay there, bruised and bloodied, the wind knocked from my lungs but soon felt a deep compulsion to reach out my hand. When I did, something soft pressed gently against my palm. I grabbed hold of it and found myself pulled to my feet, then led through the pitch-black darkness up a steep slope. Once I emerged from the dark valley and realized I was holding on to a tail—not that of a hyena, but of a huge and fearsome lion—I let go, terrified it would turn and destroy me."

I paused, taking another deep breath. In the telling, it felt as if I'd been dreaming it all over again.

"And did it destroy you?"

"No." I huffed a disbelieving laugh. "Not at all. It paced ahead of me for a few steps and then stood bathed in brilliant sunlight, its mane sparkling like stars. It roared so loudly I felt my very bones rattle from the power. And then it turned, stalking down the hill toward me. All I could do was stand frozen with fear as I waited for it to tear me apart. But instead, it brushed past me. I could feel the silken warmth of its fur against my skin and the weight of its enormous paws vibrating the earth beneath my feet. When I turned, it was standing at the edge of that dark valley again, waiting, staring at me expectantly . . . and then I woke up. The dream has been the same every single night."

When the haze of the memory cleared, I realized Samuel was smiling and nodding. As if my nightmare had clarified something for him.

"Your father told me of your dreams," he said. "Including the one you revealed to King Abibaal. It's no wonder you were led back to Naioth."

"Why is that?"

"Because for hundreds of years, the people of Israel have gone their own way. Done what was right in their own eyes. This has led to generations of idolaters in this Land, creating gods in their own image and calling them holy. I have tried, over the long years of my life, to call the *am segula* to repent. To throw away worthless idols and cut down their high places. And yet they refuse. So, I built Naioth to train a new generation of prophets and teachers along with Levites, musicians, and others who will call the people back into right worship. Back to repentance. Back to reverence and fear of the God who brought us out from Egypt."

"So my dreams *are* prophetic?"

"What did Mosheh teach about those called to prophesy?"

I paused to sift through the multitude of words in my head, reaching for a relevant passage. And soon, one rose clearly to mind.

> "But the prophet who dares to speak a message in My name that I have not commanded him to speak, or who speaks in the name of other gods—that prophet must die. You may say to yourself, 'How can we recognize a message that the LORD has not spoken?' When a prophet speaks in the LORD's name, and the message does not come true or is not fulfilled, that is a message the LORD has not spoken. The prophet has spoken presumptuously. Do not be afraid of him."

Samuel grinned. "Astounding, young man. Yes. We must test everything against the commands of Yahweh. Weigh our words carefully. And confirm it is from his mouth *before* we speak. Because if we do not take the warnings Mosheh laid out at the Mountain seriously, and thereby deliver messages that are born of our own pride or gain instead of pure Truth, our lives *should* be forfeit."

I rubbed at my brow. "That is a heavy burden."

"It is. A messenger of the Most High must fear Yahweh *alone*. It is a dangerous thing to stand in the doorway between the Almighty and his people, an office that cannot be undertaken without carefully counting that cost. For the days are coming soon when those who speak truth will be killed for doing so."

"How will I know for sure these dreams and visions are from Him?"

"The same way a child knows the voice of his earthly father, one must know the Voice of the One who calls us *his* children. Read. Listen. Study. Memorize. Meditate. Ask for wisdom. Listen some more. Weigh *everything* against what the Torah says about his character and his commands, and fear him above all. Then listen again before speaking even one word in his holy name."

My pulse raced as a thought came to me. "Did I do wrong to speak to Abibaal about my dream before I came back to learn these things?"

"Was anything you said a lie?"

"No. It was the dream exactly as I saw it."

"Did any of it contradict what you know of Yahweh's character?"

"No. Aside from the dream, I spoke only the words of Yahweh as written, to warn the king."

"Was anything you said for your own glory or recognition?"

I shook my head. "Not at all. In fact, I was fairly certain the king was going to have my head removed from my body before I even finished speaking."

"Then unless your words prove to be false, I believe you have obeyed, son."

"I doubt I will ever know for sure, one way or the other, if my words come to pass, now that I've left Tyre. And the dream itself was so confusing, full of strange imagery."

"Sometimes a message I'm given is clear as the blue sky overhead, but very often the things I am told to say are clouded in mystery. It is up to Yahweh alone to bring clarity. Or perhaps to keep the meaning hidden for the right time." He placed his warm hand on my shoulder. "And as for your lion, I think you should follow him."

I barely had time to register his words before he'd walked off, heading for a group of musicians gathered in the shade up ahead of us, which included Avi's father, Ronen. Although most of Ronen's students appeared to be around twenty, a boy no older than eleven or twelve sat on the ground at the center of the group, eyes closed as he strummed a lyre with skillful fingers.

I came to a stop beside Samuel, whose eyes were focused on the young musician as he began a haunting melody in a clear, sweet voice. The words that came from his mouth were unlike anything I'd heard: tender, yet profound, and sung with a depth of feeling that was incongruous to the youth of the boy in front of us.

When he finished the song, no one spoke, too enraptured to dare interrupt the sacred silence that followed.

Finally, Ronen stood and approached the boy, placing a hand on his shoulder. "That was truly beautiful, young man. You'll come play for us again soon?"

Clutching his lyre close, the boy nodded.

"I'm glad to hear it," said Ronen. "We could probably all learn a thing or two from you."

While Avi's father excused the rest of the students, the boy blushed furiously, which made the thick swath of freckles stand out on his cheeks. A woman who'd been listening from a short distance approached him with an adoring smile on her face. From the resemblance between them, I guessed she was his mother.

As the students gathered up their instruments and scattered, Ronen came to stand with Samuel and me. "Shalom. What are the two of you up to?"

Of all the many relatives I'd been reintroduced to since my return—so many it was difficult to keep them all straight—Ronen and Eliora were easily among my favorites.

Avidan's father not only trained the Levite singers and instrumentalists but had written hundreds of songs performed by the choirs during festivals and sacred gatherings. And Eliora, a Philistine-born woman whom Avidan favored heavily, was a grandmother to all the children in Naioth. Her extensive gardens were nearly always filled with eager little ones plucking weeds or berries under her keen supervision. None left without a kiss on the forehead from Eliora and a fistful of vibrant blooms for their mother's table.

"Just walking your nephew home," Samuel replied, then gave me a teasing nudge. "So he doesn't get lost again."

My uncle barked a laugh. "A good idea. We all know he is prone to doing so."

I didn't mind the jest at my expense. In fact, it made me feel connected in a way I'd ached for during those lonely years. Part of the family who'd missed me while I'd been gone. But it also made me wish again for impossible things: for Elissa to be the one here teasing me; to show her the beauty of the village where I'd been born and introduce her to the people who inhabited such a unique and special place; for my mother and Eliora to someday dote on children with blue-green eyes and lightly freckled noses . . .

With a start, I realized both the boy with the lyre and his mother had reddish-brown hair so similar to the color of Elissa's that it made my gut ache with yearning.

"Your son is quite the talented musician, Zemirah," said Samuel.

The woman curved an arm around the boy, who was again blushing at the praise from the famous prophet. "His talents far outpaced mine by the time he was six, although I did have the most excellent of teachers." She gave Ronen a telling nod. "But if you'll excuse us, my husband is waiting for us with the wagon. We have a long way to travel."

"Perhaps you will join us next time as well? It's been far too long since I've heard you play," Ronen said. "You'll be back soon, won't you?"

"Yishai said we will come north again once the shearing is complete."

"Excellent." Ronen scrubbed the boy's ruddy curls. "When you return, I want to hear the song you wrote about the moon and the stars. It was beautifully done."

Shyly, the boy nodded, then gave Samuel a respectful bow before continuing down the street with his mother, lyre clutched tightly under one arm.

"She's not exaggerating," said my uncle as his gaze trailed after them. "I've taught hundreds to play the lyre over my lifetime, and that boy is the most naturally talented musician I've ever met, as though music was woven into his bones in the womb. From what I understand, he even *sees* music like colors swirling in his mind. Quite extraordinary. And the songs he writes . . ." He shook his head in wonder. "Inspired. Truly. Especially for one so young. His music would calm the most turbulent of souls."

"Will he join the Levitical choir when he is older?" I asked.

"He's not a Levite. He's a shepherd from the tribe of Yehudah. His mother took refuge here many years ago, so they come to visit whenever her husband travels to Ramah to sell yearlings. I've offered for the boy to stay with us and study music for a season or two, but his father is against it. Says his place is in the fields with the sheep." Ronen shook his head in frustration. "What a waste of extraordinary talent."

Samuel's gaze remained on the woman and her son until they disappeared down the path leading to the valley. "All in due course, Ronen. The boy will come when the time is right."

My uncle and I exchanged a curious glance at the odd statement, but instead of explaining, Samuel silently turned to walk away, apparently having forgotten he'd meant to come speak to my father. And then, to my surprise, my cousin Zevi appeared at the head of the path. I'd not seen him since shortly after he'd delivered me to my family, anxious as he'd been to return to Kiryat-Yearim and his own. However, to my shock, instead of Gavi coming up from Ramah with him, Adin appeared a few steps behind. As soon as he saw me, he began jogging toward me, passing Zevi on the way.

With a grin, I strode forward to greet him with an embrace. "It is good to see you!"

"And you as well!" He slapped my back exuberantly. "From what I hear, you had quite the adventure without me."

"And I'm told you became a soldier," I said, taking stock of the leather breastplate he wore and the short sword at his side. Broad-shouldered and well-built from the training he'd received both on Shardana and with the army of Israel, he barely resembled the wounded young man I'd met in Gaza. "And a husband, too, I hear?"

He tipped his chin. "That I have. That's why I came along with Zevi. My commander gave me leave to come home until she gives birth."

I blinked at him, deeply confused. "But it's only been a few months since you left Tyre."

He grinned, blue eyes full of mischief. "That, my friend, is quite the long story. And you'll have to tell me about life in Abibaal's palace—"

"Actually, that happens to be the very reason why we are here." Zevi's interruption sobered Adin immediately. "I went to report to King Saul a couple of days ago, since it was he who permitted us to retrieve you in the first place. He was eager for news of our neighbors to the north, both friend and foe. After hearing about your position within the household of Abibaal and your unique skill with languages, he sent me to fetch you."

"For what purpose?"

"Knowing the king—" Zevi frowned, looking apologetic—"and his penchant for gathering talent that can benefit the throne, I would guess he means for you to join his court at Gibeah."

31

Gibeah, Israel

Although the royal fortress at Gibeah sat atop a hill like that of Tyre, there was little comparison between the two. Where Abibaal's sprawling palace shone like a beacon, vibrant and ornate from every angle, Saul's appeared little more than a rustic military garrison with weathered limestone towers marking each of its four corners.

The guards at the gates hailed Zevi with respect as he, Gavi, and I entered. Although my older cousin had been commander over hundreds during battles in the past, his primary responsibility now was training recruits, developing exercise regimens, and tactical instruction. However, much of his time was spent in Kiryat-Yearim, helping his father cut and deliver timber all over the region, and enjoying his growing family with Yochana.

Once the king's steward had been notified of our arrival, he led us into the dimly lit palace. The weak sunlight peering through narrow slits high on the walls was bolstered by clusters of single-wick oil lamps set in niches. Especially on a day when storm clouds loomed overhead, threatening a deluge, the atmosphere inside was nearly as gloomy as outside.

"How is he today?" murmured Zevi to the steward as we approached the closed doors of the main hall.

"About the same as when you left last week," the steward replied in a low tone. "But there was a difficult report from the coastlands yesterday, so I hope you bring good news with you." My cousins had warned me of Saul's temperamental nature and his often-unreasonable demands, so I was prepared to tread lightly. But still, the steward's warning was unsettling. Since Zevi had come to fetch me two days ago, I'd spent hours in prayer, pleading for direction, for wisdom, and for clarity, but now I simply pleaded for courage to face whatever purpose Yahweh had for me here.

"The king has been meeting with his council this morning, along with a few priests from Nob," said the steward, "but if you'll wait here, I'll let him know you've arrived."

He slipped through the doorway, leaving us in the corridor. While Gavi and Zevi quietly discussed a recent Midianite incursion, my mind wandered back to Tyre, to a palace full of light and salt air and the beautiful woman whose eyes sparkled like the sea at midday. How long would I pine for her? A year? Two? The rest of my life?

I imagined she was near the shores of Shardana now, if not already there, with her delicate toes in the creamy sands, chin tilted upward while warm sea breezes teased her silken hair, her cheeks and freckled nose kissed rosy pink by the sun.

When I'd first met Elissa, I thought her soft and pampered, a fragile woman who would never adjust to life on the island. But beneath the polish of Tyre, her backbone was wrought-iron, a product of the heavy load she'd carried all these years, and as much as it pained me to admit, she would easily adapt to life with the Shardan. Without a doubt, they would adore her. I only hoped she'd found a way to endure leaving her mother behind in Tyre.

"The king will see you now," said the steward, who'd somehow materialized in front of me while I'd been dreaming of Elissa.

Zevi put his hand on my shoulder, squeezing in silent reassurance, and Gavi gave me a somber nod, a promise of unwavering solidarity. Although Avi was not here, I could almost feel him at my back as well. My throat went tight at the unspoken reminder of the vow marked on my right hand.

After what seemed a lifetime of walking alone into every unknown, I stepped forward into Saul's royal chambers bolstered by the men who'd fearlessly entered hostile territory to secure my freedom.

Unlike the corridor, this room was lit by scores of oil lamps in niches, on tables, and hanging in clusters from the high ceiling. The air stank of olive-oil smoke and rich incense, stinging my eyes as the men gathered around the king parted to allow us through, a few giving respectful nods to my cousins.

Seated on a wooden throne nearly as impressive as one of Abibaal's was Saul ben Kish, king of Israel. Even while sitting, his towering height was apparent. He would likely look my uncle Natan directly in the eye and topped me by a few fingers, at least. But where I was long limbs and lean muscle, Saul was solid bulk from chin to ankle. Similar to Abibaal, he had both the wild appearance of a warlord and the commanding presence of a born royal.

Above each of Saul's broad shoulders, a wolf was carved into the back of the throne, fangs bared. They were at once the symbol of his tribal origins and an unspoken threat, one that caused a faint shiver to race down my spine while the three of us knelt before him until given leave to rise by the steward.

"So, this is your cousin?" said Saul in a deep and resonant voice.

"It is, my king," said Zevi. "Shalem ben Iyov."

Saul tilted his chin, gaze traveling down to my feet and back up to my face in what was likely an unconscious habit of oppositional assessment. There was something vaguely familiar about the man, which I attributed to spying on his anointing with my cousins when I was a boy.

"I'm told you've spent the past few months in the palace of Tyre."

"Yes, my king."

"Zevi reported that you served as a personal scribe to Abibaal himself."

"For a short time, yes." There was no need to explain how it had been only a few days before everything turned upside down.

The king hummed thoughtfully. "From what I understand, it seems Israel owes you a debt of gratitude for preventing war with Tyre."

"None, my king," I said, eyes downcast. "I only meant to uncover the truth."

"A man of humility, I see," said Saul.

"If I may speak, my king?" Zevi interjected. At Saul's nod, he continued. "As Shalem is a man who does not raise himself above others, I will speak on his behalf. His bravery and intelligence did indeed dissuade Tyre from coming south to fight at Gaza's side as well as prevent the Asherites from being destroyed for a lie. Although he has little memory of his life before his abduction by Sidonian traders, he has remained steadfast in his loyalty to Israel."

I wasn't certain how true that was, but I trusted Zevi's discernment in dealing with Saul, whom he'd served under for the past thirteen years.

"Yes, yes. You've told me all these things before, Commander. Now I want to hear from your cousin." Saul leaned back in his seat, the red-gold crown on his head glinting in the lamplight. A pinch of recognition hit the center of my chest. I'd seen Zahava's work only once, when Adin showed me the unfinished breastplate she was working on for Enesidu, but I recognized her skill in the snaking vines and delicate leaves encircling Saul's head. The fact that the crown he wore was not the original *Atarah Hod* made by her ancestors was a secret few would ever know.

"Well . . ." Saul prompted, waving an impatient hand. "Go on."

I furrowed my brow. "My king?"

He let out an annoyed sigh, signaling for a servant to refill his wine. "Tell me about Abibaal. The palace. Tyre. Their defenses. Their weaknesses. Anything. Everything."

A frisson of something oddly protective welled up. But if I refused to reveal what I knew about Tyre, I suspected Zevi and Gavi might be blamed for my reticence. So I told the king about the city of Tyre, its grand harbors full of sleek and sturdy ships, about the opulence of a palace paneled by cedar with soaring beams held aloft by vast columns. Of walls so thick and tall they were practically impenetrable. Of gardens full of wild animals and every exotic plant. Of a large standing army, countless chariots, and an unparalleled naval force. Of treaties with Egypt and Philistia and many other nations and tribes in the region. Of vast and lucrative trading networks that spanned the Great Sea and even into the icy north, where tin mines abounded in deep green forests.

With each detail, Saul's deep brown eyes grew wider, gradually filling with what I recognized as the same avaricious gleam I'd seen in Abibaal's gaze when he'd learned of Shardana's treasures. The king leaned forward as I spoke, large hands steepled as he listened intently.

When I paused, uncertain what else to say, the king stared at me, his intensity causing the hair on the back of my neck to rise. I imagined this must be what it would feel like to face this warrior-king across a battlefield, unarmed and vulnerable. Every muscle in my body was strung tight, and my pulse rushed hard in my veins. My cousins at my side were still as stone, as if they too sensed danger.

Finally, Saul sat back, taking a long draft from his silver cup while I willed my stomach to uncoil. Before I could brace myself for whatever came next, the king spat his mouthful of wine on the floor beside his throne.

"What sort of swill is this?" he shouted, then hurled the cup itself aside with a clatter.

Though neither one of them made a show of it, I felt both Zevi and Gavi shift toward me and a half step ahead, as if preparing to protect me from their own king. My cousins were loyal to the point of foolishness.

The servant who'd poured the wine scurried back, face aflame as he hurried to clean up the mess. "A thousand pardons, my king."

"Where did that foul drink even come from?" Saul demanded. "A cesspit?"

One of the men from behind us stepped forward, visibly shaken. "It was a gift, my king. My apologies that it was not to your liking. I'll send for a different vintage right away."

The king narrowed his eyes. "Are you trying to *poison* me, Achbar? Is that what this is? Are you in league with my enemies?"

Achbar blanched. "No, my king, of course not—"

Saul ignored his protestations, launching into a furious litany of accusations, each more vicious than the next, and to my shock, even cursed the stricken man in the name of foreign gods.

Although Zevi had warned me of shifts in Saul's moods, the severity was truly shocking to witness. Even Abibaal in all his arrogance did not fly into such irrational rages.

"Get out of my palace!" Saul screamed, spittle flying from his mouth. "You have no more place on my council!"

Face crimson, Achbar fled for his life, as Saul then tore into his steward for daring to serve tainted wine. Head down, the steward remained still as stone while the king excoriated him, obviously used to such harsh treatment. It reminded me all too well of my time with the Sidonians, who considered me and the rest of their slaves less than human.

This was the man Yahweh had chosen to inhabit the throne of Israel? To care for and defend his beloved people? Instead of representing Yahweh by ruling in righteousness and wisdom, he was consumed by bitterness, suspicion, and increasing greed. No wonder Saul had been rejected, his blessing and cover removed.

Samuel's words came to mind. ". . . *what has filled the void will do great damage.*" I had no doubt he was right. As long as this man sat on the throne of Israel, the people would remain in darkness as well. I could only hope that whoever succeeded Saul would be a man of humility and reverence for the Most High.

After a while, Saul seemed to run out of awful names to call his faithful servant and demanded fresh wine. The entire room seemed to hold its collective breath until he'd slung back two full cups.

Satisfied, the king sat back on his throne and turned his wolfish gaze on me.

My stomach twisted. There was no guessing what Saul might say or do next.

To my surprise, he merely picked up the conversation as if nothing had happened. "Zevi tells me that not only did you convince Abibaal not to go to war with us, which my spies in the north corroborated with a report that the recent military buildup ceased, but that the king of Tyre owes you his life and that of his family."

Apparently, Zevi had been selective about the details of my time in Tyre. But what good would it do to try and explain how I'd gone from trusted personal scribe to imprisoned and banished, especially when I'd been caught mid-embrace with the king's daughter?

The memory of that night once again stirred longing for her. For as difficult as it was to think of her married to Torben, I was grateful she was far away from whatever unknown dangers lurked in that palace. To me, Haldon's death had only raised more questions than it provided answers. It was far too convenient that he'd died by his own hand just as his involvement with the Sidonians was proved.

". . . and so you'll go," Saul was saying as my mind snapped back to attention. "Convince him that trade between our peoples would be both lucrative and beneficial. We control the Jezreel Valley now, and therefore the eastern route to Damascus. That should be plenty of leverage to secure access to timber to expand this palace, among other projects I have in mind. Perhaps you can even convince him to loan me a few of his architects to design the expansion."

I glanced around, confused at the turn in the conversation and uncertain who he was speaking to. But both Zevi and Gavi stared back at me, their expressions troubled. What had I missed while my mind was wandering?

One of the priests dared speak without permission. "What about the temple, my king? You did promise to build a permanent sanctuary at Nob."

Saul's jaw ticked. "Once we've secured a trade agreement with Tyre, there will be plenty of timber for a multitude of such undertakings. *I'll* decide which takes precedence once I have Abibaal's full cooperation." He turned his attention back to me. "Aside from access to trade roads, what does he covet most?"

My mouth went dry as I tried to gather my scattered wits, a dull ache forming above my right eye.

"I . . . forgive me, my king," I began, sidestepping his question in favor of scrambling for a defense against his plan to have me negotiate with Abibaal on his behalf. "But I . . . I did not leave Tyre under the best of circumstances. I was told to leave and never return."

Saul waved his hand at me, his copper and silver rings glimmering in the lamplight. "You'll be under my banner and bearing plenty of gifts for the king. Tradition dictates that emissaries are given safe passage, even across enemy lines. And, of course, I'll send a well-armed escort with you to prove that you represent me."

"With all respect, my lord, I am only a scribe. A former slave. And since I've returned to Naioth, I have been in training to perform my sacred duties as a Levite."

Almost imperceptibly, Zevi shifted closer again, and Gavi's hand twitched at his side. No matter how respectfully I'd spoken, I'd argued with a king. I braced for his ire to flare as it had done with Achbar, but Saul only took another deep draft of his wine. "A Levite, are you?"

I nodded, the hair on my neck prickling at the undercurrent of disdain.

"You look a little old to be one of those simpering fools bowing at Samuel's feet."

I swallowed hard. "After my long absence, I am certainly behind my peers in Levitical training. But I am committed to performing my sacred duties at the Mishkan as soon as my studies are complete and I am adequately prepared for service."

"I am your king." Saul waved his cup in my direction, red liquid sloshing onto the ground. "You will do as I say."

Panic clawed at my chest. I could *not* go back to Tyre. Not only was it possible Abibaal would have me arrested on sight, maybe even stripped of my freedom all over again, but I'd have to return to a place haunted by the memories of Elissa, reminded over and over that she was the wife of another man. After all I'd endured, after all my family had endured, I refused to believe Yahweh would send me back, especially in the service of a king he had rejected. Perhaps once the man Samuel claimed would one day sit on that throne was raised to power, I would willingly offer my talents for the sake of my people, but I was no longer a slave. I would not bow my knee to an illegitimate king.

I took a deep breath and prayed for clarity of mind as I opened my mouth to refuse, on the grounds that my duty to Yahweh superseded any I had to the man before me, when a vision rose up.

I saw Saul just as he was now, seated on his throne with a false crown of red-gold on his head, but the two wolves carved into the wood had come to life, their vicious fangs buried deep in the king's neck on either side, greedy eyes glimmering in victory as a bloody wound appeared in the center of his chest. Saul's eye sockets were pits of black, his face drained of life, and his mouth gaping—somehow breathing but a dead man all the same. Horrified by the sight, I lifted my eyes to what appeared to be a vast spray of stars overhead, far more plentiful and glorious than the night I'd stood atop the tower with Elissa. A bright light appeared in the heavens, outshining the moon by magnitudes. I could not look away. I did not want to. Because the source of the light came from a throne of such majesty and beauty that my feeble human words could never do it justice. The Light was All Powerful. The Light was Truth. And the Light was Love.

Then, as quickly as it had appeared before me, the vision was gone. Leaving only the human king before me, appearing far smaller than he had before.

I caught my breath, dazed and head spinning as I tried to comprehend what had just happened and what it all meant.

One thing was clear: The man seated on the throne of Israel was only there at the pleasure of the King Above All Kings. His reign would end. But that of the One seated on the throne of the heavens would never pass away. It was to *him* I owed my allegiance. I would gladly bind myself as a servant to the Master of All for the rest of my days. And if that meant following the Lion back into the darkness of the unknown, as Samuel had encouraged me to do, then I would obey. There must be some greater purpose in my returning to Tyre, or such a compelling vision would not have come to me when it did.

Although I could practically feel the impatience vibrating from Saul, I paused, dropping my head as I weighed what to say to the king carefully, making certain to listen for the Voice of the Ancient One at the center of my being and then pleading for courage to speak Truth before I opened my mouth.

"I will go."

"Excellent." Saul lifted his empty cup in salute. "I'll have—"

"However—" I cut him off, lifting an apologetic hand—"as I told you before, my *first* duty as a son of Levi is to Yahweh."

Saul's smug smile melted like wax and his eyes flared as I continued.

"From the moment Levi was set apart at the Mountain of Yahweh, it has been our responsibility to tend to his beloved people and his sanctuary. I was trained from birth to carry out those duties and to set aside all other selfish pursuits for this holy calling."

It did not matter that I had little recollection of my early years in Naioth; the weight of that sacred purpose was etched on my bones.

"So I will go and speak to Abibaal on your behalf because Yahweh has made it clear he has a purpose in my doing so. But then I must return to Naioth, continue my studies, and wait on Yahweh's direction."

The ensuing silence echoed loudly throughout the room as everyone waited for Saul to respond. On either side of me, my cousins stood like sentinels, their bodies strung taut, but neither one had tried to interject, seeming to trust that I knew my own mind, even if their natural instincts were to protect me like they always had.

"Fine," Saul said, his tone flat. "You'll act as my emissary when needed, and as a translator when foreign dignitaries come to Gibeah. Otherwise, scribble in your scrolls and play priest all you like."

After so many years of serving as Raphad's translator, I recognized the statement for what it was—a concession in a negotiation. He was giving me ground while ensuring he retained the upper hand.

Pausing, I listened. Asked for guidance. Then listened some more until I was certain of my answer. Then I bowed my knee before King Saul, telling him it would be my honor to serve as Israel's emissary to Tyre. But I bowed my heart and will to the King of Kings and prayed that just as he'd done during all the years I was lost, he would continue to walk beside me every step of the way.

32

Elissa

I stared up at the silent sky. I should have gone back to my quarters hours ago, but there was something peaceful about lying here on my back, head pillowed on the cradle of my crossed arms while staring up at the sparkling expanse as it turned slowly overhead.

"There you are!" Melita appeared at the top of the Celestial Tower stairway. "I've been looking everywhere for you. So have the Crows."

I let out a sigh. If it were possible, Abenasser was even more overprotective than he'd been before. I'd been forced to find new ways to dodge his underlings. Tonight had been fairly easy, since the newly elevated eunuch had imbibed too much wine with his evening meal. He'd fallen asleep outside my door, clearing my way to sneak up here. Abenasser would be furious, but I'd had enough of feeling like a prisoner. Everyone in the palace had been scrutinized and questioned, no matter their status, and all belongings searched for evidence of treachery—including my own. Even now, every scrap of papyrus was examined before it was carried in or out of the gates.

After my father had sent the king of Sidon the bloodless bodies of the traitorous scribe and the men Shalem's cousins had captured, there had been no further attacks on Tyre. As expected, Hannibel, the king of Sidon, denied all knowledge of the plot to overthrow my father, even sending a caravan of lavish gifts in an overture of friendship, but I doubted Abibaal would ever fully trust Sidon again.

The Gazan princes also had disavowed any knowledge of the scheme, admitting only to pushing Yarikh to join their campaign against Saul's forces. They'd sworn to have left my brother on his ship, insensible from drink, hours before the fire started, and produced witnesses to back their claim. It was determined that a torch must have fallen in the hold of his ship, spreading to a cargo ship loaded with olive oil. The fire had swept through the docks, burning many smaller vessels, along with most of the cargo that was stored nearby and even a few of the dockside inns and shops. It would take months to rebuild, but my father vowed the port would be even grander once it was complete. If only my brother could be restored to life as well.

I could not understand why he'd gotten so entangled with Enesidu's sons, who'd fled the city as soon as they'd managed to convince the king they had no part in his death, but I did not for a moment believe they were completely innocent. If only I had some way to prove what I felt in my gut. Yet another reason I needed to escape my room tonight, since terrible visions of my brother's death haunted my sleep. I patted the stone roof beside me in invitation. "Come, sister. Watch the stars with me."

Melita joined me, stretching out her long body and fixing her own eyes on the spray of twinkling lights scattered across the deep blue canopy overhead.

"It's so lovely," she murmured. "I wonder how many there are up there."

"Far too many to count."

"Do you really think the gods can see us from up there?"

From the time we were small, the Crows had taught us that deities manifested as points of light in the heavens, their chariots moving slowly across the sky as they watched over the affairs of men.

"I don't know, Meli. It seems to me that a true God would not remain on a fixed course across the sky but would set those cycles into motion. Shalem told me . . ." I paused, catching my breath as I realized it was the first time I'd said his name aloud since he'd left Tyre.

She turned her face to me, voice soft. "What? Tell me."

I kept my gaze pinned to a particularly brilliant star pulsing icy blue and white directly overhead. I took a deep breath and continued, "He said Yahweh positioned every star in the sky with only a word from his mouth. That he spoke the sun and moon into existence. And that there is no god above him."

"And do you believe that?"

I hoped it was true. That the Creator of all, the one who reigned from a glorious throne above all other gods in the vast heavenlies, was the same God who brought my mother back to life.

"How else do you explain my mother's healing?"

Since she'd embraced worship of Yahweh, she'd blossomed like a flower in the spring. No longer bound to our room locked in grief and torment, she enjoyed the company of the other concubines daily, her bright laughter once again filling the women's courtyard as she played games with the children the way she'd done when I was small. She still grieved for Yarikh—there were days her smile was a little dim, and even times I'd seen her wipe tears from her cheeks—but her newfound faith in the God of the Hebrews had freed her from whatever dark spirit had tormented her for so long.

Melita shook her head. "I have no explanation at all. Even the king seemed to take notice at the wedding."

After a few weeks to allow for the mourning of her brother, Seriyah's prince had traveled alone to Tyre to plead for his bride, insisting a large celebration was not necessary and that he only wanted my sister by his side. Our father had gladly relented, eager to confirm the covenant between Tyre and Gebal, one he probably feared might never come to fruition. I'd tried to be glad for Seriyah, but I was far too conscious of the void she'd left behind.

It was only the memory of the brilliant smile on her face as she pledged herself to the heir of Gebal atop this very tower at sunset that softened the sting of missing her.

The ache for Shalem, however, had only grown. I'd forever be haunted by the pain on his battered face as I'd turned away from him in that courtyard. And when the Shardan had arrived last month, I'd thought my broken heart would shatter completely while my father presented me as the treaty bride to solidify their bargain.

It was Shalem's lessons that saved me from being immediately swept off to their distant island, since I alone could negotiate terms with King Uvaldo in his tongue. He was easily swayed to propose a longer betrothal period to give his men a chance to learn shipbuilding techniques in the king's shipyards. Even if it was only a temporary reprieve, I was more than grateful for the extra time with my mother and Meli. But every time I used the language Shalem had taught me, it was still his low, gentle voice I heard in my mind. I missed him more every day, especially whenever I looked at the stars.

"He's quite handsome, don't you think? In a terrifying sort of way."

Confused, I turned to stare at my sister. "Who?"

"Torben. Your bridegroom. Who else?"

I huffed a laugh. He certainly was that. When Uvaldo, the grizzled pirate-king had announced I was to marry his nephew, whom he'd recently pronounced his heir, I thought my father might perish from delight.

Melita's description of Torben as terrifying was fitting, since he was in every way the embodiment of the pirates I'd imagined. His broad, thick-muscled shoulders and towering height would give even the most battle-hardened Tyrian soldiers pause in a fight. And like the rest of the Shardan men, he wore multiple braids in his shoulder-length, dust-brown hair, which was shaven on both sides of his head to reveal swirling tattoos. The scar that slashed from just under one gray eye through his top lip did little to mar what was indeed a strikingly handsome face.

And yet I missed kind eyes of golden-brown, a patch of silver in black curls, and the calm and steady presence of the man who'd never really been a servant in my eyes. And I had only a few more weeks to indulge in doing so before I must lock away those memories for good. It was the only way I would survive this marriage without falling to pieces. That, and knowing Melita would be spared my fate.

"Has Elithan brought you more gifts?" I asked. The merchant who'd shown interest in me months ago had quickly shifted his attention to Melita once my betrothal was announced.

She sighed. "Yes. Nearly every other day lately."

"You don't sound pleased."

"I am. He's quite generous, as you know. And kind. It's only . . ." Her voice drifted away.

"What?"

"He's . . ." She placed a palm over her face, groaning. "Ugh, I am terrible. He's so *short*."

A surprised laugh burst free before I clamped my hand over my mouth, but still I could not control the giggles that welled up in my throat. The man barely reached Melita's chin, after all.

"Lissi!" she hissed, pushing at my shoulder in mock frustration, which only made it worse. Soon, both of us were suppressing laughter behind our hands, tears dripping down our faces.

"I'm sorry," I sputtered, brushing the wetness from my cheeks. "I should not laugh."

"At least he's rich," she said with a shrug, wiping at her own face. "And he'll shower me with every luxury."

"As he should. You deserve to be treated like the queen you were born to be. And you won't have to worry about being sent away from Tyre."

She turned a sad smile my way. "If only you could stay too. I don't know what I will do without you. Especially now that Seriyah is gone."

I linked my fingers with hers, taking a deep breath. "You'll watch over my mother for me, won't you?"

"Of course I will. Although now that she is so changed, you won't need to worry as much. Truly, it is a miracle."

I hummed in agreement, and the two of us returned to searching the sky.

"Do you think . . ." She paused, biting her lip, but kept her eyes on the starry host overhead. "Your mother said she asked Yahweh to show himself to her. Do you think he would do the same for me if I asked? Even without sacrifices like we offered at the Temple of Astarte?"

"I don't know, Meli. But I guess it's worth a try, isn't it?"

We went quiet for a long while, listening to the gentle shush of the distant waves on the rocky shoreline as the stars continued along their fixed paths overhead. Paths that must have been determined by the One who set them into place from the beginning.

"Are you there, God of the Hebrews?" my sister whispered. "If so, will you reveal yourself?"

For so many years, I'd thought my sister timid, half afraid of her own shadow, but in this she'd been far braver than me. I squeezed her fingers tight, echoing her words in my heart.

There was no audible answer from the heavens, no booming declaration to shake the earth. We lay there for a long time, until my back began to ache from the hard stone beneath me and my arm cramped from cushioning my head for so long. Just as I opened my mouth to suggest that Melita and I get some sleep, a streak of light darted across the edge of my vision. I paused, thinking perhaps I'd imagined it. But then Meli gasped.

"Lissi. Did you see that?" She pointed to where another streak of light had shot across the expanse. And then, after only a few more breaths, yet another arced over the night sky, brighter and bolder, followed by another and another until it seemed the heavens were falling all around us, brilliant lights shooting across the deep blue expanse in all directions like loosed arrows. Melita and I watched the dazzling display in openmouthed wonder until, at some point during the astonishing answer to my sister's simple prayer, I fell asleep, feeling seen and heard in a way I never had before. If Yahweh cared enough to show himself to me, even on this tower dedicated to the gods of Tyre, then perhaps on the faraway island of Shardana I wouldn't be so alone after all.

33

Shalem

City of Tyre
One month later

I'd never felt so foolish. The heavily embroidered and fringed outer garment flapped against my shins, I was constantly forced to push back the voluminous sleeves, and the stiff leather sandals had already rubbed a blister on the pad of my left foot. A wide, striped sash was wrapped three times around my waist and tied in some sort of complicated knot I would never be able to replicate on my own. And on my head was a gaudy blue turban, woven with gold and crimson threads, the long tassels hanging down over my shoulders.

Yet even though the extravagant clothing made me look the part of Saul's royal emissary, the moment I walked through the gates of Abibaal's fortress, it felt as though I'd never left. As if I was still a powerless slave beholding this opulent palace for the first time.

However, unlike the day I had followed Raphad down the same cedar-paneled corridor, with my head down and a heavy load on my shoulders, this time I was accompanied by not only Zevi and Gavi in polished bronze armor and helmets, but also a small guard and a group of servants carrying gifts for the king. To my surprise, Komar, the king's steward, did not seem to recognize me, because as he led us through the palace, he described the advanced techniques used by the architects, pointing out each unique feature for our perusal as we walked toward Abibaal's receiving room. I was far too occupied looking for Elissa around every corner to listen to the steward's boasting, though I knew she was long gone. I even smelled the spicy-sweetness of her fragrance in the air as we entered the royal wing, the trick of my mind driving me mad with longing.

"I'm still stiff from riding that ridiculous camel for the last ten days," muttered Gavi from my right side, while Komar explained how the burbling fountains in the king's courtyard were moved by a mechanism underground. Two enormous gray birds squawked at us from perches in the shade of the portico, a recent addition to Abibaal's ever-expanding menagerie of exotic animals, if I wasn't mistaken.

"You could have walked," Zevi said dryly.

"And keep up with those long-legged beasts? They walk nearly as fast as you, Zev." He smirked. "Besides, anything is better than getting on a ship with Shay. I'd rather not end up on the seafloor."

I had very little desire to ever step aboard a seafaring vessel either. Two shipwrecks were enough for anyone to keep their feet firmly on the earth. Thankfully, Saul had provided a caravan of camels and wagons to carry us and the gifts for Abibaal on the long journey.

Zevi ignored him. "Are you ready for this, Shay?"

It should not have surprised me that Zevi and Gavi had insisted on coming back to Tyre with me. Although I'd argued with Gavi, since Zahava was so near her time and I hated for my cousin to miss the birth of his third child, he insisted he trusted his mother to take good care of his "little dove" and that his stepfather would see to it that she was attended by the best midwives his silver could guarantee.

However, I could not help but wish Avi and Adin were here with us.

Adin had been recalled to his unit days after his wife had given birth to a daughter. Avi had planned to come with us as well, but his oldest son broke an arm falling from a tree two nights before our departure, so he'd needed to remain in Naioth. Even so, I could feel his presence with me in the form of the daily prayers he vowed would be lifted on my behalf until I returned home once more.

I'd been astounded my mother had not fallen to pieces as I explained why I must travel north again. But she'd revealed she'd had her own dream while I'd been in Gibeah. While she would not tell me the details, only that Yahweh had given her a promise, she said that over the years of my disappearance, she'd learned to trust him in ways she'd never thought possible.

Since my striking vision in Saul's throne room, my own trust in the Most High had only grown. So when I answered Zevi, there was no wavering in my voice. "Yes, I am ready."

I could almost feel the vibrations of enormous golden paws leading me forward.

Komar ushered us into the king's receiving chamber, where Abibaal sat on his ornate chair with his panthers on either side, their unnerving golden eyes tracking our movements across the room.

We bowed low as Komar introduced me as the royal emissary of King Saul of Israel, a lofty title that did not settle well on my shoulders. But that title, along with the royal seal around my neck, had given me entrance to the palace. The irony that the seal of Abibaal had hung in its place three months before was not lost on me. It could only be Yahweh's doing that I'd garnered the trust of not just one but two powerful kings in my lifetime. However, one of those kings had banished me from his palace. And here I was, ignoring that command and trusting Saul's royal banner to protect me from the wrath of Abibaal.

"Up, up," said the king, waving us to our feet. "I'm eager to hear what Saul has to say—" His pause brought my chin higher. Abibaal was staring straight at me, his jaw agape.

"Is that . . . aren't you my *scribe*?"

I'd hoped the thick beard on my face and the turban hiding my silver patch of hair would hide my identity, at least for a short while, but Abibaal was far too observant for that. In fact, as his gaze darted to the bronze-clad warriors at my side, I was certain he recognized them as well.

"Yes, my lord," I replied, bowing low again. "Saul sent me to speak on his behalf. He sends his hopes that your family is well and ever-expanding, that your kingdom thrives on land and sea, and that friendship between Israel and Tyre will be established on solid ground for generations upon generations."

Leaning forward on his seat, the king stared at me with an unreadable expression. He opened his mouth, then paused, and closed it again. If I did not know better, I would almost think the King of Tyre was flustered.

"If it pleases the king, I have brought gifts from King Saul." I waved forward the first of Saul's servants, who carried a small chest containing an assortment of exquisite jewelry made by Gavi's wife.

Abibaal raised a staying palm, blinking rapidly. "Not just yet. First . . . first, there is something you *must* see. I did not know you were coming, so I'll have to tell the queen—" He paused abruptly, then began muttering to himself. "She'll understand . . . he *must* see the flame . . . explain how he would know . . ."

Now *I* was the one at a loss for words. I'd never seen Abibaal in such an agitated state. He was always in command, full of bluster and arrogance, even in private.

"Komar!" he bellowed, startling the panthers. "Where are you?"

The steward scuttled in from an adjacent room with his cone cap askew. "Yes, my king?"

The king stood, gesturing to us. "Take my guests to fresh quarters, and see to their servants as well. I'll go speak with the queen. We'll have to prepare a banquet, of course . . ." Then, as if in a daze, he strode from the room without a word of farewell.

All of us stared at the doorway in complete bewilderment. Including Komar.

"What have you done to the king?" he asked, frowning.

"I truly have no idea."

After a few moments of confused gawking at the door, Komar seemed to remember his duties and snapped into action. After assuring me he would make certain the king received the jewelry, perfumes, fabrics, and other offerings we'd brought with us, he swiftly arranged for the costly gifts to be taken to the treasury for safekeeping, our animals bedded down in the stables, and for Saul's guards and servants to be roomed at the other end of the palace. Then the steward himself led Zevi, Gavi, and me to the guest wing.

"I cannot believe I did not recognize you under all that finery, Mattaniel," he said as we crossed the courtyard once again.

"My real name is Shalem. I was . . . lost many years ago and did not know who I was until my cousins came here to find me."

"Well, *whoever* you are, you've quite shocked the king." He chuckled. "I don't think I've ever seen him so out of sorts."

As Abibaal's right hand, Komar was likely the best person to prod for information about what had happened in Tyre after I left. The man was, without a doubt, the most well-informed servant in this palace. However, since his job required tight lips, I'd have to take care in my approach. Through Prince Yonatan's spy network, Gavi had learned that tensions were still high with Sidon, but that Abibaal had abandoned plans to send his armies into Israel. The ban on Asherites in the city had been lifted as well, so our plan to entrap the true thieves had managed to prove their innocence after all.

"The reconstruction of the port appears to be making good progress," I began.

"That it is. The king's crews are working day and night to rebuild the docks on an even grander scale."

"Was it ever determined who started the fire in the harbor that night? I understand the Asherites were exonerated."

"They were." He winced. "Witnesses testified that it was simply a terrible accident. Once the wind carried sparks to a nearby cargo ship full of olive oil, catching its sails on fire, there was no stopping the blaze."

"From what I heard, the fire began on Prince Yarikh's ship."

"It did. Some even say the prince himself was at fault, but I still think the blame lies with those Philistines," he said, voice low and full of venom. "I did not trust them from the start. All they did was stir up trouble."

"What happened to the Gazans?" I asked.

"Since there was no way to prove their involvement in the fire, the king sent them away. Told them never to set foot in Tyre again and to deliver the message to their father that Gaza should fight its own wars."

"And what of Sidon?" Before Komar could answer my question, the very last voice I expected to hear asked one of its own.

"*Mattaniel?* What are you doing here?"

I blinked my eyes, thinking perhaps I was seeing things. But no, there stood two very large pirates, looking completely out of place in Abibaal's luxurious palace with their partially shaved heads and braided beards.

"What are . . . ?" I began before Torben barreled toward me, then wrapped me in a tight embrace that knocked the breath from my lungs.

"Salpa! You are here!" he said in his undulating language, using the name he'd given me in honor of a silver-streaked fish common to Shardan waters. He shook me twice by the shoulders, grinning widely. "I thought we'd not see you again, brother." He released me, but before I could catch my breath, Uvaldo yanked me into his own suffocating embrace. For as affectionate as my family had proven to be when I returned to Naioth, the Shardan were three times as expressive with those they considered friends or family.

"This city is all you and Raphad told us—and more," said the old man as he slapped my back. "The shipyards alone are a wonder!"

"But . . . why are you still here?" I asked, mind spinning with the implications. Because if Torben and Uvaldo were still in the city, then so was *she*. My stomach dropped as my gaze lifted, first landing on a scowling Shamzur before tracking to the two women nearby.

Elissa stared back at me, ocean-eyes shimmering as Melita pressed close to her side.

Uvaldo pounded my back once again, so hard my teeth rattled. "I knew I was right to listen to my nephew when he said to let you three live. Just think, in only two weeks, he'll be married to a daughter of the king of Tyre! And we have *you* to thank!"

34

Elissa

Shalem is here. The unbelievable words kept tumbling over and over in my mind while I marveled at the change in him. It wasn't just the beard or the wealthy clothing; something intangible in his bearing had shifted while he was away. I'd seen a glimpse of it the day he'd left, when he'd seemed to shake off his broken shackles to speak with surprising authority to my father about his dream and his God. But there was a new self-assurance in the way he carried himself now, like a man who'd never been enslaved in the first place.

His lovely golden eyes continued to flick to me as he told Torben and Uvaldo about the command by the king of Israel to return as an emissary. It had been so many weeks since I'd been in his arms, but I could almost feel them around me now, even though five paces separated us.

Although she understood nothing of what the men were saying to one another, Melita's steadying grip on my arm had not relaxed since Shalem had appeared like a dream come to life.

"I did not expect to find you here," said Shalem. "How long have you been in Tyre?"

"A little over two months," said Torben. "Thanks to Elissa,

we've been learning Tyrian shipbuilding methods. We don't have cloud-scraping cedars on the island, of course, but we'll adapt their ways to build our own seafaring vessels."

"She's quite resourceful." Uvaldo gave me a gap-toothed smile. "She'll make a wonderful queen for our people."

Shalem's flinch was so slight, I was certain only I noticed it. "She will indeed."

I swallowed against the burn that welled in my throat, glad no one had asked me to speak. Melita squeezed my arm reassuringly, and I lifted a silent prayer of gratitude for my sister. For so long, I'd thought Melita's tender heart and sensitive nature a weakness, something she must overcome to be a woman of strength, but it could not be further from the truth. The more she embraced the God Who Hears, as Danice had called him, the more her fearfulness diminished, allowing the true beauty of her gentle soul to shine like the sun. If I could be only half as tenderhearted as Melita someday, I would consider myself blessed.

"Tell me, Salpa," said Torben, continuing in his own language, "I've heard rumors I don't quite understand because these Tyrians speak so quickly, not like you taught me. Are there eels in these halls?"

I scrambled to comprehend the strange question, wondering if I'd misunderstood his words. What could eels have to do with this palace? And *what* was a salpa?

Shalem did not hesitate to respond. "I'm certain of it."

Torben folded his arms across his broad chest. "Tell me."

"A young scribe was found dead, by his own hand, or so it seemed, with evidence pointing to his involvement in the plot against the throne. You've heard two princes were killed?"

A dip of Torben's chin confirmed he had.

"I've stewed on it for three months now. To me, the scribe's part was minimal. He was a messenger, tasked with delivering and altering documents. But he was not even in Tyre when the ship was attacked. He'd gone home because his father and brothers were killed. Someone else—someone close to the king's inner circle—

knew exactly where his ship would be and when, and more than likely who exactly was aboard and where they were sleeping that night, even though there were last-minute changes to the passenger manifest. I also suspect there was someone aboard Prince Yarikh's ship who caused it to tarry behind ours, giving the Sidonians opportunity to attack."

The question of eels made more sense now. They were the type of creature to slither into hidden cracks and openings, waiting patiently for the perfect moment to strike. We'd been warned as children to take care not to put our hands or feet into such places while swimming in the sea, lest we suffer the wrath of needle-sharp teeth and locking jaws that twisted and tore without mercy. If Shalem was right and there were still conspirators inside this palace bent on overthrowing the throne of Tyre, they were likely watching and waiting for the perfect chance to strike again.

"Is this house built on solid rock? Or shifting sands?" asked Uvaldo, his grizzled face full of concern. "We need to know *before* we cut a covenant with them."

Shalem's eyes darted to me briefly. "Tyre's foundation is as firm as the stone it is built upon, I have little doubt. As for the eels . . . my cousins and I mean to poke around in a few crevices and see what we can uncover."

I was so wrapped up in the conversation that when Shamzur spoke in my ear, I nearly yelped. "Your gown was delivered this morning, my lady. Perhaps we should be going?"

I pressed a palm to my racing heart as I caught my breath. I'd quite forgotten the eunuch was here.

"Alterations must be made immediately so it's ready for the ceremony."

"Oh . . . yes. Of course," I stuttered, while Shalem, his cousins, and the Shardan men stared at me.

Before today, I'd looked forward to trying on the dress Shamzur was having made for the ceremony. In fact, it was the only thing I'd actually anticipated about my marriage to Torben. Now I could think of nothing more torturous. But at least Shamzur had provided me with the perfect means of escape. So I avoided Shalem's gaze as I made my excuses to the men, then let Shamzur guide Meli and me back to the women's wing, where I stood before the same copper mirror where Seriyah had admired her own wedding finery. I feigned delight as the exquisite purple-dyed Egyptian linen garment was wrapped around my body and held back my tears while Shamzur fidgeted with the embroidered hem and adjusted the pleated waistline with tiny bone pins. It made me miss my older sister just as much as it pricked at my broken heart.

Shamzur's shaven brows pulled together as he took a step back to assess, clucking his tongue. "Not quite right," he murmured, then pulled the ruby-headed toggle pin from his own neckline and jammed it through the two top layers of fabric to hike it up on one side and better reveal the fringed layer below.

"That does look much better," said Melita. "Where *did* you learn to fashion such beautiful clothing, Shamzur?"

"Hmm?" He tilted his bald head back and forth as he eyed his work. "Oh . . . my mother was an accomplished seamstress. She put a needle and thread in my hand before I could speak full sentences."

"She must be so proud of your position here in the palace."

His mouth pursed tight. "She died."

"I am sorry to hear that." Meli looked stricken by the misstep.

"It was long ago," he said dismissively, bending low to adjust the underskirts once again.

While she waited for Shamzur to finish his adjustments with the gown, Melita wandered about the room, sliding her fingers over the many colorful folds of fabric on shelves, opening drawers, and sifting through scraps.

I faced my reflection in the copper mirror, a throbbing ache in the center of my chest as I thought again of Shalem, of the shadow of pain on his face when Uvaldo spoke of me being Shardana's queen, something I had no wish to be.

I stared into my own tear-filled eyes and spoke to the God I was only beginning to know. *Why, Yahweh? Why did you bring him back now?*

Melita's voice cut into my silent pleas as she peered into a basket atop Shamzur's worktable. "What were Shalem and the others talking so intently about earlier? I did not understand more than a few Shardan words."

"The plot against the king." I quickly swiped a tear from my cheek and cleared my throat. "Shalem is convinced others are involved."

Wide-eyed, she turned, a crimson cord she'd pulled from the basket dangling from her hand. "In Tyre?"

"In this palace. Ow." I hissed at the prick of one of Shalem's bone needles against my thigh. Mouth full of pins, he grunted an apology as he continued his task.

Melita hurried over, the long, knotted cord dragging behind her. "How does he know? Are we in danger?" I hated the pinch of fear in her voice.

Still standing atop the dais, I set my hand on her shoulder and gave it a reassuring squeeze. "Shalem is the most brilliant man I've ever known, Meli. If there are others in league with Sidon, I'm certain he and his cousins will find them."

She bit her lip, blue eyes brimming with trepidation as she picked at the knots on the cord. "Torben could probably help, too, don't you think? Even though he doesn't speak our language well, he's very observant. The other day, he saw me out in the gardens and said—"

She gasped, jolting as Shamzur yanked the cord from her hand. "What are you doing pawing my belongings?"

Both of us gaped at the eunuch. I'd never heard the man so much as lift his voice to any of the women in this palace before.

"Forgive me," Melita said. "I was only curious."

He did not respond, turning his back to us as he replaced the cord in the basket.

"Go ahead and remove the garment," he said over his shoulder, his tone once again mild and detached. "Once the alterations are finished, you'll need to try it on again."

Chastened into silence, a pink-cheeked Melita helped me remove the gown and redress while Shamzur folded the garment into a parcel and tied it securely with a complicated knot before calling one of the apprentice eunuchs to deliver it to a laundress.

Annoyed with Shamzur, I scrambled for some way to bring the smile back to my sister's face while also reminding him of his place. I stepped down off the dais and grabbed her hand. "Do you know what I think?"

She peered at me shyly. "What?"

"I think we should go visit the queen."

Her blue eyes flared. "We should?"

"Don't you want to see the baby?"

As I'd guessed, the mention of the newly born heir to the throne set a smile back on her lips. "Oh yes. I only got to see him during the naming ceremony. Do you think she'd let us hold him?"

Above anything in the world, Melita adored babies. I prayed someday she would have a multitude of her own golden-haired little ones to enjoy.

"Of course. He is our *brother*, after all," I said, leaning into the designation. Shamzur pressed his mouth into a line but otherwise did not react to the jab.

I slipped my arm into hers and led her from the room, delighted that she'd seemed to totally forget Shamzur's rudeness as she launched into recounting some delicious gossip she'd heard about Thalassa from her maid that morning. How I would miss my sweet sister when I was gone. Shalem may have returned to Tyre, but nothing had changed. I would marry Torben and go, for Melita's sake. Even so, the painful fissure in my heart had been torn open all over again, a wound I wasn't certain even Yahweh could heal.

35

Shalem

Entering the king's garden as an emissary instead of a slave was like walking into another of my strange, convoluted dreams. There were numerous dignitaries scattered about, sipping wine, gossiping, or seeking someone more important than themselves to impress. Instead of being ignored by these luminaries, I was introduced as King Saul's spokesman, offered all manner of rich food and drink, and greeted with respectful bows. If I did not have my cousins by my side—Gavi making snide comments under his breath every so often—I would for certain think I'd wake any moment curled in the dirt beneath a Sidonian trader's wagon.

But here I was, mingling with the wealthy and the royal as we waited for Abibaal, who had yet to appear at his own banquet nearly an hour after it began.

The invitation to this feast had arrived via Komar early this morning, along with new sets of clothing for myself, Gavi, and Zevi, and I certainly could not rebuff a summons from the king. Especially when I'd still not been given the chance to explain Saul's proposals.

Taking advantage of our guest access to the palace, Gavi, Zevi and I had visited Tabnit in the Hall of Records, who'd been overjoyed to see me. I'd gently prodded for information about Haldon, under the guise of feigning shock over his demise, but Tabnit seemed to know little about his apprentice's movements in the days after he returned to the palace, aside from his designated duties. The head scribe spent most of his days with his nose pressed into scrolls, so it did not surprise me. He ruled his small domain well but cared little for anything beyond those four walls.

My cousins and I had split up after that—Zevi to seek out the head of the guard in the palace barracks, Gavi to try wheedling information from some of the guardsmen lurking in the corridors, and I to talk with servants I'd worked alongside for months. However, while Zevi and Gavi uncovered a few details about the extensive interrogation of every person in the palace during the months I'd been gone, I garnered little more than suspicious looks, submissive bows, or confused, blank-eyed stares. I was no longer a peer, and like Komar, all of Abibaal's servants were famous for their tight lips with outsiders. They held coveted positions here; even the lowliest slaves ate and dressed well, so the punishment for disloyalty was far too costly.

Perhaps I was wrong to worry that there were others involved in the plot against Tyre, but the loose threads had nagged at me since I'd left. If there was someone in this palace biding their time for the perfect opportunity to take down Abibaal, then I was determined to root them out before I returned to Naioth. Hopefully, that would also be long before I was forced to watch Elissa marry Torben.

As foolish as it was, I could not stop searching for her among the crowd. Seeing her yesterday had been excruciating because not only was she marrying someone else within weeks, but I'd plainly seen my longing mirrored in her eyes. Three months apart had done nothing but make me love her even more. Yet instead of pulling her into my arms like I'd dreamed of since I'd left, I'd had to offer Torben my blessings for a happy and prosperous marriage and listen to Uvaldo prattle on about all the glorious seafaring ships he would one day have because of her shrewdness in negotiating the marriage contract with her father, thanks to the language lessons I'd given her.

"There he is!" came a familiar, booming voice from my left. Raphad strode toward me, his face deeply bronzed from the sun, looking strong and healthy as he threw his arms wide to gather me into a firm embrace, then he kissed both my cheeks.

"Mattaniel!" he said, grasping my face to shake me affectionately. "I am so glad to see you again, my loyal friend."

Torben and Uvaldo had told me of their surprise when Raphad returned to their shores. Apparently the journey there had been waylaid for weeks due to bad weather, but he'd been welcomed back as a hero for bringing news of a potential treaty with Tyre.

"How well you look!" he exclaimed. "These wealthy clothes suit you!"

"What are you doing here?" I asked.

"Abibaal invited me, of course." He leaned in, whispering loudly, "Now that I'm back in his good graces and my debt to him is nearly satisfied, my access to the palace is restored."

"Your wife said you proposed a colony?"

"Indeed I did. I spent only a couple of days in the king's prison," he said. "Just enough to give him time to cool his ire. Then I pleaded for an audience through the head guard, saying I had an idea that would make certain Uvaldo would give him whatever he wanted, which I knew would pique his interest.

"So, when Abibaal finally allowed me to be brought to him, I proposed again that I return to Shardana and talk to Uvaldo myself about establishing a Tyrian colony there. Far from just taking what we need from the mines and establishing trade across the sea, there are now plans for a thriving settlement, seeded by intrepid Tyrian families and ambitious merchants, tradesmen, and artisans. That way Tyre can have a permanent presence there, and the Shardan can benefit from established businesses, more demand for their goods, and more protection from an outpost of soldiers based there. I knew as soon as Uvaldo saw Tyre itself, he'd have visions of cities like this one all over his island too."

"But why didn't Abibaal tell me he'd sent you in the first place? For months I thought you were under the lash in the shipyards or on one of the building crews."

Raphad laughed heartily. "The king is no fool. I would guess he wanted to make certain you had plenty of incentive to fulfill your part of the bargain by thinking I was in chains."

That did seem to align with the way Abibaal managed to tip the balance of every negotiation to his own favor.

"Thankfully," said Raphad, "I've fulfilled my own bargain by bringing the Shardan here, eager to cut a covenant and open their mines, and am now allowed to start rebuilding what I lost."

"I'm glad to hear it. And I'm sure Portea is grateful to have you home again."

His grin stretched wide. "That she is. And I hear it's you I have to thank for bringing Danice to her doorstep. Portea is in love with the babe, of course, and has insisted we adopt Danice as our own daughter to ensure little Otzar is always cared for."

My jaw went slack. "Even though she is Hebrew?"

He waved a meaty palm. "Two of the best men I know are Hebrew. Why would that matter?"

Before I could ask whether Elissa knew about Danice joining his family, she appeared in the garden, walking arm-in-arm with Melita, a few paces behind Uvaldo and Torben as they approached us.

Like a thirsty deer scenting fresh water, my entire being was pulled toward her, but I forced myself to focus instead on greeting my Shardan friends, who'd also been given new clothing to wear tonight.

"How do they wear these robes all the time?" grumbled Uvaldo, tugging at the embroidered outer garment wrapped around his body and secured with a decorative toggle pin at his shoulder, then at the woven belt wrapped around his thick middle. "It's suffocating. I can barely move."

"King Uvaldo," I said, bowing extravagantly low, "I'd not realized you'd be gracing us with your presence tonight."

The elderly pirate puffed out his chest at my loud and overly fawning greeting. Although he probably hadn't understood much of it, my public deference to his status had drawn the attention of quite a few curious listeners.

The corner of Torben's lips twitched with amused approval.

"I am certain, my lord," I continued on, "that King Saul of Israel will also be interested in discussing a trade agreement with you, should you be so inclined."

Uvaldo's grizzled brows arched high as I lowered my voice and translated my own words.

"Would he?"

Frankly, I had no idea whether Saul would desire a connection with some far-flung island across the Great Sea, nor how the Shardan could benefit, but if anything, it lent Uvaldo a bit more credibility.

Raphad took up where I'd left off by leading Uvaldo and his nephew away to introduce them to a few of his wealthy friends.

"I feel almost as ridiculous as those pirates look in these garments," said Gavi, frowning down at the green-fringed kilt he'd been forced to don. "And I miss my knives."

"No one is allowed to bring weapons inside this palace, aside from Abibaal's guard, I'm afraid." I gave him a sideways glance. "And probably you most of all after you sliced the finger off that Sidonian in front of the king."

Gavi grinned wolfishly. "He screamed like a little girl, didn't he, Zev?"

Zevi only rolled his eyes heavenward, then continued silently surveying the crowd around us, diligent as always.

"Yes, he did." Elissa came closer, Melita at her side. The two of them had remained a few paces away, feigning disinterest in our conversation while sipping cups of wine. But Elissa's ear had been directed toward us the entire time.

"I apologize you were witness to that, my lady," said Gavi, looking uncharacteristically abashed.

She shrugged. "He deserved it. And I doubt he would have told you anything without such *incentive*."

Gavi's grin tilted. "I knew I liked you. Reminds me a little bit of Yochana, eh, Zev?"

Zevi turned his gaze on Elissa and gave a quick nod. "My wife would be honored by the comparison."

Elissa's smile was bright as she laughed. "I suspect it is I who should be honored. Tell me, is your wife a woman of strength?"

He dipped his chin. "Without a doubt. And the most talented perfumer in all of Israel. Among many nations, in fact. Her balms and fragrances are coveted all over the region, from Egypt to Damascus."

It was rare for Zevi to elaborate on anything; every word he spoke was deliberate and guarded. But when it came to Yochana, he was practically effusive.

Elissa's lips parted. "Is it she who concocted the scents all the women in this palace are coveting today? There is talk of little else besides the exquisite perfumes the king's wives are wearing this evening."

Zevi nodded, his slight smile betraying his pride.

Komar had obviously made good on his promise to ensure the gifts we'd brought were given to Abibaal. I'd noticed a couple of Abibaal's wives wearing the finely spun woolen cloaks, and the two long-horned oryx Saul had sent for the Garden of Beasts were tied up near the fountain, allowing Abibaal's guests to gawp at the lovely desert animals, which to the people of Tyre were quite exotic.

"That may be true," Gavi interjected, not to be outdone, "but it's *my wife* who created the jewelry Saul gifted to the king and queen. There is no finer goldsmith than my little dove."

That was the absolute truth. Her pieces were coveted the world over, although she never created red-gold anymore, and most jewelry was still attributed to her father for her own safety.

"Also, Avi's wife, Keziah, raised the four horses we brought along," I added. "Her own stallion is of a famous warhorse lineage in the Zagros Mountains."

"Such talented women in your family," she said. "I'd love to meet them someday." She winced at her own words, smile dropping away.

Elissa would never meet my cousin's wives. She'd never even see her sisters or her mother after she sailed away in a few weeks, most likely never to return to these shores.

"I'm hungry," Melita chirped, then tugged on Elissa's arm. "The king is taking forever. Let's go eat something before he arrives."

It seemed Melita was just as protective of her sister's heart as Elissa was.

"All right. But first—" She turned her eyes to me. The moment stretched long, my pulse thrumming as she held me captive in her potent gaze and the warm breeze wafted her spicy-sweetness my way. For as lovely as Yochana's perfumes were, there was nothing on earth to match the headiness of Elissa's nearness. She blinked three times, as if pulling herself out of the same deep pool I'd been drowning in, then extended a small parcel. "You forgot to take these with you when you left. Thank you again for all the months you spent patiently tutoring me."

I accepted the package, wrapped in a piece of linen cloth, my heart jolting into my throat when her soft skin brushed my palm before she walked away with her sister.

Unable to remove my eyes from her retreating back until she disappeared around the curve in the path, I measured my uneven breaths, willing myself not to chase after her, kiss the ground her silken slippers touched, and beg her to run away with me right this moment. She'd walked away from me twice now with a farewell in her beautiful eyes. I did not think I would survive the third.

"What is it?" asked Gavi, gesturing to the forgotten parcel in my hand.

In a daze, I removed the cord and unrolled the item from the fabric. It was the set of inks and reed pens she'd gifted me. But also inside the wooden box was the broken shell from that night on the beach. I could barely breathe as the memory of her in my arms, her lips on mine, washed over me . . .

Someone let out a startled scream behind us, which was immediately followed by a shout by what sounded like one of the guards.

Zevi was already on his way toward the disturbance as Gavi and I met gazes in silent accord to follow. The three of us pressed through the crowd of murmuring guests, either craning their necks to see what was going on or moving toward what sounded like an argument on the far end of the garden. We followed the curving path and came around the bend to find a few of Abibaal's guards standing near his stone seat, staring at the king's black panthers lying on the ground, motionless.

"Who would do such a thing to those poor animals?" asked one woman as we passed. "They were so beautiful."

The three of us got as close as we could in the pressing crowd of onlookers. One of the giant cats lay on its side, back arched strangely, and the other was sprawled flat, its claws outstretched in distress. White foam ringed both their mouths, their mottled purple tongues lolling.

"What is going on?" The king's bellow echoed across the garden as he strode toward his throne.

"Stay back, my lord," said the captain of his guard, hands up to keep Abibaal from plowing forward. "Your panthers have some sort of disease."

"That's no disease," said Zevi quietly. "That's poison."

"How do you know?" I asked.

"Yochana," he replied. "She was called down to the valley because a herd of sheep ate some wolfsbane that got mixed into their feed. Half of them died, and the shepherds hoped her knowledge of plants would help. They looked just like that, foam around their mouths, contorted in pain. Someone gave those cats poison."

"Look," said Gavi, pointing to the stone chair while the king argued with his guards.

Abibaal's serving table, which had been set there in anticipation of his arrival in the garden, had been knocked over. What was left of the meat and root vegetables slathered in thick sauce lay on the ground.

"It wasn't the panthers who were meant to be poisoned," I murmured. "It was the king."

Zevi leaned in close, dropping his voice low. "Who has access to the king's food?"

A great many hands were involved with preparing the large and extravagant meals that were served to the king and his guests at a feast such as this one, far too many to narrow down. "Nothing gets to the king's table without his cupbearer tasting it, to avoid a situation just like this one."

"Is he here?" Zevi asked, looking around the small garden, which was now packed with a growing number of guests.

I searched for the cupbearer, whom I'd seen on many occasions during my time in this palace and would recognize easily. I shook my head.

"Do you know where his quarters are?" Zevi asked.

"I do."

"Let's go before anyone else puts these pieces together," said Zevi, then turned to push back through the crowd, Gavi and I close behind.

But then I saw Elissa, and without thinking, I veered her way.

"What is happening?" she asked.

"Someone poisoned your father's panthers. But we're sure it was meant for him. You and Melita need to go back to the women's wing right away, until we can determine who did this."

"There are plenty of people here, Shalem. Guards and eunuchs are watching over us."

I took a chance and stepped in closer, dropping my voice low. "*Please*, Elissa. I need to know you are safe. Someone meant to kill your father—likely the same person who arranged for your brothers to be murdered. Who knows what they are capable of? I *have* to know you are safe."

She pulled in a shuddering breath and nodded. "All right. I'll go. But you'll find a way to tell me what is happening as soon as you figure it out?"

"I will."

At my promise, she tugged a white-faced Melita away and headed for the closest eunuch to ask for an escort. Once they had left the garden, I turned to find my cousins, along with Torben, waiting for me. I did not pause to ask whether my old friend had been listening as I spoke to his betrothed in a far-too-familiar tone of voice. I spun and headed for the palace, knowing the three of them would follow.

The cupbearer had lived only a few doors away from the room I'd inhabited during my brief time as the king's scribe, so it was easy enough to find. The door was shut but not locked, and inside we found the cupbearer lying on the floor in a pool of what at first appeared to be blood but instead turned out to be dark red wine, the emptied cup still clutched in his outstretched hand.

"He must have drunk his own poison," said Torben.

The cupbearer looked far more peaceful in death than the panthers had, as if he'd simply laid down in a pool of wine and gone to sleep.

Gavi squatted beside the body, then turned the man over so he could see his face, then pushed two fingers into the dead man's mouth. "He didn't poison himself."

"How do you know, Gav?" asked Zevi.

"As one who has drunk copious amounts of wine in the past, I can tell you two things: There's far too much on the ground for him to have imbibed more than a drop or two. And also, his mouth is dry." He leaned close to inhale. "No odor of wine either."

"There's no foam either," Zevi agreed. "No vomit. It couldn't be the same."

"So, what killed him?" I asked. "There's no blood."

Gavi felt around the cupbearer's torso, pulling back his wine-soaked tunic, then turned him over to examine his back. No knife wounds of any sort. But then he lifted the shoulder-length hair off the back of the man's neck and pointed. "There's the answer."

A small hole had been made at the base of the man's skull, right at the top of his spine. A faint trickle of blood marked where something had penetrated his skin in a place that would be lethal but unnoticeable.

"Clean," said Zevi. "Had to be a razor-sharp but narrow weapon. Not a knife or a dagger."

What could make such a uniformly round hole in the back of a man's neck? I let my eyes travel around the room as I considered. If it wasn't a knife, then perhaps it was another kind of tool. An iron stylus, perhaps? Could a scribe have sneaked in here to kill the cupbearer after poisoning the king's food?

"Let's get out of here," said Zevi. "Guards will come soon."

We left the unfortunate cupbearer on his face in the puddle of wine and slipped from the room, closing the door behind us, then headed back out into the twilight. Most of the guests were gathered in clumps outside the gardens, discussing the events in fervent tones. But a few were loudly protesting being locked inside the palace grounds—probably an order to keep the unknown killer from escaping.

"Well," said Torben, "what do we do now?"

I let out a long sigh, rubbing at my brow. "I don't know. I've spent months trying to untangle this plot, and I am at a loss. Anyone with an obvious motive is either dead themselves or long gone from Tyre."

"Whatever we do, it must be swift," said Zevi. "When the person who did this realizes his poison failed to kill Abibaal, he could get desperate."

"Why now?" Gavi frowned, arms folded across his chest. "For the past three months, things have been quiet in Tyre. No attempts on the king. No caravan attacks. No sabotage. Until tonight. What changed?"

"I can think of only one thing," said Zevi, his dark brown eyes lifting to meet mine. "*You* came back."

My stomach sank into a pit. "He means to pin this on me, doesn't he?"

"Could be."

"Tell us everything again," said Gavi, widening his stance. "Any possible detail you can think of. Start from the very beginning of your time here. And don't leave out a thing."

36

Elissa

As soon as I walked into our room, I remembered my mother had gone to visit the queen and her baby tonight, an excuse to avoid the banquet. For as changed as she was now, she still tended to avoid the king's vainglorious displays of wealth and status. I didn't blame her. The only reason I'd gone myself was to give Shalem the items I had collected from his room after he left. Perhaps it was foolish, but I wanted him to have something to remember me by.

"What do we do now?" asked Melita as she sat on the edge of the bed, leaning back on her hands.

"I think all we can do is wait here until Shalem sends word." I went to peer out the window at what remained of the sunset in the west.

"You really love him, don't you?"

I flinched at the blunt question. I'd not even admitted that aloud to myself, let alone anyone else. What good would it do anyhow? Shalem was as out of reach as he'd ever been, and soon there would be an entire ocean between us.

Crossing the room, I dropped down beside her and lay back with a deep sigh. "It does not matter. I am marrying Torben."

Her jaw ticked as she stared down at me. "Only because you won't stand up to our father."

"He is the *king*, Meli. What power do I have? Everything I tried before failed. I won't let you be sent away with the Shardan just because I want Shalem—"

My hand flew to my mouth, my eyes wide as I scrambled for how to reel back my words.

She frowned. "What are you talking about?"

"Nothing. I'm famished. Let's see if Rahej will escort us to the kitchens—"

She grabbed me as I tried to stand and yanked me back down, then pinned me with a blazing blue glare. "We're not going *anywhere* until you tell me the truth, Lissi."

Her vehemence shocked me into complying with the demand. "Abibaal said if I don't go, you do. I couldn't let that happen. It's so far away. Shalem said the island is beautiful and the people generous. But life there will be difficult. Rugged. It is not a plush palace and kid-skin slippers. But it is my lot. Not yours."

She folded her arms, jaw set. "When did the king tell you this? From the beginning? Before you met your tutor?"

"No. It was the night he was sent away."

"Because you wanted to go with him."

Not a question. She knew me all too well.

And what could I say? It was true. My father was no fool; he'd certainly seen my heart written all over my face, which was why he'd threatened my beloved sister if I did not submit.

"It was never a true possibility, Meli. I would not have left my mother behind like that, especially without saying good-bye. Besides, our father would not have let me go anyhow. We are pieces of silver in his hands, to be traded for whatever asset he covets. And you know as well as I, Abibaal keeps close account of every last scrap in his coffers."

She lifted her chin, staring out the window at the darkening sky. "Still. You did not give me a choice in the matter."

I scoffed. "I told you, Shardana is not a place you want to go."

"Because I am too weak? Too timid?"

"No, Meli, that's not what I—"

She put up a hand to stop my argument. "You've always been my champion, Elissa. Protected me. Helped me. Covered for me. But over the past few months, I've learned quite a bit about myself. I'm stronger than I thought I was. You were too busy mooning over your tutor to notice, but I've found my voice in many ways. And you should not have decided my life without coming to me first. You should trust me to know my own heart and mind."

I blinked at her in astonishment. She was right. I'd been so wrapped up in myself that I'd not seen that she had been changing in a similar way to my mother. She stood taller now, no longer hunching to appear small. She looked people in the eye when she spoke instead of glancing away with pink cheeks. Even when Shamzur had snapped at her for touching his cords, she'd been embarrassed, but she'd not fled the room or crumpled into tears as she might have before.

I slid my hand into hers, tangling our fingers together. "You're right, Meli. Forgive me. I think perhaps I've been used to managing my mother for so long that I fell into a habit of managing you too."

She shrugged. "I let you. It's nice to be taken care of. But I need to stand on my own two feet. Even when I lose my sandals."

She grinned, and the two of us burst into giggles, falling backward onto the bed to laugh together until tears streaked down our faces. Then, when our stomachs snarled nearly in tandem, we decided to look for Rahej after all.

Yet when the two of us stepped out into the courtyard, we found only Nolam shuffling past, mumbling to himself.

"What are you doing out here?" I asked, taking his arm. Lately, he'd become even more frail, his back curved so badly he was forced to walk with the help of a short staff. I was glad, however, that Abenasser refused to send him away from the palace, insisting he should live out his final years in the only place where anyone cared for him.

Completely lost in his mutterings, Nolam startled at my touch.

"Oh! Elissa. Have you seen Abenasser? I've been looking for him everywhere."

"No, I'm sorry. Someone tried to poison my father tonight but killed his panthers instead. Abenasser is probably helping in the search for the perpetrator."

"Oh. My. Can it be? Certainly I am wrong . . ." He tugged at his sparse beard. "He's been here twelve years. I never suspected . . . I must find Abenasser."

I squeezed his spindly arm. "What has happened? Can we help?" I'd never seen him so upset before in my life.

"What? Oh . . . well." He glanced around the courtyard. "I do not want to cast aspersions without proof, but I overheard something that Abenasser needs to know."

"Tell me. Then I'll go find him."

"I was in the eunuchs' receiving chamber and fell asleep after my meal, as I'm apt to do, you know. When I woke, I heard voices. I kept still, wondering if I might hear what they were talking about since they were speaking in hushed tones."

"Is this a habit of yours?" I interjected. "Feigning sleep to listen in on conversations?"

"Once in a while," he admitted sheepishly. "People will say all manner of interesting things when they don't know the old man is listening."

Melita giggled, poking him in the chest. "You sly fox. Apparently I've been going to the wrong sources for gossip."

He winked at her, grinning.

"Does this mean during my tutoring sessions . . . ?" My jaw dropped. "Were you listening then too?"

"Sometimes." He shrugged one bony shoulder. "You and that handsome tutor were not very skilled at hiding your fascination with each other. I had to make certain you were safe."

Hot embarrassment washed over me. "*Nolam!* Shalem—I mean, Mattaniel—was nothing but respectful."

"He was. But I suspect the boy would burn down this entire palace if you asked him to."

I caught my breath. "Why didn't you say anything to Magin or Abenasser?"

He put his gnarled hand on my cheek. "Perhaps I was wrong to keep your secret. But you've endured so much with your mother's illness over the years. It was good to see you smile like that. Even if it was only for a time."

Adoration for the sweet old eunuch flooded my chest as tears pricked my eyes. But I'd gotten completely waylaid by his admission. "So, what did you overhear while you were pretending to be asleep?"

Immediately, his gentle smile melted away. "The messenger had brought Shamzur some fabric from a laundress, something for your wedding, I think. Which wasn't unusual. But then the young man mentioned a name I'd been trying to remember now for months."

"You mean the woman you were looking for in the records?"

"Yes, exactly. She was one of Ragembal's concubines. Jazeliah."

"You think this laundress is the same Jazeliah?"

He nodded, wispy white hair floating in the slight breeze.

"Your great-uncle found her in a Sidonian brothel, became enamored of her, and brought her into his household. She was a stunning woman, and a talented seamstress. The reason I'd thought of her in the first place was that a few months ago, when one of the children nearly drowned, Shamzur jumped into the water to rescue her."

I'd heard of the incident. One of Thalassa's younger sisters had misjudged the depth of the pool, panicked, and swallowed so much water she'd not been able to keep herself afloat. We'd all been glad Shamzur was there to save her.

"Once the little one was safe, he came out of the pool with his robes soaking wet and out of sorts. You know my eyes don't work all that well, but in the sunlight, I saw a lightened area of skin on his leg, covering his entire calf, as if someone had stitched a patch of pure white linen there, and I thought immediately of Jazeliah because she, too, had a similar affliction. Although her face was perfection when she entered the palace, her skin was marred by whitened spots all up and down her arms and across her chest. Over the years, it spread up her neck and over her jaw. I've never seen the like—at least until I saw that patch on Shamzur."

That must be why his garments covered him so fully, chin to toes, to hide discolorations on his skin. "What happened to her?"

He sighed. "When your father took over the palace, she swore allegiance to him to avoid execution, but he sent her away. You know how particular he is about the beauty of his women. I heard nothing of her again."

The hair on the back of my neck rose as I considered these revelations. "Did she have a child?"

"Not when she left the palace. No. But Shamzur is about the right age . . ."

"To have been born a few months after the coup," I finished for him. Was Shamzur the son of Abibaal's uncle?

"I don't know what it means," said Nolam, "but I cracked open my eyes for just a moment when they went quiet and saw Shamzur hand the messenger a cord—one of those knotted ones he uses to tie around parcels of fabric or garments—before the young man slipped out of the room. Then Shamzur left too. It all disturbed me so much, especially in light of those attacks by Sidon. Which is why I was trying to find Abenasser. If Shamzur is involved in any of this, he must know."

Shamzur had been in this household for many years. I remembered him as a young apprentice, around thirteen or so, when I was a child. He'd served the king's women faithfully all that time. Had access to every area in this palace and the full trust of my father after such long and loyal service. It was only because Abenasser had been second in command next to Magin that Shamzur was not in charge of all the Crows now. Had *he* been the one behind this plot from the beginning?

As I'd done with the broken pieces of the tablet, I examined the clues from all angles, turning them around and around in my mind to see where the ragged edges might align. The banished

Sidonian concubine. The skin disorder. The sewing talent. The cords. The mysterious laundress named Jazeliah.

I thought back to times I'd seen Shamzur bind up fabrics and garments or untie them after receiving a shipment. Each one had been knotted, all along the length. I'd even seen him tie a few of those knots, some that were quite complicated, like sailors' knots on rigging. I'd always thought it a strange quirk, since the fringes on his robes were knotted too, but what if those knots were not simple decoration but some sort of code? Just as Shalem had created symbols to represent sounds of the Shardan language, couldn't a pattern of knots do the same? And what better way to send a message than disguised as a harmless parcel of fabric sent to a laundress?

My stomach dropped as all the pieces seemed to slide into place beside one another, forming one horrible conclusion: Shamzur was behind the murder of Ahiram. Possibly even involved in Yarikh's as well. With both heirs to Abibaal's throne eliminated, tonight he'd tried to assassinate the king—perhaps he even thought he'd succeeded since I'd not seen him in the garden afterward. And if he was attempting to extinguish my father's royal line, there would be only one life left to destroy.

"Melita," I said, my blood racing nearly as fast as my thoughts, "you need to go find help. Shalem. Abenasser. Torben. The captain of the guard. Our father. *Someone* needs to know the baby is in danger."

"What do you mean?" she called out as I took off toward the royal end of the women's wing. "Where are you going?"

"To save our little brother!" I shouted. "Go! Find help!"

And then I ran, because it was not only the tiny heir to the throne who was in danger but the queen as well. And since she'd been visiting with Khamera tonight, my mother was directly in the path of a killer. One she trusted without question.

37

Shalem

With sober expressions that reminded me they were not just my cousins but highly trained soldiers, Zevi and Gavi interrogated me thoroughly about my time in Tyre, while their diligent gazes continued roving the deepening shadows of the gardens around us.

But when a black-robed Crow came flying around a corner on the heels of a golden-haired woman with terror in her blue eyes, it was Torben who reacted first.

"My lady!" cried the young eunuch, panting as he grabbed for her arm. "You need to go back—"

With a curse, Torben yanked the Crow away from Melita, throwing him to the ground so fast the eunuch had no time to cry out before he was sprawled on his back, gasping for breath.

"You will *not* touch her!" Torben bellowed in his own language.

Elissa's sister stood with her mouth gaping for the span of a heartbeat before rushing toward the enormous Shardan. "Don't hurt him! He was only trying to protect me."

Torben looked down at the young woman, chest heaving and murder glittering in his dark brown eyes.

She put a hand on his forearm. "It's all right, Torben. I am safe. I promise."

My pirate friend blinked twice, as if clearing vicious thoughts from his mind to make way for her soothing words. To my surprise, he nodded, then took a deep breath as he stepped away so she could help the stunned eunuch to his feet.

"Are you all right, Rahej?" she asked the bewildered young man.

He brushed at his black robes, setting them to rights. "Abenasser said you must remain in the women's wing for the night."

"And as *I* told *you*, Elissa sent me for help."

My blood went still. "Where is she?"

"With the queen and Leyana. She sent me to find you or someone else who could help because she thinks Shamzur is going to kill the baby."

My head rang like a struck bell as many of my questions, half-formed postulations, and vague hunches coalesced into one answer: Shamzur.

I did not know how Elissa had come to that conclusion, but my intuition instantly told me it was the right one. The somber eunuch had unfettered access to every part of this palace, and even if I had no idea what his motive might be, he had the training and certainly the intelligence to weave together a complicated plot against the throne. But there was no time to parse the reasons or the method when Elissa was in danger.

"Lead the way," I said, ignoring the sputtering arguments of the eunuch.

Melita nodded once, spun around, and showed the four of us exactly how she'd outrun the young Crow as she led us into the palace, through a maze of corridors and small courtyards, and toward the women's wing.

By the time we arrived outside the queen's quarters, which spanned three levels, Melita had breathlessly relayed everything Nolam had seen and overheard. It took little effort to guess that Elissa concluded the knotted cord he'd handed over was a coded message, an ingenious way to transmit information undetected by the guards at the gates. I had likely even delivered one of those coded messages myself to the laundress—Shamzur's *mother*—without knowing what I'd held in my hands.

There were four well-armed guards at the main door on the first level of the queen's rooms. Instead of wasting time by trying to convince them to let us through, Melita led us through a side gate and around the outside of the palace.

Although the first level of the queen's extensive suite of chambers had only narrow slits for windows, which were impossible to slide through, there were wide balconies on the top two floors. The only way was to climb a tall date palm and then leap the distance between the tree and the second-level balcony.

"Well . . ." Gavi tipped back his head to take in the height of the palm. "You always were the best at climbing trees, Shay. You told us so *all* the time."

"Did I?"

"Absolutely," he said, smirking. "Even after you fell out of one and nearly cracked your skull open."

"You'll need to protect your hands," said Zevi, already untying his belt. "Those fronds are sharp as knives."

As he wrapped the fabric around my left hand and forearm and Gavi wrapped my right, I marveled that neither of them tried to stop me. From every story Avi told me of our childhood, they'd always tried to protect me from harm, even if I'd constantly manipulated them until they included me in their adventures. But even if they had not pressed me about my feelings for Elissa, they knew me well enough not to argue when it came to her.

Even Torben only gave me a firm nod, then stood silently beside Melita, who gripped his sleeve tightly as I began my ascent toward his betrothed.

"We'll be right behind you," said Gavi.

It was fortunate they'd wrapped my hands. As I hoisted myself upward, the palm trunk scraped my legs raw with every movement. But I did not care if it stripped the flesh from my bones, I would not stop until Elissa was safe. So instead of allowing the pain to slow me, I used it to push me higher and higher along the trunk until I was above the balcony, the tree bending under my weight. Without pausing to count the cost of missing, I pushed off the tree with the remaining strength in my legs, flinging myself across the distance to grab for the parapet.

I hung there for a few moments, a little stunned I'd actually caught the edge with both hands, then pulled myself up and over the parapet. Once my feet were beneath me again, I walked with soft steps to the doorway and peered through billowing curtains into the chamber inside.

It was empty.

However, voices trickled down from above, so I went back to the parapet, caught Gavi's eye, and gestured to the top level. After swiftly unwrapping my hands, I tossed the belts over the edge and stole into the queen's chambers. Sandals removed, I climbed the narrow stairway to the top level where, to my bone-deep relief, I heard Elissa's voice.

"Don't drink that! I told you, he poisoned it!"

"Elissa," Khamera snapped, "cease these false accusations. Shamzur is a loyal servant in this household. Leyana, take your daughter out of my rooms."

"Perhaps we should hear her out—"

Elissa spoke over her mother, who seemed torn between obeying the queen and trusting her daughter. "It was you all along, wasn't it? In league with Sidon to overthrow the king."

"My lady," he replied in his odd, high-pitched voice, "I have no cause to betray your father—or any of you, for that matter."

"Does Jazeliah?"

There was a pause. A long one that spoke louder than his false protestations.

"Who is Jazeliah?" asked the queen just as the baby squawked. She shushed him, then repeated herself. "Shamzur. Who is this Jazeliah?"

He sighed, the sound resigned. "Foolish girl. You could not simply leave it be, could you? Now all of you will have to die."

"What is the meaning—" the queen sputtered.

"Hold your tongue, woman," he snapped, dropping the mask of a self-effacing servant.

To my surprise, the queen did go quiet, probably from shock more than anything. On hands and knees I peered around the edge of a cedar vanity table to find that Shamzur was too far away for me to grab without risking the women in this room. The one I cared for most stood between the queen's bed and the eunuch, her mother on the opposite side, close to where the baby squirmed restlessly atop the blankets beside Khamera.

"Jazeliah, as Elissa seems to know, is my mother."

"He did this to avenge her," Elissa said, "because the king sent her away after the coup."

He huffed. "You don't know anything."

"I know you are guilty of Ahiram's death. Probably Yarikh's too. And that you poisoned my father's food tonight and now mean to kill his last heir."

Elissa's statement drew gasps from both the queen and her mother.

"Abibaal is *dead*?" Khamera choked out.

"That can't be!" cried Leyana.

"Do you really think anyone will let you sit on the throne?" asked Elissa, wisely keeping the truth to herself. "You have no proof you are Ragembal's son. Besides, my father's men will tear you apart when it's discovered what you've done."

"I don't want that cursed throne," he spat. "I just want his line stamped out. I want every memory of him erased from the earth the way my mother was erased from this household. As if she meant nothing."

"Abibaal allowed her to live, Shamzur. Many others were not given such mercy."

"Mercy?" he snarled. "You call being sent into the streets to live like a dog *mercy*? You call having to *beg* to return to a flea-ridden dockside brothel because not even your self-righteous family would take you in, any sort of life?"

"I am sorry that happened to her, I truly am. But why destroy yourself to exact vengeance now? All these years later?"

"Destroy myself?" He barked a caustic laugh. "This is my destiny, girl. I am the redeemer of what was lost, the avenger of her suffering. No, this"—he pointed to the floor—"is *exactly* what the gods fated me to do, as the oracle of Eshmun told her before my birth. The plan she devised then has finally came to fruition."

"Your mother planned all this?"

He grinned. "Brilliant, isn't she? She knows this palace inside and out. Knew the best way for me to get access was as a Crow. She taught me *everything* I needed to know in order to be chosen."

"That's why you become a eunuch?"

He ticked a shoulder. "I did it gladly. My momentary pain was nothing compared to her lifelong afflictions."

"We trusted you, Shamzur," said the queen, indignant. "Gave you every luxury, and all this time you were plotting against us?"

"Stings, doesn't it?" His smirk was the height of arrogance. "And while you were lording over me, prancing about in clothing I made as if somehow *you* had done something worthy of the honor beyond warming a king's bed, I was preparing to humble you—all of you. And it was worth the wait."

"So none of this was Sidon? Or the Philistines?" Elissa asked.

He waved a dismissive hand. "Useful fools. Stupid enough to part with their resources while we tugged the rings in their noses to turn them whichever direction we wanted them to go."

"But why lay the fault on the Hebrews? They did nothing to you."

"They kicked her out in the first place. Hypocrites," he hissed.

"Your mother?"

"Her own family accused her of being cursed with leprosy for the patches on her skin and declared her unclean. Sent her away with nothing more than the clothes on her back. She was only twelve and barely escaped stoning when she tried to return after the coup."

I winced at the harsh and horribly misapplied application of

Torah law. Even if Jazeliah actually had been stricken with the disease, Mosheh had never prescribed stoning for lepers. True, those determined by a priest to be afflicted were sent outside the camp to protect others, but the Torah also allowed opportunity for healing and hope of restoration. After hundreds of years of living among the Tyrians, it sounded like some of the Asherites were not only confused about the condition itself, but practicing a graceless version of Torah.

"Your mother is Hebrew?" Elissa asked.

He spat on the ground at the mention of what was, apparently, half his own heritage. "That's enough with the questions. You always were far too presumptuous for my liking." Then he called her a foul name that made my blood boil.

Leyana surged toward him, eyes full of fury. "You will not speak to my daughter in such a way."

He laughed as Elissa restrained her mother. "She'd likely have gone just as mad as you, had you two not made the foolish mistake of coming here today. But alas, we'll never know, will we?"

He threw off his outer garment and stalked closer to the women. "Don't bother screaming. The guards down there have been paid a year's wage to be deaf and blind today."

Elissa pushed her mother behind her, the two of them skittering back toward the bed. The queen clutched the baby close to her breast, wide-eyed as Shamzur stalked closer, brandishing an iron toggle-pin the length of my handspan, the thin blade he must have used on the cupbearer and possibly even Haldon.

I felt, rather than heard, Zevi's arrival at my back, knowing Gavi would not be far behind. With his steadying hand on my shoulder, my cousin's presence bolstered me as I searched for something to use as a weapon. Just as I reached for an alabaster jar atop the vanity table beside me, thinking to cause a distraction, Shamzur lunged toward Elissa, tugging her out of reach of her mother. He spun her, putting one hand over her mouth while the other pressed his blade to the side of her throat.

"Back up, Leyana. *Now.*"

She did as he asked, scrambling over to stand beside the queen, one shaking hand pressed to her mouth as she stared helplessly at her daughter.

Then, to my surprise, Shamzur turned himself and his captive toward my hiding place.

"Don't bother. I've known you were there for quite some time. Come on out."

I held my breath for the count of five, mind racing, but I had no choice. Slowly, and with hands raised, I came to my feet.

"Oh, look, Elissa. Your lover is here." Shamzur grinned in delight, his shaven brows arched high as he skimmed the point of the lethal blade up to her jaw. "Quite convenient, actually. Now I don't need to worry about planting evidence, and I'll catch the perpetrator myself. Dead."

Elissa's pleading eyes met mine across the ten paces between us. *Run*, they said. *Save yourself.*

"You ladies have two choices. Drink the wine or die by my blade. I'd choose the less painful option. Either way, none of you are leaving this room. It's only a matter of who dies first."

It was useless to tell Shamzur to let her go. He knew Leyana and I would do nothing if it meant that blade pierced her. And the queen would certainly not put the baby in danger.

"Perhaps not. But you've made a mistake, Shamzur," I said. "The king isn't dead."

The self-satisfied smile dropped from his face. "What?"

"His panthers ate the poisoned food before he ever sat down. Apparently your plan wasn't as foolproof as you assumed."

The baby in the queen's arms let out a cry, pulling my attention away for only a moment, but it was enough to realize exactly what the king had wanted me to see. There, on the top of the child's small, downy head was a dark red mark, shaped nearly exactly like a fiery flame.

And somewhere, deep inside me, I felt the rumble of a lion's roar. Great, golden paws had indeed led me back here to see confirmation not only of my dream, but of the purpose I'd been called to since birth.

I dropped my hands to my sides, a wide smile curving my mouth. "It's useless, Shamzur. You have lost."

The eunuch's blade ticked at Elissa's throat. "Don't move any closer."

"I don't need to. Because the oracle your mother consulted lied. False words from a false god. But I serve Yahweh, King of All. And there is no falseness in him. He *is* Truth."

"How dare you—"

"Silence!" I demanded, a rush of something powerful vibrating in my bones as I gestured to the baby. "This child was born to be a blessing to the sons of Yaakov, to extend branches of friendship that will be inscribed with the name of the Holy One on sacred ground. There is nothing on this earth that can thwart Yahweh's will, and nothing above or below that can subvert his perfect plans. Not your mother's twisted ideas of vengeance. Not the desire of ancient enemies for land that is not their own."

Shamzur's hand was shaking, either from fury or fear, as he sneered at me. "You can do nothing to stop me, *slave*."

"Perhaps not. I have no weapons." I spread my hands wide. "But I am not a slave. I am a priest of the Most High God. And *I* am not alone."

Zevi and Gavi slipped from their hiding places, coming to stand on either side of me, unarmed as well but unquestionably lethal. Shamzur's eyes flared as he tripped back a couple of steps, dragging Elissa with him.

"Also"—I grinned at him—"there's a pirate behind you."

Shamzur jerked his head around just as Torben barreled through the balcony doorway with a bellow that would terrify the most battle-scarred of warriors. Distracted, the eunuch let the toggle-pin slip away from Elissa's throat.

"Drop!" I yelled in Shardan as I bolted forward.

Elissa obeyed, letting her entire body weight fall heavily to the floor, which yanked her free of Shamzur's grip and away from the blade.

I threw my body over hers as Torben, Gavi, and Zevi encircled the furious eunuch while he spewed foul curses against us and against the house of Abibaal, swinging his toggle-pin wildly through the air as they closed in.

As though they'd discussed their moves in advance, Torben looped his thick-muscled forearm around Shamzur's spindly neck at the same time Zevi wrenched his arm backward until something snapped. The eunuch cried out, dropping the blade. Then Gavi delivered a powerful blow to the man's smooth jaw. Torben released him and Shamzur went down, hard, his head cracking loudly on the limestone floor.

He lay unmoving. Unconscious or dead, I didn't really care. All I knew was that, at least for the moment, Elissa was safe in my arms.

38

Shalem

The bride stood radiant in Tyrian purple atop the Celestial Tower as the sun set at her back, her long, filmy veil fluttering in the warm breeze.

Dressed in finery himself, Torben carefully repeated the words of the vow the priestess spoke, even if many of their meanings escaped him, then accepted a pitcher of wine to pour at the base of the standing stone in the center of the tower—a pretense of an offering to gods he did not know or worship. Then the bride did the same, careful not to drip any wine on the fringe of her pleated underskirts. A rivulet of wine streaked toward her leather slippers and she tripped back a step, nearly toppling in her haste, but the sister at her side held her steady.

Torben grinned at his veiled bride, entertained by the overreaction before tipping his chin to the priestess in silent command to continue her long, droning supplications to false deities.

Beside me, Uvaldo's gap-toothed smile was as brilliant as the flare of sunlight limning the horizon over the sea. This final seal of the covenant between himself and Abibaal assured his receipt of not just one but two ships built by the king's ship makers, along with a small crew of skilled laborers and lumbermen to help begin his own shipbuilding enterprise. More Tyrian crews would soon come to expand the mines, and within the year, the new colony was to be rooted on one of the southwestern peninsulas, where their ships could anchor in the protected harbor. Raphad, too, had already begun preparations to move Portea, Danice, and little Otzar to Shardana before the seasons changed, determined to rebuild his trading empire on fresh shores.

Although I doubted Uvaldo himself would live to see his kingdom become anything like Tyre or Sidon, it was entirely possible that Torben and his heirs would build something worthy of a lasting inscription in the Hall of Records someday.

When the litany of prayers to deaf gods was finally complete, the priestess handed Torben a silver chalice. He took a long draft before lifting the veil of his bride and offering it to her. She accepted the wine with a bright smile and drank, binding herself to him in front of the small crowd of select witnesses while the first of the stars appeared against the darkening sky.

Shouts of blessing and celebration came from those gathered around the bride and groom as the ceremony concluded, but I lifted a silent prayer to the God Who Hears for the courageous woman who'd agreed to go to a faraway island out of deep love for her sister and a plea that both of them would be covered in His protection always.

Elissa turned her gaze toward me, a rueful smile on her lips for the distance that lay between us and would very soon grow impossibly wide. Regardless of everything that had happened over the past months, she would always and forever be out of my reach.

"A feast has been prepared in honor of the bride and groom," said the king, looking nearly as pleased as Uvaldo that the covenant agreement was finally complete. He would have silver in abundance, a kingdom spreading over the sea, and a daughter who would be queen of the Shardan someday. "Go. Enjoy the abundance of my kingdom and the meat of the sacrifices offered in honor of this union."

I stood near the parapet, awaiting my own turn to offer well-wishes to the bride and groom, when I felt a familiar presence come to my side.

"They seem to fit together well, don't they? I never could have expected it."

I inhaled, drawing the spicy-sweetness of her fragrance deep into my lungs and wishing I could hold it there forever.

"They do." I looked down at Elissa, whose eyes were trained on her golden-haired sister. "Are you certain she is not frightened to go to the island?"

She shook her head, her lips curving into a gentle smile. "She insisted Torben makes her feel safe in a way she never has before. And that even if she barely comprehends his words, she understands his heart in some mysterious way. She says that he may look terrifying to others but with her, he is like beeswax in sunlight."

I chuckled at the notion of my fearless friend melting for Melita, but I'd seen it with my own eyes the day she'd come to us for help. One touch of her hand had doused his fury.

"He'll take good care of her, I promise."

"I know. Because I threatened to board my father's fastest ship and gut him like a fish if I received word to the contrary."

My lips twitched at the threat, even if I was fairly certain she'd make good on it if Torben failed to uphold the vow he'd made to Abibaal that Melita would not only be his queen one day but his only wife as long as he lived.

The day after Shamzur had been revealed as the worst of villains, Torben surprised everyone by announcing publicly that he refused to marry Elissa—that it was Melita he desired and would marry none other. Since Abibaal cared only that the covenant between the two kingdoms was confirmed, he easily agreed.

"It does not bother you that he threw you over for your sister?" I asked, though I dreaded the answer.

She finally looked up at me, a frown pinched between her brows. "You don't know?"

"Know what?"

A smile tilted one side of her lovely mouth upward, and my mind went hazy as I stared into her ocean-blue eyes.

"It was *her* idea, Shalem. Not only did she find herself hopelessly enamored of your pirate friend, but she also knew that my heart is—and always will be—yours."

"But . . . I thought it was because of your mother that she agreed to go."

"No. My mother is well, Shalem. Your God, Yahweh, healed her broken heart. She is stronger now, mind and body, than she has been since I was a little girl—maybe ever. Her friendship with Danice changed everything."

My jaw went slack. I'd seen Leyana a few times after the events in the queen's quarters and she'd seemed a quiet but lovely woman. In fact, I'd been a little confused why Elissa said she was so disturbed in spirit. Apparently, while I'd been gone, much more had changed than I realized.

"Good. You're still here. I have something to say to you both."

It took a couple of moments for me to process that Abibaal himself was standing in front of us, arms folded across his wide chest and that awful ceremonial lion skin draped across his shoulder. Its amber eyes glittered as I bowed low before the king of Tyre.

"Enough," he said, gesturing for me to stand. "You'll be returning to Israelite territory soon, yes?"

I nodded. "Yes, my lord. My cousins and I plan to depart in a few days, as soon as the Shardan leave."

"Excellent. I'll be sending a caravan of gifts with you, including a wagonload of timber, so you'll have to stick to the main trade roads. I'll send a small contingent with you to ensure you're unmolested along the way, although I suspect my roads are a great deal safer since that madman and his treacherous mother are locked in a cell, awaiting execution."

Shamzur had survived Torben and Gavi's wrath, as well as the torture ordered by Abibaal to pull every last secret from his tight lips, but neither he nor Jazeliah would live to see the new moon. It was only for the sake of this wedding that the king had held off what would be a public display of justice in the central square of Tyre—with Abibaal himself delivering the killing blow to avenge his sons' blood.

During interrogations, Shamzur and Jazeliah had eventually turned on each other, revealing they'd been just as responsible for Yarikh's murder as they were for Ahiram's. They'd paid a disgruntled soldier handsomely to knock over a torch on Yarikh's ship while the prince was too drunk to respond. But Elissa had been relieved to hear that her brother adamantly refused to promise her to Zandar, a convenient argument that directed suspicion toward the Gazans and away from the true villains.

It had also come to light that, for many years, Shamzur had been pilfering expensive pieces of jewelry from the royal family to fund their vile schemes. Since it was he who dressed Abibaal's women, giving him access to countless costly items in the treasury, it had been easy to hide his theft. The trust he'd earned over twelve years of calculated loyalty had given the two freedom to weave a complicated plot, patiently stoking resentments of those they deemed weak enough to manipulate or bribe. I doubted the king would ever ferret out every one of their accomplices, especially since Shamzur had likely killed more than a few, but a number of guilty servants and townspeople had already been arrested.

"I have a message for Saul," said the king, "that you will deliver along with the timber—a glad acceptance of his request for cooperation between our kingdoms and a vow that our borders will remain friendly. You'll make certain he understands I have no wish to cling to the past, won't you?"

I flinched at the ingratiating tone of the question, as if the powerful king of Tyre worried whether I would omit the request. "Yes, my lord."

"He *must* know that I desire only peace between our peoples. I will *not* breach his borders." He let out a shuddering breath that seemed at odds with his large and commanding presence— almost as if he was *afraid*. "You saw the baby? My son?"

Realization began to creep in. "I did."

"I thought you were quite mad that day, you know. Even as you stood before me recounting your dream—trees and earthquakes and spreading branches and flames atop a crown—I did not believe you. But then the queen gave birth to my new heir. She insisted we call him Ahiram after our firstborn."

A new cedar, growing in the place of the first.

"And when I saw him, marked by that red flame . . ." Abibaal shook his head. "I knew I'd been wrong about you. I did not understand that you were a seer. If I had, I would never have had you beaten that way."

"Please, my lord." I lifted a palm. "I hold no ill will. I am only grateful for your mercy. It allowed me to return home and explore my sacred role as a son of Levi."

"Tell me—" The king's voice wavered. "What more can I do to escape the wrath of your God?"

I stared at him, struck by the humility of the plea. Abibaal was still brash and arrogant, still beholden to false gods and his own greed, but at least he now acknowledged Yahweh's fearsome power. If only the king of Tyre would bow his knee to the King of All Creation . . .

I took a few moments, eyes on the glittering heavens above, to ask Yahweh for wisdom to humbly convey whatever he wished me to say. Then, I listened. Carefully weighed the message impressed on me against the Word inscribed on my heart and mind, then listened again before I dared open my mouth to speak.

"In my dream, your kingdom remained long after your death, expanding to unfathomable reaches through the efforts of your son. But *only* if you and your descendants continue to extend the hand of friendship to Israel. Guard her from the nations to the north. Use your influence to buffer her against invasion on every side. And provide resources necessary for her survival and for the glory of Yahweh. If so, the mighty cedars of Tyre, along with your builders' unique ingenuity, will be remembered for all of history."

The king's mouth opened to speak but I lifted a palm.

"As you know, among the gifts I brought from King Saul are

copies of the Torah, sacred ancient writings worth far more than every text in your Hall of Records combined. Read them for yourself. Seek the Wisdom of the All-Knowing One. The promises given to Avraham spell destruction for those opposed to Yahweh's beloved people. This eternal covenant was cut by Yahweh himself, in fire and blood. I pray that you and your descendants will bless Avraham's seed, and thereby choose life throughout your generations."

The tower went quiet as the admonition died away. Everyone else had disappeared, leaving only the three of us and the flickering torches around the parapet, marking each of the four winds.

Abibaal nodded, bejeweled hand pressed to his heart. "I vow it will be so." He took a deep breath, then seemed to visibly gather himself as he released it, shaking off the uncharacteristic meekness in favor of his usual imperious tone. "And *you*, daughter, will not forget your promises either."

"Of course not, my king," she said with a submissive nod.

"Excellent." He narrowed his eyes on her. "Your mother is right. You may look like her, but you are far more like me than I ever imagined. A shrewd negotiator, aren't you?"

She grinned at her father. "I learned by watching the best."

For the first time since I'd entered the palace of Tyre, Abibaal smiled back at his daughter with genuine affection. "Leyana truly is herself again, isn't she?"

Elissa nodded, pressing her lips together as her eyes shimmered with tears. "She is. Stronger, even. Thanks to Yahweh."

"She wants to go with you, you know. Insists she can learn more about the God of the Hebrews there." His brow quirked. "Says she is of no use to me as a concubine anyhow."

"If you care for her—and I know you do, Aba," she said gently, "then it is time to set her free."

He let out a slow exhale. "All right. But *you* have only six months before you must return. Before the Feast of Awakening. My ships will depart as soon as the seasons change. Agreed?"

"Agreed."

My head spun with confusion, a slight headache forming at my temples. Apparently, I'd missed some sort of negotiation between the king and his daughter.

"Oh, I nearly forgot." The king pulled a weathered roll of papyrus from his richly embroidered belt and extended it to me. "Consider it a wedding gift. Although I owed it to you, since you did fulfill your part of the bargain."

Bewildered, I accepted the scroll, but as the king strode away, leaving the two of us alone atop the Celestial Tower as the last of the sunset faded into twilight, I could do nothing but stare at the place where he'd disappeared down the stairway.

"What—" I blinked. "What exactly just happened?"

"Open it," she replied. "You'll see."

I unrolled the document, which was imprinted with both Raphad's faded seal and a fresh one, large and ornate and unmistakably that of Abibaal, King of Tyre. Official manumission papers.

Elissa stepped in close, her honey-and-spice fragrance swirling around us on the warm breeze as she placed her hands on my chest. "What happened is that my father has unlocked the cage. I am free."

Dazed by both her touch and her confusing revelation, all I could say was, "But he said you have to return."

"That is true. We will need to travel with the group establishing the colony on Shardana. I've promised we will be liaisons between our people and theirs for a short time. It will be important for the Shardan to learn our language so trade can flow easily. Once we are satisfied with their progress, we can return home. My father was frustrated, at first, that I refused to consider marriage to one of Saul's sons, but I reminded him that a union with a royal emissary—especially an extraordinarily gifted one—has plenty of advantages." One corner of her mouth quirked, amusement sparkling in her eyes. "I know nothing about Saul's court, of course, or what weight your influence actually holds there. But neither does my father."

"Are you telling me—" I took in a breath to steady my voice

and to temper my racing heartbeat. "That you convinced the king to give *us* his blessing?"

She pressed her lips together, nodding.

"And that you are free to come with me to Naioth as my *wife*?"

Another nod.

Overwhelmed, I tipped back my head, taking in the sparkling white veil of stars spread above us like an endless covering of lovingkindness, and praised the steadfast, gracious God who'd taken me from a lonely cave, through shadowed valleys and deep waters, and into this place of glorious light.

Then, with a triumphant shout, I let the sheet of papyrus flutter to the ground and kissed my bride.

39

Naioth, Israel
Two months later

My wife and my mother stood arm-in-arm, talking with Leyana and Eliora while I listened to Ronen argue with another Levite about whether one of his songs needed another verse. As if she'd sensed me staring from across the gathering, Elissa met my gaze and gave me a soft, secret smile that felt like she'd poured warm honey into my bones. Even this far away, her presence was a balm. I would never get over the idea that she was truly mine, bound by covenant and one in flesh.

There'd been no formal ceremony in Tyre, no sacrifices or blessings lifted to foreign gods, only the two of us atop the Celestial Tower that night, under a canopy of numberless stars, vowing before Yahweh Most High to bind ourselves together and follow whatever path he chose to lay out before us. However, as soon I arrived in Naioth with a wife and a mother-in-law, my delighted mother insisted on arranging an enormous wedding feast to celebrate our union.

The women of my family had eagerly taken both Elissa and Leyana under their capable wings, patiently teaching them how to navigate daily rigors of life outside a palace. Soon, they all teased one another affectionately while joyfully sharing the burden of tending to homes and families.

I watched her now, as one of my little nieces tugged her away from the women by the hand, insistent on Elissa dancing with her as David, the young shepherd from the village of Bethlehem, plucked a vibrant melody on his lyre under the sprawling canopy of an ancient terebinth tree. I'd yet to speak to his mother, Zemirah, about my hope that she and Yishai would allow him to play for King Saul.

When I'd returned with Abibaal's gifts and the news that Tyre was eager for an alliance, I'd been told Saul was not well enough for an audience. Reluctantly, his steward admitted that melancholy had consumed the man for weeks now. Battling sleeplessness and irrational agitation, Saul could not be soothed. They'd tried everything from herbs to incantations, yet nothing calmed his troubled spirit. Somehow, as we spoke, I'd been reminded what Ronen had said about the talented young musician: *"His music would calm the most turbulent of souls."*

If that was true, then he would be doing a great service for not only his king, but also the people of Israel. The Philistines were once again stirring up trouble in the south, and Saul's leadership was desperately needed. Hopefully, David's parents would give their permission for me to bring him to Gibeah on my return.

Elissa's melodic laugh pulled me from such troublesome thoughts as she and my niece twirled in a circle, her tawny hair unbound and her rough-spun wool skirt swirling to reveal bare feet. A smile tugged at my mouth when she came to a stop, hand on her heaving chest as she caught her breath. Sensing my eyes on her, she met my greedy gaze with a piercing one of her own, a thousand secrets passing between us across the distance. I would never get my fill of her. Never cease wondering whether I might wake up one day and find that it had all been a beautiful, impossible dream.

A long arm came around my neck, jerking me backward with a playful squeeze.

"I'm stealing him, Abba," said Avi. "You two are putting him to sleep with your music talk."

Ronen laughed. "Apologies, Shalem. I'd meant to congratulate you but got sidetracked talking with Ori."

Gavi appeared at my side, grinning. "I think he was too busy staring at his wife to care what the two of you old men were blathering on about."

They all laughed at my expense, which made my face go hot, but what could I say? It was true.

"Let's go," Avi said, tugging me by the shoulder.

"Where?"

"You'll see," said Gavi. "We promise to get you back to your bride before sunset, then she can have you for the rest of the night." He gave me a suggestive waggle of his dark brows, which of course made Avi snort like an ox.

Seeing the three of us walking away from the gathering, Zevi left Yochana's side. "Where are you fools taking him?"

"The ridge," said Avi as Zevi fell into step behind us. "Have something to show him."

I really didn't care where they were taking me or why. I always enjoyed the company of these three men who'd left their wives and families to bring me home.

Following the narrow path through towering trees while Avi talked about his oldest son's new obsession with drumming on anything within reach, Gavi picked up pine cones to throw at tree trunks every so often, and Zevi stoically kept pace with me, felt very much like my faint memories of exploring the woods as children. Memories that seemed to populate more and more as time went on. In light of the way Yahweh had healed Leyana, I continued asking for full restoration of my mind but had learned to be content with small glimpses into what I now knew was an extraordinarily beautiful childhood with a family who adored me to the point of indulgence.

When we reached the ridge overlooking the valley, the four of us stood gazing down on Ramah, where Gavi and Zahava lived in his parents' enormous villa and where Samuel himself had been born decades ago. The city's grand gates and newly constructed House of Meeting—funded by Gavi's stepfather—were visible even from here.

"Why are we here?" I asked.

"This is where it all started," said Avi, gesturing toward the head of the path that curved down into the valley. "This is where we set off for Bezek, intending to fight in Yavesh."

"After you two manipulated me into taking you with me," Zevi grumbled.

"You punished us plenty by marching our legs off all night," Gavi shot back.

"Someone had to toughen you up. We were going to battle."

"*I* was going to battle," said Gavi. "Avi was going to empty his stomach all over the battlefield."

"Anyhow, as I was saying . . ." Avi interrupted, scowling at Gavi, who looked quite proud of having annoyed our mild-mannered cousin. "You probably hid here in the bushes the same way you did when we spied on Saul's anointing—waiting to follow us like the little sneak you were back then."

I laughed at the ribbing, knowing from all his stories that it was true. I'd hated more than anything being left out of their games and explorations and had gotten myself into quite a few scrapes because of it. But even though I'd been the youngest of the group, and at times an entitled little pest, I'd still been considered part of their brotherhood. I had the scar on my palm to prove it.

"So, in honor of your marriage," Avi continued, "and the ending of what turned out to be the longest adventure the four of us ever had, Gavi has a gift for you."

From a pouch at his belt, Gavriel produced a small knife, made of flint and bound to the short handle by a very old piece of leather cord. He placed it in my hand and as my curious fingers curved around it, I remembered . . .

EPILOGUE

Shalem

My knees smarted as I plucked my knife from where it had fallen into the mud when I'd tried to jump over a narrow stream, misjudged the distance, and fell.

At least Gavi wasn't here to make fun of me for tripping over my own feet. It wasn't my fault they'd seemed to have grown far faster than my legs, but my cousin never missed a chance to tease me over my lack of height, my skinny body, my hairless face, or pretty much anything, really.

Yet even though it stung whenever he poked at me in front of Zevi and Avi, he sometimes took me on hikes in the woods around Ramah, just the two of us, showing me how to track deer and other small game by looking for prints or scat on the forest floor. Not to mention he'd been the one to make my knife in the first place, just as he'd done for the others. And last year, he'd nearly lost his life protecting Avi and me, so I was fairly certain he only teased me like that because he wished he had a little brother. He'd even told me that once, during one of our treks in the forest, and I said I'd gladly exchange him, Zevi, or Avi for either one of my awful sisters. Besides, having cousins who'd vowed by their own blood to treat me as a brother was much better, because they had chosen to do so, which was far more meaningful to me.

Today, however, all three of them had left me behind. Again.

My stomach had hurt while I listened to my cousins whisper together behind Avi's house yesterday, arguing over whether to deceive their parents so they could camp near Mitzpah, then spy while the tribal leaders chose who would be the first king of Israel. They knew I would give anything to be there too, yet deliberately kept it from me.

I was not a little boy who needed to be coddled anymore. I was fourteen years old. Considered a man, whether my beard had grown in yet or not. And I refused to be left behind while they witnessed the most exciting thing to ever happen in Israel.

So I'd waited in the bushes near the trail and followed them. I'd huddled in the cold away from the circle of their firelight, while listening to Avi prattle on about some girl his mother wanted him to marry someday, while sternly telling myself that there were not sharp-toothed beasts lurking in the shadows, watching me. Perhaps it was ridiculous, but I'd half-wished Igo was there with his giant warm body snuggled beside me while I curled up in the dirt, waiting for morning. But Zevi must have tied him up before he left Naioth, for fear he'd get the three of them caught.

Igo would certainly be of great help now, since I'd gotten distracted from my pursuit when I fell and my knife flew out of the leather sheath Gavi had made for me. It hadn't taken long to search about the muddy stream bank and recover it, but it was enough to miss which way my cousins had gone.

After wiping the mud from my most treasured possession with the hem of my tunic, I held my breath, listening for their voices on the breeze, then searched the rocky ground beyond the stream for footprints. But I'd lost their trail in the thick woods surrounding the valley. With no choice but to select a direction and hope something would lead me to them, I kept walking, humming one of the songs Uncle Ronen had written.

However, instead of finding my cousins, I stumbled across a gathering of tents in a wide clearing, probably the camp of one of the clans that had come to witness the selection of the new king. A few cook-fires still smoldered around the area, as if they'd only recently been abandoned, but aside from a few pack animals tied to trees or hobbled near tents, the camp was empty.

Frustrated with myself, I decided to skirt the clearing and head for higher ground, since I'd heard Gavi say something about a high ridge with the best view of the proceedings. But I'd only gone a few steps when a deep voice rang out.

"What are you doing?"

I halted, heart racing. My father was around here somewhere, since Samuel had asked him to help prepare an altar for a sacrifice, and the last thing I needed was some stern elder dragging me to him by the ear. I'd be sent home immediately and barred from spending time with my cousins. Zevi would be here for less than a week, and since he came all the way from Kiryat-Yearim only a few times a year, I did not want to waste any of the remaining time by being in trouble.

However, I could see no one among the tents, aside from a hobbled brown donkey staring at me intently, long ears twitching.

I stared back at him. I had odd dreams from time to time, vivid ones with brilliant colors and confusing images that clung to me for days, sometimes weeks. Was I hearing voices coming from the mouths of donkeys now too?

"Behind you," said the voice, so I turned around slowly, heart pounding, to find one of the tallest men I'd ever seen leaning against a tree, arms folded across a broad chest as he frowned at me from beneath a hooded cloak. With the sun at his back, I could not see his face well, but he had to be at least Uncle Natan's height, maybe even a few fingers taller, if possible. A heavy iron sword, one I would struggle to lift with two hands, hung from his belt. All I could do was stare at him, knees trembling.

"Looking to steal something?"

I shook my head vehemently. "No, my lord. I'm only searching for my cousins."

"Are they Benjamites? I don't recognize you."

Gavi was, but admitting so might get him in trouble, so I skirted one truth for another. "I'm a Levite."

"Are you?" He sounded oddly intrigued.

"Yes, I live in Naioth."

"Why are you in Mitzpah, then? There's a gathering of tribal elders today."

Stomach writhing, I nervously blurted out the truth. "I know. My cousins wanted to watch them choose the new king, but they left me behind, so I followed them. I lost their trail, and now I don't know where to look."

The man stared at me, chin tilted as if trying to determine whether I was lying. Then, with a soft chuckle, he shook his head. "All right. Go on, then."

Relief coursed through me. It seemed I would not be eviscerated by his wicked-looking sword or taken to my father after all.

"Thank you, my lord." I took a couple of steps but then paused. "Why are *you* down here? Don't you want to see them cast lots too?"

He barked a sardonic laugh. "I already lost one round of lots today. That's why I'm stuck here, watching the baggage like a servant." He gestured to a large pile of crates and bags at the center of the campsite.

"You aren't a guard?"

He shook his head. "Just the fool whose lot was cast. Although I suspect one of my brothers tipped the scales on his own behalf."

"That's not fair."

He shrugged. "I don't mind. I'd much rather be here right now."

"But you'll miss everything! I can't *wait* to see who Samuel anoints as the king of Israel. Everyone has been talking about it for weeks."

He huffed. "And who do you think will be selected?"

"A man from Yehudah," I replied confidently. I knew the prophecies well. Had most of them memorized, in fact. "Yaakov said the scepter would not pass from him. So it must be someone from his tribe."

"Is that so?"

I nodded. "And he'll have to be the bravest one of them all to defeat our enemies."

Another rueful laugh. "It's more likely he'll be the biggest fool of them all. The nations around us have vast armies, countless weapons, and centuries of experience in warfare."

"That doesn't matter."

"Why not?"

"Don't you remember what Yahweh said about our enemies on the Mountain in the wilderness?"

"What was that?"

Immediately, I began to recite:

> "When you go out to war against your enemies, and see horses and chariots and an army larger than your own, you shall not be afraid of them, for Yahweh your God is with you, who brought you up out of the land of Egypt. And when you draw near to the battle, the priest shall come forward and speak to the people and shall say to them, 'Hear, O Israel, today you are drawing near to battle against your enemies: let not your heart faint. Do not fear or panic or be in dread of them, for the Lord your God is he who goes with you to fight for you against your enemies, to give you the victory.'"

I paused to catch my breath. "Whoever Samuel anoints as king doesn't need to worry, because Yahweh promised to fight for us. We only need to listen and be still."

He was quiet for so long I began to fidget, worrying whether I'd ever find Zevi, Gavi, and Avi now that I'd gotten distracted talking to the man guarding the baggage.

"I need to go find my cousins, or I'm going to miss everything. Shalom."

He nodded, seeming distracted as I began to walk away, but then he called out, "They're probably on the southern ridge. I was up there looking for some runaway donkeys not that long ago. Go back about thirty paces and turn to your right. There's a small path you missed."

I thanked him, waved farewell, and turned back the way I came. Sure enough, I found the tiny path he'd spoken of, probably an old hunting trail. It led me to the top of a ridge overlooking the entire Mitzpah Valley. Hearing voices, I darted behind an acacia tree, counting to ten before I craned my neck to look past the trunk. There, in the thick grasses lining the ridge, my three cousins lay on their bellies, peering over the edge.

Victory surged in my bones. I'd *finally* found them.

AUTHOR'S NOTE

And here we are, my friends, at the end of another series, and one that challenged me in ways I never could have foreseen. When I first began to map out these books, my life looked very different than it does today. We were still in the thick of homeschooling, my son just starting tenth grade and my daughter eighth. We had years of math and science and literature and history ahead of us, years of devotions around the kitchen table and discussions about the Word and the world, and years of daily time together. I could not have imagined then just how much would change before the final page of this series was written.

I was only a couple of months into writing the first book of THE KING'S MEN when a breast cancer diagnosis brought everything to a halt. Then, while I was deep in the throes of chemotherapy, both of my parents were diagnosed with severe dementia during a health crisis that shook our family like never before. My dad and mom were both brilliant, left-brained people who never quite understood the way my right-brain tendencies refused to color inside the lines, but they were incredibly proud of me, and losing them both far too early was something I was in no way prepared for.

Writing through seasons of pain and sickness and trial was not easy. Many times, it was slow and grinding and sometimes barely a paragraph at a sitting. There were months I wondered if I would finish. There were days I was certain I wouldn't.

But the Lord carried me through, day by day, grace upon grace, and the kernel of an idea during a plotting retreat to write a series around four young rebellious cousins (while we all were in complete denial that we had the dreaded "C19") somehow blossomed into eight books (four novels and four novellas) that span decades with characters that have become incredibly dear to me.

What I did not expect was how profoundly crafting these stories would shape me in return. Again and again, I sat down to write heroes and heroines who were fighting the same battle I was fighting—the ancient human battle of trying to be the king of your own life when things are spinning out of control. Each of them had to learn, sometimes painfully, to lay down their own will and instead seek the will of Yahweh. To stop straining toward their own understanding and to trust the voice of the One who sees the end from the beginning. I was writing their stories. But page after page, God was also writing something into me.

Walking through cancer has a way of stripping away every illusion of control. It places you, very simply, at a crossroads: You can grip tighter, or you can open your hands. As well, learning to lay my children down in prayer during some of the hardest trials we've ever faced as a family was one of the scariest things I have ever done. And yet the steadfast love of my Savior met me in every uncertain step, finding its way onto the pages of these books whether I planned it there or not. The catharsis of shaping these characters through their own surrendered moments, while I was fighting to surrender my own, is something I will carry with me for the rest of my life. Excruciating and holy, all at once.

Now that these books are complete, my children have grown into young adults and my homeschool table has given way to college moving days and evolving futures I can only pray over. I've gone from being a super-engaged mom in the middle of everything to relaxing into a support role, but I continue to daily lay them at the foot of the Throne while they unfold their wings and test them in new ways. I'm in awe of who they are becoming and cannot wait to see where we all are once the next series is complete.

It is a bittersweet thing to say goodbye to THE KING'S MEN, to let these characters rest now in the quiet of my imagination and set my pen to new stories. There is grief in it, even as there is gratitude. This series has pushed me and stretched me and made me grow in ways I did not ask for and yet would not trade.

None of this happened alone. I am deeply grateful to my plotting partners—Nicole, Tammy, Amy, and Christy—who encouraged me in the hard moments, flew to be with me during treatment, and challenge me to push myself in new ways with every book I write. Your friendship and support are invaluable, and I am beyond blessed to have each of you in my life.

To my editors, Jessica and Jennifer—your patience with me through all of this upheaval has been a gift I will never forget. Thank you for seeing the vision through the chaos and giving me the space and support to untangle these stories when they refused to unspool easily.

To my beta readers—Carolyn, Tammy, and Joanie—thank you for bearing with my messy first drafts (sometimes more than once) and still somehow being willing to do it again the next go-around.

To my daughter — thank you for all the hours you spent listening to me read these stories out loud over the past few years. That gift meant more than I can say, and I felt your absence on the final pass of this last book more than you know.

To my son—for being a fantastic brainstorming partner and the one who always senses when I'm struggling.

And to my husband—thank you for loving me and supporting me through every hard season. I can't wait to see what the next thirty years have in store for us, together.

To the entire team at Bethany House—from the editors to the proofreaders to the marketing team to the designers and everyone who sets their eyes and hands on my work from the very beginning to the very end—I cannot thank you enough. You make these books what they are.

And for my readers. Your support and prayer and encouragement mean so much to me. I'm still in awe that there are people all over the world I've never met but who care so much about me and my stories. I hope THE KING'S MEN reminds you that as you walk through this life, be it on the heights of the mountaintops or through the darkest valleys, the One who sits on the Throne of the Heavens holds you close to his heart. He sees you. He hears you. He knows you. And he absolutely *adores* you. Let him be the King of your life and rest in his steadfast love.

Soli Deo Gloria.

Connilyn Cossette is a Christy Award-winning, bestselling author who loves digging into the ancient world of the Bible and crafting immersive stories that encourage readers to encounter the Great Storyteller himself. As the grateful adoptive mom of two homeschool graduates and a recent breast cancer survivor, she knows firsthand how Yahweh's steadfast love redeems every unexpected plot twist. She and her husband of nearly thirty years are based just north of Charlotte, North Carolina, with suitcases always half-packed for their next adventure together.

Sign Up for Connilyn's Newsletter

Keep up to date with Connilyn's latest news on book releases and events by signing up for her email list at the website below.

ConnilynCossette.com

Follow Connilyn on Social Media

Connilyn Cossette

@ConnilynCossetteAuthor

@ConniCossette